P9-AQJ-440

The Last Drop of Hemlock

Also by Katharine Schellman

THE NIGHTINGALE MYSTERIES

Last Call at the Nightingale

THE LILY ADLER MYSTERIES

The Body in the Garden

Silence in the Library

Death at the Manor

The Last Drop of Hemlock

KATHARINE SCHELLMAN

MINOTAUR BOOKS
NEW YORK

This one is for me

This is a work of fiction. All of the characters, organizations, and events portrayed in this novel are either products of the author's imagination or are used fictitiously.

First published in the United States by Minotaur Books, an imprint of St. Martin's Publishing Group

www.minotaurbooks.com

Designed by Gabriel Guma

Library of Congress Cataloging-in-Publication Data

Names: Schellman, Katharine, author.
Title: The last drop of hemlock / Katharine Schellman.
Description: First edition. | New York: Minotaur Books, 2023.
Identifiers: LCCN 2023002002 | ISBN 9781250831842 (hardcover) | ISBN 9781250831859 (ebook)
Subjects: LCGFT: Thrillers (Fiction) | Novels.
Classification: LCC PS3619.C3482 L373 2023 | DDC 813/.6—dc23/eng/20230123
LC record available at https://lccn.loc.gov/2023002002

First Edition: 2023

10 9 8 7 6 5 4 3 2 1

The Last Drop of Hemlock

ONE

The rumor went through the Nightingale like a flood, quietly rising, whispers hovering on lips in pockets of silence.

Dead, the voices murmured. *Dead?*

On the dance floor or jostling at the bar, voices and drinks raised in equal measure, the club's patrons didn't hear it sweeping around them. They were too caught up in escaping from their daylight lives, too distracted by the music that carried them together, apart, together again, kicking up their heels for the Charleston or catching their breath in a waltz. They were too busy calling for another drink, another kiss, another song. Too busy following the rhythm of the music, shaking sweat from their eyes, enjoying being young and free or old and freer.

Dead, the voices murmured where the dancers couldn't hear. *Dead?*

Instead, the rumor went through the workers, the waitresses and bartenders, the bouncers and busboys. They dodged between the tables, guarded the doors, and flirted with customers while they mixed drinks, as light on their feet as the dancers as they moved through the club that was their second home. And the rumor moved with them.

Did you hear? they murmured. *Dead.*

When the band took a break, the rumor made its way to them too, delivered with a tray of drinks for the thirsty, curious musicians who had watched the whispers rippling around them.

How'd you find out? they murmured back. *What's she going to do?*

The rumor went through the Nightingale like a flood, creeping higher and higher before anyone realized it had traveled quite so far.

Dead, the voices murmured. *Dead?*

Dead.

TWO

Bea, where the hell have you been?"

Vivian Kelly had a moment to whisper the question as she waited at the bar. Around her, the hot summer air was filled with laughing voices, the stomp of feet on the dance floor, the clink of glasses, and above all with the sound of music. The band was in the middle of a Charleston, Vivian's favorite dance, and she couldn't stop her toes from tapping inside her shoes as she slid her tray forward for the next round of drinks.

She'd had less time for dancing since starting work at the Nightingale, but she didn't mind. Three nights a week she could still tie on her dancing shoes for the whole night. And the ones she worked, she usually managed to snag a dance or three anyway, depending on how her breaks worked out. Either way, she was there in the jazz club that had, almost without her realizing it, become her home. No matter that the whole thing was illegal—Honor Huxley, the club's owner, paid enough protection money that the club was usually safe. Vivian knew for a fact that one of the men drinking two seats down from where she stood was an off-duty police sergeant.

The band was hot that night, the trumpet and the piano competing to see who could wear out the dancers first. But the song still wasn't hitting with quite the flair that it usually did, because there was no singer up there with them.

That was usually Bea, who had just come rushing into the club an hour and a half after she'd been due on the bandstand. The staff break rooms were behind the bar, and she was heading that way when Vivian caught her arm with one hand.

"I was about to send out a search party, I was that worried," Vivian said, giving her friend a quick, concerned once-over. "I waited for fifteen minutes before I had to leave without you. And where's your uncle? Honor had to call Silence in to man the door tonight, and she's not too happy about it."

"I hope I didn't make you late, too?" Bea said, her voice shaking as she checked her reflection in the mirror over the bar. She looked her usual glitzy self, with gold beads sparkling against the black of her dress and a feather curling over her pinned-back hair. Bea loved singing in its own right, but it was also one of the few good ways that a Black girl in New York could get herself noticed, and she had confessed to Vivian that she wanted to look the part every night in case a chance to move up ever came. But tonight she was clearly upset, her fingers clumsy as she fidgeted with her hair. "I've got to get up on the bandstand, I'll—"

"Wait." Vivian stopped her from turning away. "What happened? Are you okay?"

"No," Bea whispered. She was vibrating like a plucked string, and her eyes were red, as if she'd been crying. "Uncle Pearlie's dead."

Vivian's arm dropped. "Dead? But . . . but he was just here last night. What happened? What do you mean, dead?"

"Mama is crying her eyes out at home," Bea said, her voice still low. She glanced around, then pulled Vivian toward the bandstand with her. "Doc Harris said it was a suicide. Says that he's seen it before, and maybe he had, with folks that've lost everything or got no hope left. But . . ." She trailed off, looking nervous.

"Vivian!" The holler came from the bar, where the bartender had a round of drinks ready for her. "Table's getting antsy, so shake a leg, kitten!"

"But what?" Vivian whispered urgently. She had to get back to work—the club's patrons were having too much fun that night to wait patiently for their booze—but the look in Bea's eyes worried her.

"Pearlie hadn't lost everything," Bea whispered, her voice dropping even lower as the band flourished to the end of their number. "Or at least, he was on his way to getting it back. Vivian, I don't think he killed himself. I think someone killed him."

"Wha—" Vivian stared at her friend, too stunned to even finish a single word.

At that moment, the music started up again. The bandleader, Mr. Smith, had clearly spotted Bea, because the musicians were just launching into the first bars of "It Had to Be You." "And here she comes, the Nightingale's own songbird! Beatrice, get up here," he called playfully as the dancers hollered their approval. "This one's no good without you!"

"What do you mean, *killed*?" Vivian breathed, finally finding her voice.

Bea gave her friend a single, anguished look, then plastered a smile on her face as she hopped up onto the bandstand. She made it to the microphone just in time, and the song poured out of her, rich as whiskey and smooth as honey. The energy in the room grew even brighter.

Vivian stared at her, the only one in the club shocked and still, thinking that there had to be some mistake.

Bea's uncle had arrived in the city only a few months before, following his sister-in-law and her family north from Baltimore. He had started working at the Nightingale as a bouncer less than two weeks after he turned up. Vivian had never found out what connections he had that made Honor Huxley give him a chance so quickly or whether it had just been as a favor to Bea. She hadn't asked, either—it was the sort of thing it was usually safer not to know. And Pearlie had been popular with everyone at the Nightingale, friendly and outgoing, always ready with a joke or a smile.

But there had been shadows lurking in his eyes, and he had been jumpy and mistrusting, even for a bouncer at an underground club. No one knew why he had left Baltimore, and Pearlie had never volunteered to share the story. He had turned up in New York with nothing but the clothes on his back and one suitcase, and he hadn't been there long enough to have gained much more.

Even if she didn't know the details, Vivian knew his kind of story. They were a dime a dozen in the run-down corners of the city, and they rarely ended well. It didn't surprise her that Doc Harris had ruled his death a suicide.

She made her way quickly back to the bar, where the bartender was waiting impatiently for her, his hands busy with other orders while he rolled his eyes at her. "Good of you to help us out, Viv."

"Danny." Something in her voice made him pause, the long-suffering humor in his expression replaced by concern. "Where's Honor got to?"

"She has a meeting upstairs." Danny Chin was known as the Nightingale's star bartender and smoothest talker, but he was much more than that. Most of the club's patrons never guessed that he was Honor Huxley's second-in-command, half of the brains and plenty of the muscle that kept the place running and in good with the people who mattered. There was little that happened at the Nightingale that escaped either Danny's or Honor's notice. So it only took him one look at her face to see that something was wrong. He gestured to one of the other waitresses. "Ellie, take this order. Table on the far corner where that doll in the red dress is sitting. Vivian and I need to have a chat."

"On it, Mr. Chin." Ellie was new at the Nightingale, eager as a puppy to please and fit in. She scooped up the tray as Danny gestured for Vivian to meet him at the end of the bar, putting at least a little distance in between them and the many sets of ears that might overhear them.

"What is it, kitten?" he asked, lowering his voice.

"It's Pearlie," Vivian said, swallowing nervously, not sure how to say what he needed to know. "He didn't come in tonight."

"And I'm guessing it's not because he suddenly moved to Park Avenue?" The world that the Nightingale existed in wasn't always a safe place to be, and Danny had been in this business too long not to know what the expression on Vivian's face meant. "When did he die?"

"I don't know when," Vivian whispered. "Doc says it was a suicide. Bea's a wreck."

Danny nodded, his mind clearly already working. "All right. Get her off the bandstand once this number's done," he said. "I'll tell Honor. But don't make a scene about it."

"Holy hell, did you say Pearlie's dead?" someone whispered behind them. It was Ellie, holding out Vivian's empty tray. She was too new to know better than to get close when Danny had pulled one of the club's employees aside like that.

Danny closed his eyes, sighing. "Don't blab it around, okay, Ellie?" he said, giving Vivian an exasperated look. "Thanks for handling Viv's order, but don't forget you've got your own waiting, too."

"Right, yessir." Ellie nodded. "Here you go, Vivian." She handed over the tray and hurried away, eyes wide.

"It's going to be all over the place in five minutes," Vivian predicted, watching the girl scamper off.

"Folks liked Pearlie," Danny said with a resigned shrug. "They'll want to know what happened to him. You just get Bea back to the dressing room so they don't have a chance to pester her. I doubt she's up to it. I'll let Honor know."

Vivian parked her tray on the corner of a table whose occupants were too busy gazing into each other's eyes to protest. The band had just started a new number, and she had to weave her way between couples as she made her way across the dance hall.

"Vivian, pretty girl, where are you off to in such a hurry?"

Vivian, her mind on her friend, nearly jumped out of her skin as someone grabbed her hand playfully.

"Come on, baby doll, you promised me a dance last week and you still haven't paid up." The sandy-haired man laughed. He gave her hand a tug to pull her closer to the dance floor. "You're a treat to look at running your feet off, but you don't get nearly enough time to dance anymore."

"Give me an hour, Jimmy," Vivian said, forcing a smile as she tried to tug her hand away. Jimmy, laughing, continued to tow her slowly toward the dance floor. Vivian planted her feet, using all her weight to pull against him. "One hour, I promise, then I'm all yours on my next break."

"Oh, fine," Jimmy said, giving her hand an exaggerated kiss before releasing it and waving her on her way. "I'll be pining until then, wasting away to a shell of a man."

"You'll find twelve other girls to dance with in the meantime, you goof," Vivian said, shaking her head, though her eyes darted toward the bandstand once more. Pretty Jimmy Allen was the sort of boy who was all flirtatious bluster and absolutely no follow-through, and usually Vivian liked spending time with him. But not tonight. She could see Bea's fingers locked in a death grip around the microphone, though none of the tension could be heard in her voice. "See you in a jiffy."

It took Vivian a moment to get the bandleader's attention—she had to wait until the trombone player's solo. Mr. Smith glanced around the club, taking stock of how the dancers were enjoying the music, and Vivian was able to catch his eye with a wave. He nodded back, giving her a wink and a brow raised in question. She signed a letter *H* with two fingers before raising her pointer finger toward the ceiling—and toward the second floor, where the owner's office was located. It was part of the club's private code, a way for employees to quietly let each other know that Honor wanted to see one of them.

The bandleader, who had worked at the Nightingale for years and been in more than one fight on Honor's behalf, took it in stride. When he pointed at himself, Vivian shook her head. She nodded toward Bea, who had just begun the final verse, her eyes closing as she crooned the plaintive song, as heartfelt as if she were singing to a lover and not a roomful of strangers.

Mr. Smith's sigh was visible, even if Vivian couldn't hear it over the music. Vivian couldn't blame him; he had planned out his set thinking Bea would be up there with them, and now he was losing her again after only two songs. But there was no help for it.

As the piano trilled a final flurry of notes, Mr. Smith—Vivian knew it wasn't his real name, but no one ever pestered him about it—stepped over to Bea and whispered in her ear. She stared at him, and the sparkle of the dim electric lights caught her just enough that Vivian could see a tear slipping down her cheek. She nodded and stepped back from the microphone, turning to hop down and join Vivian just as the bandleader lifted his hands.

"Change of plans, boys," he said to his musicians. "We need to liven this place up a little. 'Sister Kate,' if you please. A-one, and a-two—"

"What is it, Viv?" Bea asked in a low voice.

"Danny wants you back in the dressing room. I think Honor's going to have some questions. About Pearlie."

Bea swallowed, looking anxious, but she nodded. "Of course." Honor Huxley ruled her club with an iron will, the instincts of a born businesswoman, and a fierce loyalty to everyone who worked for her. If something had happened to one of them, she would want to know.

The dance floor was a whirl of bodies, men in white shirts who had already shed their jackets, women whose spangles and diamonds reflected the light in a hundred scattered directions. Even without a singer, the song pulled the club's patrons to their feet. Everyone that they could see was either crowded around the bar or joining the line of the dance. Vivian and Bea dodged between them, making their way to the doorway by the bar.

Bea's eyes were fixed grimly on their destination, as though she were keeping herself going through sheer determination. It fell to Vivian to smile and chat with the customers who crossed their paths, most of them wanting to know when the Nightingale's songbird would be back on the bandstand. When they finally reached the bar, Danny was waiting. He gave them a quick look up and down before lifting the hinged flap in the counter to let them behind the bar.

"In you go, songbird," he said gently. "You too, Viv. Honor's on her way."

THREE

Bea sat at her dressing table, her feet up on the chair and her chin resting on her knees. Her eyes were squeezed shut, her arms clasped around her legs. Vivian had tried to talk to her and had been told in no uncertain terms that her friend needed her to be quiet.

Vivian didn't press; grief hit everyone different, and Bea would talk when she was ready. But Vivian couldn't stay seated herself. She paced from one end of the dressing room to the other.

The room was set aside for the use of the female staff—there was another one for the men, at the other end of the bar. It wasn't large, but there were sofas pushed against two walls for the waitresses to put their feet up when they were on their breaks and a washroom off one end so they didn't have to use the same one as the club's patrons.

Bea was the only one who got her own dressing table, brought in special by Honor when Bea was promoted from waitress to chanteuse and needed to look a touch fancier than the rest of them. It wasn't even two feet across, squeezed into one corner next to a sofa, and half the time the other girls needed to use her mirror. But the gesture had almost brought Bea to tears, and she was as unlikely to cry in public as anyone Vivian knew. The rest of the staff had taken note: Bea was someone who mattered to the success of the Nightingale.

Now, Vivian checked her friend's reflection in the dressing table's mirror every few minutes, but Bea didn't lift her head until the door opened and the Nightingale's owner walked in.

Even in the world of hidden dance halls and illegal liquor, Honor Huxley could stand out in a crowd of thousands. She was dressed as she was every night, in sharply tailored trousers, a crisp white shirt, and black suspenders. But with her curly blond hair pinned back and her lips painted deep red, she didn't just look masculine. She didn't just look feminine either. Honor was her own person in every way, as comfortable on the dance floor, where she danced almost exclusively with women, as she was behind the heavy wood desk in her office, doling out bribe money to cops so they'd look the other way while she kept her operation running. She was beautiful and unreadable, ruthless and secretive, untrustworthy and loyal in equal measures.

As always when she saw Honor, Vivian's heart did a little flip in her chest. Her feelings toward Honor were unendingly complicated. She had once thought that working at the Nightingale would sort those feelings out, either through constant exposure or clear boundaries. She had learned pretty quickly that wasn't going to happen. There was no getting complacent about Honor Huxley, and no way to ignore her when she walked in a room.

Honor let the door swing shut behind her, eyeing the two of them. Her lips were drawn into a tight line. "You okay, Beatrice?"

"Yeah," Bea whispered, her feet sliding down to the floor. For a moment, she straightened her spine, trying to pull herself together. Then her face crumpled. "No."

Honor nodded. Pulling a chair over, she sat next to Bea, her legs planted firmly apart, her elbows resting on her knees and her hands clasped together. She leaned forward. "Tell me what happened to Pearlie."

Vivian made herself sit quietly on one of the sofas while they talked, though she wanted to jump out of her skin with nerves. The sound of a waltz drifted in through the closed door, the sweet, romantic sound an unnerving contrast to Bea's description of her uncle's suicide.

"They said he dosed himself with arsenic, which I guess is easy enough for someone to do, it's in half the boxes on any hardware store's shelves," Bea concluded. Her voice had gotten more brittle, more angry, as she spoke, and her hands were clenched in her lap. "And sure, I hadn't seen him for years before he turned up here. But don't you think—" She broke off, taking a deep, shaky breath through her nose. "He didn't tell you anything, did he? About why he left Baltimore?"

Honor shook her head slowly. "Pearlie had troubles, I know that much. He kept his mouth shut about what they were. But Beatrice . . . he wouldn't be the first."

"I know." Bea dropped her head into her arms, her forehead resting on the dressing table. Her voice was muffled. "But he was my uncle. I don't think it was that simple. It can't have been. And the doc just looked around, they didn't call the police or nothing . . ."

"Beatrice." Honor's cool voice cut through the increasingly frantic rush of words. Bea lifted her head, and Honor's expression softened. "Go home tonight. Go home for the week. Be with your family. Bury your uncle."

"But who's gonna sing?"

One corner of Honor's lips lifted. "We managed without a singer until a few months ago. We'll manage for a week. You take care of yourself, and we'll see you when you're ready."

Honor stood, about to leave, when Bea caught her wrist.

"Will you do something about it? Find out what happened?"

"Beatrice—"

"He worked for you, Honor. And you always say we can count on you. You know people who know things, right? Can't you find out, I don't know, something? *Anything*?"

"Only if there's something to find. If there's nothing there, there's nothing I can do."

"There's something not right about it, Honor. I know he didn't kill himself. *Please.* I can't bear for another—" Bea broke off abruptly, swallowing back whatever she had been about to say, her expression shuttering.

But Vivian could guess what it was. Bea's father had died a few years before, when influenza swept through the city. When Pearlie, his brother, arrived, it had been like getting a piece of him back for the Henry family. Pearlie and Bea had been instant buddies, and the younger children had adored his big laugh and tall tales.

For Pearlie to be gone now, another father lost, and so quickly after entering their lives . . . Vivian's heart broke, listening to her friend grow more desperate. Grief could make anyone jump at shadows or look for a reason, for any kind of explanation, in the wildest places.

But Bea was practical to an infuriating degree. She was the sort of girl who looked straight at her grim lot in life, accepted it, and did her best to come up with a plan to manage. No matter how sad she was about her uncle's death—and she was plainly heartbroken, even if she'd put on a good show up on that bandstand—she wouldn't invent excuses for it. If she said something wasn't right . . . Vivian shivered.

But asking Honor for favors was always a risk, especially if you asked before you knew you absolutely needed it.

"I can help," Vivian heard herself saying before she had time to think it through. Honor and Bea both turned in her direction, startled, and Vivian swallowed nervously. "If it'll make you feel better, Bea, I can help. What if a coroner took a second look, to see if they find anything unusual? Then you'd know, one way or another."

"How would you do that?" Bea asked, weary and wary.

If she hadn't been distracted by grief and worry, Bea would have remembered exactly how Vivian could get someone in the coroner's office to help them out. But if she wasn't thinking about it, Vivian didn't want to remind her. It would only add to her friend's unhappiness, and that was the last thing Bea needed.

"I'll figure something out," she said simply.

Honor was looking at her, her expression unreadable once more, and Vivian resisted the urge to fidget nervously again. She had a feeling Honor knew exactly what she was planning. And she wasn't sure she wanted to know how Honor felt about that.

Luckily, at that moment, a knock at the door interrupted them. Ellie poked her head in, glancing at all three of them before her gaze settled on Bea, her face falling in sympathy. "Bea? I'm so sorry about your uncle. There's someone here asking for you, though. Fella named Abraham? He says your ma wants you to come home."

"That's good," Honor said briskly, standing. "You do what I said, Beatrice. Come back when you're ready."

Bea gathered her things in a daze while Vivian brought her coat and street shoes. Bea had one pair of shoes that she wore when she was on stage, red velvet and tied with gold ribbons. She never wore them anywhere else, wanting to make them last as long as possible. When they were back in their box under the dressing table and she had her regular heels on once more, she glanced at Vivian.

"You sure you can find something out?" she whispered.

Vivian couldn't help glancing at Honor out of the corner of her eye, but the club owner's back was to them while she spoke with Ellie. "I'm not sure, but I'll give it a try." Vivian wanted to give her friend a hug, but Bea's stiff posture said clearly that she didn't want one. Vivian settled for holding the coat up while Bea slipped her arms in. "I'll be by to see you tomorrow, okay?"

Once Bea was gone, following Ellie out the door, Vivian could feel Honor's gaze on her like a hand on the back of her neck: warm, comforting, unsettling. They were alone—the first time that had been true in months. Vivian lifted her eyes, unsurprised to find Honor watching her.

"You all right, pet?" Honor asked quietly, not coming toward her, not moving at all. They could hear the music from the dance hall clearly, but inside the dressing room it faded into stillness as they stared at each other.

Vivian lifted her chin. Honor never flirted with her anymore, but that gaze was enough. Just being around each other could still put them both on edge, could remind them of everything they had left unresolved. She wished there was some way to set things at ease between them. But she hadn't figured out how. Not yet.

"I hate to see her such a wreck," Vivian said, answering Honor's question. She wondered which of them was going to be brave or reckless enough to mention the offer she had made. "Bea usually holds it together better than anyone I know. For her to be this upset . . ."

"She and Pearlie had gotten close, I think," Honor said.

"And him going is probably reminding her of her dad," Vivian added, her glance straying toward the door. She regretted it instantly; it was hard to know whether it was ever safe to tell Honor personal information. But Honor liked Bea. And there was little chance, anyway, that she didn't know that Mr. Henry's death had changed his family forever.

Honor nodded slowly. The playful sounds of a piano solo made their way into the room, pattering through the still air between them, making Vivian suddenly remember her promise to dance with Jimmy.

Vivian waited. She didn't have to wait long.

"So. You're going to ask him for help, then?" Honor didn't mean Jimmy. "Do you think he'll say yes?"

"You're not the only one who has a hard time saying no to me," Vivian said, but the words were playful rather than pointed.

Honor laughed softly. "True enough." She held open the door for Vivian, and another wave of heat and music washed over them as they stepped back into the dance hall.

Spots of light reflected from a thousand spangles danced over the walls and patrons alike. Vivian took a deep breath, watching as a young woman in a silver-and-green gown persuaded another girl to join her on the dance floor, bangles flashing and legs moving in a joyful blur as they danced, breaking away to mirror each other briefly before coming together once more. In the corner, one of the waitresses was being pulled out of her break, laughing but not protesting, by a young man with curly black hair.

To them, to so many of the other people Vivian could see, the Nightingale wasn't just a place for a drink and a smoke and a spin around the floor. Plenty of people thought the daylight world of the city was the safer place to be. But that all depended on who you were.

That wasn't true at the Nightingale. It might not be safe—it was illegal, no matter how much protection money Honor paid—but its dangers were distributed far more evenly than most other places.

Honor surveyed it all with pride, cool and elegant and dangerous as a panther on its own turf. But Vivian thought there was an undercurrent of tension in her posture. Honor had built something important in the Nightingale, and she was ruthless about protecting it. That ruthlessness didn't come with any easy choices.

"I'd do anything to help Bea out," Vivian said quietly, continuing their conversation from the dressing room. "He might say no. He might not be able to help, even if he wanted to. But I'm going to ask."

Honor looked thoughtful as she nodded. "Let me know what he says, and if you find anything out," she said. Her eyes drifted back to Vivian—was there an edge of longing to that look? Vivian could never be sure anymore—before her perfectly shaped brows drew together in a worried frown. It made Vivian shiver. Honor almost never let anyone see her worried. "You know why I can't get involved yet, right?"

"I do." And she did. The world of smoky dance floors and shady deals and drinks imported across state lines ran on what you knew and who owed you. Honor couldn't waste favors if she wasn't sure what had happened.

There was every chance Pearlie's death was exactly what it seemed, though Vivian couldn't blame her friend for wishing it was something else. And if asking for a favor at the coroner's office would help Bea find her way through the suffocating layers of grief, Vivian would do it gladly.

But even if it turned out that Bea was right, and there was something off about her uncle's death, Honor couldn't risk getting involved until she had a better idea what had happened. If she angered the wrong people by looking into it, or doing something about it, then the Nightingale and everyone who depended on it would be in danger. None of them could afford that.

"The doc was probably right," Honor said quietly. "And until we know otherwise, we treat it like sad news and nothing more. I don't need folks getting scared." She turned and gave Vivian a smile, her full red lips kicking up at the corners. Honor always smiled like she had a secret. "Which means you need to get back to work, pet."

"No rest for the wicked," Vivian said. If she took a step closer, she knew Honor would smell like vanilla and cinnamon and whiskey. But she stayed where she was. Out of the corner of her eye, she saw Pretty Jimmy on the dance floor; when he caught her eye, he spun out his partner and used his free hand to blow her a kiss. Behind the bar, Danny was leaning on his elbows, making the leader of a group of wild girls blush as she ordered drinks for her friends. Pearlie used to stand right at the end of the bar, keeping an eye on things. He had only been there for a few months, but it already seemed emptier without his larger-than-life presence. Vivian swallowed down her own sadness. "I'm not likely to turn up anything surprising about Pearlie, am I?"

Honor had been about to turn away, but she paused. "I wouldn't take that bet," she said after a moment's thought. "People will always surprise you if you look too closely at their lives. But the odds of . . . well, it's most likely nothing."

Vivian nodded. "It's most likely nothing," she repeated, trying to reassure herself as much as anything. She shivered, wondering what, exactly, had Bea so convinced that something wasn't adding up about her uncle's death. "But if Bea's right, we're gonna need your help."

FOUR

Vivian woke to the smell of ham frying. For a moment, she thought she was in heaven.

Last spring, she hadn't been sure that she and her sister, Florence, would be able to afford their rent for the rest of the year. The two-room tenement where they lived was cramped and ugly, but it had been their home for more than five years. The prospect of moving to one of the few cheaper places in the city—which were infinitely more cramped and ugly and dangerous than the dingy corner they currently called home—had left them both sick with worry.

But these days, Florence was making more money at the dressmaker's shop where she sewed and Vivian handled deliveries. And since deliveries took up less time in a day than the sewing she had previously done, Vivian had the energy to work at the Nightingale too, which brought in even more each week.

They didn't live like queens. They didn't even live like a snug little middle-class family. They were still poor, still scrimping and saving. But they could breathe a little easier.

Vivian hoped that maybe, one day, things would get even better for them. But in the meantime, there was a roof over their heads that wasn't going anywhere. And every so often, there was ham frying at breakfast.

The room's single window was wide open, trying uselessly to catch a stray breeze. But only heat and humid air blew in, along with the smell of summer in the city—the reek of garbage that had piled up on the street, the odors of a dozen different breakfasts being cooked in the style of as many countries, the smells that had seeped into the wood and stone from years of families living too close together. Maybe it would rain, one of these days, and then for a glorious twenty-four hours the world around them would be washed clean.

Vivian lay still for one more minute before dragging herself out of bed.

She dressed quickly. These days, Florence got up first and made breakfast so Vivian could get a little extra sleep after her shifts at the Nightingale. But they both had to be at Miss Ethel's dress shop by eight.

"Morning, Vivi," Florence said, yawning, when Vivian finally made her way out of the bedroom they shared.

In spite of the fatigue still blurring her head, the greeting made Vivian feel warm inside. Growing up in an orphan home and making their way in an unfriendly world had built a towering series of walls between the sisters. Those walls were slowly coming down, brick by hesitant brick.

The return of her childhood nickname had been a wall Vivian hadn't remembered was there until it had come down.

"Morning," she replied, going to the coffeepot and pouring them both a cup. Black, of course—they still couldn't afford sugar or milk for themselves, though they sometimes bought it for the neighbors. "I'm glad you didn't wait up last night."

"Woke up when you came in," Florence said quietly, spearing the two paper-thin slices of ham from the frying pan and forking them onto plates alongside their toast. "I don't think I'll ever sleep through the sound of someone coming in and out of here."

She said it without much worry, but Vivian knew that casual attitude had been hard to come by. "You were able to get back to sleep, though?" she asked, carrying the plates to the table. It took up most of the room, with a little space left over for Florence's rocking chair in the corner.

"Yes."

They sat down at the table together, a study in contrasts. They were both dressed well enough, in summer dresses that covered their shoulders and had the longest hems fashion would allow. Working at a dressmaker meant they were expected to look the part, but Miss Ethel didn't want anyone thinking the girls from her shop were fast.

The similarities ended there. Vivian, her black hair stick straight and bobbed to her chin, looked exactly like the sort of girl who spent her nights in places that needed a password before they let you in. The sort of girl who kept secrets and could be ruthless with them. Florence, with her wavy brown hair kept long and pinned back, looked as demure as a painting. But when she needed it, she had a ruthless streak as fierce as Vivian's own. That didn't mean Vivian told her sister everything—they weren't there yet. But they had always relied on each other, and now, bit by bit, they were learning to trust each other, too.

"Anything interesting happen last night?" Florence asked as they ate, and Vivian yawned into her coffee.

Vivian hesitated. She preferred to keep the seedier parts of life at the Nightingale as far away from her sister as possible. Florence didn't even swear, much less drink or smoke or think of letting a stranger hold her close in the sweaty heat of a dance floor.

But Bea didn't just belong to the world of the Nightingale. The Kelly sisters had known Bea's family for years, trading help and favors, meals and jokes, taking care of each other when they needed to because no one else in the world was going to do it. Florence would be devastated if Vivian kept news about the Henrys from her.

"Bea was a mess last night. You know her uncle Pearlie?" Vivian asked quietly. She had been looking at her coffee cup so she didn't have to meet her sister's eyes, but now she glanced up to catch Florence's worried nod. "He died yesterday. The doctor thinks . . ." Quietly, fiddling with her food now instead of eating it, she told Florence about Pearlie's suicide.

She didn't tell her that it might not have been a suicide after all. If Bea was right, Vivian wanted whatever had happened to stay as far away from her sister as possible.

"That poor family," Florence said, her voice breaking. "The little ones will be devastated. And Bea . . . He brought pictures of her father with him when he arrived, you know."

"I know."

Florence shook her head, pushing her plate away as though she had lost her appetite. "That's the third suicide I've heard about in the last month."

"Poor folks are desperate folks," Vivian said, standing abruptly and gathering their dishes. It was almost time for them to leave for work.

Florence had already made sandwiches for their lunch, wrapped in brown paper and tucked into a basket. Miss Ethel didn't give any of her seamstresses a long enough break to buy lunch, and they didn't like to spend the money in any case. And Vivian needed something she could carry with her in case her deliveries took up more than just the morning.

"I know," Florence said sadly. "And desperate folks do awful things. I just feel so awful for them. Should we take them dinner tonight?" she asked as they headed out.

Vivian carefully locked the door behind them as they left. "Sure," she agreed, hoping she would have something to tell Bea by that night.

Not an answer—she didn't have the sort of connections that could convince a coroner to drop all his work and do her a favor.

"I can pick something up and take it over once I'm done with my deliveries," she said. "I want to check on Bea anyway. And Lord knows Mrs. Henry deserves our help."

Maybe by then she'd be able to tell Bea she had set things in motion. Anything to help her friend move past the heartbreak of her uncle's death.

The deliveries ended with the morning. After four hours of crisscrossing the Upper East Side in cheap shoes, Vivian's feet were aching, her hair hung limp under the brim of her hat, and she could feel sweat trickling down the back of her legs. Summer was brutal in the city—not that she had ever experienced it anywhere else.

But her work for Miss Ethel was done for the day, which meant she had a few hours before she needed to meet Florence at home. It was time to ask for her favor.

Vivian's steps slowed as she came around the corner. The building she was looking for was a cozy brownstone that she knew had been divided up into private homes—only one or two rooms each, but still worlds of comfort beyond where she and Florence lived. The door was only a few steps away when she paused, her mouth twisting in a grimace as she tried to decide what to do. The landlady, who lived on the first floor, was a stuffy, old-fashioned woman who would think only one thing about a girl coming to see one of her male tenants. Vivian didn't much like the idea of being looked up and down, thoroughly judged, and sent on her way.

But her mind was made up for her when someone came out the front door only a moment later. Tall and lanky, with arms that swung awkwardly by his sides as he walked, he wasn't the man she was there to see. Before she could talk herself out of it, Vivian hurried down the sidewalk and caught the door before it could swing closed behind him. The man, who was muttering what sounded like a shopping list under his breath, continued down the street without noticing, and Vivian was able to slip inside. Stepping on her toes, as light as if she were dancing a quickstep, she made her way up to the third floor.

There she paused, hesitating again, before taking a deep breath and crossing the hall to one of the heavy, old doors. She was raising her hand to knock when the door swung open, the room's occupant just putting on his hat and ready to step out when they came face-to-face.

Vivian held in a yelp of surprise and took a quick step backward. But the man was clearly used to a particular kind of unexpected visitor, his hand going faster than she could follow to the back of his waistband.

Before she had even caught her breath, she was staring down the business end of a revolver, pointed unwaveringly at her chest.

FIVE

"God almighty," he swore, though he kept his voice down, as he tucked the gun back under his jacket. "Don't sneak up on a fella like that."

"I wasn't sneaking," she protested as he grabbed her hand and hauled her into the room, closing the door behind them before anyone could see her in the hall. "I mean, I snuck past your landlady, sure. I'm not an idiot. But that was just bad timing."

"And you couldn't give me a call to warn me you were coming by?"

"I should have," Vivian said, her voice shaking. She'd forgotten how fast he could move when he thought he was in for a fight.

"You should have," he agreed, running his hands from her shoulders down her arms in a quick, soothing gesture. "Hey there, Vivian Kelly."

Vivian laughed, and the sound was only a little forced. "Hey there, Leo Green."

Leo took a step back, looking her over from head to toe. Vivian felt her cheeks getting warm. She and Leo had been on a few dates, and gotten a little frisky a time or two, but his line of work—and the fact that he had lied to her about who he really was for the first weeks they had known each other—made him a hard man to trust completely. She had forgiven him for the lies, but forgiveness and trust were two different things. Aside from a dance here and there, she had kept her distance since she learned the truth. Leo, to his credit, hadn't pushed.

Now, he hooked a knuckle under her chin, lifting it gently as he looked her over. "It's been a few weeks."

"You haven't been around," she pointed out.

He shoved his hands in his pockets, shrugging. "I've been busy working."

"For your uncle?" Vivian couldn't help the way her voice dropped as she said it. His uncle was the police commissioner, a cold, ruthless man whose job was as much—or more—about protecting the interests of the wealthy New Yorkers who kept him employed as it was about policing the city.

The commissioner was cold and ruthless to his family, too: when his sister had married a Jewish man, he and the rest of his family had turned their backs on her. And he hadn't shown any interest in her child, Leo, until that child was grown up and useful to him. Leo had been a supplier in Chicago when his uncle finally reached out, offering work rather than affection.

He still didn't acknowledge his nephew as family. But he paid Leo well when the police needed someone who could work outside the law, or who knew firsthand the intricate web of loyalties and rivalries that connected the city's mobsters and bootleggers.

Vivian suppressed a shiver. That work had brought Leo back to New York a few months before, and she had come face-to-face with his uncle on the worst night of her life. He wasn't a man she had any desire to see again.

But she was willing to use the particular set of connections that he provided—if Leo was willing to help out.

Leo shrugged. "Sometimes for my uncle," he said. "I've gotta find other work when he's not knocking." He grinned. "Sometimes it's even honest."

Vivian snorted. "Color me skeptical."

"But I hope you're not here to talk about my uncle, sweetheart."

"Not directly." That made Leo's eyebrows rise, and Vivian took a deep breath. "Do you know anyone in the coroner's office?"

"The coroner's office?" Leo's eyebrows were nearly at the brim of his hat now. "And here's me hoping you'd come to ask me out for dinner and dancing. You sure know how to keep a fella on his toes, Viv."

"Do you?" she pressed.

"I might," he said after a long pause. "Why? Don't tell me you're mixed up in something—"

"No, it's not like—"

"Because after what happened last time—"

"It's just a favor for a friend," Vivian said firmly, shaking her head.

Leo scowled. "This isn't for Honor, is it? Because doing favors for her got you in a whole mess of trouble before."

Vivian rolled her eyes. He wasn't wrong, but there was still a hint of jealousy in his voice. Another time, she might have liked hearing it. But right now, she was only thinking about her friend. "It's for Bea. Her uncle offed himself, except she doesn't think that's the whole story. And she doesn't think the medical examiner will look closely at the body of a broke joe who killed himself unless someone tells him to."

"She's not wrong," Leo said cynically, crossing his arms over his chest and leaning against the door.

"Never said she was. But I figured if you knew someone, we could ask him to be a little more thorough. Then when he comes back and says yes, it was a suicide, she'll maybe be able to move on." Vivian smiled hopefully at Leo, but the angle he was leaning at had pushed his hat down over one eye, and the shadows it cast across his face made it hard to read his expression. "Nothing to it. So what do you say? Be a pal and help me out?"

He didn't reply for several moments, and her heart began to sink. She didn't want to go back to Bea and admit that she couldn't help after all.

"What's in it for me?" he asked at last.

Vivian scowled, crossing her own arms in imitation of his posture. "Didn't know things were so tit-for-tat between us."

"If word gets back to my uncle that I'm calling in favors with the medical examiner, he might get testy. And the last thing I want is to be on the outs with the man who has every cop in the city at his beck and call."

"So we won't let word get back to him," Vivian suggested, uncrossing her arms and sliding close enough that she could nudge him with her shoulder. "You just pointed a gun at me, Leo, the least you could do is help a girl out."

Leo grimaced, looking embarrassed. "I didn't mean to."

"I know." Vivian was struck by a sudden thought. "Tell you what. Why don't we get Bea to take us to her uncle's place? She can tell you herself why she thinks there's been some funny business. You can see if there's a good enough reason for it to be worth sticking your neck out."

"And if I'm not buying it, case closed, no favor?" Leo asked. "And no looking sour at me next time I ask you to dance?"

"You got it." Vivian smiled up at him. "But I think you're going to say yes, just to set her mind at ease."

"What makes you so sure?"

"Because there might still be a hell of a lot I don't know about you, Leo, but there's one thing I do know." Vivian poked him playfully in the chest. "You're a big softie underneath that tough-guy attitude. You won't be able to resist helping out once you see the state she's in."

Leo shook his head, but he was smiling at her again. He caught her hand before she could poke him a second time and pulled her close enough that he could brush a quick kiss against her cheek. The brief spark of contact left her skin tingling, and she had to stop herself from raising her fingers to the spot where his lips had been.

Things were good just now. Easy. Straightforward. She didn't need to go making them complicated by wondering what sort of possibilities Leo Green represented.

"All right," he agreed before she could protest the kiss. "But just because I've missed you. Now, let's see how good you are at sneaking past my landlady."

"Leo, huh?"

The unhappy note in Bea's voice was impossible to miss.

"Say what you want about his work for his uncle, it does give him some helpful ins," Vivian said, unpacking the bag of food from the automat. There was no one there to eat it at the moment, but she needed something to do with her hands.

She wasn't the only neighbor who had brought food, either. An entire chicken pie sat on the table, still steaming, next to a bag of apples. Other neighbors had stopped by to see that the Henrys were fed for the day before promising to bring meals in the days to come; without an icebox, keeping too much food fresh would be too difficult.

Another time, Vivian might have pointed out that it was unfair for Bea to stay sour at Leo but give Honor a pass. But that wasn't quite true: Bea knew Honor, knew why the Nightingale's owner had acted the way she had. She had reasons to trust her boss, even if she knew Honor could be untrustworthy. Bea and Leo didn't have that kind of history. And anyway, even if Vivian had wanted to have that argument, this certainly wasn't the day for it. "Can you think of another way to get a second look?"

Bea grimaced, glancing over her shoulder. But no one else was in the apartment. Her mother was at work, and her brothers and sister were at school. They'd be back soon, and it was Bea's task to get them settled and fed before Mrs. Henry got home. On normal days, Bea would kiss everyone good night and head to her job at the Nightingale not long after that, and Mrs. Henry would wait up after the kids had gone to bed, sewing or reading or just praying until all her children were safe under her roof once more. But this wasn't a normal week. Bea had nowhere to go, and she paced around the room like a cat in a cage.

"Mama wanted me to stop by Pearlie's today to pick up some of his papers," Bea said, looking a little lost as she glanced around the room. "She wants to see if there's anyone in Baltimore who needs to know he's . . ." She trailed off, biting her lip. "Anyway, I need to be back before the kids are home. They'll need me to get their dinner."

"Well, we've got that covered," Vivian pointed out gently, pulling an entire apple pie out of the bag and setting it in the center of the table. "And we've got an hour or so. As long as your mother's not home before us, we should be in the clear. If you're sure you're up to it?"

Bea hesitated, then nodded. "Let's get it over with. Leo's waiting for us?"

"Have you told your mother you don't think it's a suicide?" Vivian asked as they made their way downstairs, stepping wide to miss the spot with the broken tread halfway down the flight. "What did she say?"

Bea shook her head. "Not yet. Not until I can prove something. Pearlie wasn't her brother, but she's still . . ." Bea stopped mid-stair, pulling in a shuddering breath and dropping her forehead against the wall. Vivian took her friend's hand, and Bea squeezed it like it was a lifeline. "She's having a hard enough time now, between managing her own self and trying to explain things to Baby. The boys are old enough that they get it, they're sad but they're not confused. But Baby . . ."

Bea shook her head again, and Vivian caught a glimpse of something wet on her friend's cheek before Bea brushed it angrily away. Vivian didn't say anything. One thing they had in common was hating to let anyone see them cry. Bea gave her hand a final squeeze and straightend up. "Anyway," she continued. "I don't want to say anything until I know it for sure."

Leo was waiting for them outside, watching the door, hands in his pockets while he leaned against a streetlamp and whistled. When he saw them emerge, he stopped whistling, took his hands out of his pockets, and pulled off his hat.

"Beatrice," he said, his voice more somber than Vivian would have expected. "I'm sorry to hear about your uncle."

Bea eyed him, clearly surprised by the gesture but unwilling to let it change her mind about him. "Did you know him?" she asked coldly.

"No," Leo said, unoffended. "Saw him a time or two at the Nightingale. But I know losing family's hard."

He said it with sympathy, but Vivian heard a roughness to the words. Leo had once mentioned that his father lived on Long Island, and she was pretty sure he had been telling the truth. But beyond that, she knew little about his family. He was estranged from his mother's relatives, except his tenuous connection to his uncle the commissioner, but she didn't know anything about where his father's family was or what kind of relationship he had with them or even whether his mother was still alive. That had never struck her as odd before—folks who met over a cocktail and a dance in a jazz club didn't tend to share more about their lives than they had to. And Leo held his secrets close to his chest. But now she found herself wondering who he had lost, and when, and how.

"Appreciate it," Bea said. "But you're still going to make me prove he didn't do it himself, aren't you?"

"You don't have to prove it," Leo said. "But if I'm going to ask the medical examiner to do me a favor, I need to be able to tell him why."

Vivian watched them, her eyes darting from one face to the other. But Bea only sighed. "Come on, then." She turned and started walking, her shoulders tense and her stride so brisk it looked like she might collapse if she stopped moving. She didn't turn to see if they would follow.

Vivian glanced at Leo, not bothering to hide her worry. He gave her shoulder a brief squeeze before following Bea, with Vivian bringing up the rear.

It's not much to look at," Bea said quietly as she looked around Pearlie's onetime home. There was only one room; like the building where Vivian lived, the shared washroom was out in the hallway. A large iron bedframe was pushed up against one wall, made up for the summer with lightweight sheets that had been tossed back over the footboard to air it out, presumably after Pearlie's body had been taken away. In the center of the room was a heavy wooden table, dented and nicked by the many families that had likely used it over the years, and one wall was taken up with a stove, washbasin, and cupboard.

But in spite of the sparse furniture, the room was cluttered in a way that felt cozy and lived in. Books were piled on the floor and table, and a basket at the foot of the bed held blankets waiting for when the weather turned cold. Vivian felt an ache in her chest, thinking of the winter that Pearlie wouldn't be there to see, and she turned quickly, looking for something else for her eyes to rest on. There was a typewriter sitting on the table, and on the wall hung three photographs, faces in shades of gray smiling out of the frames.

Vivian stepped closer to look at them. Two were groups of people, but one showed two men. One of them was Pearlie, younger than when Vivian had known him but still broad-shouldered and tall, with a playful lift to one eyebrow. The other man was a little older, sharply dressed and with a wide, gentle smile, one arm around Pearlie and one holding a little girl with an enormous bow in her hair.

"My father."

Vivian jumped; she hadn't heard Bea come up next to her. Her friend was staring at the photograph with hungry, sad eyes. "We hadn't seen Pearlie since my father died until he turned up here at the beginning of the summer. I was so happy that he came to find us. We don't have much left in the way of family, and ever since . . ." She cleared her throat. "He had a lot of fun stories about Dad from when they were growing up. Left Baby and the boys in stitches every night after dinner. Me too," she added in a whisper.

"And that's you?" Vivian asked quietly. The little girl smiled sunnily at the camera, her head resting contentedly on her father's shoulder.

Bea nodded without saying anything.

"It's a nice place," Leo said, making both girls start a little. "Small, but nice."

It was nice, Vivian thought, looking around. There was no wardrobe, but hooks on the wall held two suits, each with a matching hat hung just above it. She stepped closer. She had only ever seen Pearlie in the black suit he wore when he worked at the Nightingale, but she had spent enough years sewing clothing to appreciate the other: sharply cut, made with elegant lines and expensive fabric. She frowned. There was a nightstand between the suits and the bed; Vivian pulled open the top drawer and found a box of carefully folded handkerchiefs and ties. She reached out to touch them, even though she didn't need to. She could tell what the fabric was just by looking.

She glanced up to find Bea watching, her apprehension clear in the nervous way she was biting her lower lip. "Where was Pearlie getting his money, Bea?" Vivian asked quietly.

Bea swallowed. "Pearlie can't have been one of those poor joes so in despair that he couldn't see any way out," she said in a low voice. "He wasn't poor, not anymore, and he could see a way out." She glanced at Leo.

"What did you find, Viv?" he asked.

"Silk for his handkerchiefs and ties," Vivian said. "The suit he wore to work at the Nightingale was nothing special, but the other one is top quality. And so is the hat."

"Money isn't always enough to stop folks from falling into despair," Leo said gently, but he sounded uneasy.

"I noticed the suit first," Bea said, coming to stand next to Vivian. "Guess it comes of spending so much time with you, Viv. And then I noticed the neckties." She glared at the drawer, then abruptly shoved it shut. "I asked Pearlie what was going on. And he told me. A big payout from a mob boss, he said, and he spent a little, but most of it he squirreled away. And another one coming soon. Just one more job to finish, and then he was moving out of this sad little place. On to bigger and better things. He was going to take my whole family with him."

"Out of New York?" Vivian said, suddenly feeling like a vise had squeezed around her chest. She wanted what was best for Bea and her family, she truly did. But what would she do without her friend?

"To Harlem or something. Somewhere better than here." Bea cast a critical eye around the small room, but Vivian suspected she wasn't really seeing it. Bea gave every penny she made to her mother, hoping to buy a better life for her brothers and sister than a precarious living in two rickety rooms in a neighborhood that most of the city forgot even existed. "He wasn't despairing. He was the most hopeful person I knew. He was downright *jaunty*. He said things were just getting better and better. He had a plan." Bea shuddered. "And now he's dead, and I'm supposed to think he just couldn't take it anymore and swallowed arsenic? Fat chance. I think someone killed him, and I want to know who."

"Did he say where he hid the money?" Leo asked.

"Does it matter?"

"It does if we want to make sure he was telling the truth. Maybe he just stole those things and didn't want to tell you that."

"You can't steal a suit like that," Vivian pointed out. "Not and have it fit."

"He said it was here," Bea said.

A quiet gasp echoed through the room, and all three of them wheeled around to find a woman in the doorway. Her eyes, already large and dark and fringed by extravagant lashes, were wide with shock as she stared at them.

"Alba?" Bea frowned, taking a step forward. "How long you been standing there?"

The woman, Alba, was older than Bea and Vivian, but not by much. And she didn't answer, just stared at them without speaking before turning abruptly and hurrying away.

"Alba!" Bea yelled, but she was already gone.

"Who was that?" Leo asked, looking wary. "Do I know her?"

"Alba," Vivian said slowly. "Alba Diaz." Alba had come and gone so fast Vivian felt as though she had imagined seeing her. But the pain and surprise in her expression had been all too real.

"She works at the Nightingale," Bea said, eyes still on the doorway where Alba had been. "You've probably seen her around there. That's where she and Pearlie met. They've been seeing a lot of each other recently."

"They're a couple?" Vivian asked, surprised. "I never saw them together."

"They've been keeping it quiet at work, I think. And from her family." Bea scowled, and her voice was brittle and bitter as she spoke. "Apparently her people wouldn't have liked her stepping out with someone like my uncle. I hope she didn't hear what we were saying," she added, lip curling. "She's probably dumb enough to blab it all over."

"She heard something," Leo said grimly. "And I don't think it made a good impression. Can't believe we left the door open."

"We didn't," Bea said, rubbing at the spot between her eyebrows. "Lord, my head hurts something fierce."

"Should we go after her?" Vivian asked hesitantly. "She looked . . ."

"We'll talk to her tonight," Bea said firmly, going to close the door once more. "If we're here now, we're getting this done, because I don't want to come back." She gestured toward the bed. "Help me slide that out, will you? I'll prove it. Pearlie didn't do this to himself."

Pearlie had been too clever to hide anything under the bed, Vivian realized. Instead, Bea instructed them to slide the bed toward the door until there was a foot and change of space between its head and the corner where it had rested. There, in the spot that had been behind the headboard, a rectangle of knotty wood covered up a hole in the wall. It looked like the sort of shoddy, slapdash patching that Vivian was used to seeing in her own building. It didn't even have nails in each corner.

But the hole for one of the nails that was there was a little too big. Bea pulled it out of the wall easily, and the board slipped out of place, swinging around the remaining nail to hang with its long edge down. Behind it, a neat cubby had been cut into the wall.

"Smart," Leo said, nodding. "Did he make it himself, or was it here already?"

Of course Leo would admire a good hiding spot. He probably had more than one in his own home. Vivian was about to say something sharp when she caught sight of Bea's face. "What is it?" she asked.

"The money," Bea said. Her voice was quiet, but there was an edge of panic under her words. "It's not here."

SIX

The hidey-hole wasn't empty. There was a bottle that no doubt held Pearlie's bootleg liquor. But there was no money, not even a handful of quarters, and certainly not anything like a mobster's payout.

"I don't understand," Bea said, her voice going high-pitched. "He showed me. There was cash . . ."

Leo moved her gently aside and inspected the hole. His face was impassive as he pulled out the liquor bottle and handed it to Vivian. There was an envelope as well; he handed that to her, too, before running his hands around each side of the hiding spot. "No other compartments," he said, stepping back and dusting his hands off. "But that doesn't mean there isn't somewhere else he was hiding things. Let's look around."

He and Bea began to search the rest of the apartment, moving systematically around the room as they felt the walls and searched behind the furniture. Vivian didn't join them. Bea knew her uncle, and Leo knew how folks with things to hide tended to think. They were more likely than she was to find anything else Pearlie might have tucked away.

Instead, she looked at the bottle Leo had handed her. It was unmarked, but that wasn't a surprise. It was mostly full of deep, amber-brown liquid, though it looked as though Pearlie had enjoyed a drink or two from it already. Vivian uncapped the bottle and took a sniff. For someone who spent as much time at a bar as she did, it was easy to identify: brandy, and high quality, too. She put the cap back on and set the bottle down, turning her attention to the envelope.

Inside was a simple sheet of paper, folded once and unmarked with any sort of monogram or address, though that was no surprise. What was written on it wasn't the sort of thing anyone in their right mind would put their name on.

A bottle of the good stuff for a job well done. Drink a toast to our continued work together.

It was signed only with the letter *H*.

A shiver went skating down Vivian's back. "Well, we know for sure that he was taking work from some shady folks," she said, raising her head.

Bea and Leo had met up on the opposite side of the room, neither of them having found anything else hidden away. But at Vivian's words, they both looked at her.

She held up the letter. "Looks like the booze was a thank-you for whatever job got him so flush. And it says there was more work to come."

It took Leo only a few strides to cross the room. "May I?" She handed him the letter without protesting, and he scanned it. His frown deepened. "Any chance it's from your Ms. Huxley?" he asked, pointing to the *H*.

"It's not her handwriting," Vivian said. "And I never heard of Honor sending liquor to any of the staff." She turned to Bea. "Have you?"

Bea took her own turn examining the note. "Nah, she just lets us drink on the job. If she was going to treat anyone to a little something special, my guess is it would be Viv here. Don't you think?"

This last was said with a deliberate lift of her chin, her gaze slightly taunting as she met Leo's eyes. Vivian could see his jaw tighten—Bea knew exactly which buttons she was pushing—but he let the jab slide.

When Bea saw she wasn't going to get a rise out of him, she shrugged, handing the paper back. "Viv's right, it's not her handwriting. And she's got too much class to send a note that someone else wrote for her."

"And anyway, who would she get to do it?" Vivian pointed out. "Danny?"

That made Leo chuckle, and even Bea cracked a smile. All of them knew Danny, and none of them could picture him writing out Honor's letters for her like some sort of Park Avenue social secretary.

"Well, in that case—"

Leo broke off, whatever he might have said lost to the sound of the door opening. They all turned, Leo stepping forward to put himself in front of both girls as the door swung open.

All of them stared at each other.

Bea found her voice first. "Abraham? What are you doing here?"

He gave them all a wary look before answering. A young Black man who drove a cab and had lived in New York City his whole life, Abraham had a skeptical streak a mile wide and plenty of rough experiences to back it up. Vivian thought he had probably just gotten off work: his hair, which he wore parted along one side and pomaded down, was still perfectly in place, but his white shirt wilted around the collar, and he was holding the jacket of his suit over one shoulder. That made sense; from what Bea had told her, Abraham tended to work nights and mornings, which made their schedules conveniently compatible.

"Looking for you," he said at last. "I stopped by to see you, and when you weren't home, I thought you might have come here to get some of Pearlie's things."

Vivian didn't know Abraham well, and the look he turned on her and Leo made her want to take a step back. The hand that had been holding his jacket up dropped to his side, the fingers curling into a fist in the fabric. Tall, wiry, and good-looking, with a pair of round spectacles perched on his nose, Abraham wasn't the sort to seek out a fight. But he was protective enough of Bea that Vivian wouldn't put it past him to start swinging if he thought he needed to. He stepped closer to Bea and put an arm around her shoulders. "Everything all right?" he asked, casting another baleful look at Leo. "You one of Pearlie's associates?"

"No," Leo said, his own shoulders set warily, as though bracing for a fight. "Just helping out Beatrice here. As a favor."

"He's one of Vivian's many admirers," Bea put in. She was leaning into Abraham's arm as she spoke; for all she wanted to stand on her own feet and act like she didn't need anyone to take care of her, Bea had admitted to Vivian that she liked how protective he could be. It was nice, she had said quietly, almost as if she were embarrassed to say it out loud, to have someone looking out for her for a change, instead of her being the person who took care of everyone else. She gave Abraham a little smile as she spoke; her eyes were still sad, still tired, but she clearly wanted to reassure him. "Don't mind Leo. He just hangs around the Nightingale making eyes at her whenever he gets the chance."

Leo scowled, but he didn't argue with the description. Abraham's mouth twitched as though he was about to smile as he glanced around the room. "What are you . . ." His eyes fell on the bed, which was still pulled away from the wall. Frowning, he dropped his arm from around Bea and went to it, one hand rising to the hidey-hole that was plainly visible. When he lifted his face back toward Bea, his worry was clear. "Something going on?"

Vivian looked around, but both the bottle and the letter had disappeared. Leo must have tucked them away quickly, with those hands that were used to hiding illegal things from curious eyes. She wondered where they had gone, but there was no chance to look.

"Like you said, we're looking through Pearlie's things," Bea said quietly. "I told you last night, remember?"

Abraham nodded. "You don't think he did it to himself," he said quietly, his hands tightening into fists once more. "So you're going through his things to find . . . what?"

"Proof of some kind," Bea said, sounding desperate. "There used to be money, there, Abraham, but it's all gone. And we found—"

"Bea, don't do this to yourself," Abraham pleaded. "Whatever you found or didn't find, do you think your uncle would want you mixed up in it?"

Bea's reply was an angry accusation. "You don't believe me."

Vivian's eyes were locked on Bea's face, but behind her, she felt Leo give one of her hands a tug until it was hanging behind her back. The cold neck of a bottle pressed against her fingers until they closed around it.

"I think that if you're wrong, you're going to cause your family a whole mess of grief. And if you're right, you're going to get mixed up in something even worse." Abraham glanced at the bed. "And I think either way, you shouldn't leave things this way. If someone was messing with Pearlie . . ." He trailed off. "Let me take you home," he said, more gently this time. "Pearlie cared about you too much, Bea, he wouldn't want you doing this."

Bea wavered, suddenly looking unsure.

"I'll help," Leo said, stepping forward. "He's right that we shouldn't leave it there, anyway." After a moment, Abraham joined him. It took the two of them a moment to get a grip on the heavy bed, then they slid it back into place with a matched set of grunts. When they were done, Leo came to stand next to Vivian once more, side by side, their bodies hiding the brandy bottle from view.

"Will you let me take you home?" Abraham asked, putting his hands on Bea's shoulders. "And you just forget about this whole thing?"

She swallowed, then nodded. "Okay." But she gave Vivian a quick glance, and her fingers flicked out rapidly. Vivian's hands tightened around the bottle, still hidden behind her back.

Abraham saw the look. "You need something?" he asked, an edge to his voice.

"Mrs. Henry wanted some of Pearlie's papers," Vivian pointed out. She could feel her palms growing sweaty and slipping against the glass of the bottle's neck.

"I think I can help her with that," Abraham said, a protective arm back around Bea's shoulders as he sent another suspicious look toward Leo.

"Then we'll beat it," Leo agreed, placing his hat back on his head and picking up his own jacket from the chair where he had tossed it. "Sorry again for your loss, Beatrice. Come on, Viv."

Somehow, as he placed one arm around her shoulders and turned her toward the door, he managed to let his jacket fall over his arm at just the right moment to cover the bottle from view once more. And then Vivian felt its weight disappearing from her arms as she was herded out the door. Vivian's heart was pounding like a set of drums played by a drunk. Never mind Abraham—what were they thinking, walking out into broad daylight with a bottle of booze in their arms? What if someone saw? What if they walked past a cop on the beat?

Leo glanced at her face as they made their way outside. "Relax, sweetheart," he murmured. The hand that wasn't holding the bottle under his jacket slipped around her waist and gave her a quick squeeze. "I've been running liquor for years, and I ain't been caught yet."

"Were you usually this dumb about it?" Vivian hissed as they turned toward her own building, which was only a few blocks away.

"No. But I also usually had more than one bottle to worry about. This is nothing." He grinned sideways at her, dropping his arm. "Cheer up, buttercup. I'll get you home, and then I'll head to talk to my friend at the coroner's office. Unless I should just pour this down the drain? Did Beatrice really want us to drop the whole thing?"

"No." Vivian shook her head, remembering the quick signal Bea had given her. It was another one of the signs from the club: two fingers up, then down to meet her thumb. A sign that looked like a mouth saying no. "She told Abraham yes, but she told me no. Which means she wants us to keep going." She glanced at him. "But why do you need the bottle for that?" She shivered even as she asked. There could really only be one reason.

Leo didn't answer for a long minute. "Come meet me tomorrow, okay?" he said at last. "Once you're done with your deliveries, stop by my place. I'll take you to meet my pal the medical examiner, and we'll see what he can tell us." They were at her building now, and he bent down to give her a quick peck on the cheek. "But first, can you run upstairs and get me a bag or something to stash this in? I'll need to have my jacket on if I'm going to look presentable enough to ask for a favor."

SEVEN

Vivian was halfway through her shift at the Nightingale when she spotted Bea.

It was a beautiful night outside, fluffy clouds flirting with the moon and glowing silver in its light. And it was a wild night inside, the smell of smoke and champagne hanging in the air. The sultry, humid heat of the night had made its way onto the dance floor, in spite of the electric fans. More than one person had tried to prop open the back door to the alley, hoping for a breeze to find its way in, but each time some member of the staff kicked it closed. Everyone wanted a breath of fresh air, but no one wanted to risk a curious or stupid policeman coming to see what all the music and fuss was about.

The band was playing Charleston after quickstep after Charleston, almost daring the dancers to keep up. White shirts were plastered to broad backs, and Danny had already called for a second case of gin to be brought up from the cellar.

A pretty redhead at the end of the bar had been smiling at Vivian for most of the last half hour. Vivian wasn't opposed to asking the girl for a dance when she had her next break, but things were so busy she could barely take time to breathe, let alone flirt. While she waited for her order of drinks to be shaken up, she glanced around, meaning to catch the redhead's eye. Instead, she saw a familiar figure on the dance floor.

Bea was dressed to the nines, her hair perfectly styled and pinned in place with sparkles and feathers, her dress cut to perfection with eight inches of indulgent fringe that leaped and spun as she danced. She was partnered with someone that Vivian had never seen before, but she didn't lean into him as she danced, didn't look for comfort or closeness like she had with Abraham. He was just another fella at the club, someone nameless and forgettable, there for a dance and never again.

Vivian met Bea's eyes as she spun away from her partner, and they stared at each other for a heartbeat before Bea was caught up once again and disappeared into the swirl of bodies.

When the song ended, Bea was nowhere to be seen. Vivian wanted to go looking for her, but she held back. If Bea had wanted to talk, she wouldn't have made herself scarce. Vivian worried, but she understood.

Some days, it was just too much to look real life in the face. Some days, the only thing to do was to lose yourself in the music for as long as you could manage.

EIGHT

I don't think I can go with you."

Bea spoke in an undertone, glancing over her shoulder. Alba was seated at the Henrys' kitchen table, hands locked around a cooling cup of coffee as though it were a lifeline. Behind her, Mrs. Henry stood with her hands on Alba's slumped shoulders, head bent down as she spoke softly.

"Alba told my mother about me poking around Pearlie's place yesterday," Bea said, her mouth twisting. "I could slap her for that if she weren't clearly so broken up about him. But Mama's not happy. And I want to find out what Alba saw."

"Is that what they're talking about?" Vivian asked, her own voice not much more than a whisper. She was standing in the doorway, hesitant to come in but still trying to get a good look at Alba without being too obvious. Bea had said she and Pearlie were a couple, but Vivian hadn't seen them together before, and she couldn't help her curiosity.

Alba wasn't anything like the sort of person Vivian would have pictured big, brash, friendly Pearlie being attracted to. She was much younger than he was, lithe and pretty, with big dark eyes and a perpetually sarcastic edge to her smile. She was always fashionably dressed at work, but today her hair had been pinned back sloppily, as if she hadn't bothered with anything more than getting it out of her eyes, and she clutched a man's coat around her shoulders like a blanket. Vivian thought it must have been one of Pearlie's, because it swamped her tiny frame. She looked like her grief was a physical weight. She barely lifted her head, her eyes fixed on her mug, though she nodded at whatever Mrs. Henry was saying.

"I don't know," Bea said, looking nervous. "Alba showed up here maybe thirty minutes ago. Last time I saw them together, I didn't think Mama even liked her. But now . . ." She glanced over her shoulder again. "I mean, it's gotta be about Pearlie, right? But I dunno what—"

"Beatrice, we need you to—Oh, hello, Vivian." Mrs. Henry had straightened and was now frowning at the two of them. "Why are you lurking in the doorway, honey?"

Vivian lifted the basket that she had set down by her feet. "I picked up some groceries for you all. There's fresh milk for the kids. And sugar for your coffee."

Mrs. Henry nodded, one hand rubbing her back where it always ached from being on her feet too many hours of the day. She wore the uniform for the restaurant where she worked six days a week as a waitress, and even in that she was beautiful. Mrs. Henry was a woman who had presence, no matter what life seemed to throw at her—and it had thrown a lot. From the grim set of her mouth and eyes, it was clear that Pearlie's death was just one more tragedy to soldier through. "That's sweet of you, honey," she said, not really paying attention. "Will you and Beatrice put them away, please? The little ones will be home soon, and Alba and I have to head to the coroner's office."

Vivian, already walking toward the kitchen cupboard, froze. She and Bea exchanged a nervous glance. After a moment of silent panic—eyebrows raised, heads shaking quickly—Bea spoke up.

"Why're you going there?"

"We have to claim your uncle's body," Alba said, her voice tense and miserable.

Vivian shuddered a little. Too often, when someone in their rundown little neighborhood died, the family struggled to scrape together the money for a decent burial. Those who couldn't afford it had to leave their loved ones' bodies with the coroner's office, destined for a mass grave on Hart Island, where the unknown and unclaimed of the city's morgues were sent. Technically, the Henrys should have close to two weeks to claim Pearlie's body for burial. But the rules weren't always followed, especially when it came to poor folks.

Vivian couldn't blame Mrs. Henry, or even Alba, for wanting to hurry. But if there hadn't been time for Leo's favor yet . . .

"Can it wait a day?" Bea asked, earning herself a look of confusion from her mother and one of disgust from Alba. "Please, it's important."

"What could be more important than treating your uncle with respect, when it's the very last thing we can do for him?" Alba demanded, setting down her coffee so forcefully that it splashed over the cup's edge and spattered the table. She didn't seem to notice, but Mrs. Henry grimaced.

"Why do you get a vote, Alba? You're not even part of this family," Bea snapped. Vivian suddenly wished she were anywhere else.

The emotions flew across Alba's face in quick succession: pain, then sorrow, before settling into pure rage. Her eyes were full of angry tears, her mouth already open on a torrent of sharp words, before Mrs. Henry gripped her shoulders.

"You need to keep yourself calm, remember?" she murmured, just loudly enough to be heard where Vivian and Bea were standing. "She's hurting, same as you. But you think about what Pearlie would want you to do, hear me?" She turned to Bea before Alba could argue. "Why on earth would we want to wait?"

"Because . . ." Bea looked to Vivian, who shook her head uselessly.

It wasn't her uncle, wasn't her family. It couldn't be her choice whether or not to say anything. Bea grimaced, then took a step forward, squaring her shoulders. "Mama, there was a hiding spot behind Pearlie's bed, and there used to be money in there, cash from a—"

"From a job he did for some mobster, I know," Mrs. Henry interrupted. The ugly words were jarring, delivered in her soft voice with no emotion.

Bea stared at her mother. "You know?"

"Of course I know, girl. Pearlie was no good at keeping secrets when he was excited about something." Mrs. Henry shook her head. "Thought he'd at least have the sense to keep it from you, though. I'd wring his neck if he was . . ." She broke off, looking suddenly stricken.

"Well, then, you'll know why I don't think Pearlie killed himself," Bea said, her voice suddenly hoarse.

"What?" Alba stood, pushing off Mrs. Henry's hands. "What do you mean—"

"I think someone else must have wanted him dead." Now that she had started, Bea seemed like she couldn't stop. The words poured out of her, like a river of music from an untuned piano, heartbroken and angry. "Because who's going to kill himself when he's got cash enough to change his life, and more coming in—It doesn't make sense, Mama, you have to see that. So if we just wait a little, we can find out who—"

"No."

"Mrs. Henry, we can be careful about it, I promise," Vivian put in, glancing at Bea's stricken face. Part of her wanted to stay out of it, but even more of her wanted to back up her friend. "Someone I know has connections at the coroner's office, so he's asking them to look into it. They should be able to—"

"No."

The sharp word hung in the air, startling all of them. Even Mrs. Henry looked surprised by how forceful she had sounded. She took a deep breath. "You don't need to be prying into Pearlie's life," she said.

Her voice was soft; thawed of its frost, Vivian could hear a current of fear running underneath. "No matter what happened, no good comes from getting mixed up with those kind of people, or from getting in their way. I know you and your uncle were close, Beatrice. But you let things be, you hear me?"

"Wait, do you mean you don't think he killed himself either?" Alba demanded. Mrs. Henry tried to urge her back into her chair, but Alba shook her hands off, stepping away from the table, her movements quick and jerky. "Why didn't you say something? What do you think happened? You have to tell me, Della, you *have* to—" Her voice was rising as she spoke, her breathing coming faster.

"Alba, you have to calm down—Think of the—Alba!"

It was no use. Alba shook off Mrs. Henry's hands once more, then kept shaking her head, growing more hysterical.

"Bea, get Dr. Harris," Mrs. Henry ordered. "Tell him Alba's in a state and he needs to come quick. It isn't safe for her to be getting agitated like this."

"Mama, what—"

"Do what I say. *Now.*"

Bea nodded, already sliding her feet into shoes. "Yes, Mama." She didn't waste time arguing or asking more questions—when Della Henry spoke like that, her children listened.

"Do you want me to come with you?" Vivian asked as they hurried out the door.

Bea looked as though she wanted to say yes, but in the end she shook her head. "You find Leo and get to the coroner's office. We need answers, and we need them quick."

"What if the coroner says nothing strange happened, it was just . . ." Vivian couldn't bring herself to say the word *suicide,* not to Bea. Not yet.

Bea's jaw tightened, but she didn't have time to argue. "Get going and find out, will you? I need to find the doctor."

Walking through the halls to the coroner's office made Vivian shudder, and not just because she could picture a corpse on the other side of every door.

The city's chief medical examiner kept his offices as part of Bellevue Hospital, a large, ominous building overlooking the East River. Not many years ago, the position had been held by a man who knew nothing about science but was very good at taking orders from the sort of people who put politicians in power. But there had been a scandal that had made so much of a splash in the papers that even the Tammany political machine couldn't protect their man. The old medical examiner was out and a new one had taken his place.

"He's a fair man," Leo said as they stopped in front of a door. "Doesn't touch a drop of alcohol, but he's a decent fella in spite of that." Leo grinned when the joke made Vivian giggle a little. "I don't know whether we're dealing with him or one of his staff. But either way—" He knocked on the door with his knuckles, a quick, businesslike series of raps. "—he should be able to tell us something. Or nothing, which is something in itself. Don't be nervous."

There was no way to not be nervous, not there, not for her. What if the commissioner found out they were there? Would he cause trouble? Would that trouble follow her back to the Nightingale? For a moment, Vivian wished she hadn't asked Leo for help. But she would do anything for Bea. And it was too late, anyway.

"Come in."

She had been worried that she would find herself in the place where bodies were autopsied, but the room that greeted her was like any other office, full of overstuffed shelves, a desk covered in papers, and old coffee cups scattered about waiting for someone to remember them and clean them up.

Vivian had read about the coroner and his staff in the paper, men who used newfangled science to unmask killers, particularly the city's poisoners. He was younger than she expected, but friendly, approachable, even a little portly. If she'd run into him on the street, she never would have guessed that he mangled bodies and chopped up their organs for experiments and who knew what else, all to catch murderers.

But she couldn't remember his name, though knew she had to have read it at least once. She stepped forward, not wanting to hover in the doorway, and waited for Leo to introduce them.

The coroner looked at her in surprise. "You brought a friend?" he asked, a hint of disapproval in his voice.

"I told you I needed a favor for someone else," Leo said, giving Vivian a sideways smile. "She's the someone."

There weren't going to be any introductions, Vivian suddenly realized. Leo didn't want to give her name, and the medical examiner, it seemed, wasn't going to insist on it. She felt a rush of relief—the last thing she wanted was someone knowing exactly who she was and why she was there. But she didn't want the coroner to overlook or dismiss her, either. She shook off her nerves and stuck out her hand.

"Pleased to meet you, mister. Thanks for your help."

Looking bemused, he took the offered hand and shook it. "Wait until you know what I have to tell you, young lady. Then you can decide whether to thank me or not." He gave them another quick once-over, then nodded, as if he had just decided something, and stood. Shrugging off his jacket, he tossed it onto a hook on the wall and pulled on the white lab coat that was waiting there. "I have five minutes. Walk with me."

"Where are we going?" Vivian asked nervously as they were ushered back into the corridor. The tap of their shoes on the stone floor echoed around them, and while the air was heavy and humid, the summer heat didn't seem to penetrate inside the heavy walls. She was hard-pressed not to shiver as they followed the coroner.

"I have an autopsy to do," he said. Glancing sideways at her suddenly white face, he chuckled. "Don't worry, young lady, I'm not expecting you to watch. But I have to stay on a schedule. And the bottle Mr. Green asked me to test is still in the lab." He swung open a heavy door for them. In spite of his fatherly features, his eyebrows were raised as if in challenge as he ushered them inside.

She stopped in the hallway, hands on her hips. "Are you waiting to see if I panic or faint or something?" she asked, not wanting to admit that part of her was afraid of doing exactly that.

He laughed. "A little. We don't often have visitors here, and especially not pretty girls. I have to find my entertainment where I can since I'm going to be working past midnight tonight."

"Busy day in the morgue?" Leo asked, his cheerful tone at odds with the dark implications of his questions.

The coroner's smile was tight. "Ever since they passed the Eighteenth, there's always someone on the wrong side of a mob boss or a jumpy cop or a bottle full of moonshine. And the wrong side of any of those things means you turn up here. But they won't give me more men or more funding, because I don't toe any kind of party line. It's always a busy day in the morgue. So, like I said, I have five minutes, and only three of them are left." He looked at Vivian again. "Are you coming in?"

She took a deep breath and stepped into the lab.

It was cold. One wall had shelves from floor to ceiling, each one crowded with equipment: glass bottles, rubber tubes, stands and clamps and other things she couldn't begin to imagine the names of. Another was full of bookcases holding more books than Vivian had seen in one place in her life. Some were as thick as two fists placed end to end. Others, in long lines with matching spines, looked more like sets of magazines. The third wall, across from the door, was end-to-end cabinets, their glass doors displaying hundreds of bottles and boxes, each carefully labeled.

In the middle of the room was a long metal table with a white sheet to cover the ridges and contours of what was clearly a corpse.

Vivian shivered, then turned to the coroner, who was watching her with quietly smiling expectation. She swallowed, trying to ignore the sinking feeling in her stomach as she realized what it must mean that they were in the lab and not his office.

She had thought, when she suggested this, that it would make things easier. She couldn't bring Pearlie back, couldn't save the Henrys the pain of losing him. But putting Bea's fears to rest—that much she could try to do.

She hadn't really believed anyone wanted Pearlie dead, not even after she had seen the empty spot where he had hidden his money. Folks spent money all the time, even when they said they were going to save it for something important. Maybe he'd had debts he couldn't escape. Maybe he'd been robbed. Maybe he'd just gone out drinking or gambling and wasted it all and was ashamed, and losing the money he'd worked so hard to get had been enough to push him over that edge.

There were a hundred maybes to choose from. But now . . .

"I'm guessing if you're keeping the bottle in here, you don't want anyone accidentally drinking it after all," Vivian said, pleased when her voice came out with its normal saucy lilt and none of the sudden panic she was feeling.

The medical examiner laughed at her lack of distress. "Right first guess, young lady." Vivian felt as if her stomach had taken a sudden, nauseating drop. But she kept her fear hidden as he continued. "It only took one test to show that the brandy in that bottle was laced with arsenic. And not in a way that would build up and kill someone slowly and carefully, either."

"What do you mean, slowly and carefully?" Leo asked, frowning.

The coroner tugged on his coat to adjust the shoulders. "Arsenic is a metal. Given in very small doses over time, it will build up in the body. The victim gets sick slowly, maybe has stomach pains every once in a while, and then eventually, poof, dead. It's horrible but looks natural enough, so unless there's a reason to get a coroner involved, they can get away with it, too. Poor bastard just seems like he's getting sicker and sicker over time and then suddenly drops dead all on his own."

"Jesus, Mary, and Joseph," Vivian blurted out, unable to keep silent even though she wanted to appear cool and unaffected.

"Sorry," the coroner said, grimacing a little. He looked genuinely apologetic as he shook his head. "I'm usually talking to folks who are in the same line of work when poisons come up."

"But that's not what happened here, right?" Leo said quickly, looking ill himself. Leo's work as a supplier would have taken him into all sorts of illegal business, and Vivian wouldn't have been surprised to know that he'd had a hand in a death or two, though he had never admitted it, even when she'd asked. But he was a straightforward guy who used his fists and, occasionally, the revolver tucked in his waistband. Poison wasn't in his line at all.

"No." The coroner shook his head again. "Whoever prepped that brandy just dumped the stuff in there. If someone drank it, I can't imagine they lived through the night."

"So what happens now?" Vivian asked, hating the quiet, unsteady way that the words came out. But she couldn't help it.

Bea was right. Pearlie had been murdered.

The coroner rubbed his jaw thoughtfully, where the shadow of a beard was beginning to appear under his skin. "Well, that depends. Mr. Green here only told me that he needed a favor for a friend. There have been three arsenic deaths here in the last two weeks. One was a straightforward murder"—the calm way he said that made Vivian shudder, but either he didn't notice or didn't care—"very poorly done; a fellow from Brooklyn poisoned his brother after they got into a fight over their family's business. And this isn't evidence from that, or you wouldn't be the ones bringing it in. So." He fixed first Vivian then Leo with a stern look. "Are you going to tell me which of the two suicides we've got on file might actually be murder?"

Vivian looked at Leo, but he was watching her impassively, waiting for her decision.

On the one hand, if Pearlie had been murdered, they couldn't just ignore that.

On the other hand, if he had been involved in mob business, who knew what the police would uncover. Bea's work put her on the wrong side of the law nearly every night. Or what if the boss he'd been working for didn't like the attention and came after the Henrys?

She couldn't decide without talking to Bea first.

She had no idea how to say that to the man in front of her. But apparently her silence had gone on long enough to speak for itself.

"That wasn't part of the deal," Leo said. He sounded cheerful enough, but the glance he gave Vivian as he checked to see whether she wanted to say anything more was wary. She swallowed nervously and shook her head.

"Our deal was that I do you a favor," the medical examiner replied testily. "I could always tell your uncle about it, and I don't think he'd be happy."

"Calling him my uncle is a stretch," Leo said, still cheerful, but there was something cold in his voice. "As he'd be the first to tell you. And then he'd be unhappy with me, and I wouldn't be able to warn you when he has some new bee in his bonnet that you should know about."

"Leo, it's all right," Vivian said. She didn't want him to burn any bridges on her account, and she especially didn't want any of this coming to his uncle's attention. She met the coroner's eyes and said simply, "I'm here as a favor, too. It's not my choice whether to say anything."

He sighed. "Can't say I'm surprised. Our police don't give regular folks much reason to think highly of them these days. And depending on who was involved . . ."

He glanced back at Vivian, and it took all her concentration to keep a straight face. He might suspect that one of the city's mob bosses was involved, but he wouldn't know anything for sure if she didn't give it away.

He sighed again. "Not as if I didn't know what I was getting into with this one." He fixed Leo with a stern glance. "You're trouble every time you walk through that door."

"I've only been here four times," he protested.

"As I said. Trouble. Each time." The coroner's words were clipped, but there was a small smile on his lips as he said them. "And I don't envy you, your uncle, or this young lady, whatever hard choice she has to make, so I won't push. For now."

"Thanks for your help, mister," Vivian said, meaning it sincerely. He didn't have to help them. Hell, he could have called the cops in as soon as he'd figured out what was in that bottle and had a full police welcome waiting for them when they arrived. That he hadn't gone that route told her that he actually cared something about helping folks in the city.

"Take care, Doc," Leo said, giving a small salute as he turned to go. He stepped into the hallway, holding the door for Vivian. "You ready?"

"Sure." She gave the medical examiner one more nod then followed Leo out.

"A moment."

The quiet call came once they already were several paces down the hall. Vivian hesitated as she exchanged a glance with Leo. She didn't like the thought of what else the medical examiner might have to say. But odds were, even if it wasn't good news, she needed to know it. She gestured for Leo to wait where he was as she went back.

She paused in the doorway, and she and the doctor considered each other for a long moment. He rubbed his jaw, looking torn. Vivian waited silently, unable to stop herself from glancing around the lab. It still gave her the creeps. She realized she was shifting nervously on the balls of her feet and planted her heels firmly on the ground.

"How a crime happens tells you something about the person who did it," he said at last. "We usually see that sort of slow poisoning I mentioned in very particular circumstances. It's usually someone close to the victim, someone who didn't want to get caught and could afford to wait. Someone with a grudge, so maybe they didn't mind seeing their victim suffer. Maybe they liked it a little."

Vivian nodded. That made horrible, stomach-churning sense. "And when they just dump the poison in and walk away?" she asked, trying to sound matter-of-fact and failing, even to her own ears. "What does that usually mean?"

"That they wanted the job done fast," he said, talking quickly as though he was telling her this against his better judgment. "Which probably tells you one of two things. Either your poisoner wasn't afraid of getting caught, because he has the right sort of connections or reputation to keep him safe."

As anyone in the mob might have. Vivian nodded. "Or?" she prompted when he hesitated again. She understood why. It had to make him uneasy that they wouldn't tell him who had been the victim of the poisoned brandy.

"Or it was someone who was feeling a little desperate, and he wanted to get it done before he lost his nerve."

"I thought poison was usually a woman's weapon," Vivian pointed out. "That's what everyone says, anyway."

The coroner smiled grimly. "I've heard that, too. And in the slow cases, that's often true. Women who feel like they don't have any other options, who've been badly treated or think they've been wronged, might poison their husband or mother or brother because they wanted to escape them or to punish them. But I've seen plenty of men use poison too. I wouldn't rule anyone out on sex alone."

Vivian nodded slowly. "How long are you giving us before you take this to the police?"

The coroner rubbed his jaw again. "Depending on who your victim was, there's no guarantee they look into it. Not if it's a case they've already closed. On the other hand, poisoning sells papers, so journalists are usually happy to pick those stories up. And if it got some kind of press attention, that might earn enough public interest that the police would have to do something about it."

"How long until you take it to a newspaper, then?" Vivian tried not to shudder, imagining a reporter prying into the Henrys' family life. What if they wrote about where Bea worked, and some politician decided to earn points with the temperance crowd by making an example of her? That sort of thing happened to Black girls who got caught stepping outside the law if they didn't have someone powerful or popular keeping them safe. And Vivian didn't know if Honor's bribes and connections would be enough to protect her friend.

The doctor met her eyes. "I'm keeping a record of those two suicides. If there's another arsenic poisoning from either neighborhood, anything that could be connected to one of them, that's when your time runs out. I'm not going to leave a murderer running around this city."

Vivian nodded. "Thank you."

He sighed. "Let's just hope I don't regret it."

NINE

"Alba's pregnant."

The news was delivered in a whisper almost as soon as Vivian walked in and Bea closed the door behind her. Vivian stared at her, then at the open bedroom doorway, where she could just see Dr. Harris sitting with Alba, who was lying down on one of the beds. Della Henry hovered nearby, all three of them talking softly together. Dr. Harris nodded, jotting something down in his notebook before taking out his stethoscope and bending toward Alba once more.

"What do you mean, pregnant?" Vivian demanded. At Bea's annoyed look, she added, "Does that mean Pearlie was . . ."

"The father? Yes, unless Alba is a lot sneakier than I can give her credit for," Bea said. She sounded dazed as she spoke. "She was working herself into a full-blown panic fit after I said that about him being killed. It was a good thing Mama had me run for Doc Harris, and lucky he was in his office when I got there."

"What are you going to do?" Vivian asked. They both spoke in whispers, still staring through the door at the examination happening there. Dr. Harris made another note.

"That depends on what you found out," Bea said, turning away abruptly. She glanced down at her hands, as if wondering what to do with them, before giving herself a shake and going quickly to the basin in the kitchen. It was full of dirty dishes, and she threw herself into washing them as she spoke. "Tell me quick, the kids'll be home soon. Bad enough if they find out about the baby tonight, they don't need to overhear us talking about . . . about Pearlie."

Vivian picked up a towel and began drying the dishes as Bea handed them to her. She opened her mouth to speak, but nothing came out, and she found herself staring at the dish she was holding, wiping it over and over, to avoid looking her friend in the eye.

Bea's hands moved into her line of sight, taking the dish away. "Just tell me," she said quietly. "It's bad news whether I was right or wrong. And I can't stand wondering any longer."

"You were right," Vivian whispered, her voice catching in her throat. Bea sucked in a sharp breath. When Vivian looked up at last, Bea's eyes were dry, but her jaw was tense with misery. "Leo took that brandy bottle we found to be tested. Turns out it was chock-full of arsenic."

Bea took a slower breath this time, shuddering as she let it out. "So someone did want him dead. Did your Mr. Green tell the coroner who was on the receiving end of the poison?"

Vivian shook her head. "No, but that doesn't mean he won't figure it out. So we have to decide what we're doing, and fast." The dishes forgotten in front of them, she told Bea what the coroner had said about slow poisoners compared to fast ones. "And your uncle did say that he had been working for some mob fella. If that was who did the poison, it makes things . . . tricky."

Bea snorted. "That's one way to put it. As much as I want to find out who did it, there's no chance I'm putting my family in the way of some mobster with a grudge. Not even because Pearlie was murdered. But maybe we could—"

"What the hell do you girls think you're doing with that sort of talk?"

They both jumped, and Vivian held back a shriek. Whirling around, the dish towel clutched in her hands like the most useless sort of weapon, she found herself face-to-face with Dr. Harris, who stood behind them, his black exam bag in one hand and the other planted firmly on his hip.

"God almighty, Doc, my heart just about gave out," Bea gasped, one hand pressed against her chest. "Don't sneak up on a girl like that."

"I wasn't sneaking," he said, a sardonic lift to his eyebrow.

He was a young man still—and he hadn't been born to this part of town, so he looked younger still, his face free of lines carved by worry and poverty and too much cheap moonshine. And he'd never look like he belonged, too polished and polite, without the swagger and grit that men like Leo or Danny wore as armor against the world. But he could walk down the street and not a single person would hassle him, expensive suit or not. He had moved to the poor, mixed little neighborhood west and south of Central Park three years before, wanting to serve as a local doctor to people who would otherwise never be able to afford to see one.

Three years of broken bones and midnight fevers. Vivian didn't know him well; she and Florence weren't often sick. But she knew more than one child that Dr. Harris had nursed through croup, more than one young fella he had patched up after a night at a bar turned into a brawl, treating them all whether they could pay or not.

Now, though, he did not look pleased with them. "If you hadn't been so busy whispering like children, you'd have heard me coming." His arms were crossed against his chest, and his voice dropped as his head tilted forward. "Tell me I didn't just hear what I thought I heard."

Vivian glanced at Bea. "I guess it depends on what you think you heard."

Dr. Harris scowled at her. "Don't play coy with me, young lady. I've got a patient in there pregnant with a baby whose father just killed himself. She's on the verge of a nervous collapse, which would be dangerous for her and the baby. And apparently that's because *you* got her all riled up with some wild ideas about murder. I can't allow that to happen. She needs *calm*."

"They're not wild ideas," Bea snapped, but she said it quietly, glancing once more toward the bedroom door, which was now closed.

Dr. Harris's scowl grew, but Vivian spoke up before he could say anything else. An argument was the last thing Bea needed after getting such awful news.

"We won't say anything to Alba," Vivian said quickly. "But Bea's right. Pearlie was poisoned."

Dr. Harris shook his head, his expression softening. "He took arsenic, Beatrice. The police found it under his sink."

"Rat poison," Bea pointed out.

"Which is full of arsenic," Dr. Harris said. He wasn't a good-looking man, but his face was kind as he laid a hand on Bea's shoulder. Vivian saw her friend stiffen, but the doctor didn't notice. He spoke quietly, still using the calm voice that could soothe upset or scared patients. "I know your family is hurting. But I saw the symptoms myself, and the coroner confirmed it."

"That's not all he confirmed," Vivian said quietly. "I just came from Bellevue. We found a bottle of brandy at Pearlie's place, and when the coroner tested it, he found that it was full of arsenic."

The black bag dropped from the doctor's hand, and he took a step backward as if trying to distance himself from her words. If the situation hadn't been so serious, he would have looked almost comically stunned, like an actor in the moment before a dialogue card appeared. He stared first at Vivian, then at Bea. "He what?"

"Pearlie was poisoned," Vivian repeated. "We just don't know who did it."

"What . . . ?" Dr. Harris swallowed visibly, glancing at the bedroom door once more before lowering his voice. "What are the police going to do?"

"Nothing," Bea said quietly. "Viv didn't tell them who the brandy bottle had belonged to."

"Are you going to tell them?" he asked. He added quickly, "You still can't let Alba know."

"You don't think she deserves to know the truth?" Vivian demanded.

Dr. Harris shook his head. "Not in the state she's in." He looked about to say something more, but all of a sudden, his expression shifted from worried into a look of quiet horror. "I've had two patients in the last couple weeks who mentioned getting unsigned letters that threatened them with poisoning if they didn't do exactly what they were told. I didn't think much of it at the time: they had no idea who sent them, and people will say all kinds of things to get attention. But if Pearlie got the same kind of letter . . ." He trailed off, looking nervous.

"Letters?" Vivian's stomach gave a lurch, and her heart felt like it was beating at double its normal speed. "Who were they?"

The doctor shook his head. "I can't talk about my patients. But they live around here. One was even in the building next to Pearlie's. So maybe whoever was responsible for those letters sent him one, and—"

"Stop."

Vivian and Dr. Harris both turned to Bea, who was shaking her head. "We don't need to know more, because we're not doing anything about it. Right now the police don't know, and we're going to leave it that way. Pearlie was working for some mobster, right? That's where he got his money. The last thing I want is to get on the wrong side of whoever was in charge there."

Vivian stared at her friend, too stunned to respond. After all that, Bea was just going to drop everything? But Dr. Harris was already nodding.

"That's smart of you, Beatrice. My brother and father used to be caught up in that line of work," he said quietly. Vivian and Bea gave him twin looks of surprise—he seemed far too starchy and aboveboard to have family who made their money doing illegal things. Seeing their disbelief, he smiled sadly. "It didn't end well for my brother. People like that are dangerous, girls. You're right to put it behind you. And it wouldn't change anything: poor Pearlie is dead, and Alba will be raising that baby on her own."

"Not on her own, if I know Mrs. Henry," Vivian put in.

"That's true enough. What a born mother that woman is." He picked up his bag and fetched his hat from the table. "You be careful now, girls. The last thing this family needs is more sorrow."

"Yes, sir," they both said quietly.

He turned toward the door, then hesitated, grimacing before he turned back. "By the way, Vivian, how is your sister?"

Vivian had expected more of a lecture, and she was left gaping at him for several awkward moments before she managed to reply, "She's fine, I guess? Why?"

"No reason." Dr. Harris crammed his hat on his head, looking embarrassed as he turned away. "Give her my regards, if you would."

Vivian stared at him as he hurried out the door. But she didn't have time to worry about Dr. Harris. When he was gone, the door closed firmly behind him and no one else in the room, Vivian turned back to Bea. "You're going to let it go, just like that? After we found out—"

"Don't be stupid," Bea said, turning back to the dishes. Vivian bristled, but she kept her mouth shut, knowing it wasn't worth arguing over—not with everything else going on. "Of course I'm not letting it go. But the last thing I want is people gossiping about my family. Folks talk to the doctor about everything, and he talks right back."

"Oh." Vivian took the dish Bea handed her, nodding. "Plus, I wouldn't put it past a fella like him to go to the cops to keep us safe. And folks would notice them asking around long before they noticed us."

"God, he would, wouldn't he?" Bea shook her head. "He probably thinks the police actually help people."

"They do," Vivian said, an edge of bitter humor to her words. "Just not people like us."

"That's for damn sure," Bea agreed. "So we'll help each other, right?"

The look she gave Vivian was pleading. But it was also certain: there clearly was no doubt in Bea's mind that her friend would be willing to help her out.

Vivian swallowed, suddenly nervous, but she nodded. Dr. Harris might have been relieved to think that they would let the matter go, but what he had told them made that far less likely. "Of course. And if there are other folks around here who have been getting threats, they're going to need help too. I'd guess if the doc has heard about a couple, there are more out there he hasn't heard about. And maybe . . ." She hesitated. "Maybe if we learn enough, I tell that coroner what really happened, and he can do something about it."

Bea gave Vivian a sharp glance as she handed over another clean, dripping dish. "Don't you go saying anything to him without asking me first. I've got the kids to think about, and Mama, and now that baby . . ." She shivered, her fear visible for a moment before she turned away. "I'm not putting me or my family in that kind of danger until I know for sure it's worth it."

"Of course," Vivian agreed. "Not a word until you say so. You all right if I take off? If I don't get home before Florence, she'll worry. And I'm working tonight."

Bea's jaw was tight as she plunged her hands into the basin of soapy water once more, but after a moment she nodded. "I'm all right. Maybe you can ask around at the Nightingale, anyway? All kind of rumors end up there."

Vivian nodded slowly. "That's true. And I'll tell Honor," she added. "She said she wanted to know what we learned."

Bea gave her a quick glance. "Did she know you were asking Leo for help?" When Vivian nodded, Bea almost cracked a smile. "Was she jealous?"

"Do you think Honor would ever let anyone see she was jealous?"

Bea's expression grew into a real smile. "When it comes to you? Sure."

"Things aren't like that anymore," Vivian protested.

"Sure they are," Bea said, handing over another dish. "And one of these days you're going to have to decide if you ever want to do something about it." She smirked at Vivian's scowl before her expression grew serious again. "But Pearlie first."

"Yeah," Vivian agreed, drying her hands on the thin towel. Florence would be expecting her home soon. "Pearlie first."

Vivian and Florence arrived at their building almost at the same moment, Florence unlocking the door while Vivian dashed across the street, holding her hat on her head with one hand and ignoring the angry honking of the car she had nearly cut off.

"Where have you been?" Florence asked as they trudged up three flights of creaking stairs. Not long ago, Florence's question would have been a brittle accusation, a line drawn between them that Vivian longed to cross but couldn't. Now, it was genuine curiosity.

"With Bea," Vivian said as she unlocked the door to their tiny home.

Florence nodded, yawning as she kicked off her shoes and settled into her rocking chair. "How are they doing?" she asked, letting her eyes drift closed for a moment. "I'll get up, I promise, I just need a moment."

"It's fine," Vivian reassured her. "I'll fix us something for dinner. I picked up some groceries on my way home. You sit and rest."

Days sewing at Miss Ethel's dress shop started at eight in the morning and didn't end until it was too dark to sew. In the summer, only the fact that the city buildings blocked the sun around dinnertime made that bearable. Florence looked dead-on-her-feet tired, but at least tomorrow was Saturday. Ever since the spring, when Vivian had struck a bargain with Miss Ethel, they had Saturdays off. Florence didn't even have a bag of sewing that needed to be done at home, a luxury that would have been unimaginable just a few months before.

"How are they?" Florence asked at last, opening her eyes to watch Vivian puttering around the kitchen. "Anything new I should know?"

"They're sad," Vivian said. "But no, nothing new."

She didn't even hesitate before lying. Florence had spent years taking care of her little sister. The least Vivian could do was to take care of her in return. And that meant not making her worry.

"Nothing new at all." She handed Florence a plate with a sandwich on it. "I've gotta get ready for work."

TEN

It felt strange to walk to the Nightingale alone.

Most nights, Vivian had Bea beside her, coats over their dancing dresses even in the summer, so no one stopped to wonder, or maybe ask where they were headed so late, all dolled up. They couldn't afford a cab, not every night, so they walked. Bea, focused and determined, would stride exactly where she needed to go, confident, brisk, and careful, always careful, watching the alleys and shadows and doorways for anyone who might turn into trouble for two girls walking at night.

But Vivian's eyes and steps always lingered, taking in the pools of golden light under the streetlamps, the shop doors barred and bolted for the night, the glimpses of night sky peeking between the buildings where no stars could be found. Sometimes there were sounds of laughter floating from windows, thrown open to catch whatever breeze might be stirring the heavy city air. Sometimes there were strains of jazz or blues rolling out of a carelessly opened door, behind the buildings or back in the alleys, hidden but waiting if you knew where to find it.

There were nights Vivian longed to go wandering, to cross the grid of streets to where mansions stood shoulder to shoulder, each trying to outdo each other with light and splendor and drama. She wanted to know what it was like to live that way, without worry or fear or anyone to tell you what you couldn't do.

The Nightingale was waiting. And she could find those things there, even if it was only for a few stolen moments on the dance floor.

But it still felt strange to walk alone. With Pearlie's death, the streets that for a while had felt safe were full of shadows again, spots where unknown bodies slumped, drunk or asleep or just too tired to stay on their feet, where strangers lingered and called out to passing girls.

Vivian glanced at the sky, black and purple without a star to be seen, heavy and sultry with the summer heat. She checked the change in her purse and, before she could talk herself out of it, she flagged down a cab.

The band was in a mellow mood that night, brassy and slow to match the heat outside. Bodies swayed on the dance floor, cheeks and chests pressed close to each other, lovers and strangers and friends carrying each other through the smoky, boozy rhythm.

Vivian was glad. In her current mood, she didn't think she could take the manic rush of energy that came with a Charleston night. She had already forgotten one order and delivered a bottle of champagne to the wrong table, a mistake that could have come out of her pay. Luckily for her, the accidental recipients had been decent enough to point out the error instead of just drinking it before she realized she'd gotten it wrong.

"What's wrong, kitten?" Danny asked as she came rushing back for the cocktails she had left waiting on the bar. Instead of his regular killer smile, he gave her a worried look. "Your head's all the way up in the clouds tonight."

"Thinking about Bea," she said. It was a true enough answer, even if it was the easy version, no explanations necessary.

At least, there wouldn't have been with anyone but Danny. But he rarely took anything at face value. He put down the bottle he had been about to pour from. "You find anything out?" he asked, throwing a towel over his shoulder and leaning forward, his voice dropping to just above a murmur. "Anything Hux should know?"

Vivian lifted her tray in a smooth motion, the six glasses on it barely shivering. "Yeah," she admitted. "It ain't good."

Danny nodded slowly. Making up his mind, he called out to the other bartender. "You got it handled for a minute? Have to go find the boss lady."

"I'm on it."

Danny smiled as he came around the bar, an easy grin to show anyone who might be watching that everything was normal, there was nothing to worry about. "Go on, kitten. Those fellas are going to get rowdy if they have to wait any longer for their drinks, and it's too damn hot to be breaking up a fight tonight." He gave Vivian a gentle nudge between her shoulder blades. "Hux'll find you when she's ready."

Vivian did her best to focus on work, but every time her eyes strayed to the bandstand where Bea should have been singing, or the spot by the bar where Pearlie should have been standing, her thoughts jumped back to the coroner's face when he told her what was in that bottle. She felt disoriented and unstable, like she was in a dream that could turn into a nightmare at any moment, knowing something that no one else there did.

The Nightingale had its regulars, same as any other place, and by this point she knew most of them. But over the hours of any given night, two or three dozen strangers might whisper the password at the door, pull aside the velvet curtains that kept the sound of the band from sneaking out, and make their way down the steps into the crowd. And they could be anyone: factory workers or debutants, politicians or mobsters.

Had Pearlie met whoever had killed him here at the Nightingale? Could that person be on the dance floor at that very moment?

Vivian was glad when her break finally came. A pretty fella in a gray suit had been making eyes at her for the last hour, a smile on his face and an invitation in his eyes. She had smiled back, glad for the distraction and yearning to spend a few minutes losing herself in the music. As soon as she set down her tray, he ordered two glasses of champagne and turned her way, one in each hand.

But before he could reach her, a long-legged figure in sharp trousers and a crisp white shirt came between them.

Honor gave Vivian a smile. "Dance with me, pet."

The band was just striking up a waltz. Honor loved a waltz, but Vivian knew that wasn't really why she was asking. Still, she hesitated.

They had danced together only once, before Vivian knew that Honor had, both accidentally and deliberately, sent her into danger. Honor'd had her reasons, but knowing that still didn't make Vivian trust her completely. Especially when she knew that Honor could do it again. And she would probably agree to it.

But Pearlie was dead, and there was no knowing if Bea was in danger because of it. Honor held out her hand, and Vivian took it.

The dreamlike feeling intensified as Honor's other palm pressed against the small of Vivian's back. Vivian took a slow breath, trying to find her mental feet, even as Honor swept her into the dance with a silky, confident lead. The slow, crooning melody made the air and Vivian shiver.

She met Honor's eyes at last and was surprised to find the same hint of vulnerability there that she was feeling. "Feels like old times," Honor murmured, her voice laced with regret.

They didn't have old times. They had danced together only once, kissed only once after that. But Vivian knew exactly what she meant. Something about them fit together—or it would have fit, if they could trust each other.

Vivian shifted her weight back, just the smallest bit. She didn't want to pull away, not in the middle of a dance. But she needed that breath of air between them to keep her mind steady. "Did Danny talk to you?"

Honor had felt the shift, and for a moment the look in her eyes was sad. But then her smile was back in place, dark lashes sweeping down as she sent a quick look to the left and right. No one was paying them any attention. She nodded. "I didn't want anyone to see me take you back to the office, just in case they got curious. But if we're on the dance floor, no one's going to look twice if we're whispering at each other. So. Tell me what happened."

Vivian let herself sway close again, until her head was almost on Honor's shoulder. Lifting her chin, her voice no louder than a murmur, Vivian told her everything she had learned, both at Pearlie's place and at the coroner's office. When she finished, Honor led them into a slow turn, Vivian spinning away for a brief moment only to find her way back into Honor's arms. She wanted to rest her head on Honor's shoulder, to breathe in the sweet, spicy scent of her perfume. But Honor didn't pull her close again.

"And you're going to help Beatrice find out about those letters? The ones the doctor told you about?"

Vivian nodded. "I promised her I would. I don't want to, but she's hurting so bad right now. And she's scared. What if the folks Pearlie got involved with come after her family? What if they do something that tips that coroner off and he talks to the papers and—"

"You don't have to explain it to me," Honor said quietly. "Just tell me how I can help."

Vivian's feet slowed, and for a moment she was surprised enough to lose the rhythm of the dance. "Just like that? Because Pearlie worked here?"

"And Bea works here. And I look after my people." Honor pulled her close again to murmur in her ear, "Including you, pet. I've got some trust to earn back."

Vivian pulled back, far enough to look Honor in the eye. "I seem to remember not long ago you telling me that I shouldn't have trusted you."

"And you shouldn't have. Then." Honor's expression was deadly serious. "Things are different now."

"Are they?" Vivian asked, her voice prickly. She knew better than to let her guard down around Honor, no matter how much she might want to.

For more than two bars of music, Honor was silent. Her eyes closed briefly, and when she opened them again, the regret was back. "I'd like them to be. But even if . . ." She hesitated. "Folks out there need to know that I look after my own. That's part of what the Nightingale means. So. What can I do?"

Vivian bit her lip. "Can you get a message to someone we know? Busy boss lady like her wouldn't give me the time of day, but she might pay attention if it's coming from you. And I want to talk to her."

Thankfully, Honor understood right away without Vivian needing to say the name out loud. She didn't think anyone was listening in, but she couldn't be sure. "You said the note was signed *H*."

"Yeah. It's not a sure thing. But she might know something, one way or another."

"I'll see what I can do."

The song ended with a single, lingering note from the piano. For a moment they stared at each other, not moving, neither of them sure what to say. Something like a possibility hung between them. Then Honor looked over Vivian's shoulder and frowned. "Do I recognize that fella?"

The band swung into a bouncy Baltimore as she spoke, and the moment was broken. Her mind stumbling to catch up, like a missed step in a dance right when the tempo changes, Vivian turned to see where Honor was looking. She found herself frowning, too.

Abraham was standing near the bar, his hat in his hand as he looked around and his anxious expression making him stand out in a way no one in their right mind wanted to stand out at a speakeasy.

"That's Bea's fella," Vivian said, a wave of worry hitting her. Forgetting about Honor for a moment, she dodged through the dancing couples to reach him as fast as she could. A couple of grumbles and more than one "Hey, watch it!" followed her, but she ignored them.

"Abraham," she gasped when she reached him. "Is Bea okay?"

The look that met her didn't make her worry any less. "Hard to know," he said, fidgeting with the brim of his hat as though he didn't know what to do with his hands. She had no idea, Vivian realized, whether Abraham drank or danced or even ventured out to where places like the Nightingale opened their doors. He often drove the night shift in his cab, but that was all she knew. "I stopped by after dinner to see her, and she asked me to drive her here. Said she needed to get out for a bit." He nodded toward a corner table. "She asked me to get drinks. But I'm worried about her. She should be home with her family."

"Sometimes a girl needs a break from her family," Vivian pointed out.

"Yeah, well." Abraham fidgeted with the brim of his hat again, glancing around nervously before picking up the two cocktails that the bartender slid his way. "They're worried about her. And so am I. Can you talk some sense into her?"

Vivian sighed. "No promises, but I can try."

But she didn't get a chance. When they reached the table, she found her friend chatting with another man. Vivian could tell by the tense set of her shoulders and the way one hand was tapping against the table that Bea was some kind of nervous or excited.

"Please, mister," she was saying in an urgent whisper. "If you know something, please, you gotta tell me."

"Everything okay?" Abraham asked, eyeing the other man warily.

Both of them jumped a little when they realized they had company. The man stood, looking ready to move off, but Bea grabbed his sleeve. "Mr. Guzman here knew my uncle," she said, her voice light and casual, her expression anything but. "He heard about Pearlie dying and came over to give his condolences."

"Lived near him," Mr. Guzman said, looking uncomfortable. He was about the same age as Pearlie had been. There were lines around his eyes but none on his forehead, and his hair had only a touch of silver at the temples. "Started coming here because Pearlie mentioned it was a good time. Sorry again about your uncle, Songbird. But I'm due on the dance floor, so excuse me but—"

"But here's the funny thing," Bea continued, her eyes boring into Vivian's. "Seems Mr. Guzman got a pretty odd letter a few weeks ago."

"I got nothing to say about that," Mr. Guzman said through clenched teeth. His chin tucked just the slightest bit toward his chest, and he shifted his weight, as though he was fighting the urge to step back.

"All right, he said no, so that's that," Abraham broke in, setting the drinks down so abruptly that they spilled a little. He shook his head, looking anxious. "Come on, Bea, we should get going. You need to—"

"You sure we can't persuade you to give us a minute of your time?"

The group startled again when Honor spoke. None of them had noticed her approach the table. But where she stood, she easily blocked Mr. Guzman's path back to the dance floor.

He stared at her, suddenly looking nervous. "Ms. Huxley. You planning to shake me down for something?"

"Just information," Honor said smoothly, a dollar appearing between her fingers. She held it out to him. "And it's not a shakedown, just a request. Sit down and have chat with me."

"Oh?" He eyed the money, but instead of taking it he crossed his arms. He eyed them all warily. "I don't much like talking to strangers these days."

Vivian tried to look as unthreatening as possible. She was used to watching dancers move; she could tell he was balanced on his toes, ready to flee at a single wrong word. Something had him on edge for sure. "And we won't take up much of your time, mister, I promise," she said earnestly, giving him a small, hopeful smile. "But it's real important. Please? It'll just take a minute."

Guzman looked her up and down, and his posture relaxed slightly. "All right, baby, since you asked so sweet. But make it quick."

They all sat down again, crowded around the small round table, and he took a long drink, grimacing as he set down the glass and looked them over. "What do you want to know?"

"Those letters," Bea said, leaning forward. "Can you tell me anything about them?"

Guzman let out a slow breath. "You didn't hear nothing from me, little girl. You understand? But if your uncle got a letter, I'm guessing he ignored it, poor bastard. You can't ignore one of those letters."

Vivian's heart sped up. "You got a letter?" she asked. "What did it say?"

"That someone knew I had a real pretty silver hairbrush, and if I didn't want something bad to happen, I should leave it in a certain spot on a certain night and not ask any questions." His mouth twisted bitterly. "It was the only valuable thing I had. My mother brought it with her when she first crossed the border. And now I got nothing of hers left."

"And you did what the letter said?" Honor asked, her brows rising in surprise.

"Goddamn right I did. After what happened to the folks the floor below me? I don't have a death wish. It might have been a family treasure, but that's no good to me if I'm dead."

"What do you mean?" Vivian demanded. "What happened to your neighbors?"

"And where does the poison come in?" Honor added.

Guzman hesitated, then seemed to make up his mind all in a rush. Speaking so quietly that they had to lean forward to hear him, he murmured, "They got a letter before I did, and they ignored it. The day after they were supposed to leave their valuables, someone sent a package addressed to their kids. There was a box of rat poison in it."

"Sweet Jesus," Abraham bit off. Bea reached for his hand, her own eyes fixed on Guzman; Abraham took it and pressed it against his mouth.

Vivian was too terrified to say anything; her breath felt like it was tangled in her throat.

"Were the little ones all right?" Honor asked.

"They were. But the threat was clear. Another letter arrived that day, and they did exactly what it said. So yeah, I handed over that hairbrush." He sighed. "I'm sorry about your uncle, Songbird. But if he got one of those letters, you should just do what it says."

"Do you still have yours?" Vivian asked. "So we know what to look for?"

He shook his head. "I burned it. Didn't want that sticking around in my life."

"You didn't want to take it to the police?" Vivian asked, not because she thought the answer would be yes—it clearly wasn't—but because she wanted to know what he would say.

"They tried that," he said shortly. "My neighbors. They didn't have the letter, but they told the cops what had happened after that poison arrived. Want to know what they said?"

"No," Abraham said, looking queasy. Vivian didn't blame him. Whatever it was, it wouldn't be good.

"Yes," Bea said quietly.

"They said that if they couldn't keep dangerous substances away from their kids, the little ones would be taken away. Police don't care about someone trying to steal from poor folks, because they don't think poor folks have anything worth stealing. So no, I didn't try to go to them. I just left the damn thing where I was supposed to. And you should do the same."

Bea stood up abruptly, her breath coming in short, frantic bursts. "I need to find out if Pearlie got one of those letters," she said. "I can't remember seeing anything in his papers. I need to go. Right now."

Abraham had jumped to his feet. "I'll take you, baby," he said quickly, putting an arm around her and pulling her close. "It's going to be okay."

Bea cast a look at Vivian. "Will you—"

"Of course. First thing in the morning, I'll come tell you anything else we find out," Vivian said. "Go, it's okay."

Mr. Guzman watched them leave, shaking his head. "Poor kid," he said. Downing the rest of his drink and standing up, he cast a quick look at Honor. "Was that all?"

"Not quite." She was watching him closely. "So you just left the hairbrush and that was it?" Honor asked. There was a note of skepticism in her voice, verging on suspicion, and Vivian turned to look at her in surprise. But Honor was watching Guzman. "Nothing else?"

Honor was good at reading people. She had to be, in her line of work, had to be able to tell when someone was lying or holding information back from her. Vivian didn't know what had tipped her off this time, but Guzman's jaw tightened. For a moment, Vivian thought that he would walk away.

Then he let out a short, humorless laugh and shook his head. "No. You're sharp, lady. That wasn't it. I hid. I wanted to spot whoever was coming to pick it up and beat them to a pulp."

"What happened?"

"Whoever it was got to me first. I heard someone behind me, and before I could turn around they had bashed me over the back of the head. I was out cold. Woke up at least an hour later. Someone had taken my shoes, and I got sick every time I walked up the stairs for a week." His mouth twisted bitterly. "Had to spend three dollars I couldn't afford on new shoes, on top of everything else."

"You know anyone else who got one?" Vivian asked. He was almost done talking to them, she could tell, and she couldn't blame him for it. Just thinking about what had happened to him and his neighbors made her shudder. "Anyone else you gave that advice to?"

He shrugged. "Word gets around about something like this, especially after a few months of it happening."

"Months?" Vivian breathed, exchanging a quick, shocked glance with Honor. But Guzman wasn't done. In spite of his hesitation, it seemed like he was relieved to be talking about the whole thing.

"There were a few people next street over. Anyone who didn't pay up right away got a can of poison in the mail. One fella even woke up to find someone had come up the fire escape and left it inside his window. There's probably folks out there who know of more, if you could get them to talk. But I doubt they will."

"What did your neighbors have to hand over?" Honor asked.

He shrugged. "Gold locket with a rose on it. Pretty thing. Probably worth a tidy little bit. But not worth more than their kids' lives. Like I said, just do what the letter says. And that's all *I've* got to say about it. So I'll take that cash now." He held out his hand.

When Honor pulled out another two bills for an even three dollars, his eyes widened in surprise. He nodded his thanks as he took it. "Thanks for your help, mister," Honor said.

"Yeah. Do me a favor, and don't drag me into this again. And tell your songbird sorry again about Pearlie," he added as he turned away. "Poor bastard. Shoulda just paid up when he got that letter."

Once he was gone—he made a beeline for the stairs—Vivian and Honor stared at each other. "Do you think," Vivian said slowly, "if he comes here, and he knew Pearlie . . . do you think whoever is writing these letters has something to do with the Nightingale after all?"

"I hope not," Honor replied quietly, her eyes hard as she stared past Vivian's shoulder, her expression closed off. "But it looks like I need to do that favor for you sooner rather than later if we want to learn anything more."

ELEVEN

"Are you going to tell me what's going on?"

Vivian was startled out of her distraction so suddenly that she pushed her needle through the fabric too quickly, stabbing it deep into her own hand. She yelped and dropped the mending without thinking, cursing loudly.

Florence frowned at her. "You know it's not ladylike to swear like that," she said before turning back to the pot of beans and broth she was stirring.

"Well, we're not ladies," Vivian snapped, still shaking out her hand. "God almighty, that hurt. Or at least, I'm not a lady."

"I'm well aware," Florence said dryly, but there was a smile hovering around her lips that would not have been there a few months ago. "Don't bleed on my clothes, please."

"Thanks for your concern," Vivian grumbled, retrieving the dress from the floor and setting to work again. They had both been trained as seamstresses in the orphan home—"Respectable work," one of the nuns had reassured them, "and always in demand"—but Florence was the one who still had to sew daily for work. Vivian had taken over the household mending ever since she started doing deliveries for Miss Ethel instead of bending over tiny beads and tinier stitches every day.

"I'm still waiting for an answer, though."

Vivian grimaced. She had hoped Florence would forget her question. "What do you mean?"

"You know exactly what I mean." Florence turned away from the stove, the ladle sticking out at an awkward angle as she crossed her arms. But underneath the disapproving stare, Vivian could sense the sharp edge of worry. It was there in Florence's clenched jaw, the rigid set of her shoulders. "You've been distracted, and you were tossing about after you got home last night."

"You were asleep when I got home," Vivian said defensively, scowling down at her work so she didn't have to meet her sister's eyes.

"I'm never asleep until you're home, Vivi." The soft answer made Vivian flinch. "Not completely. Are you going to answer the question?"

"Nothing's going on," Vivian insisted, resisting the urge to stab her needle into the fabric. As much as she might want to, she had been a seamstress too long to take her nerves out on the mending. "Last night I had to help Bea out with something. That's all."

She was hoping that mentioning Bea would convince Florence to stop asking questions. She and Florence owed the Henrys so much. When the sisters had moved into their shoebox rooms after leaving the orphan home, Florence had fallen sick almost immediately. With influenza still fresh in everyone's minds, no one would come near them, and Vivian had been too scared and poor to know what to do.

Della Henry had heard about the two Irish girls who needed help, so she had showed up at their door one morning to do exactly that. And both Kelly sisters knew they would never be able to repay her for it.

But when Vivian looked up, Florence was watching her still, her worry plain as day.

"Do you remember the last time there was something going on?" Florence asked quietly. "And you didn't want to tell me what it was—I don't blame you for that," she added quickly, raising her hand to cut off Vivian's protest. "You had no reason to think I would listen. So I'm telling you here and now, this time I'll listen. Is there something else going on at work?"

Vivian hesitated, then wished she hadn't. She didn't want her silence to make Florence worry. "Nothing's going on at work," she said. It was true enough, though she knew Florence might take issue with that definition of true if she knew the whole story. But this time it wasn't anything that put them in danger, so Florence didn't need to have it weighing on her. She worried enough about Vivian working at the Nightingale. There was no use adding to those fears. "I'm just worried about Bea. Pearlie's death has been hard on her."

"I can imagine. I envied her when Pearlie arrived, you know," Florence said. "I used to dream about our own family showing up like that. That they would care enough to come find us someday." She had turned back to the stovetop, and she spoke softly. But Vivian, her sewing forgotten for the moment, heard every word. "But I guess more family just means more people to lose. So maybe we're lucky, after all."

It was so rare that Florence said anything about their unknown family. Vivian stared at the fabric in her lap, her hands still, not quite brave enough to raise her eyes. "You don't dream that now?"

The room was quiet enough that she could hear Florence's barely there sigh. "Not much room in our life for daydreams, is there? Besides, they've had two decades since our mother died. If they wanted to find us, they would have by now."

"Maybe they didn't know where to look." Vivian had never been able to shake the hope that one day someone from their mother's family—or even their unknown, unnamed father's family—would manage to track them down and welcome them back. It was a hope she held on to out of stubbornness more than any actual chance of it happening. "Maybe they didn't know we were there to look for at all."

Or at least, it had felt like stubbornness until a single day in Chinatown, only a few months before. Less than a single day, really. A brief moment, when she and Danny had been helping a man who collapsed on the street. Vivian, unable to understand what anyone was saying around her, had been cradling the man's head in her lap when he opened his eyes, looked right at her, and called her by her mother's name.

She had felt like her own heart would give out, like she might collapse right next to him on the sidewalk. But a moment later, the man had been whisked away by his neighbors in search of the local doctor. Vivian had been left staring after him, wondering if she had imagined the whole thing.

Before that moment, they'd had only one link to their mother and their past: a sour, unhappy neighbor who had lived in the building when their mother was there and who, in spite of resenting the responsibility, had made sure they stayed together long enough to be sent to the same orphan home. She never spoke well of their mother, though she had known her only a few months before she died. But she had always said Vivian and Florence looked like her, though they both had dark hair and their mother's hair had been bright red.

Florence had dismissed the possibility that the stranger's words meant anything, unwilling to let that hope flicker back to life. But since that day, Vivian had been torn. She wanted to track down the man, to find out whether he did know something about her mother, about their family.

And she was terrified that if she did, she'd discover they had known all along that Mae Kelly had left behind two daughters when she died, and they just hadn't cared.

"Come on." Florence's brisk order broke into her thoughts as she wrapped two dish towels around the pot's handles and took it off the stove. Vivian could tell by the tone of her sister's voice that Florence, too, was thinking painful thoughts and didn't want to admit it. "The beans are ready. Get your shoes on and get the bread and let's take this over to the Henrys."

"Yeah, sure." Vivian sniffed, but she didn't wipe her eyes. She had learned long ago that crying took up time and energy that she couldn't afford to waste. Folding the mending back into its basket, she gave Florence a sideways glance. "Oh, I forgot to tell you. Turns out, a girl from work was Pearlie's sweetheart. And she's having a baby."

"What?" Florence stared at her, then let out a heavy breath. "Well. That's going to be a fun complication for everyone."

The Henrys were just finishing their breakfast when Florence knocked, bowls of oatmeal in front of the children and a can of Klim powdered milk still out on the table between them. "Can we drop off some lunch?" Florence asked, poking her head inside the open door, since Vivian had taken over carrying the heavy pot of beans.

"Florence, honey, you girls are angels." Mrs. Henry, dressed for work, was hovering over her children while Bea handed her a steaming mug of coffee. She looked even more worn and weary than usual. Vivian's heart ached for Mrs. Henry that she couldn't afford to ask for time away from the restaurant, even after a death in the family.

"You'd do the same for any of us," Florence said, going and putting her arms around Bea's mother. "And you have, many times."

Mrs. Henry held on to her for a long moment, then pulled herself together as she always did, giving Florence a brisk pat on the cheek. "Put it on the stove, thank you. Bea can give it to the little ones while I'm at work. I'm hoping Mr. Chandler will let me off early today, in any case."

"And since I'm not working today, I can help out with whatever needs to be done around here while you're at the restaurant," Florence said firmly.

"Honey, you don't have to—"

"There's laundry," Bea interrupted, giving her mother a pointed look. "We'd be grateful for the help, thanks, Florence. Mama's working herself to the bone. And someone needs to go over Everett's math lesson with him because he's falling behind." Everett, fifteen and small for his age, scowled at her, but Bea scowled right back. "You are. And girls who sew are good with numbers."

Mrs. Henry probably would have argued more, but she didn't have the time. A few minutes later and she was out the door in a whirlwind of tight hugs and tired eyes. Her oldest son went with her. The laundry needed to be washed; once that was done, Bea and Vivian took over hanging it on the rack above the stove while Florence sat with the other two children to go over their schoolwork.

"Did you find a letter?" Vivian asked, lowering the rack and tying its pully rope in a knot to keep it in place while they worked.

Bea scowled. "Alba took his papers, fat lot of help she is. Said she had to look through them to find things she'd need for the baby. And Mama said not to bother her. I could barely sleep last night, wondering what to think about this whole mess. Do you think he got one? What else did Mr. Guzman say last night?"

Vivian glanced at the three heads bent over the table and lowered her voice as much as she could. "Not much more," she said, filling Bea in on Mr. Guzman's admission that he had tried and failed to catch the letter writer.

"God almighty," Bea swore quietly. "Do you think this means it wasn't a mob angle at all?"

"It still could all be," Vivian pointed out. "Making folks scared like that, so they hand over their valuables? Sure sounds like a smooth operation to me."

"And it's the sort of thing the police aren't going to take notice of. Plenty of things in a normal home have arsenic in them, so if someone tried to report it—"

"Like that family did," Vivian interrupted.

"Right. They tried to report it, but the police just think it's lazy poor people who got careless and left out a can of some everyday thing." Bea shuddered. "Then a death like Pearlie's, that looks like a suicide? No one looked twice at that. But why the change?" There was a pleading note in her voice, and her hands shook as she raised the rack once again so that the drying clothes hung over the stove. "Everyone else, it was just threats. Why did Pearlie have to be the one to die?"

"If he got one of those letters—"

"And he must have, right?" Bea interrupted. "With that bottle being full of arsenic . . ."

"But everyone else did what the letters said," Vivian said softly. She didn't look at Bea as she said it, wanting to give her friend as much space as she could to work through her messy feelings. "And the money was gone, which means whoever was after it got it, either before or after he . . ." She didn't want to finish that sentence.

Bea was silent for a long moment, her hands braced against the edge of the counter, her expression tight and angry. Vivian didn't blame her. Sometimes, anger felt easier than sorrow.

"But here's the question, right?" Bea said at last. "Pearlie must have thought that bottle was from whatever boss he was working for, whoever paid him that money. Are they the same person?"

"I don't know." Vivian grimaced. "Before we can figure anything out, we need to get those papers from Alba and see whether there actually is a letter there."

Bea shook her head at the mention of Alba. "I still can't believe Pearlie left behind a baby. Poor Alba. I don't even like her, but I wouldn't wish that on anyone, being left alone and pregnant like that."

"She's not alone," Vivian whispered, reaching out to squeeze her friend's hand. "She's got all of you. And you're going to love that baby to pieces, even if you never come around to liking her."

After a moment, Bea squeezed back. "Let's go see if she's home."

Alba, it turned out, lived in the same building as the Henrys, one floor down. She opened the door quickly enough when they knocked, looking surprised. Then her face drew into a scowl. She was a beautiful mess, her hair pinned haphazardly on top of her head, wearing only a wrapper and her step-in, as though she had been in the middle of getting dressed when they knocked. "Here to gloat? Or planning to help me pack?"

Bea and Vivian glanced at each other in confusion.

"Pack?" Vivian asked. "Are you going somewhere?"

Alba laughed, bitter and a little wild. There were tear tracks on her cheeks. "They could probably hear the shouting all the way over in Brooklyn, I just assumed you heard it, too. My mother kicked me out. She wants me gone by the time she gets home."

Vivian felt a wave of phantom nausea, and she swallowed rapidly. It was every girl's nightmare, of course, and the reason she never let herself get so friendly with any man she met when she was dancing or working. It was bad enough that once women had babies, they never seemed to stop having them. But being unmarried and with a kid on the way was a steep drop into a ditch that could be impossible to climb free of. Especially if you had the sort of family that would kick you out when that happened.

"What did she say?" Bea asked softly.

"That she can't keep such a sinful girl under her roof. But I think she just doesn't want another mouth to feed. Especially since it'll be hard for me to work right after the baby comes." There were tears in Alba's eyes again, but she brushed them away and tossed her head, her pretty mouth trembling before she pressed it into a tight line. "I'll manage. I don't care."

"Well, I care," Bea said. "Fine model of Christian charity she is, stupid cow. You're coming home with me."

"You don't have to do that."

"Like hell I don't," Bea snapped.

Alba glared at her. "Don't suddenly start pretending you like me now, Beatrice."

"I'm not pretending. I still don't like you. But that doesn't mean

I'll let someone throw you to the wolves like that. We're not letting anything happen to you or that baby, and you know my mother will say the same. So go pack whatever you've got that matters to you. Are those Pearlie's letters?" Bea added, almost like it was an afterthought, as she pointed to a stack of papers on the table. Alba nodded. "I'll gather those up."

Alba lifted her chin, proud and angry, looking like she wanted to argue, but Bea cut her off impatiently. "Don't be all high and mighty and stupid about it. Just say yes and get your things."

They stared at each other. At last Alba nodded and, without another word, disappeared into the back room. Vivian watched her go, remembering Dr. Harris's instructions not to upset her. The last thing they needed was Alba overhearing whatever they might say while going through Pearlie's papers. Luckily, Alba didn't seem to be at all suspicious of what they were doing, and she yanked the door shut behind her.

Vivian turned back to the table. Beside her, Bea took a deep breath and pulled the stack of papers toward them.

There wasn't much to them—jotted notes, a few letters from friends in different states all dated more than a year ago. Bea put those aside for her mother, who had wanted to write to those folks and let them know about Pearlie's death. There was a handful of receipts from what might have been a pawnshop.

Bea stared at those for a long time. "He only had one suitcase when he arrived in the city," she said quietly. "And he always insisted on paying for his room and board before he got a place of his own." Sniffing a little, she pushed the receipts aside with a jerky motion.

They fluttered to the floor, and Vivian bent to gather them up, her chest feeling tight. Pearlie had always been outgoing, friendly and playful and proud. She wondered how many of his things he'd had to pawn to feel like he was pulling his weight before he got that job at the Nightingale. And she wondered if he had been able to buy them back before his death.

Vivian was just shuffling the receipts into a pile when she heard Bea suck in a breath. She looked over and found her friend staring at a single sheet of paper.

Without a word, Bea slid the paper across the table, only her fingertips touching it, as though it would burn her or poison her if she held it too tightly. Just as gingerly, Vivian picked it up.

The letter was written in blocky, ugly capital letters. Unlike the tidy little note that had come with the brandy bottle, this one looked as though the person writing it had been barely literate. Or, maybe, they'd been trying to disguise their handwriting. It was just as Mr. Guzman had described: a demand so simple it almost seemed like a joke, telling Pearlie to put the one thousand dollars he had into a bag and leave it in a certain spot at exactly one in the morning. The date it gave for the drop-off was two weeks before. *Don't stick around or try to see who's coming to get it,* the letter finished. *You won't like the consequences if you do.*

Someone trying to disguise their writing, then, Vivian thought. Her mind latched onto the details of the note to avoid thinking what they really meant. No one who was barely literate wrote out words like *consequences*.

"One thousand dollars?" Bea breathed. Her hands were trembling, but Vivian couldn't tell whether it was from shock or sorrow or anger. A mess of all that and more, most likely. "How the hell did he get that? And what the hell are we supposed to do with this? And why did they just rob everyone else, but my uncle was the one who they killed? Why'd they have to decide to change everything then? Why *him*?"

Her voice was rising as she spoke. Vivian tried to gesture for her to be quieter, but it was too late.

"What are you talking about?" Alba demanded. She was standing in the doorway when they turned guiltily around, wearing a cheap, fashionable dress, her hair pinned more tidily, a bag in one hand and a notebook under her arm. But she somehow looked even wilder than before, her eyes darting between them with more angry, jittery energy than her small frame looked like it could contain. "Who was robbed? Who was murdered? What—"

"It's okay," Vivian said, trying to sound soothing, her hands held out as if she were trying to placate a feral cat in an alley. "Really, it's nothing you need to worry about. You just finish packing and—"

"You shut your mouth," Alba snapped. "You ain't part of this family, so it's got nothing to do with you." She rounded on Bea. "What were you saying about Pearlie? Tell me. I deserve to know. Tell me right now, or I swear I will throw open that window and—"

"God almighty, Alba, leave her alone. And shut your own mouth for half a second so I can answer you," Bea finally yelled. The two of them stared at each other, both of them breathing as heavily as if they had just run up the building's five rickety flights of stairs. So much for keeping calm. Vivian didn't even want to think about how Alba might have been planning to finish her threat.

Bea took a deep breath. Her voice was steady when she answered, but Vivian could see her hands shaking. "We found out some things about Pearlie," she began slowly.

"Some of them I'm guessing you already know?" Vivian broke in. "The money, maybe?"

Alba stared at her for a moment. "What makes you think I know about any money?"

"Because you saw us at his place, even though you hightailed it out of there pretty damn quick. And as far as I know, you haven't asked what we were doing there." Vivian glanced at Bea as she spoke; her friend, looking surprised, nodded slowly. "So you know Pearlie was working for someone and got a hell of a payout from it, don't you?" A sudden thought occurred to her. "Is that why you were there? Were you coming to look for the money?"

The silence stretched through the room, answering the question even before Alba spoke. "Yes," she said at last. "Of course I knew about it. Pearlie and me, we told each other everything. He knew about the baby," she said, a defensive note creeping into her voice. Her free hand pressed instinctively against her lower belly, her fingers splayed wide as she took a deep breath that didn't seem to do much to steady her. "He was going to take care of us. But then . . ." She shuddered. "The doctor said he killed himself, and the money wasn't where he'd hidden it. I thought maybe he spent it, or lost it, and couldn't bear to tell me. And I was so . . ." Her words came out in a sudden rush. "I was so *angry* at him for leaving us like that."

"He didn't leave you," Bea said. She was angry too, an icy anger that made Vivian feel chilled herself. "Someone sent him a bottle of brandy, with a note thanking him for a job well done. Vivian has a friend who knows a fella in the coroner's office. They tested it, and it was full of arsenic."

Alba's bag and notebook fell to the ground, and she grabbed the doorframe with one hand to steady herself, her other hand tightening protectively across her belly once more. "But who—Why would someone—"

"For his money, looks like," Vivian said quietly. "Someone's been threatening folks around here, sending them letters demanding whatever pretty or precious things they've got, and threatening them with poisoning if they don't pay up. And Pearlie got one of those letters, because someone must have talked and found out about the money."

"What?" Alba was shaking her head, her back pressed against the doorframe as though she were trying to run away without realizing it. "That doesn't make any sense. How . . ." She trailed off, eyes wide and mouth trembling.

"Pearlie didn't pay up," Bea said, holding out the letter, relentless in the face of Alba's denial. "We just found the letter in his things. He didn't pay up, so they killed him and took the money."

"And now word's going to get around," Vivian said, realization dawning. "That's what they're hoping for, I bet. Word gets around, and then people really will pay up, because they don't want to die and have it just dismissed as a suicide or an accident—"

"And of course the police aren't paying any attention, because that's exactly what it looks like," Bea agreed bitterly. "And we can't even tell them, because who knows what kind of reach this group has and who they'll come after next."

"No. That doesn't make sense." Alba was still shaking her head. "That *can't* be what happened, you don't—"

The door to the apartment opened, and all three of them turned in panic. But the woman who was standing there looked too old to be Alba's mother, her white hair pulled into a soft, old-fashioned knot on top of her head and her face a spiderweb of cozy lines and folds. She looked as kind and gentle as it was possible for an old woman to look as she stared at the three of them in surprise and confusion. For a moment Vivian relaxed. But then the woman's gaze moved from Vivian to Bea, her expression growing pinched and suspicious. When she finally rounded on Alba, her eyes were hard and flinty, her mouth twisted as though she were tasting something disgusting. An angry, disapproving torrent of words exploded out of her, her voice starting loud and getting louder. Vivian flinched; even though she couldn't understand, it wasn't hard to figure out the meaning as the old woman gestured dismissively at Alba and pointed toward the door. Alba spoke to her rapidly in the same language, but the old woman just got more insistent, pointing at Vivian and Bea as she shook her head.

"Me voy, Abuela, me voy," Alba finally snapped. Stalking to the table, she gathered all the papers into a pile and shoved them at Bea, who was left with her arms full, papers sticking out at all angles. Vivian picked up the bag and notebook, planning to carry them for her; the notebook was actually a sketchbook, she saw, full of little drawings, birds and plants and buildings around the city. But Alba snatched them both from her, glaring at Vivian as though daring her to argue. Then, head held high, she stalked toward the door. She didn't look back, and Vivian and Bea were left scrambling to catch up.

Vivian looked back as she turned to close the door behind her. The old woman, silent now, was watching her granddaughter go. There were tears in her eyes. But when she saw Vivian looking at her, her expression grew flinty again. She stepped forward just enough to yank the door out of Vivian's hand and slam it closed.

Vivian stared at the door, her heart aching for Alba in ways that she could never say out loud.

Maybe Florence was right. Maybe it was better not to have any family at all.

TWELVE

Bea and Alba were back at the Henrys' apartment by the time Vivian caught up to them, and they weren't the only ones there. Abraham had arrived, hat in hand as he cast sideways glances at Florence, who was still sitting with the children. When Bea walked in, he practically leaped forward to catch her hand.

"Where have you been?" he asked. "I was worried you were trying to—"

"Just taking care of a few things," Bea said firmly, jerking her head toward her brother and sister in a clear warning to watch what he said. Abraham winced and nodded. She shoved the letters into his hands. "Here, hold on to these, okay? I just need to get Alba settled."

Alba met Abraham's eyes briefly, and they stared at each other before Alba, head held high, let Bea usher her into one of the bedrooms to unpack her things. Abraham watched them go with a frown on his face.

Vivian watched him in turn. She wasn't surprised that he had come to check on Bea—it was good that he had. And she wouldn't be surprised if he wanted to ask what she and Honor had discovered. But he looked downright unhappy, twisting his hat between his hands as he watched Bea and Alba. He had been friendly with Pearlie, she knew. Maybe he didn't get along with Alba, who could be prickly and melodramatic if you rubbed her the wrong way. And Abraham himself wasn't the most easygoing of people.

Vivian looked away quickly as Abraham turned back to the room, not wanting him to know she had been watching him. Still on edge from the discovery of the letter in Pearlie's things and the ugly confrontation with Alba's grandmother, she leaned against the kitchen counter and closed her eyes, listening to Florence. Once, when they were much younger, Florence had told her stories about their mother, about her dreams for their life together. Those moments hovered at the edges of Vivian's memory, and trying to catch them was like trying to learn a dance she could only watch out of the corner of her eye. But the sound of Florence's quiet voice still made her feel safe for a brief, distracting moment.

"It's the fanciest thing I've ever worked on in my life," Florence was saying. Everett and eleven-year-old Baby—whose real name was Della, after her mother, but no one called her that—were sitting at the table with cups of milk in front of them, watching while Florence sketched a picture of a dress on a crumpled sheet of brown grocer's paper. "The gems go right here around the neckline, see? Almost like a necklace themselves. And then also around the hem. I have to sew on teeny, tiny metal brackets to hold them in place, and they have to be in just the right spots."

Vivian opened her eyes at last to find Abraham flipping through the papers Bea had handed him. His face fell, likely when he realized whose letters they were, and his mouth twisted unhappily. But a moment later he grew still, staring at one of the papers in the pile. Vivian could guess which one.

"What kind of gems?" Baby asked, wide-eyed, the line of milk on her upper lip making her look even younger than she was.

"Aquamarine and topaz," Florence said, her smile wistful as she wiped Baby's face with her fingers. Florence loved beautiful, delicate things, and she could never afford them for herself. "They make the prettiest pattern, pale blue and gold. And the dress is a deep navy blue, so they really do seem to shine against it. Miss Ethel calls them semiprecious stones, but they seem pretty precious to me."

Abraham's head shot up as he finished reading. "Bea!" he began, before Vivian slid close and nudged his ankle with her foot. He turned to her, scowling.

"She won't want you yelling about it," she murmured. "Or waving it around."

"But what—"

"What's going on?" Everett piped up, looking over at them.

"Nothing," Abraham said quickly, putting the pile of papers on the counter and trying to smile. "Just going to check on your sister." He strode into the bedroom.

As soon as he was gone, Vivian pulled the letter out of the pile. Bea wouldn't want to risk her brothers or sister finding that. Vivian put it in her pocket, just to get it out of the way. She would ask Bea what to do with it later.

"She locks the dress and the box of stones up every night before the store closes," Florence continued. "I can't start work until she unlocks it for me in the morning."

"She also checks everyone's pockets before they're allowed to leave at night to make sure no one has stolen any," Vivian put in as Bea and Abraham reemerged, shutting the door of the bedroom quietly behind them. "She's terrified Mrs. Blake is going to count the stones on the dress and discover one of them is missing."

"Who sews their gems into their clothing instead of just having a jeweler set them?" Everett asked, trying not to look too interested in a story about a dress.

"Rich folks who already have more jewelry than they know what to do with," Bea said shortly. She turned to Abraham. "Did you have something you needed to tell me?"

He seemed about to answer, then his eyes darted toward the children. "Doesn't matter," he said, giving a weak smile. "I'll be right back. Gonna go ask Alba if I can bring anything by for her. My sister's littlest has outgrown a lot recently."

"Too much jewelry sounds like a nice problem to have," Baby said dreamily, still thinking about the dress. Vivian couldn't help a snort of laughter. Then Baby turned to look at her sister. "What's Miss Diaz doing here?"

Bea sighed, rolling her eyes heavenward. "Not a moment's peace," she muttered, but she crossed the room to stand between her brother's and sister's chairs. "Miss Diaz is going to be staying with us for a while."

"Why?" Everett asked. His round face had the world-weary look of someone much older than his fifteen years. "Is it something to do with Uncle Pearlie?"

Baby's mouth trembled. "I miss Uncle Pearlie," she whispered. "It's too quiet at dinner without him."

"I miss him too, honey," Bea said gently. She looked up at Florence. "Thanks for keeping an eye on them. we're going to have a family chat right now."

"You're always welcome, Beatrice," Florence replied, gathering up her things. "We'll get out of your hair, but you let us know if you need anything else, okay?"

"Sure thing."

"Bea—" Vivian began, but her friend shook her head.

"Later, okay, Viv? I've gotta deal with these two troublemakers." She gave each of their shoulders a little shake before crouching down so she was closer to eye level with them. "Will I see you tonight?"

"Tonight?"

"Yeah." Bea nodded. "I'm ready to go back to work. I know it's your night off, but if you wanted to stop by—"

"Sure," Vivian said. She couldn't tell Bea no. Not after what they had just learned.

Bea nodded, giving her a quick, grateful smile. "And you two—" She turned to Everett and Baby, a bright smile on her face that made Vivian's heart ache. Bea always put on a good show for the kids, determined to spare them the worries that plagued her and her mother. But they were getting older, and it was hard to tell how much it fooled them anymore. "I have some exciting news to tell you."

Florence waited until the door was closed behind them and they were going down the stairs to ask, "So what really happened?"

Vivian sighed and explained about Alba's family as they walked back to their own tenement building. By the time they reached their front door, Florence was wiping her eyes. "That poor girl. Thank God you and Bea stopped by when you did, or who knows where she might have gone."

"Flo . . ." Vivian went to pick up her mending again, and she kept her eyes on the fabric as she spoke, too nervous to look at her sister but unable to stop herself from asking the question. "You'd never do that, would you, if . . . if I . . ."

"Of course not, I—" A loud *thunk,* as though Florence had been holding something and set it down abruptly. "Vivi, you're not—"

"No!" Vivian did look up then, long enough to meet Florence's stricken eyes. She laughed humorlessly. "Glad to know that's how you'd react, though."

"Well, you can't blame me for asking, after a question like that. And don't make that face at me. I know what people get up to in places like your Nightingale."

"No, you don't," Vivian said, more sharply than she intended, then stopped herself before she said anything she might regret. It had been months since she and Florence had fought over the Nightingale, and she hadn't missed it. She took a deep breath. "It's just a place folks can go out dancing, have a few laughs, that sort of thing."

"And drink, and smoke—"

"Yes, those happen too," Vivian said, the mending forgotten in her hands. "But they aren't the point, Flo. The point is that it's a place to be yourself, or not yourself. To not worry about all this—" She gestured, the sweep of her arm taking in their unlovely home, the shouts of neighbors that were filtering through the walls, the plight of Alba two blocks over. "—and just exist, like you're the equal of every other person there, even if it's just for a few hours."

"You make it sound so high-minded," Florence said, clearly skeptical.

Vivian laughed. "Well, high-minded is maybe stretching it a bit. And yes, sure, some people are there to drink too much and get sweaty with strangers."

"Vivian!" Florence didn't like that kind of talk, which was why Vivian couldn't help it sometimes.

But Vivian pressed on. "But it's also a place for folks who wouldn't be welcome anywhere else." She eyed her sister curiously. "Don't you ever just want to have fun? To have a night where you don't think about any of it and just be free?"

"Who says dancing with strangers is my idea of fun?" Florence said defensively.

"Well, then, what is?" Vivian demanded, starting to feel exasperated. She didn't think her sister was being deliberately obtuse, but she had worked so hard to change their lives for the better. Why couldn't Florence see that things weren't the same as they had always been?

Florence ran her fingers along the edge of the counter, a frown between her brows as she stared at their aimless path. "I don't know. I've never had a chance to find out."

"You've got two days off every week now," Vivian pointed out, a hint of a challenge in her voice. She waited until Florence looked up and met her eyes. "You could do something with them, you know."

"And you think I should come to your dance hall?" Florence asked, crossing her arms.

"Why not?" Vivian replied. "You like music. You'd figure out the dancing fast enough. Nothing I say is going to convince you that it's not some hotbed of sin."

"No, it's not."

Vivian ignored the comment and pressed on. "So why don't you actually go there and see what it's like for yourself?"

"I couldn't."

"Why not?" Somehow, now that she'd said it out loud, it felt important to Vivian that she convince Florence to go. Maybe she wanted to shake her sister out of her tired, lonely routine. Maybe she just wanted a chance to prove Florence wrong. Maybe both.

Florence was saved from having to answer by a knock on the door, a quick, syncopated series of raps, as if the visitor were playing a jazz rhythm on the wood. Both girls jumped.

"Are you expecting someone?" Florence asked, going to answer it. "Oh!"

Danny was standing in the doorway. He and Florence stared at each other in surprise, as if neither one knew what to make of the other's presence there, before Danny scrambled to take off his hat and give her a friendly smile.

"Sorry to startle you," he said, with more genuine politeness than Vivian had ever heard from him before. "I'm looking for Vivian."

"Oh. Yes, of course." Florence turned toward Vivian, her cheeks pink with embarrassment. Men didn't often come to their home, and Vivian suspected she was worried about what the neighbors might think if any of them saw. "Vivi, there's—"

"Yeah, I can see him," Vivian said, unable to keep the amusement from her voice. "Mind if he comes in?"

"Oh," Florence said for a third time, her blush growing as she turned back to Danny. "Do you want to—I mean, you heard her. Come on in."

"Thank you," Danny said, stepping past her. For a moment, Vivian was worried that her sister's obvious discomfort had made him uncomfortable. But a moment later her fears were put to rest as Danny gave Florence a big smile and a wink. "If I'd known Vivian had such a pretty sister, I'd have stopped by long ago."

"Easy there, lover boy," Vivian said dryly as Florence's eyes went wide and Danny chuckled.

"Sorry, Miss . . . Florence, I think? Have I got that right?"

Florence nodded. Her back was still pressed up against the open door from when she had stepped aside to let him in, and she didn't seem to be capable of moving.

"Danny Chin." He held out his hand, and Florence, without seeming to know what she was doing, shook it. "I work with your sister, here."

"I guessed as much," Florence said, her voice sounding strangled. Her cheeks had gone past pink and were now bright red.

Vivian had to hold back her own laughter. She had never seen Florence flustered like this before. But she took pity on her sister. "Did you stop by just to flirt, Danny, or is there another reason?"

"Can't a fella do both?" he teased, his eyes still on Florence. But when she didn't seem to know what to say, his smile became a little softer. "I really am pleased to meet you, Miss Florence. From what I hear, Vivian's lucky to have such a swell sister looking after her."

"She needs a lot of looking after," Florence managed at last, casting a not very subtle glare in Vivian's direction. "If she's hanging out with flirts like you."

Vivian would have let herself be drawn into an argument, but Danny laughed. "No need to look so grumpy, kitten, I deserved that," he said to her, still smiling. But his expression grew more serious. "I can't stay long, I'm checking inventory soon. But Hux asked me to come by with a message."

Vivian felt like her heart had just sped up to twice its normal rate. "Yeah?" She wasn't supposed to work that night, so if Honor was sending her a message, she had a good idea why.

"There's someone coming by tonight to see you. And she's not the sort of person we should keep waiting."

"No, I imagine not. Guess I'll be there." She shivered, remembering the note that she and Bea had found tucked in Pearlie's things. "Did Honor tell you what it's about?"

Danny raised his brows. "Not much she doesn't tell me. You know that."

"I do." The letter was still in her pocket, she realized, and she pressed one hand against it, feeling the paper crinkle through the fabric. Danny hadn't given a time, which meant there was no knowing when their guest would turn up. She'd have to arrive at the beginning of the night and wait to see what happened. "Tell Honor I'll be there."

"Then I'll see you tonight, kitten." Danny gave Florence another smile. "Nice to meet you," he said, putting his hat back on and giving the brim a jaunty little tip.

"Likewise," Florence said. Her voice still came out a little strangled, but there was a smile pulling at the corners of her lips.

That smile made Vivian pause after she closed the door behind Danny. Maybe Florence wasn't as immune to fun and flirtation as she seemed. Vivian cast a sideways glance at her sister. "Did you make up your mind, then? You coming with me tonight?"

"What?" Florence asked, looking baffled for a moment before her eyes grew wide. "You're serious, aren't you? Didn't that Mr. Chin just say you have a meeting with someone?"

"That'll only take a few minutes out of the whole night. Come on, Flo," Vivian wheedled, her voice sweet and persuasive and a little mocking. "What are you scared of?"

As soon as the words were out of her mouth, she regretted them. There *were* things to be scared of. Pearlie's death was a reminder of that. And depending on how the meeting that Honor had arranged for her went, she could end up a lot more involved in that than she wanted.

But before she could say anything, Florence had lifted her chin and nodded. "Fine. I'll go out with you tonight." The pink was back in her cheeks, but that hint of a smile was still there. "If you say it's safe, I trust you."

I trust you. The words were so welcome that Vivian didn't have the heart to take back her challenge.

THIRTEEN

Here you go." Danny slid two glasses of champagne across the bar to them. He gave Florence a wink. "On the house tonight. Welcome to the Nightingale."

"Thanks, Danny. You're a peach." Vivian smiled back at him, then spun around on her stool before taking a long drink. The bubbles struck the back of her throat like a jolt of electric light in a dark room, and she sighed with pleasure at the bright rhythm of the music. Florence, copying Vivian's movement, took slow, careful sips of her drink as she eyed the dance floor.

Bea had met Vivian for the walk to the Nightingale that night, eyebrows raised when she saw Florence coming along with them in a borrowed dress, nervously touching her hair, which Vivian had pinned up in a faux bob. But she didn't say anything aside from telling Florence that she looked nice.

She had held back from the rest of the staff, not ready yet to be her usual, outgoing self. But her act was still top-notch. She was, at the moment, up on the bandstand, belting her heart out for the foxtrot.

Vivian couldn't help tapping her heels against the rung of the barstool in time to the song. But Florence stared around, looking uneasy. Her eyes grew wide as one man stopped dancing just long enough to strip off his jacket, wider as a group of well-dressed young men crowded the bar next to them and shouted orders for drinks, then wider still as she spotted two women foxtrotting with their cheeks pressed together.

"This was a bad idea," Florence whispered, her own cheeks crimson, her fingers fluttering against her glass. "It's not the sort of place for someone like me."

"Flo, it's a place for everyone," Vivian said, trying to sound encouraging enough to convince both of them. She didn't want to admit that she was thinking the exact same thing.

"Not for folks who like to keep their clothes on in public," Florence retorted. Her voice rose just enough to draw curious glances from a few patrons crowding around the bar, and her blush deepened when she saw them tittering. "I should go."

"But you haven't even had a dance yet," Vivian pointed out, starting to feel desperate. She didn't need her sister to love the Nightingale the way she did. But she wanted Florence to understand, to see why it meant so much to her. She wanted Florence to have a moment of fun, an escape of her own, even if it was only for one night. It felt like a gift that Florence had decided she didn't deserve, and Vivian wanted to prove her wrong. "Let's find you a fella before you call it quits for the night, okay?"

"Vivi, I can't dance like these people," Florence whispered as the song ended with a flourish and the dancers applauded.

"Sure you can," Vivian said. "See, they're starting a waltz next. You know how to waltz."

"I can do a one-two-three just fine, but nothing fancy. I'd be terrified if I had to follow any of those men."

"Well, then we'll find you someone who likes to keep things simple." Vivian gave her sister's hand a squeeze. "Don't be scared, Flo. It's just for laughs."

She glanced around the room, hoping to catch someone's eye. Maybe one of the older gentlemen who frequented the Nightingale? Their manners would go a long way to setting Florence's nerves at ease. They could always find her someone younger once she was feeling a little calmer.

But the dance floor was crowded, and there were too many bodies around the tables for Vivian to spot any of the familiar faces she was hoping for. In the moments she spent looking, Florence was already shaking her head, her shoulders drawing together in discomfort and disappointment. "No. This was a nice thought, really, but I should just go home before I spoil your fun."

She spun her stool back around, but before she could set her drink down on the bar a cheerful voice spoke up.

"Care for a waltz, miss?"

Danny had just come around the bar and stood by them, leaning one elbow against the counter. He was clearly eavesdropping on their conversation but looked so friendly that it was hard to hold it against him. His suspenders cut sharp black lines down his chest, emphasizing the fact that he certainly wasn't wearing a coat, and his shirtsleeves were rolled up over muscular forearms. For a moment Vivian thought her sister would refuse, but Danny continued before Florence could gather her objections.

"My break's just about to start, and I'd be honored to take a turn around the floor with you." Danny gave Florence another smile, one that almost had a hint of shyness to it. Before Vivian could decide whether that was an act for her sister's benefit or the real deal, he was holding out his hand. "How 'bout it?"

Florence hesitated, glancing down at his hand then sideways at Vivian. But she had at least met Danny before, and this time, he was being friendly rather than flirtatious.

Before Florence could respond, though, a slurred voice broke in.

"A girl like her doesn't dance with the help."

Vivian was almost knocked off her stool as one of the rowdy young men from the group next to them, already sloppy and reeking of gin, pushed forward to leer at Florence. "How 'bout it, doll? You know you'd rather go for a spin with a fella who can afford to buy the drinks instead of mixing them."

Vivian tried to push him away, but he just laughed and reached for Florence. Danny tensed, his hands clenching into fists and his feet shifting into a wide stance. For all his easygoing charm, he had learned to throw a punch when he was just a kid growing up in a tough neighborhood, and he could be a vicious fighter when provoked. But before Vivian could decide whether it was better to haul her sister out of harm's way or yell for the Nightingale's muscle, Florence had swatted the drunk young man's hand away.

"If I'd known the bouncers let children in here, I wouldn't have come," she said, the scorn in her voice cold as ice. "Isn't it past your bedtime, little boy?"

The young man's face flushed red with embarrassment as he gaped at her, too surprised to come up with a retort. That was all his friends needed; they howled with laughter, clapping his shoulders and shouting "little boy!" as they hauled him away.

Danny was the first to recover, flashing a quick hand signal at the other bartender and pointing to the knot of young men. Vivian knew that it would only be a few minutes before Silence or Benny appeared to forcefully suggest that they find another place to spend their time and money. Already dismissing them from her mind, she turned to Florence, who was sitting up very straight and breathing heavily.

"You all right, Flo?" Vivian asked quietly, putting a hand on her sister's arm. The fierceness didn't surprise her—it might take a lot to provoke Florence, but Vivian had seen it happen before. She could also guess how much a confrontation like that would rattle her sister, who had been so uncertain about coming to the Nightingale in the first place.

"I'm fine," Florence said quietly, but she didn't sound like she meant it.

Danny turned his attention back to them before she could say anything else. "Where the hell did that come from?" he demanded, staring at Florence.

She met his eyes. "I don't like people who think they're something special just because they have money to throw around," she said, the words all the more intense for being delivered in her soft voice. Vivian could feel Florence trembling under her touch and was about to suggest that they leave after all when her sister abruptly stood up. "Well, Mr. Chin?" she said, taking a deep breath. "Are you still interested in that dance?"

He blinked at her for a moment before a slow smile spread across his face. "Absolutely," he said, holding out his hand once more. Before Vivian understood what was happening, Florence had taken it, and he was leading her toward the floor. "You don't mind if we keep it simple, do you?" he asked. "I'm not much of a waltzer, but I can give it a go."

"You don't need to pretend you weren't eavesdropping, Mr. Chin," Florence said tartly, but Danny just laughed, and soon they were too far away from Vivian to hear any more.

Danny did keep it simple, Vivian could see as she finished her drink and claimed her sister's abandoned glass. Simple, gentle, but still elegant, an easy lead for her sister to follow. They looked good together, she realized in surprise, with the top of Florence's curly head reaching just under Danny's nose until he bent down to say something in her ear, their bodies swaying in time with the music.

Florence, when the dance next turned them in her direction, was smiling back at him.

Vivian let out the breath she had been holding. But underneath her relief was a pang of some emotion she didn't want to think too closely about. Tossing back the rest of Florence's champagne, she reached out almost blindly and caught the elbow of the first man going past. She didn't know him, but he was young and handsome, with high cheekbones, carefully pomaded hair, and a natty striped suit.

"Fancy a spin on the floor?" she asked.

His surprise at being stopped quickly gave way to a broad smile. "I'm game for anything, baby," he purred, taking her hand and leading her to the floor.

Vivian fell into step easily with him, trying to lose herself in the dance. But no matter which way they turned, her eyes kept finding Danny and Florence, who never once looked around to find her.

When the song ended and the band struck up a Baltimore, she expected Danny to lead Florence back to the bar, and she thanked her partner absently as she looked for them. But she didn't catch sight of them until she was back on her stool.

They were still on the dance floor. Danny had a cajoling look on his face, and Florence was laughing as he coaxed her through the footwork at half the tempo of the actual song. But Florence was a quick study, and soon she had at least the basic steps down. Beaming, Danny sped up, and Florence held tight to his hand and shoulder as if determined to keep up through sheer force of will. But she was still smiling.

Vivian frowned before she realized what she was doing. She had wanted Florence to have some fun, to have a life outside their home. So why wasn't she feeling happier to see her on the dance floor with Danny?

"Viv! Thank God, I was hoping I'd find you here."

Vivian shook herself out of her unhappy thoughts, surprised to see Leo sliding onto the barstool next to her. He gestured to the bartender, calling out an order for two glasses of champagne. "Not working tonight?"

"No." Vivian shook her head. "Actually, I came with Florence."

"Your sister? Where . . ." Leo trailed off as he followed her line of sight and spotted Danny and Florence on the dance floor together. He chuckled. "Damn if they don't look good together. Don't you think?" He nudged Vivian's shoulder.

She forced a smile. "They sure do. I'm glad Danny persuaded her to try it out." If she said it out loud, maybe it would end up actually being true. She took the glass the bartender handed to her and clinked its rim against the one Leo was holding. "Why were you looking for me?"

Leo glanced around before dropping his voice. "Did you tell Bea what we found out?"

It felt like a year since they had visited the medical examiner together. Vivian shivered, taking a gulp of champagne to cover her nerves. But she drank it too quickly and ended up gasping for air. "Yeah," she said, once her throat had cleared from the sharp fizz of the bubbles. "We've learned a few more things since then. In fact—"

"Hello there, girlie."

The voice, slick as spilled oil, made Vivian tense, even before she fully realized who it was. She met Leo's eyes, trying to communicate a silent warning, before turning on her stool to face the man who had appeared next to her. "Hello, George."

Bruiser George, a thin, weaselly man in a suit that wasn't too expensive to get blood on, smirked at her. "Sorry if I startled you, girlie. I thought you'd be expecting me. You *were* the one who sent that message, weren't you?"

"I expected your boss," Vivian said, eyes wide with false innocence. "I thought you'd want to steer clear of the Nightingale. You know, since the last time you were here you tried to knock Honor down a peg and almost got taken out in pieces."

His eyes narrowed and his smirk grew a little forced, but he didn't let it drop. "And here I thought we wanted to be friendly. Why don't you be a good girl and order me a drink?"

Behind her, Vivian heard the creak of the barstool as Leo stood, and she could picture the cold expression that was likely coming over his face. But she didn't turn around to look. Instead, she gave Bruiser George a dismissive smile. "If your boss is here, I'll talk to her, not to her errand boy. And somehow, I don't think she's paying you to booze it up at the bar. So, why are you here, George?"

His expression twisted, growing the sort of ugly that was scary on a man who liked using his fists. But a moment later he laughed. "Fair enough, girlie. She's talking to your boss upstairs."

Vivian frowned, not sure whether to believe him. "I didn't see her come in." And his boss—who ran a bootlegging empire that dabbled in all kinds of other unsavory business—was a hard woman to miss.

George shrugged. "She don't use the front door. Came in through one of this place's back entrances or tunnels or what have you. Anyway, I'm supposed to bring you up." He stood. "You coming or not?"

"Vivian." Leo's voice was soft, but the worry and the warning were clear. She didn't think he knew Bruiser George, but he clearly didn't like the idea of her going anywhere with the man.

Vivian didn't blame him. But she hated for anyone to know she was afraid, even when she was shaking in her dancing shoes. "You go on ahead, George. I'll be up as soon as I finish my drink." She lifted her glass of champagne in a mocking toast.

He gave her a head-to-toe look. "Suit yourself." Scooping his hat off the bar, he tucked it under one arm and turned to go. But to her surprise he paused, his mouth pursing in a sour smile. "You know, we're more alike than you want to think."

"We're nothing alike," Vivian said, soft and cold. "I don't make my cash by hurting people."

He shrugged. "Maybe not, but we're all just gears in their machine, right? Your boss, my boss . . . someone else is always calling the shots, and they sure as hell don't tell us why. We just hop when we're told and hope we don't get arrested or worse because of it." He smiled. "See you up there, girlie."

Vivian didn't look away until he had disappeared into the back hall, presumably to climb the stairs toward Honor's office once more. She set the glass down on the bar without finishing it, her hands shaking.

"You know him?" Leo asked quietly.

Vivian was glad Leo couldn't bring a gun out dancing. She wouldn't have wanted to risk him pulling it on George. Not that Leo wasn't equally dangerous bare-handed. She shivered again. "He works for Mrs. Wilson. You remember her?"

"Hard to forget," Leo said grimly. "You shouldn't follow him."

"I was the one who asked her to come. That's why I'm here tonight, to meet with her. Pretty rude not to show up."

"Then I'll come with you," Leo said. She could see the tension in his shoulders as he eyed the doorway where George had disappeared. "Fella like that is too dangerous for you to go after alone. For all you know, he's got friends up there, just waiting."

"I'm not scared of him," Vivian lied. The look Leo gave her said he knew it wasn't true. She sighed, glancing at the dance floor full of couples, but she couldn't spot her sister in the crowd. "I'm just going upstairs for a chat. Stay here, please? Keep an eye on Florence. If Danny ever gets back to doing his job, she's going to need someone to keep her company for a little bit. And if anything ugly does happen—" She shivered at the thought, though she told herself there was no reason to worry. Honor wouldn't have told her to come that night if it was dangerous. "—someone needs to make sure she's safe. Okay? Please?"

His expression made it clear that he didn't like it, but at last he nodded. "Okay. But if you're not back in half an hour, I'm coming up, and I won't care what sort of closed-door meeting I'm barging in on."

"Fair enough." She gave him a little pat on the cheek. "I'll be fine. She's just here to talk, and anyway, Honor's got my back up there. She looks out for her people." Vivian hopped off her barstool, smiling like nothing was wrong. "See you soon, pal."

"Good luck up there."

The door past the bar opened into a hallway where customers could find the ladies' powder room or men's dressing room. At the very end, a door opened into a narrow alley, a place where folks would go to cool off, catch a breath of air, or get a little frisky away from prying eyes. Before that, though, was a staircase leading up to Honor's private office.

Vivian was halfway up the stairs when she slowed to a stop, suddenly wondering if she should have listened to Leo's warning. She could see George standing a few steps below the landing where the door to Honor's office was; a few steps below that, another man waited. He was built along different lines than George—tall, lean, slick-looking—but she could see the scars on his knuckles, and one across his cheek, even in the dim light. Another of Mrs. Wilson's bruisers, then, and both of them staring at her. Vivian felt panic surge through her chest like a heart attack, and for a moment she was terrified of what might have happened to Honor behind that door.

But then George stepped up, knocking on the door smartly. "She's here," he called.

And it was Honor's voice that called back. "Get out of her way, then, instead of skulking around trying to listen in."

George scowled, clearly unhappy with both the order and the fact that someone other than his boss was giving it. But the expression was replaced a moment later by his usual oily smile. He gestured toward the door. "In you go, girlie."

The stairs weren't wide, and she hated having to pass so close to both men in order to reach the door. The back of her neck prickled with sweat when they were behind her. She paused on the landing, her fist raised to knock, meeting each of their eyes in turn. "I think you were supposed to be going?" she said, relieved that her voice wasn't shaking.

George bristled, but the other man smirked. "Sure thing, sweetheart. Come on, George, boss lady said we get fifteen once she showed up. Let's go get a drink."

Vivian watched until they were both gone before knocking. But she didn't wait for Honor's reply before going in.

On the other side of the door, the scene that met her was surprisingly cordial. Honor was behind her desk but not seated. Instead, she perched one hip on the windowsill behind it—the window itself looked onto a blank brick wall only inches away—legs crossed at the ankle and a glass of her private stash of whiskey in one hand. The bottle sat on the desk in front of her. And on the other side of the desk, just turning her head to glance at the door, was the person Vivian had come to see.

Hattie Wilson was the sort of woman whose wealth surrounded her like a cloud of perfume. She wore black still, and she had spent the time since her husband's death mostly secluded from the Manhattan and Long Island society in which she moved. But her dress was silk, trimmed with jet beads around its high neck and where the sheer sleeves gathered at her wrists. It was cut with the precision and elegance that only custom dressmaking could achieve. In fact, Vivian recognized the design and style. It had come from Miss Ethel's shop, where she and Florence both worked. Vivian narrowed her eyes, wondering if Mrs. Wilson had worn the dress as a not-so-subtle reminder of the differences between their positions in life. Her hair—no bob for her, nothing that might open her up to accusations of being loose or fast—was perfectly curled and pinned back. The hat she wore perched to one side of her head was draped with black netting, making her wide eyes and pouting mouth look even more vulnerable. She was like a china doll in her prettiness and perfection.

But those eyes were steely with determination, and the smile on that mouth was cold. There was no hint of softness or kindness there. Hattie Wilson was a survivor, and she was ruthless. She had to be, to get where she was.

"Miss Kelly," she said, giving a little nod before taking a sip from her glass. "Here I am. What can I do for you?" She glanced at Honor. "This is excellent, by the way. Who's your supplier?"

Honor laughed. "You know I'm not giving that up," she said.

Mrs. Wilson smiled, and Vivian tried not to think about what George had said. The two women had plenty in common, sure. But they were nothing alike.

There was a second chair in front of the desk, and an empty glass rested next to it, waiting for her. Vivian took a deep breath, crossed the room, and sat. "Thanks for coming," she said as Honor poured her a finger of whiskey. She took the glass, just to have something to do with her hands, but she didn't drink it. "Why did you?"

Mrs. Wilson raised her brows. "You were the one who asked me for a meeting. Would you rather I hadn't listened?"

"No. But you've got your reasons, and I doubt they've got much to do with me."

"They're not the same as yours," Mrs. Wilson said softly. "But you're very wrong if you think they have nothing to do with you."

Vivian glanced at Honor out of the corner of her eye. But the club owner said nothing. Clearly, in spite of her own interest in Pearlie's death, she was there only as an intermediary, setting up the meeting but not planning to get involved. Vivian, trying not to look nervous, took refuge in rudeness. "I was surprised to find out you'd been sneaking around to get here. I'd have thought you had the guts to use the front door like a normal person."

Hattie didn't rise to the bait. "I'm far from normal, Miss Kelly. And in any case, I can't be seen visiting a place like this so soon after having a baby."

Vivian read enough of the gossip columns to know that Mrs. Wilson had announced the birth of her son mere weeks before.

"How is the little fella?" Vivian glanced down at her glass, adding softly, "And how is your sister?"

When she looked up again, Hattie's eyes were boring into her, hard and flinty and full of rage. But a moment later that brief glimpse of emotion was gone. "My sister is well," she said, as calm as if she was at a garden party. Women like Mrs. Wilson saved all their emotion for private moments; out in public, she was as pretty and hard as a diamond. "As is my son, thank you for your kind inquiry."

Vivian let it pass.

"So you'll answer my questions, then?"

"If I can."

Vivian glanced at Honor, who still hadn't spoken, expecting her to chime in. But Honor continued to watch them impassively. Vivian held back a frown. "Then do me a favor first." She reached across the desk, retrieving a sheet of blank paper and the fountain pen from its holder. She slid them toward Mrs. Wilson. "Write something. Please," she added, almost as an afterthought.

Mrs. Wilson uncapped the pen, each of her movements precise and graceful as she held it hovering over the page. "Anything in particular?"

"How about, *See you on Saturday, thank you, Hattie.*"

Her handwriting was beautiful, of course, like something that had been engraved on a copperplate invitation rather than written by a regular person. But Vivian could tell at a glance that it didn't match the note she had taken from Pearlie's hiding place.

Mrs. Wilson was watching her face. "What am I supposed to have written, then?" she asked, looking curious but not particularly concerned.

Vivian hesitated. But there wasn't much reason not to show it to her. If she knew something about it, her reaction might give it away. And if she didn't, she might still have an idea who sent it. Mrs. Wilson, after all, probably knew something about the other folks in her line of work in the city.

The note that had come with the brandy was folded and tucked into the seam pocket of her dress; Vivian pulled it out and handed it over.

If Mrs. Wilson's expression hadn't changed at all, Vivian would have suspected that she had something to hide. But instead, her forehead creased in a slight frown, and Vivian could see her eyes slide back and forth along the paper a couple of times, rereading it more than once, before she looked up again. "I'm guessing it didn't arrive accompanied by roses and chocolates?" Vivian shook her head. "What did it come with?"

"A bottle of poisoned brandy."

A bare movement of her chin, a flinch that was quickly suppressed. Mrs. Wilson might be willing to play the cruel games that her line of work demanded, but Vivian wondered if it bothered her more than she allowed herself to think about. "I don't recall seeing anything like that in the papers," she said thoughtfully.

Vivian shook her head. "Police called it a suicide. They still don't know the bottle was poisoned."

"Not a fan of the police, Miss Kelly?"

Vivian matched Mrs. Wilson's cold, mocking tone when she replied, "Folks like me can't pay the bribes you can, so they don't tend to look the other way when they catch us doing something not strictly legal."

Mrs. Wilson didn't argue with that. "And was the recipient someone I know?"

"Friend of a friend," Vivian said evasively, not willing to let the name *Henry* become part of the conversation. "Fella who worked here, actually."

"Was the *H* supposed to be you, then?" Hattie asked, glancing at Honor.

"Could have been the idea," Honor said, looking up from her glass and shrugging. "Not my writing, either, though. And not my style at all."

"I thought maybe you'd know something about it," Vivian continued, watching Hattie Wilson closely. "Seems like the fella was moonlighting for someone in your line of work and got himself smoked for his trouble."

"Well, he didn't work for me, and that note didn't come from me." Hattie's smile was mocking. "If I wrote something like that, I'd sign my name."

That, Vivian could believe. "But maybe you know someone who works like that. Someone who takes care of problems with a subtle hand. He thought it was a present for a job well done. Anyone in your line of business who might do a thing like that?"

"What was his name?"

Vivian hesitated. "Pearlie," she said, hoping she wouldn't regret it.

But Hattie only shrugged. "If you want my expert opinion, I doubt this came from whoever he was working for."

"Why do you say that?" Honor asked, sipping her drink as if she didn't much care about the answer.

"Because something this subtle"—she handed the paper back to Vivian—"doesn't send a message. When people in my line of work punish someone, we want the rest of our boys to know about it. That's how you keep people in line."

"Kill many people, then?" Vivian asked, feeling sick and trying not to show it.

Hattie Wilson shrugged. "I prefer not to. Killing is messy. Killing means you owe the police a lot of money to keep it quiet." She took another ladylike sip of her whiskey, then tapped the note. When she spoke next, it was with the condescending inflection of a much older sister who also believed she was much smarter. "I'll give you a tip, Miss Kelly. Ask yourself what kind of message a death like this sends, then find out who would want to send it."

She finished her drink and slid the empty glass across the desktop to Honor, who caught it easily. "I'm curious to see what you turn up."

"Who says I'll tell you anything more?" Vivian asked, taunting and defiant. Mrs. Wilson made her nervous, and she never wanted the other woman to guess that.

Mrs. Wilson smiled, her voice cold and careless as a shrug. "I have my ways of finding out what I want to know. See you around, little girl. If you survive that long."

"Is that a threat?" Vivian asked, her hands balling into fists. She glanced at Honor, who had set her glass down and was watching the exchange, her face impossible to read.

"Oh no, Miss Kelly." Mrs. Wilson shrugged. "Just an observation. Girls who poke their noses into this kind of business take an awful risk. And I almost like you. I'd hate to see you end up a corpse in an alley."

Vivian sucked in a breath. It was how Mrs. Wilson's husband had died, and everyone in that room knew it.

"That's probably enough," Honor said before Vivian could reply, her voice so mild it made Vivian gape at her. She still stood on the other side of her desk, eyes on her whiskey glass as she swirled its contents in a circle. Lifting it to take a sip, she glanced up at Mrs. Wilson. "No need to get testy with each other."

She didn't look at Vivian as she spoke—didn't show any emotion at all, in fact. Vivian felt like the bottom had dropped out of her stomach. She had seen Honor jump to the defense of just about every other employee with far less cause. But she didn't seem to mind the threats, or whatever they were, that Mrs. Wilson was casually tossing out. In fact, she looked like she had barely heard them.

"You're probably right." Mrs. Wilson shrugged again. "In any case, I've got a baby to get home to." She smiled. "No need to see me out, Ms. Huxley. I remember the way just fine. And Miss Kelly?" She paused with her hand on the doorknob, and the small lift of her brows felt like a warning snaking its way down Vivian's back. "I came here as a favor, yes, but also to tell you one other thing. If you ever let slip to anyone what you know about my sister, you will . . ." She paused, as if searching for the right word. "Regret it."

The understatement in her words would have been chilling, but that threat, at least, Vivian didn't need to worry about. She shook her head. "I wouldn't do that," she said quietly, meaning it. "Your sister went through enough. She didn't deserve what happened to her, and she doesn't deserve people hounding and judging her for it now."

Hattie studied her, as if trying to decide whether she was sincere. Then, without a word, she nodded and opened the door. Bruiser George and his slick-looking buddy were waiting just outside. Hattie motioned to them without speaking, and they fell in step behind her. She strode down the stairs without looking back.

Vivian stood in the doorway, waiting until they were firmly out of sight before slamming the door closed and rounding on Honor. "What the hell was that?" she demanded, stalking toward the desk. "How could you let her say that and just *stand* there?"

Honor flinched. "What was I supposed to do, Vivian? She was here to talk to you."

"You could have said something when she was threatening me," Vivian snapped. "Anyone else, you'd have jumped down her throat, told her not to talk to one of your people like that. Anyone else, you would have threatened her right back!" She was shaking, on edge from dancing through the dangerous terrain that was a conversation with Hattie Wilson and furious at Honor for leaving her to navigate that terrain all on her own.

And Honor wouldn't even look at her, her hands braced on the desk in front of her, her eyes fixed on its surface. Vivian didn't yell, didn't want to risk anyone outside the door hearing her. But she couldn't keep the hurt and the anger from her voice. "What am I, the one person at the Nightingale who's not worth bothering to look after?"

"Do you want Hattie Wilson knowing how I feel about you?"

Honor demanded, her voice husky. When she lifted her head, her cheeks were flushed with emotion. Her cool facade was finally cracking. Vivian stared at her. It was not what she had expected Honor to say at all. "Do you want to find out what she'd do with that kind of information? I don't."

"How *do* you feel about me?" Vivian met Honor's eyes without flinching. "You don't want Hattie Wilson to know, sure. I don't know how much your business crosses paths with hers, but you know best on that front. But what about me? Because *I* still don't know. I'm starting to suspect you don't either, and I don't have time to be yanked around like this."

Honor flinched, then took a step around the desk. "I'm not trying to—"

"You might not be trying, but you are." Vivian's own breathing was coming faster now. There was longing there, and distrust that she still hadn't let go of. But more than anything, it was the uncertainty making her feel reckless and angry. She thought of Florence dancing downstairs, Dr. Harris's embarrassment when he asked *How's your sister?*

What would she be left with if Florence was gone?

"You gave me a job here, Honor. And I'm grateful for that because you didn't have to, and it made my life a hell of a lot easier than it had been. And maybe we both thought it would make things simpler if we had some clear line between us, some role to play. But it hasn't, and we both know it."

"Do you want to quit, then?" It was impossible to tell how Honor felt about that idea. She had herself back under control now, and Vivian hated her for it a little.

"No, I want you to make up your mind."

Honor smiled then, an almost mocking expression. "Rich words coming from you, pet. We both know you haven't made up your mind either."

"It's not the same," Vivian insisted, stung. They were only inches from each other now. If she reached out, she knew Honor wouldn't pull away, and they would have their answer. But that would only make things simpler for a moment. "Your life is here. Your *world* is here. Mine would be completely upended. My sister . . . I wouldn't even know how to explain it to her, never mind whether she'd actually want to see me again." She thought about Alba, cut off and thrown out because her family couldn't see past the choice she'd made. And a baby was so much more commonplace than what being with Honor would mean. "It's not safe for me to make up my mind until you do."

"I told you once, pet. I'm not the sort of woman who makes promises." Slowly, deliberately, Honor took a step back. Her smile was sad. "It's safer for me not to. Just like it's safer for you. And right now, neither of us is sure losing that is worth it."

It hurt to hear those words. Vivian had spent so much of her life knowing that most of the world—and maybe even her own family—didn't think she was *worth it*. "That's that, then," she said slowly, taking a step back.

"Is it?" Honor shook her head. "You thought that once before. But here we are again, because *not sure* isn't the same as *no*. Are you actually making up your mind this time?"

"I'm going back downstairs is what I'm doing," Vivian snapped. "Thanks for arranging the meeting with Mrs. Wilson."

"You're welcome," Honor said softly. She waited until Vivian was almost at the door before asking, just as quietly, "Are you going to be at work on Monday?"

Vivian glanced over her shoulder. "Am I?"

"You always have a place here, Vivian. No matter what happens between us. I do look out for my people."

"Well, that's something, then."

Vivian wanted Honor to say something else. But there was just the slightest tremble to her hands, a brief moment when she caught her lower lip with her teeth before her expression returned to its normal smoothness. Vivian wasn't the only one who had been hurt by the exchange. They stared at each other in silence, both waiting, until Vivian turned away once more and left.

FOURTEEN

The sound of the door clicking shut echoed in her head as she made her way downstairs into the music and heat, the sounds and scents of the dance hall a familiar balm to the sharp, angry places inside her.

She immediately glanced around, looking for her sister, and found Florence back at the bar. She still looked nervous, which made her smile a lot at everyone around her, and that, combined with her fresh-faced beauty, was drawing plenty of eyes. But she didn't seem to notice as she sipped gingerly at a glass of champagne. Bea was on her break now and sitting with her, the two of them chatting as Danny, working once more, leaned over the bar to make some joking comment.

Vivian jumped when someone caught her hand, and she swung up her other hand without thinking, planning to push them away. But it was just Leo, who was watching her with concerned eyes. "Your sister's fine. Mrs. Wilson and her boys left a bit ago, and they didn't look twice at her. How did it go up there?"

"Okay, I guess?" Vivian said, trying to put Honor from her mind. "Thanks for keeping an eye on Florence."

Leo grinned. "She remembered me as the fella who brought you dinner that one time. Gave me a hell of a skeptical look until Danny vouched for me."

"I hope you took it easy on her on the dance floor."

"I would have, but she turned me down flat, though she was real sweet about it." He eyed Vivian, his expression growing more serious, until she wanted to squirm away. She didn't want him to guess what had passed between her and Honor. "Come dance with me," he said, giving her hand a gentle tug. The band was playing a slow foxtrot, the trumpet crooning lovingly enough that the song didn't even need a singer, and the dance floor was crowded with couples pressing their cheeks close together. "You look like you need it, and you can tell me about what happened up there."

Honor was right: Vivian wasn't sure making promises to each other was worth it, either. How could she be? She really didn't know Honor at all. "I should check on Florence," she said. But she didn't pull her hand away from his.

"You can keep an eye on her from the dance floor," he suggested. He had to stand close for her to hear him over the music, and his breath brushed across her temple as he spoke. "Come on, you've got that look in your eye like you're all jittery and mixed up inside. And I know you like to dance when you're feeling like that." When she still hesitated, he eased back, watching her face.

"Mrs. Wilson said she didn't have anything to do with it," Vivian said, trying to distract herself from her unhappy, confused thoughts. What had happened to Pearlie should matter more, anyway.

"Do you believe her?" Leo accepted the change of topic without a protest, watching the dancers as Vivian quietly filled him in on the conversation upstairs. And then she told him what they had discovered about the arsenic letters, as she had begun thinking of them. He deserved to know that much, given how he had helped out with the medical examiner.

"So whoever is behind the thefts wants them to be whispered about, so the people receiving the letters will be scared into doing what they say. But they don't want things to look so suspicious that the police get involved, which means making Pearlie's death look like a suicide." Leo frowned as he spoke. "Whoever's doing this is scum. It's bad enough on its own. But stealing from folks who are already poor, taking the one or two valuable things they own?" He shook his head. "Absolute scum."

"That makes me think Mrs. Wilson was right," Vivian said, thinking it through as she spoke. "Why would some mob boss want to rob poor people for such a small payoff? Would that be worth it? There are much easier ways to make a lot more money."

"So you think you need to look closer to home?"

Vivian glanced around the dance hall. It was filled with laughter and music and dancing lights reflected off a million spangles. But it was also filled with secrets. She knew that as well as anyone. "Pearlie spent a lot of time here before he died," she said slowly. "He got pretty cozy with the rest of Honor's muscle."

"Well, you're the one who works with them now," Leo pointed out. "They don't seem like a chatty bunch, but you might be able to weasel it out of them." The foxtrot was just drifting to a close, and almost immediately the brass section was on their feet, launching into the first Charleston of the night. Leo shook out his head and shoulders, as if clearing his thoughts. He smiled. "But before you do, how about that dance? I know you can't resist a Charleston."

"I should . . ." Vivian trailed off as she glanced back over at the bar. A blushing Florence was just being urged onto the dance floor once again, Danny grinning and cajoling her as he held both her hands. She was laughing, but stood her ground, clearly hesitant to join the couples moving at lighting speed. Danny relented, and instead of pulling her into the sweaty crush, he held her hands and walked her slowly through the steps just at the edge of the crowd.

Bea caught her eye, her own brows raised as she gestured toward Danny and Florence. Her *will you look at that?* expression was clear, even at a distance. But before Vivian had any sort of chance to respond, Bea was off, striding across an empty corner of the dance floor and catching the hand of the bandleader so he could tug her up onto the bandstand with a flourish. She arrived at the microphone just in time to launch into the song's lyrics. The club filled with cheers and whoops as her voice joined the music, notes tumbling through the air as lightly as any dancer moved across the floor.

"Okay," Vivian said, relenting. It was hard to keep her feet still when the air was filled with movement. And Florence . . . she looked away. Why did the sight of the two of them together make her chest feel like someone had wrapped a giant hand around her heart and squeezed? "Just one dance."

Leo followed her gaze to where Danny and Florence were laughing together. But he didn't say anything, just took her hand and tugged her onto the dance floor. When she finally looked back at him, he placed her hand on his shoulder, gave her a smile that was pure challenge, and took off.

And for a few minutes, Vivian was too breathless to think of anything else. No matter where she spun or what she did, he was there, a touch on her wrist sending her in the other direction, where he would catch her around the waist and spin her back the way they had come, heels kicking up, hips pressed against each other for a brief second before they broke away to mirror each other and come back together again.

If heaven meant not needing to think about anything else but the joy and ease of a single moment, then Vivian was in heaven. She laughed, reckless and free for the length of the song, and Leo grinned back. He caught her around the waist and spun them in a tight circle, finally slowing to a stop as the music ended. "There's that smile," he murmured, his words barely loud enough to reach her ears.

Vivian, still catching her breath, relaxed against him for a moment, resting her head against his chest so she could feel his heart racing at the same tempo as her own. "Thanks, pal," she whispered. "I needed that."

"I know." He kissed the top of her head, a quick, friendly gesture. "Now get back to your sister. At some point Danny will have to drag himself away from those smiles of hers, and she'll be looking for you. I see a girl over there who looks like her fella left her high and dry tonight—"

"Coulda been her gal," Vivian pointed out, the tension in her still eased by the dance and Leo's comfortable presence.

"Either way, she looks like she needs someone to ask her to dance, and I'm too much of a gentleman to leave a girl in the lurch like that."

"Yes, such a gentleman." Vivian laughed, rolling her eyes.

He winked. "Always. Now scoot along."

Vivian had to weave through the throng of dancers leaving the floor, and her path took her close to the corner where Pearlie had often stood, keeping an eye on things. Mostly the bouncers kept folks from getting too rowdy as the night went on. But there had been enough trouble not long ago—a police raid, a break-in, threats from people in high places looking to settle scores—that Honor had hired extra muscle that spring. Pearlie had been one of those hires, and he had fit in quickly with the fun-loving, world-wise crowd that made up the Nightingale's staff. And even though he hadn't been there long enough for anyone to know him well, he had been chattier than the normal muscle that worked for Honor. Vivian had never seen Benny or Saul smile, and Silence, who often worked the door, rarely spoke at all. But she had noticed them talking with Pearlie more than once.

So when she saw Silence standing in Pearlie's old spot by the bar, arms crossed as he surveyed the night's crowd and kept them in check through sheer hulking presence, she changed directions and headed his way.

Stationing herself at the end of the bar nearest the mountain-shouldered bouncer, Vivian gave the bartender a little wave. He nodded back to let her know that he'd seen her, even though he was currently swamped with customers who had carried their buzzing energy with them from the dance floor.

"French seventy-five if you have a bottle to use up, but no rush," she said when he was able to tilt an ear in her direction. The bartender nodded, and Vivian turned, leaning back to rest her elbows on the bar as if she were surveying the dance floor. Beside her, Silence—his real name was Silas, but his preference for glowering looks over actually speaking had earned him his nickname—glanced her way for a brief moment.

Vivian smiled when she caught his eye. "Drink for you, too? Or do you have to say no when you're working?"

She couldn't tell if he was scowling at her or if that was just his permanent expression, but after a moment he nodded. "Little glass ain't gonna do much to me," he grunted.

Vivian laughed. The coat he wore could fit two of her inside it, and it still looked like it barely squeezed over his shoulders. "That I believe. Hey, honey, two if you can!" she called to the bartender, who raised one fist and bobbed it up and down twice—the club's signal for *yes*.

"How'd you come to work here, Silence?" she asked, hoping to soften him up while she decided how to steer the conversation in the direction she needed. Silence didn't do small talk, as far as she could tell. But she was pretty good at getting people to chat when she wanted to. "Fella like you could probably get a job anywhere he wanted."

He gave her another brief, sideways glance, as if surprised she was talking to him, before turning his gaze back to the floor. "Benny."

"Really?" Vivian leaned her elbow on the bar, resting her cheek on her fist. "I didn't know you two were friendly."

This time he didn't even look at her. "Brothers."

"Brothers?" Vivian tried not to frown. One-word answers weren't going to get her anywhere. "You two don't look much alike. Well, aside from both being twice my size and very handsome," she teased, relieved to see him crack a small smile. It was barely there, just a slight lift at one corner of his mouth, but it was progress.

"Different mothers." He said it simply, but Vivian could guess that there was a whole story there.

That was usually the case with people who found their way to places like the Nightingale. No one was ever as simple or straightforward as they seemed. Part of her itched to find out more, but just then the bartender slid two glasses her way, each a pretty, fizzy mix of champagne and gin. Vivian caught them both, blowing him a kiss as he returned to work, before turning and handing one to Silence.

It was comically small in his bear-paw of a hand, and Vivian had to bite her lip to hold back a smile. "Well, cheers, pal," she said, raising her glass. "Shall we drink a toast to Pearlie, who will be missed?"

Silence had been lifting his own glass as she spoke. But when she mentioned Pearlie, his expression darkened, and he put the glass back down so sharply that the drink sloshed over the edge and spattered across the wood of the bar. "Shouldn't drink on the job," he said, turning back to his narrow-eyed study of the dance floor.

Stunned, Vivian lowered her own glass, her mind sifting rapidly through all the possible things she could say in response without setting his back up. She finally settled on "Guess you didn't like him, then?"

Silence's jaw tightened. "Loyalty matters."

"Loyalty to who?"

"To here." Silence scowled. "To Honor."

Vivian took a sip of her drink while she thought through that statement. "And you thought Pearlie wasn't loyal? What did he do?" When Silence's scowl deepened, she dropped her voice. "You know Bea's my friend, Silence. If there's something she should know . . ."

He didn't reply for a moment, and Vivian had the sense that he was gathering his words together. "Tried to get me on board for another job," he said at last.

"Well, lots of us have other jobs," Vivian said practically. "I do. Doesn't mean I don't care about folks here. Or about everything Honor does to keep us safe."

Silence shook his head. "Dressmaking's got nothing to do with this work."

Vivian took another sip. She didn't want to seem too interested or press too fast. Silence was exactly the type of fella who would clam up and refuse to talk to her again if she rubbed him the wrong way. "And he tried to get you working for someone in a similar line of work? Someone who was Honor's competition?"

"Mighta been. Shady, at least."

She lowered her voice. "What did he ask you to do?"

"Said they needed a driver."

Vivian put down her drink so she could take a step closer to him. "And do you know who they were?"

"No." He crossed his arms, the gesture straining the fabric of his coat across the width of his shoulders. "Didn't ask. I don't drive." He glanced down at her, his expression as closed off as she had ever seen it. "I got work to do."

"Of course." Vivian picked up her drink and smiled brightly, not wanting him to guess that the conversation had been at all deliberate. She didn't need him watching her or telling anyone else what they'd been talking about. "See you around, pal."

He grunted, not looking in her direction as she moved back down the bar. Her thoughts tumbled and tripped over each other. What had Pearlie been mixed up in, and who was running the show?

"Vivi!" Florence was back on a barstool waiting for her, her cheeks flushed with the heat and her hair starting to escape its carefully pinned curls. "Where have you been?"

"Sorry, got caught up in a conversation." Vivian looked her sister over, relieved to see that Florence was smiling. "You having fun, then?"

"I guess I am," Florence said, a little shyly. "I didn't have the nerve to dance with anyone else, but Mr. Chin kept me company." She glanced at the bandstand. "Gosh, Bea's a wonderful singer, isn't she?"

"Sure is," Vivian agreed, but her eyes were on Danny. He was back behind the bar, pouring drinks and chatting up customers, but whenever his eyes didn't have somewhere to go, they were on Florence. Vivian turned away, just in time to see Florence covering a yawn and looking embarrassed. "Are you getting too tired?"

"I think I am," Florence admitted. "I'm not used to this the way you are. Will you hate me if I want to go home?"

"Of course not," Vivian said firmly. "I could never hate you. And it's too crowded for me here anyway."

Florence eyed her, a small smile on her lips. "Liar," she said, but she sounded grateful for it. "Just let me say goodbye to Mr. Chin."

"You can call him Danny, you know."

That made Florence's blush deepen. "No," she said. "I don't think I could. Not yet."

Vivian didn't want to think about what that *yet* might mean. "He looks awful busy," she said abruptly. "I'll tell him goodbye for you later. Let's shake a leg."

FIFTEEN

Florence, who usually collapsed into bed as early as she could after long days spent hunched over her sewing, was a yawning mess the next morning. Vivian, more accustomed to late nights followed by early mornings, had been the first one up. They couldn't have breakfast until after they took Communion, but she had coffee ready to help them shake off sleep.

"I'd've left you to snooze," Vivian said, loving but mocking, as they pulled on their hats, rushing to make it to mass at the Catholic church on time. "But I thought you might want to go to confession today."

Florence's blush could have lit up an entire city block, but she kept her mouth pressed into a tight line, refusing to take the bait by either arguing or agreeing. In fact, she was remarkably close-lipped the entire walk there, and there was a distracted look on her face as they sat and stood and sang their way through the service. Afterward, she did duck into the confession booth to speak to a priest. But she didn't say what they had talked about, and Vivian couldn't ask.

Since it was Sunday, it was time for their weekly good deed: when they stopped to pick up groceries for themselves, they also bought them for their upstairs neighbor, Mrs. Thomas, and what Florence often called her unreasonable number of children. She wasn't wrong. Two marriages at very different points in her life had left Mrs. Thomas with too many children, and the oldest ones now often left grandchildren with her to care for while they worked. It had all left Mrs. Thomas a sarcastic, flinty, unpleasant woman. But she had been the one who had kept them together after their mother died. They owed her for that, no matter how much they disliked her.

"You take it," Florence said when they reached the front door of their building. "I'm too tired to stay polite if she gets testy with me today."

"Sure thing."

A sharp, unpleasant smell was creeping under the door across from the stairs as they passed by.

"Have you seen Widow Kaminski recently?" Florence asked as they both wrinkled their noses, glancing at the door where the smell seemed to be coming from.

"Not in a few days," Vivian said, frowning as she tried to remember. "Why?"

Florence sighed. "I think she's getting too old to take care of herself. Smells like she had some kind of accident in there. We should take her some dinner tonight and check in."

"Well, you go start cooking, and I'll handle Mrs. Thomas."

The Thomases lived one floor below them; Vivian went to knock on their door while Florence headed upstairs.

"Door's open," a man's voice rumbled.

Vivian poked her head around the door, feeling shy. Mr. Thomas worked six days a week at a factory, so he was rarely home. Wiry from too much work and not enough rest, with a bushy beard and a bass voice that seemed wrong coming from his thin body, he was a temperance man living in a corner of the city that couldn't have given less of a damn about Prohibition if it tried. He wasn't unkind—in fact, he was gentler than his wife—but he was exactly the sort of man Vivian had no idea how to deal with.

"Morning, Mr. Thomas," she said, holding up the basket. "Florence and I picked up some groceries. There's canned peaches as a treat, and condensed milk, and a ham bone. Should I put it to boil?"

"I'll do it," Mrs. Thomas snapped, striding into the room with a child on each hip. She plopped both of them unceremoniously on the floor to squabble over an empty box, then went to fetch a pot from the precarious stack of them in the kitchen. "Sarah!" she called, and a young girl appeared at her side. Mrs. Thomas handed her the pot, and Sarah scrambled off to fill it up at the tap in the hall washroom. The heavy pot banged against her knees as she went.

From next door, where Mrs. Thomas's grown daughter lived, came the sound of a child's hacking cough, before it was interrupted by a crashing sound from the bedroom where the older children slept. Mrs. Thomas sighed. "Never a moment's peace."

"I won't bother you anymore," Vivian said quickly before she could get roped into watching the children. She reclaimed her basket and headed for the door. "Have a good Sunday."

Out in the hallway, she didn't immediately head upstairs. Instead, she leaned back against the door, eyes closed, as she let out a shaking breath.

Florence thought of Mrs. Thomas with irritation, anger, and gratitude all mixed together. But for Vivian, thinking about Mrs. Thomas brought on quiet, sinking fear. She dreaded the thought of ending up like her: worn down by pregnancy and poverty, with too many mouths to feed and no expectation of her circumstances ever changing.

Florence thought her sister was careless, flirting with anyone she liked the look of, drinking too much, dancing with strangers. But with the specter of Mrs. Thomas hanging over her life, Vivian was more careful than someone might have imagined from looking at her. She had worked hard for the little bit of freedom she had in her life. She wasn't about to risk that.

"Vivian?"

Her eyes flew open, and she shook her head to clear her confusion and her grim thoughts. Dr. Harris was standing in the hallway, his sandy hair and brown suit both looking trim and tidy as ever in spite of the heat.

"Are you all right?" he asked.

"Peachy," she said, straightening quickly. "Just taking a quick breather. It's just sweltering, isn't it? You here because someone is sick?"

He nodded at the door next to Mrs. Thomas's place. "Poor baby has croup," he said, sighing. "And this heat isn't helping. The air is terrible today."

"I heard the coughing," Vivian said. "Sounded rough." She gave him a critical look, noticing the shadows under his eyes. "You look like you've had a hard time of it recently, Doc."

He gave her a weak smile. "It's an uphill battle in this neighborhood sometimes. If it's not sick babies, it's grown men poisoning themselves with moonshine. And if it's not either of those, it's something else." He shook his head, then tried to change the subject. "How is your sister?"

"She's fine," Vivian said, a little wary.

He didn't seem to notice. "That's good to hear. I hope she's not taking on too much. I went to see Alba this morning and found that she was living with the Henrys. The children said you and Florence were there helping out. The kids had lots to say about her and her stories," he added with a smile. "Seems they like her."

"Everyone likes Florence."

"She's likable," the young doctor agreed, and Vivian tried not to bristle, still a mess of protective and possessive feelings after watching her sister spend half the night dancing with Danny. "But I overheard Beatrice and Alba talking when I arrived, and something they said . . . Vivian, tell me truthfully. Beatrice said she was going to leave well enough alone about her uncle. Is she?"

Vivian hesitated for just a beat too long. "Yes," she said, but as soon as she met his eyes, she sighed. "No. We're not leaving it alone."

"I thought not," he said. "You know that's dangerous, right?" There was real worry in his eyes, and Vivian remembered what he had said about his brother.

"I know. But Bea's real cut up about her uncle, especially with Alba's baby on the way. And it's bigger than just Pearlie. We've been asking around. Seems someone's got the people in this part of the city running scared."

"The letters," he said, looking embarrassed when she glanced at him. "I couldn't keep my nose out of it either. After we spoke, I went and talked to those patients again. Someone has quite a tidy little business going on."

"It's rotten is what it is," Vivian said, her voice shaking. Her hands balled into fists. "Stealing from folks who can already barely afford to feed their families—" She broke off, frowning at him. "What's that noise?"

There were raised voices coming from one of the floors below them. The worry and confusion were plain to hear, but Vivian couldn't tell what they were saying. Without waiting for the doctor's response, she left the basket on the floor and hurried to the stairs.

"Everything all right?" she called down.

Will Freeman, young and stylish and what some people called a "determined bachelor" in roundabout fashion, appeared at the bottom of the stairs. "Do you smell gas up there?"

Vivian sniffed, trying not to let her worry bubble up too sharply. Gas in the building was dangerous for everyone. "Not up here," she said, starting to make her way down. "How bad is it?" She might have to run back upstairs and start banging on doors to get people out of the building if they couldn't find the source.

"We found it!" someone yelled from the ground floor. "It's coming from Mrs. Kaminski's."

Vivian and Will arrived at the same time, and he pounded on the door. "Mrs. Kaminski? Anna? Are you in there?"

"She's a little deaf these days," someone said behind them. Vivian turned, startled to see that it was Dr. Harris. But of course he would have followed her down. "Can we get the door open?"

Will turned away. "I'll go grab—"

"Wait, it's unlocked." Vivian stared in surprise as the doorknob turned in her hand and the door creaked open. "Does she usually leave her door unlocked?"

It was dark inside, with all the curtains pulled shut, and swelteringly hot. The air was thick with the smell of gas. Vivian nearly gagged.

"Mrs. Kaminski?" she called, hesitating.

"No." Dr. Harris pushed past her, his handkerchief held over the lower part of his face, heading for the old stove tucked in the corner. In the light from the front door, Vivian could see him fiddling with the knobs. "Vivian, open the windows, quick. Will, tell them to prop open the front door and every window they can in the building. We've got to get it aired out."

"Right away, Doc," Will replied. Vivian could hear the sound of him running and shouting as he went.

She pulled her own handkerchief out of her pocket and held it over her nose and mouth. But that didn't stop her coughing and gagging at the smell of gas as she went to the room's two windows. They were shut tight, in spite of the hot, heavy weather, and she had to drop her handkerchief and use both hands to shove them open. When she had, she darted back to the front door, taking deep, gulping breaths of fresh air.

Dr. Harris appeared beside her, his face grim.

Vivian didn't want to say it, but it wasn't hard to guess what he had found. "She's dead, isn't she?" she asked.

He nodded, his jaw tight. "The gas in the stove was still on, even though it wasn't lit. With all the windows closed, she suffocated." He let out a shaking breath. "Folks her age sometimes have trouble remembering things like turning the gas off," he added, almost too quietly for her to hear. "Especially when they used to live with someone else but are now on their own."

Vivian felt her eyes stinging, and she didn't know whether it was from sorrow or the lingering smell. She blinked away any tears that might have fallen.

Dr. Harris was already talking to the neighbors clustering on the stairs, telling them what had happened. Will could be heard upstairs shouting for people to open the windows. Someone else was sent to call for the police, who would have to take the body to the morgue once Dr. Harris had certified the death. Vivian shivered, cleared her throat, and pulled herself together.

Dr. Harris, once he wasn't immediately needed, leaned back against the wall, staring at the ceiling. His face was a jumble of unhappy emotions, and his shoulders were tense. He looked like he wanted to be sick. It was the first time Vivian had seen him—normally a bulwark of confidence and intellect—seem so unsure. She had often thought that he saw himself as a sort of missionary, even a savior, setting up his practice in a part of the city where he couldn't make the kind of money other doctors made, bringing his work to the defiant poor who otherwise would have suffered in resentful, unnoticed silence.

But you couldn't save everyone, no matter where you were or how much money they did, or didn't, have. She could have told him that, but she had to admire him for trying, anyway.

"You don't need to feel guilty, Doc," Vivian said quietly. "There wasn't anything you could have done."

"Wasn't there?" He let out a sound that might have been a laugh if it hadn't been so desolate. "I should have done a better job checking on her. I knew she was having trouble taking care of herself. And when I was here last week, she was so anxious, nothing she could really explain, just about her mail, of all things. I've been worried that her memory was going, but she kept insisting she was fine, even without her husband here any longer." He closed his eyes, leaning back against the wall again. "My fault."

Vivian wanted to point out that it wasn't, not by any stretch of the imagination. But she had a feeling that nothing she said would get through just at that moment. So when she noticed Florence peeking over the banister, she left him alone and went to speak to her sister.

"Is it true?" Florence whispered, coming down the stairs. Standing in Mrs. Kaminski's doorway, she looked around, ignoring Vivian's hissed warning about the gas. "She's dead?"

Once Vivian had explained, Florence's mouth thinned to a tight, sad line, and tears filled her eyes. But she nodded and pulled herself together, just as Vivian had. Whether it was poor widows or sick babies, death was too close a companion where they lived for anyone to be too surprised by its presence.

She shook her head. "Poor Mrs. Kaminski. She was clearly struggling. We should have noticed that she needed more help. For her to be pawning her things . . ."

"What do you mean, pawning her things?"

With the windows and door now open, light streamed into the room, and Vivian could see that the room was a jumble of odds and ends. Three brooms leaned against one wall, two of them broken; an entire shelf held chipped cups and teacups paired with saucers that didn't match. A basket by the rocking chair was overflowing with old clothes and rags, and there were so many piles of newspapers in a corner of the kitchen that it was a wonder they hadn't caught fire. Clearly, Mrs. Kaminski had hated to throw anything out. Vivian didn't see how Florence could tell if something was missing.

They were interrupted by a sudden babble of voices and orders as two police officers arrived. The residents of the building, wary of the officers, didn't protest their instructions to clear the first floor. Some went back to their homes on the upper floors, but Florence grabbed Vivian's hand and towed her out of the building. They weren't the only ones to seek fresh air; the gas smell was fading, but it was still there.

Outside, the sticky humidity dampened some of the nervous energy that had filled the hall. Vivian and Florence settled onto a low ledge that ran around the building across the street, their backs pressed against the stone wall as they tried to steal some of its chill. Next door, the cobbler's wife was pouring glasses of lemonade in exchange for gossip.

They were silent for a while, watching their neighbors, each alone with her thoughts. They could hear scattered bursts of conversation as everyone tried to remember the last time they had seen or spoken to Mrs. Kaminski. Vivian watched the open door of their building, the figures moving inside it looking sinister and secretive. She wondered how they had found Mrs. Kaminski, whether it had been a peaceful death, a night's sleep that she just never woke up from, or something worse. In spite of the sultry heat, she shivered. She was glad she hadn't seen the old woman's body.

"Her family won't be able to claim her," Florence said quietly. "They'll have to take her to Hart Island, eventually."

Vivian nodded. Mr. Kaminski had died several years before, leaving his widow to putter on alone in the home they had shared for most of their lives. The only child Mrs. Kaminski had ever mentioned had moved across the country to work on the railroads some thirty years ago and never moved back. Even if someone knew how to track him down, he'd never make it back in time. Mrs. Kaminski would end up a line in a ledger and one of dozens of bodies in a single grave.

"Maybe we can get the neighbors to chip in for a real funeral," Vivian said, the words catching in her throat. Their mother was on Hart Island, somewhere. Neither of them had ever tried to find out where.

Looking away from the door, Vivian watched a handful of children playing a game that involved hopping in and out of the street, until one of them slipped, tripping another, and the whole thing dissolved into a shrieking mess. Their parents, fanning themselves with hats and newspapers, didn't bother trying to intervene, and in a moment the fight was forgotten and the kids had moved on to a new game.

"Maybe," Florence said, though she didn't sound hopeful.

Vivian didn't blame her. As much as they might have wanted to help, folks around there needed to keep what cash they had.

A police hearse came puttering down the street, sliding to a stop in front of their building. It looked like one of the vehicles that Vivian had noticed outside the morgue, and sure enough, one of the men who hopped out wore a regular dark suit. The other wore a police uniform, and together they went to open the wide doors at the back of the car. The children continued their play, but the adults on the street watched as the two men unloaded a stretcher and disappeared inside the building.

"If she hadn't pawned her candlesticks already, we could have sold those to pay for it," Florence said as the low buzz of conversation resumed. "I don't know if anything else of hers is valuable."

Vivian frowned. "How do you know she'd been pawning her things?"

"Her candlesticks are gone," Florence said sadly, kicking her heels against the stone wall. "They were always on her table. She told me once that her mother brought them from Poland. And they were so beautiful, silver filigree and decorated all over with vines and grapes and poppies." A tear slipped down her cheek. "She wouldn't have sold them unless she was desperate."

Vivian felt cold all over. The door unlocked when it shouldn't have been, a death that looked like an accident, and the old woman's silver candlesticks missing. "When was the last time you saw her?" she asked slowly. "How did she seem to you then?"

Florence shrugged. "I don't know. Two weeks ago, I think. Why?"

Vivian was saved having to decide how to answer as the police and the coroner reemerged, two of them carrying the stretcher with its white-shrouded burden. The neighbors had fallen silent once more, and even the children stopped their play to watch as the men carried the stretcher to the back of the car. The buzz of conversation didn't resume until the hearse had departed once more.

The two remaining police officers stood in front of the building, awkwardly clearing their throats as everyone drifted closer to hear what they had to say. Vivian didn't miss the wary look in their eyes as they eyed her neighbors, who watched them back with equal distrust.

"It is the coroner's assessment that your neighbor met with an unfortunate end after leaving her gas on overnight with the windows closed," one officer said, speaking quickly, as though he couldn't wait to be gone. "Gas is dangerous if it builds up within a space. We urge all of you to double-check your own stoves each day to avoid a similar accident. If you have any other elderly neighbors, make sure they know how to work their own stoves and lights properly."

"Is it safe to go back in?" Mrs. Gonzales called, cradling one of her twins on her hip while the other one clung to her skirt, chewing on the side of his fist and watching the officers with wide eyes.

"It is, but keep your windows open for the rest of the day." He glanced up at the bright sky. "Not that I think anyone will want to have them closed in this weather." Glancing around to make sure no one was going to argue or ask questions, he nodded firmly.

It didn't take them long to depart after that, and the neighbors slowly rounded up their children and made their way back into the building. Dr. Harris had come out with the officers, and now he stood by himself, alone in the crowd of chattering and yelling residents, a cigarette dangling from his fingers while he stared moodily at the sky and fanned himself with his hat. His black bag slumped at his feet.

"I'll catch up with you," Vivian told her sister, changing course to head toward him.

"Her windows should have been open," the doctor said as Vivian came up next to him, though he didn't turn to look at her. "In this heat, there was no reason for them to be closed. And I should have paid more attention the last time I was there. Lot of good I'm doing," he added, with bitter self-deprecation. "University degree and what do I have to show for it? Can't even keep one old woman alive through the summer."

"She was near ninety," Vivian pointed out quietly, distracted from her reason for coming to speak with him. She didn't want to dismiss Mrs. Kaminski's life or death, but she didn't think the doctor should have been so hard on himself either.

"No," said the doctor simply. He took a long drag of his cigarette. "No, this one was my fault." He tossed the cigarette down, grinding it out angrily with the heel of his shoe. "Vivian, I think she got one of those letters."

Vivian didn't argue. She had already been thinking the same thing. And the cruelty of it took her breath away: an old woman, too alone to really tell anyone what had happened, too frail to follow the letter's demands. "You said she was upset about her mail."

He nodded, still staring at the ground. She could see a muscle jumping in his jaw as he pulled out his cigarette case and fumbled for a new one. "And I didn't pay any attention, because I just thought she was a sweet old lady whose mind was maybe drifting away a little bit. I don't know what she might have had that was valuable, but—"

"Candlesticks," Vivian said, quiet and heartsick. She wished he would offer her a cigarette, or better yet a drink at a bar. Something to steady her nerves. But men like him seemed to think it was polite to pretend women didn't do those kinds of things. "Florence told me. Two silver candlesticks. Now she's dead, and they're not there anymore. Just like Pearlie." A sudden thought occurring to her, she grabbed his arm. "Did you tell them? The police? That you don't think it was an accident?"

"How could I?" he demanded, shaking off her hands. His own were trembling as he stuck the cigarette between his lips and struck a match. It took him two tries to light it; once he did, he held it between two fingers and blew out a frustrated breath of smoke. "What are they going to believe? That they need to look for some shadowy thief who's robbing people in this miserable little corner of the city? Or that another old woman got careless with her gas line and died in a sad accident?"

"It's going to be impossible, in all that mess, to find Mrs. Kaminski's letters, isn't it?" Vivian asked, feeling hopeless. His words, *this miserable little corner of the city,* echoed in her head, a tinny song made of equal parts anger and despair. Miserable it might have been, but it was her home, and the people there mattered. She could still see Florence inside the open door of the building, talking to Will Freeman as they collected yesterday's mail from the boxes in the front hall. "But you think that's what she was talking about, don't you? You're a doctor. You're not like most of the folks here. They might listen to you—"

"Not without proof," he said, bitter with frustration. He tossed his second cigarette down before it was even finished, and the butt of it glowed like a fallen star before he crushed it with his heel. "And no one has any of that, do they?"

"The bottle," Vivian said suddenly. "The brandy bottle. It's still at the coroner's office." She hadn't wanted to tell the coroner where it came from when she was still afraid Pearlie's mobster boss had sent it. It had been too big a risk, then, that they might come after the rest of the Henrys next. But if Hattie Wilson was right, whoever was running this operation wasn't out for revenge. They wanted things kept quiet, with no evidence left behind and folks running scared. And the medical examiner had seemed to believe her. If she told him where it had come from, he might be able to convince someone official to look further . . .

"That might . . ." Dr. Harris let out a slow breath. "It'd be a stretch to convince them where it came from. But if you could do that, it might lead somewhere." He frowned. "Offices at Bellevue are closed today."

"Then I'll get my friend to take me back tomorrow," Vivian said, her heart racing with nervous energy. She'd have to check with Bea first, anyway. "Maybe the police'll actually be good for something."

"You're a pretty determined girl, aren't you?"

Vivian couldn't tell if it was a compliment or not, but she lifted her chin anyway. "I sure can be," she said, and her voice only shook a little. "Determined and foolish. Just ask my sister."

"Tell me what the coroner thinks," he said grimly. "Maybe I can add my two cents."

"I'll let you know, Doc." Vivian hesitated, then gave him a gentle pat on the arm. "See you around, I guess."

"You're a good girl, Vivian," he said with a half-hearted smile. "I'll see you around."

Inside, people had mostly gone back to their homes, but the building hummed with gossip. Vivian climbed the stairs slowly, feeling like there were weights in her shoes. She didn't want to think about Mrs. Kaminski. She didn't want to think about Pearlie. She just wanted to leave behind everything heavy and ugly and sad in her life. The doctor's words echoed cruelly in her head. *Miserable little corner of the city.*

She wanted to go dancing. She wanted to run away.

Instead, she went home, three flights up that felt like three miles, and slumped against the door as soon as it was closed behind her. Slowly, too tired to keep standing, she slid down to the floor.

Florence was sitting at the table looking through a catalog that had come in the mail. Beans simmered on the stove. There were canned pears waiting to be opened and a loaf of bread from the day-old bin at the bakery. They had so much, Vivian reminded herself. They were so lucky. Things were better than they had been ever since she could remember.

"Vivian?"

The odd note in Florence's voice, like one instrument playing off-key in an otherwise perfect song, made Vivian's wandering mind snap back to attention.

"Vivian, I . . . I think someone is threatening me."

Florence was holding a letter.

SIXTEEN

Vivian stared for a heartbeat that felt like a year, then stumbled to her feet, a cold stab of fear in her chest. "What does it say?"

"It says . . ." Florence frowned, shaking her head. "This is so strange. How could anyone know about this?"

"What does it say, Flo?" Vivian tried to keep the panic out of her voice but knew she wasn't succeeding.

"Someone wants me to take the dress from Miss Ethel's shop. The one with the aquamarine and topaz stones. They want me to *steal* it. And then I'm supposed to leave it . . . This makes no sense." When Florence looked up, the paper was trembling in her hands. She was pale, but more than anything else, she looked confused. "Why would someone write this?"

"Let me see it," Vivian demanded. Without waiting for an answer, ignoring Florence's softly uttered protest, she snatched the letter from her sister's fingers. It was written in the same awkward, blocky hand as the letter that they had found in Pearlie's papers. Its demands were just as simple and deadly. "Did this just arrive today?"

"Well, it would have come yesterday, I guess," Florence said. "They don't deliver the mail on Sunday, and I didn't check the box yesterday." She frowned, then shrugged. "I guess it's someone's idea of a joke, but I can't say I find it very funny. Especially not today."

Vivian stared at the letter in her hand, unable to meet her sister's eyes. "It's not a joke," she choked out at last. Her legs felt wobbly beneath her, and she had to stumble into a chair at the table before they buckled. How could the thief have chosen Florence?

"What? Of course it is; just some stupid prank. What else could it be?" Florence's voice was rising, and underneath the growing fear Vivian could hear the anger. "What aren't you telling me?"

Vivian closed her eyes and dropped her head until her forehead rested against her palms, the heels of her hands pressing against her eyelids. She didn't move from that position as she quietly explained about the letters, not stopping until she brought the story back around to the discovery of Mrs. Kaminski's body. "Even Dr. Harris thinks there was something not right about it," she said, still speaking to the table. "It's not nothing, Flo. I wish to God it were."

When she finally lifted her head, Florence was staring at her. There were two bright, angry patches of color on her cheekbones, and her eyes were snapping with fury.

"I asked you," Florence said, her voice so quiet it made Vivian flinch. "I asked is something wrong, what's upset you, is there something I should know about. You said no, there's nothing. And now you tell me *this*?"

"I thought it had nothing to do with us," Vivian whispered. She could feel her fear, hot and angry, pressing against the back of her eyes, but she refused to let it become tears. "I didn't want it to have anything to do with you."

"So you lied to me?"

"It wasn't a lie," Vivian pleaded. "Not really. I just . . . I didn't want you to worry. I didn't think you needed to know."

"Well, I'm plenty worried now!" Florence yelled. Her hands were locked around the back of the chair in front of her like it was the only lifeboat on a sinking ship. "Vivi, what are we supposed to do? I can't get that dress."

"You don't have to," Vivian said firmly, jumping to her feet and going to put her arms around her sister. Florence was shaking, and to Vivian's relief, she didn't try to pull away. "I promise, Flo, I'm not going to let anything happen to you. I know how to fix it."

Florence laughed, grim and disbelieving. "You know a lot of people, Vivi, but I don't think even you could possibly know someone who can make this go away."

"Maybe not go away," Vivian admitted. "But I know exactly what to do next. Go pack a bag, Flo, with whatever you'll need for a few days. Maybe three or four, just in case."

"Am I going somewhere?" Florence asked.

"You sure are," Vivian said. "Somewhere safe, until I can fix this." She and Florence had never been girls who hugged, but all of a sudden, she didn't want to let her sister go. "I promise, I won't let anything happen to you. Ever."

"Circle two-four-four-one, please," Vivian whispered into the receiver, trying not to glance around nervously.

The hotel lobby was a busy, bustling place, with visitors coming and going, bellhops pushing trolleys stacked with luggage, and the constantly shifting line of those waiting to use the bank of telephone booths. Vivian hadn't wanted to let Florence out of her sight, not even for a moment, so they were squeezed into the booth together. They couldn't close the door, and the clerk at the desk was scowling in disapproval. Florence looked embarrassed, but Vivian didn't care. With two ratty suitcases wedged between their legs and coats over their arms, Vivian suspected the desk clerk could tell they didn't have enough money to actually stay at the hotel. Any other day she might have bristled at the way he stared down his nose at them before turning to continue his survey of the lobby. But they weren't the only people who were there just to use the telephone, and she had more important things to worry about.

Vivian let out a sigh of relief when the operator finally connected her call and Leo's voice answered. "Hey, pal, it's Vivian," she whispered, cupping one hand around the mouthpiece. The lobby was loud with conversation and movement, but she wasn't taking any chances. "Florence is in trouble." Vivian swallowed. "She got a letter."

Vivian nearly crumpled with relief when he asked simply, "What do you need me to do?" It didn't take long for her to explain. "Okay, got it," he said when she had finished. "And then I'm coming to meet you. Where will you be, at your place?"

"God, no," Vivian replied, ignoring Florence's scowl. She didn't have time to worry about unladylike language. "We can't risk staying there right now. I'm taking her to the Nightingale. It's the safest place I can think of."

"Yeah, probably." The words sounded as though they had been dragged reluctantly out of him. "I'd offer to let you girls bunk here, but my landlady would have a heart attack. And then she'd throw us all out in the street."

A laugh bubbled up through the tension in Vivian's chest and came out as a snort. "That doesn't sound so helpful, no. See you there when you're done, okay?"

"I'll take care of it as quick as I can," Leo promised. "And Vivian?" His voice dropped, low and soothing. "She's going to be okay, and so are you. You won't let anything happen to her, and there's plenty of folks won't let anything happen to you."

"Thanks, Leo," she whispered.

Once she had ended the call and paid her two cents, Vivian pressed her forehead against the hot, flimsy wood of the phone booth, eyes closed, wishing she could go to sleep and wake up to find it was all a dream. A sweating, shaking hand found hers and held on tight; Vivian gripped it with equal intensity. She couldn't afford to fall to pieces. Florence—Florence who kept her head down and followed the rules, who did everything the world demanded of her and rarely dreamed of more, never mind asked for it—Florence needed her.

"Is that safe?" Florence whispered. She had been close enough to hear nearly every word of the conversation, even though Vivian had been speaking in a whisper. "Trying to get them involved?"

"It's the best thing I can think of right now," Vivian replied, shrugging, though there was barely room to move her shoulders. Bea was going to be furious, and Vivian wouldn't blame her for it. But if breaking her promise meant saving Florence, she would do it. "I don't like the idea of them poking around any more than you do. But I like it a whole sight better than the thought of you getting arrested for theft." *Or poisoned,* she thought but did not say out loud. She didn't need to. They both knew what the alternative was. Vivian shuddered.

"Okay then," Florence said, nodding firmly, though she was still pale. Her curly brown hair was limp underneath the edge of her hat. Vivian could feel sweat that was only partially due to nerves tickling the back of her own neck. It was sweltering with the two of them crammed into the tiny space together. "I trust you. Where to next?"

Just walking down the street was an exercise in fear. Vivian had no idea how many people were involved with the letters, so she had no idea whether they had the manpower to follow the people they were trying to rob. They had to get around enough to pry into people's lives, otherwise they'd never know to ask for things like Mrs. Kaminski's candlesticks or the dress from Miss Ethel's shop. But those were the sort of details that could be picked up from gossip. Something like Pearlie's cash, though . . . he wouldn't have been talking about that, not even somewhere like the Nightingale. That took some doing to unearth.

And who was to say they didn't also do the sort of work that included following Florence or Vivian around, making sure neither of them went to the police?

But they couldn't stay in their home, waiting for trouble to find them.

The back of Vivian's neck prickled for five blocks from the hotel before she saw a cab pull over for its passengers to climb out. Grabbing Florence's hand and ignoring her sudden *oof* of surprise, she towed her sister toward it at a half run and shoved her into the back seat as soon as it was empty. That earned her an offended scowl from the suited gentleman just emerging, but Vivian ignored him as she slid in after her sister and slammed the door shut.

She gave directions for two blocks east of the Nightingale, then heaved a sigh of relief once they were on their way.

"Can we afford this?" Florence's whisper was so quiet her lips moved almost silently, as she looked toward the cabbie.

"Today, I don't think we can afford not to do it," Vivian whispered back, squeezing her sister's hand. Anyone who had been keeping an eye on the Kelly sisters would know they didn't waste money on things like cabs. If there *had* been someone following them—if—they wouldn't have been prepared for a cab ride. And Vivian hadn't seen any other cabs on the block when they climbed in.

"Where are we going?" Florence asked nervously, glancing out the window.

Vivian leaned her head against the glass of the window, wishing it was cooler. "Somewhere we can stay for a while. I hope."

"What about work?" Florence asked, always practical. "We can't just disappear for days. Not if we want to keep our jobs. And not if . . ." She swallowed, clearly thinking of the beautiful dress that someone wanted her to steal.

"You leave that to me," Vivian said. "I think I can keep going, since the letter wasn't for me. And anyway, Leo's taking care of things, so it shouldn't need to be for long. I'll just say you're under the weather and need a few days at home to recover."

"She'll never go for that," Florence argued, shaking her head. "She doesn't believe in days off."

It was true. The last time one of the seamstresses was too sick to come to work for more than a day, Miss Ethel had told her not to come back and promptly found a replacement. There were, as their boss reminded them often, hundreds of girls in New York willing to hunch over a sewing machine for hours every day, making pretty things for people who lived a life of luxury far beyond their dreams, if it meant they got paid at the end of the week.

"Miss Ethel won't argue with me," Vivian said. She could feel Florence's eyes on her, feel the unspoken questions like a physical touch. But she didn't look over, and eventually she heard her sister sigh and settle into her seat. When Vivian finally glanced at her, Florence was staring out the window, head tipped back.

"What are you looking at?" Vivian asked.

"I'm trying to see the sky," Florence answered. The cabbie honked at a pair of men who had staggered into the street, arguing drunkenly though it was still only mid-afternoon. "I know it's there somewhere. But it sure can be hard to spot it sometimes."

"So, can we stay here?"

Vivian watched Honor hopefully. They were in her apartment above the Nightingale—past the second locked door on the landing, up the rest of the flight of stairs, and behind another locked door that hid a surprisingly domestic space. Honor didn't stay there all the time—as Vivian had learned after a police raid, there were times it was safer for her to be away from her club. But most of the time, the upper floor of the building was her home. And it would be, Vivian had explained in a breathless rush, the safest place for her and Florence to stay until they could go home again.

She had a hard time meeting Honor's eyes as she spoke, too conscious of how they had left things between them the night before. Vivian wished she had been less honest, less blunt. But she was also sure that, no matter how uncertain things were, Honor cared enough about her—as an employee, if nothing else—to want to help.

Honor gave her a long, considering stare, then looked past her to where Florence waited. Vivian glanced back at her sister, sitting with her legs pulled tight toward her body and her suitcase leaning against them. Honor was seated in front of her fireplace, though it was unlit, with the two of them across from her. On the low table in front of them sat a sweating pitcher of lemonade, a surprising concession to the summer heat from Honor, who Vivian would have never pictured drinking something so wholesome.

Florence's eyes were wide as she stared at the club owner. Vivian glanced down at her own glass of lemonade, trying not to grimace. She couldn't blame Florence; Honor was a lot to take in the first time you saw her, and not just because of the way she dressed. Everything about her, the way she held herself or spoke or even moved, turned heads, made you want to watch her until you could figure her out. But she hoped Honor wasn't offended by her sister's obvious surprise.

"No."

Vivian's head snapped back up, and now she was the one who stared at Honor, dumbfounded. "No?" she repeated.

"Not because I don't want to help," Honor said gently. She leaned forward, elbows resting on her knees and her hands clasped in front of her. "I just don't think staying here would be safer. Think about it, Vivian. If whoever sent that letter knew so much about where Florence works, who's to say they don't know as much about where you work?" She shook her head. "I can't stop people from coming and going without shutting the club down, which I can't afford to do. And if the wrong person made it past one of my boys and found their way up here . . ."

"Then what can we do?"

Honor stood and paced toward the window, frowning out at the rooftops and brick walls that surrounded them. It was propped open, a rickety electric fan whirring away. Vivian felt like she was being smothered, like she was drowning, like maybe it would be easier if she melted away and didn't have to worry anymore about keeping the person she loved most in the world safe. Beside her, Florence said nothing, her lips pressed together in a thin, nervous line.

"Downtown," Honor said at last, turning back to them. "You and Danny barely ever see each other outside the Nightingale, right? Unless he's delivering a message from me. Even if someone knows you work here, the odds of them thinking to find you there are small."

"He doesn't have his own place," Vivian pointed out. "And the odds of his folks being okay with some strange girls staying there are small, too."

Honor grimaced. "Won't know until you ask. He's downstairs running inventory right now. And if it doesn't work, we'll figure out something else, I promise." She went to the cabinet in the corner and, to Vivian's surprise, took out a small stack of cash. "Here," she said, holding it out. "I'll get someone downstairs to call you a cab so you're not walking away from here."

Florence, at last, spoke up. "Do you mean Mr. Chin?" she asked. Vivian could see her sister's hands trembling around her glass, but Florence's voice was steady.

Honor nodded. "His family has a restaurant down on Spring Street, and they live above it. It's where he works when he's not here. It might not be the safest part of town, but it's certainly no rougher than where you girls live." She seemed about to say something else, then shrugged. "I'll go get him."

Florence was silent for a long moment after Honor left. Then, "That's the woman you work for?"

"Yes," Vivian said shortly, feeling defensive. "She owns the Nightingale."

"All on her own?"

"Yes." Vivian struggled to keep her voice even. Florence worked for a dressmaker who owned her own shop. Owning a jazz club wasn't so much more outlandish than that. Vivian was already exhausted from worry as it was; she didn't have the energy to guide Florence through the evolution of the New Woman that was happening in the world around them. And even that would fail to fully encompass someone like Honor.

Or like herself, Vivian thought with bitter, anxious humor. That was a conversation she definitely wasn't ready to have yet.

"Oh. She's . . . very glamorous," was all Florence said in response, her voice very small. She stared into her glass again, looking overwhelmed.

Vivian felt a pang of guilt. It wasn't Florence's fault she'd been dragged into this world, one she never would have thought about if it weren't for her sister. She had to be terrified. Vivian reached out and squeezed her hand.

"It's going to be okay, Flo. We'll get you somewhere safe, and the police should be on it by the end of the day. It'll all be fine, I promise."

There was a thumping sound of someone hurrying up the steps. Without thinking, Vivian stood, putting herself between Florence and the door. There was a quick knock, and then Danny was there, his worried gaze going first to Florence, then back to Vivian. Then he smiled, the friendly, flirtatious smile that said everything was all right with the world, and if it wasn't, then he knew exactly what to do to fix it. "Hey girls," he said, stepping aside so Honor could join them. "I hear you're looking for a place to stay."

It took a little more work to convince his father.

Just to be cautious, Danny took them out through one of the club's several secondary exits, this one accessed through a trapdoor behind the bar. A ladder led them to a narrow brick tunnel that wound underground until it sloped up again, bringing them up through another trapdoor into a narrow alley. Danny had them both wait in the alley, jittery with impatience and brushing dust from their clothes, while he stepped out to the street to hail a cab.

"Are you sure it'll be safe for us there?" Vivian asked as they climbed into the cab.

She was taken aback when Danny gave her a sour look, all his normal playfulness gone. "Why, are you scared of all the Chinese folks?"

"No, I just meant . . ." Vivian could feel her face heating. "We'll stand out, is all. Two Irish girls in that part of the city are bound to attract some attention, aren't we? And that's the last thing we need right now."

Danny sighed as he ran a hand through the hair that continuously fell across one eye. "Oh. Well, don't worry about that, kitten. You won't stand out nearly as much as you think."

They rode in awkward silence for a while, Florence sneaking uncomfortable looks at both of them. Vivian was trying to decide whether she needed to say something else when Danny abruptly spoke.

"All the papers can talk about these days is the Tong Wars, and there are plenty of folks calling for the Chinese to be sent packing." He was stoic as he stared out the cab window. "Never mind we've lived here longer than half of them. But they can't shut up about gang fights." Seeing Vivian's curious expression, he added, "Makes a fella sensitive from time to time."

"They aren't real, then?" Florence asked curiously. "The Tong Wars?"

Danny laughed humorlessly. "They're real. Every neighborhood has its gangs these days, and we've got ours, too. They're not all bad, you know," he added, the look he turned on them defensive and defiant. "They look after their people. They don't agree on much, though, and they're happy to fight it out. But there wouldn't be so much of that if the government stopped making it so hard for Chinese men to live their lives and have families."

"Have families?" Florence glanced out the window, clearly confused. They were turning off Houston Street now, and the streets and sidewalks were crowded. "There are plenty of people with families here, aren't there?"

"Some, but not as many as there should be."

Vivian eyed the clusters of men who stood around on corners and outside shops as they drove past. Some of them looked like shopkeepers or restaurant owners. Others just stood there, smoking and eyeing the people passing by.

And most of them were men, Vivian realized. Children darted in and out of buildings from time to time, and there were women running errands or heading to work, but there were not nearly as many families going about their business as she would have seen in other parts of the city.

"Chinese men who come here can't bring their wives or families," Danny continued quietly. "And they don't let Chinese women in anymore."

Neither of them had to ask why. Men alone provided labor. But letting women in meant families, and families put down roots. Florence sighed. "And men without jobs and wives and kids have a lot more time to start gang fights?"

Danny nodded, but something else occurred to Vivian, and she frowned. "But your mother lives here."

"She was born in the United States, out in California," he said, the defensive note back in his voice. "And anyway, she's only half Chinese herself. Her mother was Korean."

"Oh." Vivian was quiet again, feeling ignorant and not liking it. "I didn't know all that, Danny," she said, hoping he believed her. "Honestly, I just don't want to risk anyone finding Florence. Or cause any trouble for your family because we don't fit in."

To her surprise, that made Danny laugh. "Chinese women can't come to America, so our men end up marrying whoever they can. Half the children in Chinatown have mothers who came from poor

Irish and Italian families." Before she could respond, he slowed and gestured at a tall, narrow building. "We're here."

The cab had brought them to a bustling street downtown, a part of the city where Florence had never been before and Vivian had visited only once. It felt like a different world from the corner of the city where she lived. The clamor of voices as they climbed out of the cab rose in a mixture of languages. But the buildings leaned drunkenly against each other the same as they did at home, as though if you slid one out of place the rest would topple over like dominos. Vivian couldn't read the bright signs painted with Chinese characters, but the window full of bolts of cloth clearly belonged to a tailor, the one with plucked birds hanging from the ceiling had to be a butcher, and the sweltering heat was the same as any other part of New York.

When they climbed out of the cab, Florence's hand squeezed Vivian's arm almost painfully as she stared around them. "A chop suey place?" she whispered, seeing the building Danny was leading them toward. "Is that his parents' restaurant?"

"I guess so," Vivian whispered back. "I've never been here before."

Danny glanced back at them, and Vivian was surprised to see a look of uncertainty on his face, the first time she had seen the devil-may-care bartender look anything less than fully confident. But there was also something in his expression that might have been pride.

Vivian cleared her throat. "Leo said your family owns two restaurants."

Danny grinned, suddenly back to his normal swagger. "My uncle took over their old place on Mott Street, and my parents opened this one last year. Everybody loves chop suey these days, even outside the Chinese neighborhood." He gave them an encouraging smile as he swung the door open and gestured expansively. "Welcome."

The interior was bright, painted in red and gold, cream and black, the floor filled with spindly tables set in neat lines. Electric bulbs decorated with shades of gold paper hung from the ceiling, but not many of them were turned on at this time of day; most of the light streamed from the front window. To one side, a staircase leading up had a twisted red rope strung across it. A door at the back of the room was outlined in light, and from it came a clattering of pans and the wafting aroma of dinner being prepared.

Vivian took a deep breath. The food was different than in their part of the city, but the smell of good cooking was comforting, no matter where you were.

The room was currently empty of customers, and Vivian glanced nervously at Danny. "Is it all right for us to be here?"

"They close between lunch and dinner to give everyone a little break. But no one's going to throw you out," he said, just in time for a man to shout from the kitchen, "We are not open for business!"

"Only me, Ba!" Danny called back. "Me and some friends."

A man's head poked around the kitchen door so quickly that Vivian nearly jumped, though she should have been expecting it. His face was lined and his hair beginning to gray around the temples, but otherwise he could have been Danny's twin, down to the sharp line of his jaw and his expressive eyebrows. Currently those eyebrows were drawn into a scowl, and as he came into the front room he began speaking rapidly in what Vivian assumed was Chinese.

Danny responded in the same language, his voice relaxed in spite of his father's obvious displeasure, then gestured at his small entourage. "Florence, Vivian, meet my father, Mr. Chin. Ba, Vivian's a friend from work, and Florence is her sister."

"How do you do, Mr. Chin?" Florence said politely, holding out her hand. "I'm very pleased to meet you." Vivian quickly echoed her sister.

Mr. Chin's scowl faded as he shook Florence's hand, then Vivian's, his expression polite but wary. And he still gave his son a narrow-eyed glance. "You have not brought people from your other job here before."

"No, but the girls are in a bit of a jam and need some help."

Mr. Chin held up a quick hand. "I do not want to know."

"It's not about work," Danny sighed. "Their neighborhood's a little rough right now, and they need somewhere to stay until things quiet down."

"Eh, New York." Mr. Chin shook his head, a look of reluctant sympathy on his face. "It is a hell of a place to live these days. So you want these girls to stay here?"

"Ma would say yes, and you know it."

"Your mother would let every—" Mr. Chin gave the girls a sideways glance, then switched languages again. He and Danny exchanged quick words before he finally threw up his hands. "Fine, fine. Sit, all of you. Food first, and then we will talk about it more. And then you will put in your hours in the kitchen?" he asked, turning sharply to Danny, who nodded. Mr. Chin sighed, then nodded, rubbing one palm across his thinning hair and muttering under his breath as he pushed back through the door into the kitchen.

"Everything okay?" Vivian asked as they settled into a table. "We don't have to stay if it's causing any trouble."

"It's fine," Danny reassured her. "Ma will say yes, and she'll bring him around. They just don't want anyone finding out about my second job. And they worry about me." He sighed. "I don't like making them worry. So we usually don't talk about it. I get a nap in the morning, then work the kitchen in the afternoon with my cousins. But the cash helps—that's how they were able to buy this place and still have money to send home. Besides." He leaned back in his chair, his grin returning. "I like my job. More than the restaurant, to be honest."

"It's a very nice restaurant, though," Florence said, looking around. She was sitting on the edge of her chair and fiddling with the handle of her purse. Her suitcase perched beside her chair, as though they might be told to leave at any moment.

"The food's good too," Danny said, that edge of nervous pride once again clear in his voice. "Not many businesses Chinese folks are allowed to own in this city," he added, a scowl briefly creasing his handsome face before he shrugged. "It's restaurants or laundromats. Murder on your back either way, but food's more fun than cleaning clothes."

There was a clatter from the kitchen, and he sprang up as a tiny, dark-haired woman, the skin around her eyes creased with laugh lines, came out bearing a large tray of food. She paused for a moment, sizing them up before she handed the tray to Danny. When Florence and Vivian tried to stand up to help, she waved them off.

"Sit down and let him do the work. He does not have to suffer through high heels on his feet." Her own shoes, Vivian noticed, were flat and practical. Danny rolled his eyes, but he didn't seem offended as he laid out the food. "Don't tell your father I gave you the newest batch of buns," she whispered as he laid the final dish on the table.

"You're the best, Ma," Danny said, giving her a quick, one-armed hug.

"Of course I am," she agreed, smiling and giving him a pat on his cheek as she took a seat at their table. "Introduce me to these girls."

"Ma, this is Florence Kelly and her sister, Vivian."

"How do you do, Mrs. Chin?" Florence said politely, holding out her hand.

"Oh, no," Danny said with a chuckle. "We don't—"

"Mrs. Chin is fine," his mother said, nodding as she shook Florence's hand. "They are polite girls, at least." She shook Vivian's hand, too, and she gave each of them an assessing look, her eyes lingering on their carefully sewn clothes, catalog shoes, and old suitcases. Florence's pinned-back curls earned a nod of approval. Vivian resisted the urge to touch her own bobbed hair, hoping she wasn't making a bad impression.

"So," Danny's mother said once he was done. "Some people in your neighborhood are causing trouble, yes? And you need to get away for a bit while it dies down?"

Danny started to answer, but she held up her hand. "I want to hear it from these girls, please. I need to know whether they are people we want living here before I say yes, and I can't do that if you never let them open their mouths."

As nervous as if there were a spotlight shining on her, Vivian glanced at her sister. Florence stared back with an expression that clearly said she was out of her depth. So Vivian took a deep breath and answered. "That's the idea, yes. We'd really appreciate a place to stay, just for a few days. They aren't nice folks."

"Lots of those in the city these days," Danny's mother sniffed. "This trouble, is it likely to follow you here?"

"We're hoping no one will know we're here," Vivian said.

"That's why they came to me, instead of someone in their own neighborhood," Danny put in, before Mrs. Chin shushed him again.

"We don't want to make things difficult for anyone else." Florence's voice was soft and polite as she spoke up for the first time in several minutes. "We wouldn't dream of imposing if it makes you uncomfortable."

Mrs. Chin gave her a look that was not completely disapproving before she glanced at Vivian. "I can see you are the one my son knows from work. But I do not picture you there as easily," she said, looking back at Florence.

"I'm a seamstress," Florence said quickly. "Vivian is too. Or, she used to be. She does deliveries to women who order the dresses now. We work in a shop uptown."

"Clothes for rich people?"

Florence smiled a little. "Yes, ma'am."

Mrs. Chin sniffed again but looked pleased. "It's good for a woman to know how to work. We don't have anyone sitting around doing nothing in this house. What can you do here?"

"We can wash dishes," Florence suggested. Apparently Mrs. Chin's brusque manner didn't bother her at all. "I don't know that I'd be able to cook without you standing over my shoulder telling me what to do, and that's not less work for you. But washing dishes we can manage."

Danny's mother nodded. "All right. Feed these girls," she said to her son. "They're too skinny. I will talk with your father while you eat and see whether we can help them or not." She stood, giving them one more assessing glance before disappearing back into the kitchen.

Vivian sagged back in her chair, feeling as exhausted as if she'd been through a police interrogation instead of a few reasonable questions from a short, cheerful cook.

"I like your mother," Florence said, a little smile still hovering around her lips in spite of her obvious nerves.

"She's easy to like," Danny agreed as they all settled in to eat. "And she's a fantastic cook."

As soon as she took her first bite, Vivian agreed enthusiastically. Florence nodded her own agreement but didn't answer; she was too busy eating with unladylike concentration. Neither of them had had any food yet that day, just a cup of coffee each before church, and for a few minutes they were silent as they filled their plates with rice, vegetables, eggs, and the contraband buns. Danny, eating more slowly, regarded them with satisfaction as he poured them cups of mild, fragrant tea that were far more pleasant than the bitter coffee Vivian was used to drinking.

At last, Danny's father emerged from the kitchen, still frowning. Vivian stood up as he approached, and she felt Florence's hand sneak into her own behind her back. Vivian squeezed, trying to offer some comfort.

"All right," Mr. Chin said as he stopped next to the table. He might have been frowning, but Vivian could see that his eyes were kind, and they rested on his son with no small amount of pride. Some of the tension in Vivian's shoulders relaxed. "Your mother has browbeaten me into submission. And we do not, as she forcefully pointed out, turn away young ladies who need help. So you may stay, girls"—he held up a hand to forestall their thanks—"as long as there is no trouble."

"There won't be," Vivian promised quickly. "Thank you, really."

"It's very kind of you," Florence added. "Would you like us to come back to the kitchen now?"

Mr. Chin waved away the offer. "Get settled in first. There will be plenty of dishes to wash when we reopen for dinner. Yu-Chen, show them upstairs. And carry their bags for them," he added, a twinkling look coming into his expression as he saw the girls pick up their suitcases. "We have raised you to be a gentleman." He hesitated, then added, "You seem like nice girls. And my son is a good judge of character."

"You have to be, in my line of work," Danny put in, smiling at his father.

His father shook his head. "Yes, I imagine that's true."

"Yu-Chen?" Vivian asked once Mr. Chin had returned to the kitchen. "Is that what your parents call you?"

Danny raised his eyebrows at her, the expression somehow both a look of discomfort and a challenge. "My Chinese name. Daniel was the English name they picked for me when I was baptized."

"Does it mean anything?" Florence asked.

Danny took her suitcase out of her hand over her mild protest, then scooped up Vivian's as well. "All names mean something, don't they?" he said, his voice teasing. "My parents picked mine to mean that every day with me is like a precious gem. Which is true." He gave her a wink, which made Florence look away, though she smiled as she did so.

The upstairs apartment where Danny led them wasn't fancy, but it was nicer and more spacious than their own home, filled with the sort of cozy clutter that collected over years and that Vivian assumed was part of belonging to a family. Danny led them up a second flight of stairs to a small room that was half storage but had enough space for both of them to sleep. "I'd offer you girls my own room, but I share it with my cousin Lucky, and he'd throw a fit if I kicked him out."

"This is swell, Danny, really," Vivian said, looking around. "You're a peach, and you've got the nicest parents I've ever met."

"I'm glad to help you out," Danny said softly, but his eyes were on

Florence, who was running a hand over the gauzy material of the curtains. When she turned and found him watching her, she fell still, a shy smile creeping over her face.

Vivian, who had finally begun to relax for the first time in hours, felt as though someone had squeezed her heart. She might as well not have been there, so focused were they on each other for that brief moment. Vivian found herself remembering her argument with Honor the night before, and loneliness began to prickle behind her eyelids.

She turned away quickly, not wanting to let the feeling linger, and cleared her throat. "Well, we're glad to help out in return. Which means we should probably get downstairs and do our part in the kitchen. Come on, Flo."

"Of course." Florence glanced around, on edge once more, but her smile returned when her eyes met Danny's. "Are you coming, Mr. Chin?"

"Danny," he suggested.

Florence hesitated, then nodded. "Danny."

"Come on," Vivian said, yanking the door open, angry that she could feel anything other than relief and gratitude. Florence was safe, and that should have been all that mattered. "Let's go down."

It was late—after the dinner rush—and Vivian's hands were wrinkled from hours spent washing dishes when she finally started dressing for work. Florence was already sitting on the room's only bed, which they would be sharing, her knees drawn close and tucked under her chin. She watched as Vivian shimmied into one of her dancing dresses and rubbed Mrs. Chin's lotion into her hands to soften them.

"Are you sure it's safe for you to go to work tonight?" Florence asked quietly, fiddling with the hairbrush that was lying on the bed next to her. "If it's not safe for us to be home, then shouldn't . . . shouldn't we just stay here?"

"No one's going to get me at the Nightingale," Vivian said with more confidence than she felt. "And anyway, I don't think whoever wrote that letter will be coming after me yet. They want that dress, right? They'll be waiting for us to hand it over."

"But the note said tonight," Florence reminded her. "So after today—"

"Don't worry about it," Vivian said quickly, sliding the brush out of her sister's nervous fingers and using her reflection in the window as a mirror to style her hair. Sliding a pin decorated with feathers and beads into place, she gave Florence a smile, trying to reassure herself as much as her sister. "By tomorrow, Leo should have things in motion for us. And then it should just be a little while until whoever is doing this is either caught or slinks back into the shadows."

"I'm glad you have a plan," Florence said, easing herself down onto the pillows, still curled into a tight ball. "I'm still angry with you, by the way. For keeping this from me."

"I didn't have a good reason to share it," Vivian protested.

"I just thought we were telling each other everything now," Florence said quietly, her words a forlorn accusation that made Vivian flinch. "No more keeping secrets."

"Are we?" Vivian asked, thinking of the way Danny and Florence had kept sneaking glances at each other as Danny went in and out of the kitchen that night. "Do you tell me everything, Flo?" Her sister didn't answer, and Vivian sighed as she picked up her shoes. "Anyway, I've got work. Danny's off tonight, so he'll be sticking around here to keep an eye on things. And no one but Honor knows we're here, so you don't need to worry, okay?"

"And you'll be careful?" Florence asked as Vivian turned to leave.

Vivian gave her a quick smile over her shoulder. It was a pretend smile, the kind that she gave customers who wanted someone to flirt with, a girl with no worries so they could forget about the worries in their own lives, too. She hoped Florence couldn't tell the difference. "I'm always careful. I'm just not always good."

Florence shook her head. "That's not funny."

Vivian relaxed into a real smile. "Sure it was. Cheer up, Flo. I'm taking care of it. I promise."

Danny's parents hadn't wanted her walking through the restaurant to head to work—which Vivian couldn't blame them for—so Danny had promised to show her the trick for getting out the back and down the fire escape. She wasn't surprised to find him waiting for her in the family's common room.

But the man waiting with him did catch her off guard. The last she had told Leo, she had expected they would be staying at the Nightingale; if he was standing there now, hat in hand while he met her eyes, that had to mean he had gone there looking for her and Honor had sent him downtown. Which meant . . .

Vivian caught her breath. "Did you already see the medical examiner?"

"I did—" Leo began, but he didn't get any further than that before she threw herself forward, wrapping her arms around him. Leo, completely caught off guard, just managed to catch her; his answering embrace was not nearly as enthusiastic as she expected, but that didn't dim her relief. Stepping back to catch her breath, she didn't let go of his arms as she asked, "You did it, then? Already? Thank you, thank you. What did he say?"

"What were you up to, pal?" Danny asked from behind her. "Whatever it is, you don't look happy about it."

Danny was right, Vivian noticed, her relief beginning to seep away like cold water trickling down a drain. "Leo? If you talked to him already, what's got you looking so flat-footed?"

"I know his home address," Leo said quietly. "So I went to see him this evening. And he seemed relieved when I told him what I knew. He'd been worried ever since our visit. Bellevue is technically closed on Sunday, but as soon as I told him what I needed, he said we could go right away. Well, not right away." He was babbling, something she had never heard him do before, as if he didn't want to tell her what had actually happened. "He had to have his Sunday dinner first, his wife's pretty particular about that. But as soon as that was done he met me there."

"Leo," Vivian said, cutting him off. She forced herself to meet his eyes, trying to smile and failing. "Just tell me what happened. Please."

"I'm sorry, sweetheart. He'd been keeping the bottle in his office, hoping that we'd be willing to tell him more. But when we got there tonight . . . It was gone. Someone had taken it."

Vivian felt as if she'd been spinning in circles to music that was going faster and faster and the music had suddenly disappeared, leaving her staggering and about to fall. "But . . . but that was our evidence. That's the only proof we had that . . ." Without the brandy bottle and its deadly contents, they couldn't prove that Pearlie's death had been anything other than a suicide. And without that, the letter that he received—and the letter that Florence had received—were just odd mail. The police would never look twice at that.

How had someone known it was there? And how in God's name could she keep Florence safe now?

Beside her, Danny let out a long string of whispered curses, only half of them in English. Vivian wanted to do the same—wanted to yell them—but her brain felt too numb to think of anything ugly enough for how she was feeling.

Vivian stared at a point on the floor, not seeing it. She should have told the coroner right away. She felt cold all over at the thought that someone had thrown that bottle away on purpose. Someone who didn't want its contents to be tested and scrutinized again.

But it could just as easily have been tossed by accident. There was no way to know for sure. Either way, the result was the same. They had played this all wrong, start to finish.

"Viv?" Leo's voice was cautious. "What do you want to do now?"

"Now?" Vivian looked up to find both of them watching her. She took a deep breath and let it out slowly. "I guess I'm going to steal a dress."

—•—

"Where have you been?" Bea grabbed Vivian's arm and pulled her to a corner as soon as she walked into the dressing room. A few other waitresses were chatting and resting their feet before the rush and aches of the night ahead of them; Bea cast them a wary look before lowering her voice. "I went by twice today to find you, but no one was home. And then I heard someone in your building died? Is everything okay?"

Vivian stared at her friend, wondering how much to tell her. On the one hand, she and Bea told each other practically everything. Bea never would have brought her to the Nightingale in the first place if they hadn't been sure they could trust each other. But on the other hand, if Bea knew Florence had received a letter . . .

She would guess right away what Vivian had tried to do, and she would know Vivian had gone to the medical examiner without telling her. And even though it hadn't worked, she would feel furious and betrayed that Vivian had gone behind her back, maybe even put her family at risk, for Florence's sake.

Vivian couldn't blame her for that. But she also didn't regret doing whatever she could to keep her sister safe.

And it hadn't worked anyway, which meant there was no reason to confess and cause that sort of trouble between them. And if Bea wasn't furious, when she found out what Vivian was planning next, she might insist on coming along.

Vivian couldn't let that happen. She wouldn't put anyone else in danger if she didn't have to.

"Everything's swell," Vivian said. She gave her hair a quick fluff, checked the back of her stockings in the mirror, and smiled her pretend smile once again. "Can't wait to hear your set tonight. We've missed you. And so have the folks out there." She gave her friend a bump with her shoulder. "You'll be famous one of these days, I just know it."

She could feel Bea's eyes on her in the mirror, but she bent to fuss with her shoes so she didn't have to meet them.

"What aren't you telling me, Viv?" Bea asked quietly.

"Nothing," Vivian answered, straightening at last. "Nothing at all. See you out there, okay? I need to find Honor and ask her something."

Vivian caught up to Honor by the end of the bar, where the club owner was coolly surveying her domain, lights dim, liquor stocked, band just striking up the first tune of the night. Soon, the doors would open and patrons would trickle in by twos and threes, laughing as they found their way to the bar. Later there would be larger groups tumbling out of cabs and down the steps, men and women slipping in by themselves to look for a friend or a stranger to keep them company for the night. Honor looked it over with unmistakable pride.

"There you are, pet," she said when she caught sight of Vivian. "I was wondering when you were going to show up. I was worried something had happened."

She had only been fifteen minutes late, but trust Honor to notice. Honor noticed everything. She would notice instantly that something was wrong, too—her brows were already creasing into a frown as she took Vivian in from head to toe—so Vivian didn't bother dancing around her request.

"Honor," she said, her whisper urgent as she glanced around to make sure no one else was close enough to hear. "I really hope I'm going to owe you a hell of a favor after tonight, because that means you've said yes to what I'm about to ask." She took a deep breath. "Danny told me that you know how to pick locks."

SEVENTEEN

There were places in New York that Vivian never went at night.

The elegant avenues, with mansions spilling light and sound into the air, where drivers waited next to cars that cost more than their year's salary, the tips of their cigarettes glowing in the night as they waited for the party to finish and the revelers to stumble out in the small hours of the morning.

The vast park, with its stately trees and too many shadows, where you were equally likely to stumble on a quiet, dangerous meeting taking place in the dark or someone with nowhere else to go who just wanted to find a few hours of rest.

And she never went to the pretty little row of shops, on as quiet a street as New York had, where you could find a perfectly tailored suit with a hat to match, elegant heeled shoes made in emerald velvet and tied with gold ribbons, a dress sewn with ten thousand glass beads that would turn the head of every drunk, careless partygoer at a Long Island mansion.

Vivian used to sew those dresses. Just thinking about them made her fingers ache with the memory of a thousand needle pricks. She never wanted to think about Miss Ethel's shop, or Miss Ethel's demands, when she left them behind her each night. She was even less interested in swinging by for a visit or a stroll.

When Vivian's feet took her across the city at night, they carried her to places where she could find her escape. A few hours in a cinema sitting next to a fella with a million-dollar smile and a flask tucked in his jacket. A knock on a door, a whispered password, a dance hall filled with light and music. A drink, a smoke, a chance to flirt. She didn't want a reminder of what she didn't have.

But there was a first time for everything.

EIGHTEEN

Vivian stood in the shadows next to Miss Ethel's shop, trying to ignore the way her heart felt like it was going to jump out of her chest.

"You sure you want to do this, pet?" Honor, in a dark sweater and trousers, was barely visible in the gloomy night. But she was close enough that her murmur brushed Vivian's cheek like a caress.

"I don't have a choice," Vivian whispered back, glad that the darkness hid her shaking.

She had done illegal things before. Buying liquor. Working at the Nightingale. Blackmail. That last one she had hesitated over—but she had still gone through with it, and her life was better because of it.

But blackmail was one thing. Outright theft felt like a completely different game. She shivered again, grateful for Honor's presence at her side.

"All clear," came Leo's quiet whisper from out on the sidewalk. He lounged against a streetlamp in his most respectable-looking suit and hat, which really just meant his most expensive looking. Vivian could see the tip of his cigarette glowing, like a beacon, like a warning. He had bristled at being asked to keep watch while Honor and Vivian did the dangerous work of actually getting the dress, but he hadn't argued. They all knew he was the one least likely to be hassled if someone came along.

Danny had wanted to come. As soon as he realized what they were planning, he had pointed out that he was better at picking locks than Honor—a skillset Vivian hadn't realized either of them possessed, but hadn't been surprised by at all when he told her about it. But though no one said it out loud, they all knew it would be much more dangerous for a Chinese man to be picked up than for the rest of them.

It was risky for them too, of course. But the chance of jail time was less scary than the risk of a beating from the police. And someone needed to be in charge at the Nightingale.

That left her with just Honor and Leo for help. Another time, she wouldn't have wanted to put them anywhere near each other, too conscious of the not-quite-history she had with each. But tonight she didn't care.

Florence was in danger. That was all that mattered.

"Won't your Miss Ethel get suspicious when she finds herself robbed and neither you nor your sister shows up for work in the morning?" Honor whispered.

Vivian shook her head. "I told Florence she was going to work tomorrow after all. We'll show up like usual and look shocked along with everyone else. Just gotta hope Flo's got her poker face on good and tight, because she'll realize what I did as soon as she gets here."

It was a cloudy night, but there was still light from the streetlamps catching the edges of buildings, making everything look twice as large as it did in the day. They didn't want to risk carrying a light of their own, so that was all they had to work with. Vivian blinked again and again, straining her eyes against the way the shadows twisted her perception.

"Okay," she whispered to Honor. "Let's give this a whirl."

She could hear the smile in Honor's soft voice as she replied, "I always did like how you keep me on my toes."

Honor moved like silk and water through the shadows, sliding toward the heavy, half-hidden little cellar door that Vivian had pointed out to her. It was set at an angle, half in the wall, half in the stone of the street, and if you didn't already know, it was hard to tell which shop it would actually take you into. But Vivian had worked at Miss Ethel's for a long time. If you were breaking and entering, it sure helped to know the joint well.

There was always a lock on the door, a heavy padlock that was almost never opened. And if anyone passing by glanced down the alley, they would be able to see two figures crouched awkwardly against the wall. Anyone out for a casual stroll would know to keep walking, rather than risk upsetting a group of criminals who might be either more violent or more well-connected than they expected. But that didn't mean they wouldn't telephone the police. And if the police happened by . . . well, they wouldn't hesitate to start making arrests.

"Hurry up," Vivian muttered as Honor slid two slim metal tools into the padlock.

"Talent can't be rushed," Honor murmured, her voice barely louder than the gentle click of her tools.

"Where'd you learn to pick locks, anyway?" Vivian asked, as much to distract herself from her nerves as to learn the answer.

For a moment, Honor was silent. In the shadows, Vivian couldn't see her face well enough to tell whether that was because Honor was concentrating or because she didn't want to answer. Just when Vivian was beginning to regret asking, Honor replied, barely loud enough to be heard, "I had an occasionally criminal childhood."

It was far from the answer Vivian was expecting. She desperately wanted to ask more, but it wasn't the time for anything resembling a real conversation.

"Evening, fellas."

Leo's clear greeting echoed down the alley, a warning that someone was about to go past. Honor and Vivian flattened themselves against the wall, trying to blend into the shadows in case someone looked their way.

It was a raucous group of young men, hats and bodies both tilted drunkenly as they strutted down the street with as much swagger and dignity as they could manage. They looked harmless, but even the mildest-looking fellow could be dangerous, especially when he was surrounded by his friends.

"Got a smoke, pal?" one of them slurred, giving Leo what looked like a none-too-gentle sock in the shoulder.

It was the sort of treatment that Leo wouldn't normally let slide without a response. But he couldn't do anything in return, not if he wanted to keep Vivian and Honor from being noticed. Instead, he took refuge in good humor; but Vivian could hear the edge in his voice as he replied, "Glad to share. But I wouldn't linger if I were you; cops are thick on the street tonight."

"Then what're you doing standing here?" one man asked belligerently.

Vivian didn't realize she had grabbed Honor's hand until Honor squeezed back gently. "He can handle them," she said, her voice barely more than a breath next to Vivian's ear.

In spite of the humid night, Vivian shivered. But Honor was right. It was easy to picture Leo's smile as he replied, "Following orders, my friend. Which I don't recommend getting in the way of."

A murmur went through the group; they might have been drunk, but they knew better than to ignore that sort of warning. Getting in the middle of someone else's business was a good way to end up beaten or worse in an alley.

"Thanks for the cig," one of them called, while a friend gave him a shove to get him moving down the street with the rest of the group. "Good luck with your night."

As soon as the sound of their footsteps had started to fade, Honor was back at the door. Vivian thought she must be working more by feel than anything else; it was certainly too dark to see the keyhole. Vivian stayed where she was until she heard the click of the padlock's hinge and Honor's quietly triumphant "Open sesame." A flicker from the streetlight caught her smile as she turned to Vivian. "Shall we?"

The door was heavy enough that they had to work together to ease it open and lower it, silently and slowly, toward the ground. Vivian tried to trick her mind into thinking of it as a game, just like sneaking out to go dancing, back when Florence had looked at her nighttime excursions with such bitter disapproval. But her heart felt like it was pounding right in her throat, making her breath come in shivering bursts that couldn't quite pull enough oxygen into her lungs.

"After you," Honor murmured, and they slipped inside, light on toes that were used to keeping up with the rapid tempo of a Charleston or a quickstep. There were five stairs going down on the other side, and they had to stand on them to ease the door back into place so it wouldn't come crashing down and tell the whole world that something shady was going on.

When it was closed, it was inky black in the basement, where the only window was barely seven inches high and looked out over the dank ground of the alley. Honor pulled out a flat pocket light, and the weak, narrow beam darted around the crowded little storage room like a firefly trying to find its way back to the sky.

But there was no sound from outside. So far, so safe.

"This way," Vivian whispered, sliding carefully past stacked bolts of fabric, crates of notions and trimmings, and two broken sewing machines in need of repair. Honor was a shadow moving behind her, nearly silent, but Vivian was all too conscious of the other woman's presence, the faint sound of her steps, the smell of her perfume, the electric feeling when their hands happened to brush against each other in the dark. It was the first time they had ever been together outside the Nightingale. Vivian wondered if Honor was as scared as she was. She wondered if Honor was scared of anything. "The safe is upstairs."

The narrow staircase up to the first floor crackled beneath them, a sound that would have barely registered in the daylight but at night, in the quiet, sounded as loud as a gunshot. Vivian's breath came faster as she darted up.

Halfway up, Honor put out her light, and when they came to the top of the stairs they paused once more, listening and watching. A streetlight shone right outside the store, making it easy to see what they were doing. But it also meant that anyone who happened to glance through the window would be able to spot two people moving around inside a store that was clearly closed, even if they wouldn't quite be able to tell who those people were.

They couldn't see Leo; he was standing a few storefronts down, so that he wouldn't call attention to which shop they were in. Vivian wished she could see him, just for a moment. But they needed to get in and out quickly.

The safe was in a cabinet under the counter; Vivian pulled out the stacks of fabric samples that hid it from view. Once she was bent down, the counter hid her from the view of the front window, and she felt her shoulders unknot just the barest amount. Standing back up was going to be all kinds of unappealing.

Honor crouched down beside her, pulling out her light once more to illuminate the safe's lock. Vivian could hear the unhappy hiss of a sharply drawn breath. "I can't pick a combination lock, pet. And I don't know a damn thing about cracking them."

For the first time that night, Vivian felt confident about something. She put her mouth close to Honor's ear and whispered, "You don't have to." She thought Honor might have shivered, and she wondered if it was from nerves or something else. "Miss Ethel isn't exactly what you'd call trusting. But she has a real lack of imagination. Since she can't do two things at once without losing her place in both, it never occurs to her that any of her busy seamstresses might be watching when she has to open the safe."

Honor turned so they were looking in each other's eyes, their faces mere inches apart, closer even than when they were dancing. Vivian could practically feel the curve of Honor's lips as she smiled. "But you haven't worked as a seamstress in months," she murmured. "How do you know she hasn't changed the combination?"

"Like I said," Vivian replied, unable to help smiling in response, in spite of her nerves. "Lack of imagination." She turned back to the dial. "Shine the light this way?"

The last time she had seen Miss Ethel open the safe, the combination had been the address of the shop. And when she spun the dial and felt the click of the latch giving way, she let herself believe that maybe, just maybe, they would get away with this.

The safe contained two modest stacks of cash, the money that Miss Ethel put in the register each morning. Vivian pushed it aside without a moment of hesitation. She might despise the shop owner, but she had no intention of robbing the woman beyond what she had to do to keep Florence safe.

Behind the money, the light caught an edge of folded fabric, striking blue and golden sparks from the gems sewn into it. Taking a deep breath, Vivian pulled it out slowly. The silk of the dress slithered through her fingers, unfolding like a woman stretching after a nap. She and Honor both stared at it for a moment.

Honor let out a low whistle that was mostly air. "That is a pretty thing and no mistake. Your sister is an artist."

Vivian stared at it. Drinking and dancing was one thing, but stealing was a different kind of breaking the law. Was she really going to go through with it?

They were the only ones who had received a letter asking for something to be stolen. As far as she knew, every other victim had owned their valuables.

Had the thief gotten greedy? Had their plan always been to eventually persuade other people not just to hand over their own things, but to do someone else's dirty work in exchange for safety? Or was there something else going on?

"You said it's not finished, right?" Honor's voice broke through Vivian's thoughts. She had pulled two small, lidded tins out of the safe and was peering inside them one by one. Glancing over her shoulder, Vivian could see that they held the remaining topaz and aquamarine stones. There weren't many of them left, but there were enough to be valuable. "Are you going to take these too?"

Vivian hesitated. "The letter just said the dress," she whispered. "Miss Ethel's going to be in a jam either way, but if she has these to give back, it might go a little further toward proving she's not the one who did the stealing."

She could feel Honor eyeing her with surprise. "Do you really care what happens to her, one way or another?"

"I'm not doing this to hurt her," Vivian hissed, stung. "Besides, if she ends up in jail for theft, her store closes, and then all the girls who work for her are out of a job. I don't want to do that to them."

"If you leave them behind, though, you might get another letter," Honor pointed out. "And once your boss realizes she's been robbed, she'll change the combination of this safe. You won't be able to get back in."

Vivian hesitated, then shook her head. "Guess that's a risk I'm taking, then. But I think if they knew enough to ask for these, they would have already done it." Deliberately, she took the two tins from Honor's hands and shoved them back inside the safe, clicking the door shut and giving the dial a spin to lock it. The gentle buzz of the tumblers felt unbearably loud in the silent shop. Vivian hoped she wasn't making a horrible mistake.

Before Honor could say anything else, the large clock leaning against the wall chimed the hour, and they both jumped. Vivian wound the dress into a bundle, then shoved it into a bag that she could sling over her shoulder and back. "Come on, we should get out of here."

She glanced around the edge of the counter to make sure no one was visible outside, then motioned for Honor to put out her light and follow. To her relief, the Nightingale's owner didn't try to argue or make her second-guess herself, just followed her through the maze of shadows toward the cellar steps.

They had almost reached them when a beam of light darted through the window and swept across the shop.

"Hey," a deep voice called out. "Is someone in there?"

NINETEEN

Honor grabbed Vivian by both arms and pushed her flat against the wall. They were right next to the clock, their bodies barely hidden in its shadow. The door to the cellar was only a step away, but neither of them moved as the beam of the flashlight swept past them.

A second light joined the first, making a slow path around the shop. "I don't see anyone," a gruff voice replied.

"Could have sworn I saw movement in there, though. Check the door?"

Vivian held her breath, glad they hadn't come through the front. She was trembling as she peered over Honor's shoulder, trying to make out what was happening outside without being seen herself. In the glow from the streetlight, she could see two men in uniform.

"Cops," she breathed to Honor, who let out a short breath that might have been a laugh under any other circumstances.

"The one time they decide to stop some real criminals, we're the ones they find."

They could hear the two men outside still debating, though their voices were more muffled, until suddenly there was a loud banging on the front door. Vivian jumped, and Honor held her more firmly against the wall to keep her from giving away their hiding place. Another time, all of Vivian's attention would have been focused on the feel of Honor's body pressed against hers. But there was too much at stake.

"Hey!" the deep voice called. "If anyone's in there, we're ready for you. You ain't getting out so easy!"

Vivian glanced at Honor, her face barely visible in the dim light, wondering what the hell they were going to do.

And then, suddenly, she heard singing. Horrible, off-key, drunken singing.

"'Five foot two, eyes of blue, but oh, what those five foot could do,'" the voice yowled, loudly enough to make them wince even from inside the shop. "'Has anybody seen my girl?'"

"It's Leo," Vivian whispered, holding back a terrible urge to laugh.

"Hey!" she heard one of the cops yelp. "What the hell? Where did he come from?"

"Now see here, fella, ain't you heard of Prohibition?" the gruff voice said with a long-suffering sigh. "You can't just wander the streets when you're blotto."

Leo's serenade continued unabated. "'Turned-up nose, turned-down hose, never had no other beaus. Has anybody seen my girl?'"

Vivian felt Honor shift slightly as she glanced around. "Come on," she whispered, her lips against Vivian's ear while Leo kept singing. "We can get to the door while he's distracting them. We need to get out of here before they decide to bust in and check the place out."

"Can they do that?" Vivian breathed.

"If they think they're going to catch a robbery in progress? I'm guessing they'll break first and ask questions later."

"God, send him on his way already," Deep Voice said impatiently. "He's clearly got the money to manage just fine, and if someone takes it off him before he makes it home, well, that's what he gets for breaking the law."

The moment the flashlight beams were pointed in another direction, Honor slid along the wall, keeping the clock and its heavy shadows between her and the front window. The door wasn't far, and she slipped through without swinging it all the way open. Her voice whispered back from the shadows. "Come on, pet."

Vivian took a deep breath, willing feet that were numb with fear to move. Copying Honor, she slid along the wall until she could squeeze through the open doorway.

"There!" the deep voice called out. "There, I saw something moving."

"I didn't see it."

"'Has anybody seen my girl?'" Leo bellowed, more aggressively now.

Balancing on her toes on the top step, Vivian nudged the door closed. Every sound seemed magnified to a hundred times its normal volume as she turned the handle back slowly so the latch would catch without clicking. As soon as the door was shut, she let out the breath she had been holding.

"Honor?" she whispered. "Can we get out the back while they're busy at the front?"

She could just barely make out the two voices through the cheap, flimsy wood of the door. Honor's soft exhale brushed her cheek, and she felt Honor fumble for her hands before pressing the pocket light into them. "You stay here and listen for them. I'll get the door open while they're busy up there. Count to thirty, then come down, unless it sounds like they're going around back. If that happens, flash that thing down the stairs quick as you can, okay?"

"Got it." Vivian pressed her ear to the door, beginning to count slowly in her head and trying not to jump at the creak of the stairs under Honor's feet. If she had stopped to think at all, she would have been terrified, but there was no time for that. She strained to hear both the faint voices on the other side of the door and the rustle and bump of the cellar door as Honor eased it open. They were going to make it, she thought, heady with relief. Soon they'd be out in the night and slipping away.

Then, just as her count reached thirty, a tremendous crash echoed through the shop. Vivian flinched, instinctively ducking into a crouch on the top step at the sound of shattering glass. The sound of gruff and deep male voices suddenly grew louder.

Feeling like her heart was trying to leap straight out of her throat, and all too conscious of the valuable dress slung over her back, Vivian slipped down the stairs, still in a crouch, as though that would somehow save her if they found their way to the cellar door. Her path through the storage room was faintly illuminated by the dim square of night where Honor had the alley door open. She was waiting at the top of the steps, one hand outstretched.

Vivian grabbed it, weak with relief as Honor helped her scramble out of the shop's basement. Without a word, they both grabbed the edge of the heavy door to ease it shut. Vivian was shaking so much she could barely keep her hands on it. There was a faint *thump* as it closed, and then Vivian was searching the ground to find the padlock. Honor snatched it from her hands, clamping it into place. Though Vivian knew a sound that quiet would be lost in the noise of the city, it still seemed to echo through the alley. She and Honor both crouched against the wall of the building, half-hidden among the broken crates and trash bins, waiting to see what was going to happen.

"Can we leave down the other end?" Vivian whispered. Worried about what the dress might be pressed against, she slid the bag off her back and clutched it in her arms.

She felt Honor shake her head. "I checked. Dead end. It's a solid wall. We get out toward the street or not at all."

Vivian held back a whimper. She could hear the crunch of glass, now, and the sounds of the two cops having a heated argument in low voices.

"I told you there wasn't anyone in there. What the hell did you want to go breaking the glass for?"

"I'm telling you, I saw someone moving inside. Who's going to fuss over a little broken window when we catch the bastards robbing the place?"

"Yeah, but I don't see us catching anyone. So we'd better beat it out of here unless we want to be the ones accused of breaking and entering."

"Keep your shirt on, pal, we still haven't finished looking around yet. There's an alley or something down there."

Both women tensed. "Vivian, get behind me," Honor whispered.

But Vivian couldn't move. They were half-hidden, pressed against the rough brick wall of the building. As long as no one actually came toward them . . .

Two figures appeared at the end of the alley. Silhouetted in the glow of the streetlamp, they loomed menacingly against the night, their faces dark and unreadable.

Vivian took a deep breath. It was her fault that Honor was there, and if Honor was arrested for burglary, everyone at the Nightingale would suffer. If Vivian turned herself in, it might distract them enough for Honor to get away and turn over the dress. Vivian would be arrested, there was no way around that. Her stomach turned over at the thought. But both Honor and Florence would be safe.

Vivian took a deep breath. "Don't move," she whispered, pressing the bag with its valuable cargo into Honor's hands.

"What are you doing—" Honor tried to grab at Vivian, to keep her where she was, but she was just a breath too slow.

But just as Vivian stood up, the night erupted in song once more.

"'Everybody loves my baby, but my baby don't love nobody but me, nobody but me!'"

The two police officers both jumped and spun around, one of them making a gesture like he was reaching for a weapon before he realized what was going on. Vivian froze, stunned into stillness.

"Jesus, Mary, and Joseph, he's back," Gruff Voice groaned loudly.

Neither of the cops was looking at the alley now. Honor grabbed Vivian's arm and yanked her back down. "What the hell do you think you were *doing*?" Honor hissed. Vivian could hear her voice shaking.

The singing was still going. "'Everybody wants my baby, but my baby don't want nobody but me, that's plain to seeeee . . .'" Leo stumbled into view, throwing an arm around one of the two stunned men. "Fellas, who's up for a nightcap?"

"Buddy, you must really want to end up in the drunk tank tonight," Deep Voice said through gritted teeth. Vivian could see him struggling to dislodge Leo's arm.

"I wish it were true," Leo went on, his voice wobbling up and down like he was trying not to cry. "She *doesn't* want me, you know. I should be singing that other one instead. 'After you've gone and left me crying . . .' You know that one?"

"Look here—"

"She kicked me out tonight," Leo wailed. "And now I've got nowhere to go at all!"

"Well, it's your lucky day, pal," Gruff Voice said, grabbing Leo by the scruff of his neck and hauling him off his partner. "We've got a place for you to sleep it off. Grab his other arm, will you? We're taking this one back to the station. Come on."

Vivian watched, stunned, as they disappeared from sight. She made her way down to the end of the alley, peering around the corner in time to see them frog-marching Leo down the length of the street. He was still singing at the top of his lungs as they turned the corner and disappeared. Vivian looked back in time to see Honor standing and brushing herself off. She still looked cool and stylish as ever. Vivian, meanwhile, felt like a shaking mess. She hadn't expected it to be such a near thing.

"Do you think he'll be okay?" she whispered.

"Of course he will," Honor said confidently. "He'll call a friend to bail him out, and they won't look at him twice once they've got his cash. If things do get dicey for some reason, he'll call his uncle."

Vivian grimaced. He had gotten himself arrested on purpose to help her out, and there was no way for her to return the favor if he needed it. She didn't have the cash to bail him out. "What if his uncle won't help out?"

"He will," Honor said confidently. Her voice was wry with cynical humor as she added, "Fella like Leo, who knows all the suppliers in Chicago and is getting his feet under him here in New York quick as a wink? He's way too valuable to give up. His uncle will keep him out of trouble, you can bet on it."

"I hope so," Vivian said, her eyes still fixed on the street where Leo had disappeared.

"Well, either way, there's nothing you can do about it tonight." Honor handed Vivian the bag she had left behind. "We're on a schedule, and you've got a deadline you can't afford to miss if you don't want your fella to have been arrested for nothing."

"He's not my fella," Vivian said, automatically and a little defensively.

In the dark, she couldn't see whether Honor was smiling or not. But her voice was soft as she replied, "I know."

Part of Vivian wanted to argue further, but she suspected that was mostly because she didn't want to face what she had to do next. She slid out of the alley, glancing up and down the street as she did. There was no one else around, though she could hear the sound of the elevated train and a lazy shouting match happening not far away. A moment later Honor stood next to her, both of them caught in the pool of yellow lamplight.

"You're shaking, pet," Honor said quietly, one hand rising to brush Vivian's hair behind her ear. "Are you sure you want to go through with this?"

It was impossible to guess what she was thinking as she asked that question. Vivian glanced at the storefront, where the shattered window left a jagged, taunting hole in the middle of the door. The windows around it were pristine, the shop silent and empty.

If they left without calling the police, it wouldn't stay that way for long, not with the front door busted wide open. And if something happened to Miss Ethel's shop, who knew what would happen to the people who depended on it to buy their groceries and keep a roof over their heads. Just a few months back, Vivian and Florence wouldn't have known what to do if they missed even one paycheck. They might have lost their home. She was pretty sure most of the other girls who worked there were in the same boat.

They could look for a telephone, call the police, keep an eye on the shop until they arrived. And if they spent their time doing that, they would probably miss the deadline that the letter had set. There was no knowing what would happen then.

Vivian clutched the bag to her chest, wishing Honor would tell her what to do—Honor, who knew so much more about this world where there were no black-and-white choices, no clear right and wrong. But she had a feeling Honor would refuse to answer. She had agreed to help, but Vivian was the one who had to choose.

Vivian slung the bag over her shoulder. "All right," she said firmly. "Let's go."

They had to go several blocks, to the busier streets that were still crowded with cars and revelers, before they felt comfortable hailing in a cab. This late, they couldn't depend on the subway or the streetcar. And in case the police tried to hunt down whoever was responsible for the burglary, they didn't want to risk some cabbie coming forward with a story about two women leaving the area late at night.

And anyway, Honor pointed out, Vivian was carrying something pretty valuable. Hopping on a streetcar with that was asking for trouble.

Vivian was shaking with nerves and fatigue when they finally poured themselves into the back of a cab. She felt close to falling over and wanted to just curl up against the door and go to sleep. Honor, by contrast, looked wide awake as she folded her elegant legs into the back seat and gave the driver the cross streets they were heading toward.

Her expression softened when she turned to give Vivian a head-to-toe look, and she lifted one arm. "Come here, pet." When Vivian hesitated, she smiled gently. "You know I don't bite. And you look like you could use a hug."

Vivian's entire body ached for that embrace. She desperately wanted someone to comfort her, to reassure her that everything was going to be all right. But if she let that line slip with Honor, she didn't know if she could keep her distance the next time she needed to. "You never struck me as someone who gives out hugs."

Honor's smile was wry. "I'll make an exception for you."

Vivian was too worn out to resist anymore. Sliding across the seat, she tucked herself under Honor's arm. They had never sat like that before, so close and easy, the tension that usually sharped the air between them smoothed out by fatigue, by the light and music that floated through the cab's open window, by facing danger together and coming out unscathed.

"You made the best choice you could," Honor murmured, her lips brushing the hair by Vivian's temple. The words sent a shiver skating down her spine.

Honor hadn't said *the right choice*. There was no right choice, not tonight. There was just the best she could do. Vivian thought of Leo, hauled off to jail to keep her safe, of the jagged hole in that window. "I hope you're right," she replied. She didn't want anyone else to end up hurt because of what she had decided that night. Even Miss Ethel, who she very nearly hated.

"And your sister is going to be okay."

The soft reassurance was so surprising that Vivian turned her head without thinking and found her mouth only inches from Honor's. Vivian felt her heart jump. But Honor's friendly, reassuring smile didn't waver, as if she didn't even notice how close they were. "Who are you and what have you done with Ms. Huxley?" Vivian asked, hoping it sounded like a joke, hoping Honor wouldn't be able to tell how flustered she was.

Honor chuckled quietly and gave Vivian's shoulder a little squeeze. "Call it a moment of weakness."

Vivian didn't know how to respond to that, so instead she turned to glance out the window. "We're almost there," she said, shimmying out from under Honor's arm. "You can head on home after you drop me off."

Honor blinked at her, clearly caught off guard. "What?"

"You can head home," Vivian repeated, giving her a smile as harmless and friendly as Honor's own had been a moment before. *Nothing to see here,* her smile lied. *Nothing at all.* "And yes, I know, I owe you a favor. I'll be ready whenever you want to call that in."

"Vivian . . ." Honor shook her head. "I can't just leave you on the corner."

"Sure you can," Vivian said. She glanced toward the front of the cab and chose her words carefully. "I'm just going to put it where I'm supposed to and go to bed. It's not like that's something I need company for."

"You sure?" Honor crossed her arms, watching Vivian with skeptical brows.

Vivian swallowed, her smile still in place. "Honest. I don't need to be on anyone's bad side, and neither does my sister. I just want tonight to be done."

The trickle of sweat making its way down her back wasn't just from the summer heat. She was lying through her teeth, and she could only hope that Honor didn't realize it.

Honor didn't look convinced. But she didn't protest when Vivian told the cabbie to pull over and hopped out alone. As the cab drove away, Vivian felt a pang of hurt that Honor had left her so easily. But she told herself it was stupid to be upset when she had gotten what she wanted.

For what she was planning, it was better to be alone. No need to put anyone else in danger. There had already been enough of that for one night.

The note had said to leave the dress wrapped up and under the front stoop of her building. Vivian, after a quick glance up and down the street to make sure there was no one else there, did just that before going inside.

But instead of climbing the stairs to her own home, Vivian headed toward the door to Mrs. Kaminski's empty apartment.

To her relief, the door was still propped open to let out any lingering gas. With one more nervous check over her shoulder to make sure there was no one else in the hall, Vivian slipped inside.

She didn't close it all the way behind her, afraid it might lock or that not all the gas had been let out. She tried not to breathe deeply. The room still had a heavy, musty, animal smell to it. Vivian told herself it was just the scent of a home that needed to be cleaned and not the lingering smell of death.

Navigating around the crowded room mostly by feel—barely any light filtered through the curtains—Vivian made her way to the window. On the way she nearly knocked over a stool, and she grabbed it to keep it from toppling over. Pausing, she listened, ears and eyes straining in the dark, to make sure no one had been alerted by the sound. Then she carefully tucked the stool under one arm and brought it with her to the window.

Mrs. Kaminski's curtains were heavy old things, but it was easy enough to tuck back a single corner, one that hopefully wouldn't be noticed from the outside. As dark as it was inside, Vivian hoped she would be invisible to anyone who glanced her way from the street. Setting the stool down, she inched closer to the tiny gap until she could just see the corner of the stairs where she had left the dress. She settled in to wait.

At first Vivian's mind couldn't settle, filled with worry over what she was doing, what she was risking. She was being careful, as careful as she could be, but it could still go wrong. And if it did, she wasn't going to be the only one who suffered. Florence was the one who had received the letter. She was the one who would be most in danger. But Vivian couldn't convince herself to go upstairs. She could let the letter writer—or whoever worked for them—take the dress. If she did that, she would probably never hear from them again. Unless, of course, she and Florence came in the path of some other money and ended up in the letter writer's sights again.

Or if not them, someone else. The thought made Vivian's fury gather into a bitter weight in her chest, even as sweat prickled her skin in the hot, still room. Whoever was writing those letters was coming after desperate people, families with so little that a necklace counted as wealth. Then there was Pearlie. Whatever shady business had brought him his money, he hadn't deserved to be killed for it. And Florence . . . with her, the letter writer had expanded their awful business into forcing other people to take on the danger of theft and crime for them.

The anger inside Vivian twisted, becoming something more complicated as her thoughts turned toward Florence. She closed her eyes for a moment as if that could hold those thoughts back, pressing her forehead against the windowpane that was the only cool thing in the room.

If she could keep Florence safe, they could go back to their quiet life together, the two of them against the world, just like it had always been. Nothing needed to change.

The sound of quick, deliberate footsteps broke into her thoughts. Vivian started, her head bumping the glass as she realized she had dozed off. She winced, shrinking back behind the curtain and hoping that no one had seen her there. When the footsteps outside paused, she risked a glance.

There weren't many streetlights in this part of the city, and the shadows between them looked even darker when compared to those pools of golden light. But there was enough of a glow reflected off the steps for her to see a dark figure, hat pulled far forward to shadow his face, retrieve the bag from where she had left it.

Vivian's heart was pounding like it would come out of her chest as she watched the figure check the bag, glance around—she shrank behind the curtain again but didn't take her eyes off him—and then walk briskly away.

Vivian, after only a moment of hesitation, stumbled her way back to the door and into the hall. She peered out the front door just in time to see the figure disappear around the corner.

This time she didn't hesitate. Closing the door as softly behind her as possible, she hurried after.

She had nearly reached the end of the block when she realized the strange thumping noise she could hear was the sound of heavy feet behind her. Vivian turned in time to see a second figure, moving toward her at a pace that was almost a run. She had enough time to see that he was tall and heavyset, but he dodged around the pools of yellow lamplight so that his face never caught the light.

Vivian froze, and then it seemed like everything happened at once.

The figure raised a hand, and the streetlight glinted off something metallic pointed right at her. There was a clicking noise, so faint she could barely hear it. Before she had fully realized what was happening, before she could do anything to react, a third figure, this one slim and quick, had barreled into the man, knocking him off balance just as the bursting sound of a gun firing tore through the night air.

The shot went wide, striking the side of the building Vivian was next to and spraying chips of stone into the air. She didn't even flinch as one caught her shoulder, slicing through her sleeve. She just stared at the hole the bullet had made, her mind refusing to understand what had almost happened.

She was shaken out of her stupor by the sound of cursing. The heavier, larger figure wasn't putting up nearly as much of a fight as he could have. Instead, he swore loudly, pushing away and holding up one hand, as though wanting to make sure his face wouldn't be seen. The slim figure tried to catch him, but he shook her off, shoving her away before dashing across the street and disappearing into the warren of alleys.

Vivian would have gone after him, but she was too busy staring as Honor stumbled into the lamplight.

"Are you all right?" Vivian asked, grabbing Honor's arm to make sure she stayed upright. "Where did you come from?" She craned her neck to catch a glimpse of Honor's face, trying to see if she was hurt.

"Am I all right?" Honor demanded, catching Vivian's upper arms in a painful grip. Her hair was wild from the scuffle, and there was a mark on one cheekbone that was probably going to turn into a bruise. "Am I all *right*? What the hell, Vivian?"

Vivian tried to shrink back, but those furious hands didn't let her go.

"You *lied* to me."

"I didn't want to put you in any more danger—"

Honor didn't wait for her to finish. "What were you thinking?" she demanded, shaking Vivian by the arms. "Don't you have any idea how these things work? They're sniffing out dozens of people's secrets. That takes manpower. They got evidence removed from the coroner's office. That takes connections. Whatever this operation is, it's not just one person, and they're not small time. They've killed two people." Another shake, and just when Vivian was about to push herself away,

Honor hauled her close, holding her so tightly she could barely breathe. "Goddamn it, Vivian, did you *want* them to get you next?"

"Better me alone than me and anyone else," Vivian managed to say. It was the only thing she got out before Honor grabbed her face in both hands and kissed her.

Vivian's mind stuttered to a halt. If she had been thinking, she might have come up with a word like *overwhelmed* or *shocked,* though neither of them came anywhere close to capturing how stunned she was. But she wasn't thinking at all. The only thing she was aware of was the feel of Honor's mouth on hers, the press of Honor's fingers against her jaw, the smell of hot skin and night air around them.

And then, before she even fully realized what had happened, Honor let her go, her hands dropping abruptly as she turned away. Vivian stared at her back, which was ramrod straight and tense, as her mind struggled to catch up with what had just happened.

"Don't say that." Honor's voice was cool and controlled as ever, as if her sudden burst of emotion had never happened. She ran a hand over her hair, smoothing her blond curls back into place, and gave each of her cuffs a little tug. "There are plenty of people who would be very sad to see anything happen to you, Vivian."

Vivian's fingers were on her lips, she realized, brushing back and forth as though trying to find a trace of Honor's kiss, though she didn't even remember raising them. She dropped them deliberately and turned away.

Something on the ground caught her eye, and she flinched away as she realized what it was. In the scuffle, the man had dropped his gun.

Honor saw where she was looking and stooped to pick it up. It was a short, snub-nosed little revolver, and Vivian saw Honor's jaw tighten as she stared at it.

"I don't know much about guns," Vivian said slowly. "But isn't that a little . . . little?"

"It's a Fitz Special," Honor said, and something that might have been a shiver chased over her shoulders. She tucked the stubby revolver into her pocket. "Come on, you're not staying here tonight."

She didn't give Vivian a chance to protest. Grabbing her arm in a tight grip, she hurried them both in the opposite direction from where the two figures had disappeared. Vivian would have objected, but one look at Honor's stony face was enough to make her close her mouth. There were times to argue, but this was definitely not one of them. She didn't say anything as Honor whistled up a cab and bundled her inside.

"Where are we going?" she finally asked after Honor gave directions to the driver.

She received a narrow-eyed glance in return. "Somewhere I hope you won't end up dead by the end of the night."

It wasn't a comforting answer. Vivian shivered and stared out the window, not asking any more.

The cab took them to a quiet little street farther uptown. It wasn't more than a couple miles away, but it might as well have been a different world. The buildings here stood straight, their brick fronts smooth and clean, with window boxes of flowers on the first floors and the sidewalks swept mostly clear of trash.

The apartment Honor eventually hustled her into was on the third floor, a clean, unadorned little room with electric lights and barely any furniture. There were curtains at the windows but no pictures on the walls. Vivian looked around as Honor threw the deadbolt behind them.

Vivian drifted across the floor a little aimlessly, not sure what she was supposed to say or do. She stopped next to the neatly made bed. It was only a few steps away from the stove and sink, not even room enough between them for a table and chair, though there was a small chest of three drawers next to the bed. "So this is where you live when you're not at the Nightingale?" Vivian asked, the first thing she had said since they got into the cab.

Honor's laugh was short. "It's where I stay sometimes when things are a little too hot for me downtown. I'd hardly call it a place to live."

"You didn't have to push me around to get me here," Vivian pointed out, rubbing her arm. "I wasn't arguing."

The look Honor gave her was withering. "Excuse me if I'm feeling a little sour on trusting you at the moment. Do I need to tell you why that was a stupid thing to do?"

Vivian shivered, trying not to remember the shot that had just barely missed her. "No. Are you going to tell me what a Fitz Special is?"

Honor sighed as she took the gun from her pocket. She turned it over, eyeing it warily, before setting it carefully on the chest of drawers. "A man named Fitzgerald makes them out of a regular Colt revolver. The barrel is shorter, and . . . well, there are a lot of changes to make them work. But the point is, he makes them so officers can carry a gun more easily when they go undercover. The smaller the barrel, the easier it is to hide."

Vivian felt cold all over, and her legs suddenly seemed to stop working. She sat down abruptly on the bed before they gave way completely. "So you're saying that second fella was a cop." Honor nodded. "And he was there to make sure no one followed or caught the other fella, the one who scooped up the dress." Honor nodded again, still standing, her arms crossed.

Vivian wished she would come closer, would offer her arm like she had in the cab after they left the dress shop. She wished Honor would kiss her again, even if she was still angry. Anything to chase away the fear that was creeping through her. But Honor seemed determined to keep some distance between them. Vivian tucked her knees under her chin, wrapping her arms around her legs, needing comfort from someone, even if it was just from herself. "That other fella, the one we talked to after Pearlie died. He said he tried to catch the letter writer and got knocked out for his trouble. He didn't say anything about someone trying to shoot him."

"Guess their operation is getting more serious." Honor's voice was soft. "Or more desperate."

"What made you hang around?"

In the glow of the single electric light, it was hard to read Honor's expression, but Vivian thought it might have been something close to a smile. "Instinct."

"Yours are better than mine, then." Vivian sighed, dropping her head down onto her knees. "I just thought . . . I wanted to make it all stop. I wanted to make sure they never bothered my sister again. I wanted—"

She was surprised to feel the sudden weight of Honor sitting on the bed next to her. "I know. You wanted to fix it. But some things can't be fixed. Just survived." Vivian lifted her head to see Honor watching her, her expression unreadable. Then her face softened, and she reached out to flick off the light. The room was so small that she could reach the switch with only a little effort. "Come on," she said, kicking off her shoes. Sliding up the bed and leaning back so that she was propped up against the headboard, she gave the pillow next to her a little pat. "We've got a few hours to get some shut-eye."

Vivian glanced around the room. She had noticed it was small. Now, she realized for the first time what that meant. The room barely had space for furniture. There certainly wasn't a second bed. "Both of us?"

Honor laughed shortly. "You can stay awake if you want, but you'll be kicking yourself while you're at work. Come on." She patted the pillow again. In the light that drifted through the window, Vivian could see that her wry smile was back. "I'm pretty sure we'll survive."

Vivian wasn't nearly so sure, but she toed off her shoes and scooted up the bed anyway, until they were shoulder to shoulder against the headboard.

"Why did you kiss me?" Vivian asked, deciding to be blunt. She didn't look at Honor as she asked the question, though. She couldn't play it quite cool enough for that. "You made it clear we've got no future together, not that you want, anyway. I'd have thought that meant no kisses, too."

"Even I get impulsive sometimes," Honor said quietly. "I shouldn't have done it."

"Well . . ." Vivian couldn't help herself. She wanted, so badly. And her heart ached to be wanted in return. She met Honor's eyes. "I didn't mind all that much."

They stared at each other, and then Honor shook her head slowly. "I shouldn't have done it," she repeated.

"Why not?" Vivian couldn't help whispering. She could tumble head over heels for Honor if she let herself, fast and dangerous as falling into freezing water, and she knew exactly why that would be such a risk for her. But the day they had squared off in her office, Honor had said it was a risk for her, too. Vivian couldn't figure out what that risk might be.

Honor was quiet for so long that Vivian thought she wasn't going to answer at all. "I'd let you get too close," she said at last. "And I can't afford to give myself that kind of weakness." She gave Vivian's shoulder a little squeeze. "Try to sleep, pet. Nothing else is going to happen tonight."

Vivian waited, hoping she would say something more. But Honor was silent. After a moment, Vivian sighed and slid down the pillow, stretching out as carefully as if the sheets were filled with pins that she needed to avoid. Honor did the same beside her.

Even though they were fully clothed, even though neither of them had bothered to slip under the sheets, Vivian was conscious of every inch of Honor's body next to her, every soft breath in and out. She felt hot all over and still jumpy with fear. She wanted to roll just the few inches it would take until she could cuddle up close to Honor, search through the dark for her mouth, forget everything that had happened that night.

But neither of them moved. And at last, worn out, Vivian fell asleep.

She woke when the sounds of the city outside changed to the clamor of morning, shops opening up, a paperboy on his route, the wail of a child impatient for breakfast. The dawn light was just creeping through the window as Vivian glanced around, her body still for a moment as her mind floundered, trying to remember where she was. Then her eyes fell on Honor, still sleeping next to her.

Even in sleep Honor's expression was serious, her brows pulled toward each other as if her dreams required concentration. In the dawn light, the fan of her dark eyelashes cast little shadows on her cheeks, and the pillowcase was smudged with traces of makeup that she hadn't washed off the night before. With her cheek resting in the curve of one hand, she looked more vulnerable—more human—than Vivian had ever seen her.

But vulnerable wasn't something that Honor Huxley was willing to be. And as much as she wanted to, Vivian really couldn't blame her for that.

She slid out of the bed, retrieving her shoes but not putting them on yet. Her eyes fell on the little revolver, still glinting dully on the chest of drawers. Vivian hesitated. She didn't like guns. But she was a practical girl. She eased her fingers around the handle and lifted it soundlessly, sliding it into the pocket of her jacket before turning toward the door. The click of the dead bolt was loud in the quiet room, but the door swung open noiselessly.

The back of Vivian's neck prickled, and she glanced over her shoulder. Honor was lying still in the bed, not moving. But her eyes were open, and they stared at each other, neither of them saying a word.

After a moment, Vivian turned away and left, closing the door softly behind her.

TWENTY

Walking through the morning bustle and noise wasn't too scary; there was no reason to think anyone who might be looking for her had any idea where she'd spent the night. But when she turned onto her own block, Vivian glanced around nervously, her shoulders creeping up and her eyes darting back and forth. She always walked briskly when she was out, but now she was hard-pressed not to run, to dart from doorway to doorway like a mouse trying to keep out of the way of the city's cats.

But she didn't let herself. Instead, she walked straight to the front door and unlocked it, nearly bumping into Will Freeman on his way out.

"Morning, Vivian," he yawned, the toolbox under his arm jangling as he stumbled to a halt to avoid barreling into her. "Long night?"

"The longest," she agreed, more emphatically than she meant to. She hesitated, then asked, "Any chance someone came by asking about me?"

"Asking about . . . ?" Will frowned, then shook his head, looking puzzled. "Not that I've run into. Everything all right?"

"Yeah, it's all jake." Vivian forced a smile, sliding out of his way. "See you around."

She was still jumpy as she climbed the stairs, wishing she could go to work just as she was. But her clothes, borrowed from Honor the night before so she had something other than a dancing dress to wear, were wrinkled and dusty and didn't fit her right. Miss Ethel would have a fit if she showed up like that. If there even was a store left to show up to. Vivian shuddered, imagining what state the shop might be in. But there was nothing she could do except get dressed, get Florence, and show up to work on time, looking as innocent as possible.

If she even got that far. Vivian's steps slowed as she reached the top of the stairs. She could see down the hall from where she stood, and the door to her home was clearly standing open. Vivian froze, heart pounding. But before she could decide what to do, someone pushed the door open from inside.

Bea stepped out into the hall.

"Viv!" She frowned in worry. "What's wrong? Why are you such a goddamn mess? And why are you wearing *trousers*?"

"Jesus, Mary, and Joseph, Bea, you just about made my heart give out," Vivian gasped. She had been clutching the banister for support, but she managed to straighten her spine and walk forward on legs that were shaking from relief. "Get inside, will you? I've gotta get changed for work." She glanced around, hesitating. "Was the door locked when you got here? Did it look like anyone had been by?"

"Locked?" Bea frowned. "Of course it was locked. What would it look like if someone came by?"

"I don't know," Vivian said, going to the bedroom. Two neatly made beds were just as she and Florence had left them, both with Saturday's laundry still hanging on the foot and headboards. As far as she could see, everything was where it was supposed to be. "Never mind. I don't think . . . Never mind."

"You look like you slept half the night in an alley," Bea commented as she closed the door behind them. "You gonna tell me what happened?"

"Yeah," Vivian said, checking the washbasin. It was still half-full from the day before, the water tepid and a little dusty, but it would do. She didn't feel like making the effort to go to the washroom and get a new bucketful. She yanked her shirt over her head, her voice muffled as she said, "If you tell me why you're here."

"I was looking for you," Bea said. She still looked worried, Vivian saw as she emerged from the unfamiliar clothing and began scrubbing her face and arms. "You disappeared last night, and the neighbor said you and Florence haven't been around since yesterday. And I couldn't find Honor—" Her eyes widened. "Were you with Honor last night? Are those *Honor's trousers*?"

Vivian glanced down, then quickly stripped off the clothing in question. She grabbed one of the dresses from the footboard of her bed and pulled it on quickly. Changing clothes in front of Bea didn't bother her, but talking about Honor made her feel exposed. "Sort of, but not the way you mean—"

Vivian broke off, staring at Bea, noticing for the first time that her friend was wearing a new necklace. It was a beautiful gold pendant that looked like it might be a locket, hanging so that it just nestled in the hollow of her collarbone. And etched into it was a single, stemmed rose.

Vivian had heard someone describe a necklace like that just a few days before.

"Bea," she said slowly. "Where'd that come from?"

"Where'd what—Oh, this?" Bea asked, seeing where her friend was looking. Her fingertips brushed against the pendant, and her smile took on a pleased, self-conscious edge. "Abraham gave it to me last night. Said he wanted to get me something pretty to cheer me up. He's such a sweet fella. Honestly, I think I end up more crazy about him each day."

"Where did he get it?" Vivian asked.

"What do you mean, where did he get it? At a store, I guess?" Bea laughed.

It was the first time she had laughed since Pearlie died, and Vivian wanted to be happy about that. But she couldn't when she felt cold all over.

She liked Abraham. He was quiet, sure, but he was kind and reliable and friendly enough when he was in the mood. And most of all, she liked how good he was to Bea. But if he had something to do with those letters . . .

Bea had just noticed she wasn't laughing along. "Viv, what's going on?"

"Have you ever asked Abraham where he goes when he's out nights?" Vivian asked.

"Have I asked . . . He drives a cab, he's all over the city every night. Why would I ask him where he goes?"

"And I bet he hears a lot of gossip from the back seat," Vivian said slowly. "Maybe about folks who've come into a little money, or who have a little something pretty stashed at home."

Bea was staring at her now. "Are you trying to say you think Abraham has something to do with those letters? You think he had something to do with *Pearlie getting killed*?" Tears welled in Bea's eyes as she said her uncle's name. When she spoke, her voice was shaking. "How the hell are you jumping to that conclusion? Because he owns a *cab*?"

"Bea—"

"Are you really so sore that I'm feeling a little happy with him?" The hurt in her voice was painful to listen to, but she didn't give Vivian a chance to interrupt. "That I've got someone who thinks I'm a catch and a half and likes to show it?"

"That's not—"

"You couldn't stop glaring at Danny the other night, and all he did was dance with your sister. Now you're coming for Abraham?" She shook her head, brushing the tears from her lashes with impatient hands. "Look, I know you were upset about how things went with Leo, but you've got no call to be pointing fingers at *my* fella just because you don't know how to pick 'em."

"I'm not upset about Leo. I'm just worried that Abraham—"

"Then why does it matter that someone who likes me bought me a necklace—"

"It matters if he's the one threatening my sister!" Vivian finally yelled.

Bea stared at her. "What the hell does that mean?"

Vivian felt like she couldn't breathe. How much should she share? Bea knew her too well. If something was threatening her sister, Vivian would do anything to fix it. She hadn't hesitated to send Leo to Bellevue to keep Florence safe, even though she knew her friend wouldn't want her to. And she knew what Bea would say to that, so she had kept Florence's letter a secret.

But if Abraham was behind the letters, then Bea could be in danger, too. And avoiding her friend's anger paled in importance to keeping her safe.

All that flashed through her mind quick as an electric light flipped on in a dark room.

She met Bea's eyes. "We disappeared yesterday because I had to get Florence somewhere safe. She got one of those letters."

"She got . . . Why didn't you tell me?" Bea's eyes narrowed with sudden understanding. "What did you do?"

"I tried to get the coroner to tell the police," Vivian said quietly. There was no use trying to hide it anymore. "Or a journalist, or someone."

"I told you—"

"I know. I'm sorry," Vivian said simply. "But I'd do it again. She's my sister."

Bea let out a slow, shaky breath, the kind that said she was keeping a tight rein on her temper. Vivian flinched, but she didn't back down. "But now you think it's Abraham?" Bea said, her voice sharp as static that would jump at the next touch. "What in God's name gives you the right—" She broke off, taking another deep breath. There were tears in her eyes again, but this time she ignored them. "Do you think

I wouldn't have the sense to notice if my fella was going around trying to bump people off? Including my own uncle?"

"I didn't say he was the one responsible for hurting anyone," Vivian pointed out. "But he's involved somehow. I know it."

"How?" Bea snapped.

"Your necklace." Vivian felt sick as she said it, as she watched her friend's face, but it was too much of a coincidence to look past. She nodded at the pretty gold locket. "It's got a rose carved on it."

"So?"

"So that's exactly what Mr. Guzman said his neighbors had to give up. A gold locket with a rose etched on it. How many of those do you think are lying around the city?"

"There's a lot of people in New York, Viv. Stands to reason there's a lot of jewelry too."

"Did you ask Abraham where he got it?" Vivian asked quietly.

"Did I ask—Of course not." Bea jaw and fists were both clenched. "Abraham likes giving presents. He does it all the time."

"And where does he get the money for them?"

"He has a job!" Bea yelled, losing the battle to control her temper. A clatter of toppling pots from the neighbors reminded them both how thin the walls were, and Bea lowered her voice. "He works like a dog, and that means that sometimes he can afford to buy me something pretty. I don't care if you don't like it. You know how hard it is to find a nice fella, so why're you trying to ruin this?" The hurt in her words made Vivian want to take it all back, but she couldn't. Not if there was any chance she was right. When she didn't answer, Bea's expression grew cold. "I hate to say it, Viv, but jealousy's not a cute look on you."

Vivian felt as if she'd been slapped. It was a struggle to keep her voice even. "Just ask him, Bea. That's all I'm saying. You can yell at me all you want afterward, but just ask him."

The two of them stared at each other. Finally, Bea gave a single jerky nod. "I will, just to prove that you're wrong."

Vivian smiled weakly. "I'd love to be wrong, believe me."

"You are," Bea snapped, spinning on her heel. The slam of the door behind her made the walls shake.

Vivian sighed, rubbing her eyes, then pressing her fingers against them so hard she saw stars. She wanted nothing more than to curl up in bed and sleep for days. But she and Florence had to be at work, smiling, tidy, and unremarkably on time, in just a couple hours.

The money from Honor was back in Chinatown, but the cash box under Florence's bed had enough in it for a few cab rides. Vivian shoved a small bundle of bills in her pocket and began to hunt around for her hairbrush.

She had the cab drop her off several blocks from where she wanted to be, then dodged down an alley, listening for the sound of footsteps or any other indication that someone might be following her. Peering around the corner, back the way she had just come, she scanned the crowd. No one, as far as she could tell. Still, she wasn't about to take any chances with Florence's safety. Skirting a stinking pile of trash and the rancid puddle that had gathered beneath it, she ducked down a second alley, before emerging and dashing across the street between two cars. The drivers honked and yelled, but she was already past, quick footsteps carrying her through another alley where she ducked under countless lines of laundry before emerging on Spring Street.

The restaurant was just ahead.

The bell at the door tinkled when she opened it, and a few heads turned in her direction when she walked in. The room wasn't crowded. It was early in the day, after all, and this part of the city was a lot like the one where Vivian lived: anyone who could work did, keeping food on the table and the landlords at bay.

Most of the diners who were there were Chinese, many of them older men who spoke in animated voices that Vivian couldn't understand as they gestured expansively with their chopsticks and poured each other cups of tea. In one corner, a few younger fellows ate with the focus and speed of men who would have to be at work soon and needed all the calories they could get first. And a couple of young Black men sat at a table in the corner, sipping their drinks and eating slowly, with the droopy, exhausted look of folks who had just got off the night shift and might fall asleep in their plates if they weren't careful.

A table full of gray-haired men scowled in her direction, and Vivian felt her face growing hot, wondering whether they objected to an Irish girl barging in or the fact that she was a woman wandering around by herself. She wanted to scowl right back at them, but she wouldn't make trouble or cause a scene, not in the Chins' restaurant. So instead she pretended not to see, keeping her expression carefully polite as she walked toward the kitchen.

Danny's mother emerged a moment later, a tray covered in small, steaming bowls held in her hands. She stopped in surprise when she saw Vivian weaving between the tables, and her wary, worried expression made Vivian halt in her tracks.

Mrs. Chin sighed, then nodded. She paused as she passed Vivian to whisper, "Go on upstairs. Danny is with your sister."

Vivian wondered about that moment, that look of disapproval or worry or maybe resignation. Had something happened to Florence? Had someone dangerous found their way to the Chins' door because of her? But there was no way she could ask about it, not in the middle of the busy restaurant.

"Thank you," Vivian started to say, but Mrs. Chin had already moved on with her tray. Trying not to look at the steaming food on the tables—how long had it been since she had last eaten?—Vivian made her way toward the stairs.

With customers in the restaurant, the rope slung across the bottom of the staircase sported a sign warning them in multiple languages to stay in the dining room. Vivian took one last quick look over her shoulder, making sure no one had followed her in, before unhooking the rope on one side and scooting past.

The stairs were narrow and rickety, and the aromas of food chased her up until she came to the door at the top. On edge, nervous about what she would find, Vivian didn't think to knock before she pushed the door open and stepped in.

"No, no," Danny was saying as she entered. "Don't put your thumb there unless you want it to break when you hit someone."

"Well, what else am I supposed to do, detach it from my hand?"

Vivian was stunned into motionlessness as she took in the scene in front of her. Danny and Florence were in the middle of the sitting room as he showed her how to curl her fingers into a fist. Both of them were facing away from Vivian, and neither had yet realized they had an audience.

"Here, on the outside," he said, adjusting the position of Florence's fingers. "Not curled under the others. And when you swing, it shouldn't come from your shoulder. Put the force of your whole body behind it if you want to do some damage."

"I don't even know what that means," Florence said, shaking her head and laughing. "I don't exactly spend my time thinking about how to damage anyone."

"I'll show you. Try swinging like you're going to sock some sleaze-bag right in the kisser. But do it slowly."

Vivian's jaw fell open in shock as she watched Danny step behind her sister, his hands going to her hips. As Florence swung her fist in a slow arc, Danny pressed one hip forward so that her body turned with the punch.

"See?" he murmured as he guided her through the motion again. His lips were right next to her ear. "Let your feet turn with it, too. If you use your whole body, you get more force behind the hit. And you're less likely to hurt your shoulder or your wrist while you're doing it."

Vivian felt something pricking at her eyes as she watched them, something hot and confused and almost angry. She didn't want to know what the feeling was, too afraid that it would be ugly or pathetic or something else she didn't have the energy to confront just then. But she also couldn't stand there and watch them any longer. She let go of the door, which banged closed behind her.

Florence and Danny both jumped, turning so fast as they tried to step apart that their feet tangled together. Florence had to grab Danny to stop herself from losing her balance, and he caught her in his arms in the same moment, so when they finally faced Vivian they were in an even more awkward position than they had been before.

The three of them stared at each other in wordless surprise before Florence yanked herself out of Danny's grip. "Vivi!" she gasped. "Where did you come from?"

"The stairs," Vivian said. "And I wasn't being what you'd call sneaky about it, neither. Fat lot of good you are as a bodyguard, Danny."

To her surprise, he looked embarrassed. He was dressed for a morning of work downstairs, but his tie hung in a loose knot under his open shirt collar. He busied his hands with tightening that up and rolling down the cuffs of his sleeves, which let him do an excellent job of avoiding her eyes. "No one's getting past Ma without her making a big stink of it downstairs," he said. He spoke with his normal ease, but his cheeks were flushed. "I'd have heard trouble coming."

"'Course you would," Vivian agreed quietly.

Danny cleared his throat, glancing at Florence. "Did you . . . how was work last night?"

"Just fine," Vivian said, trying to smile. "Bit dicey, but Honor kept everything in line."

"She's good at that," Danny said, looking relieved.

Vivian hesitated. "You heard anything from Leo last night? Or this morning?"

"Leo?" Danny frowned, shaking his head. "Was I supposed to?"

"Thought he mighta called you for bail money," Vivian said, trying to sound unworried and failing.

"Bail?" Danny's eyebrows shot up, while Florence's hands rose nervously to press against her lips. "What happened last night?"

"Nothing," Vivian said. "I'm sure everything's fine. I'll just try to find a telephone today and give him a call, make sure he got home okay."

"There's one downstairs," Danny said. "We pay for a line so folks on the block have somewhere to make calls. Why don't you check on him now? You've got me all worried."

"I'll do that," Vivian agreed quickly, happy for the excuse to get out of the room.

"Are you okay, Vivi?" Florence asked, clearly concerned.

Vivian managed a smile. "Peachy. Let's get to work, okay? We don't want to be late." She glanced at Florence, with her hair still in a braid and her feet bare. "I'll meet you downstairs, okay?"

She turned on her heel and left, closing the door behind her before either of them could say anything else. Standing with her back pressed against the door, she took three deep breaths. Then she forced her shoulders down and went downstairs.

The telephone was at the back of the restaurant, with a pretty wooden screen around it for privacy. Vivian picked up the receiver nervously. Leo was fine, she told herself. She was just making sure, was all. "Circle two-four-four-one, please."

Her knees nearly buckled with relief when Leo answered, his voice fuzzy with fatigue. "Hello?"

"Leo. Golly, I'm glad to hear your voice."

"Hey, Viv." She could hear the shaky inhale of a yawn on the other end of the line, but his sleepy voice sounded like he was smiling when he spoke again. "You calling to check on me, sweetheart?"

"Of course I am," Vivian said. "You made it out of the drunk tank okay?"

"Clean getaway," Leo said, chuckling. "I'll tell you all about it if you tell me about the rest of your night."

Vivian shivered. She didn't want to have that conversation in the middle of the Chins' restaurant. "Tell you what, how about you come by the Nightingale tonight? I'll fill you in then."

"Just tell me now, is Florence okay? The two of you gonna be safe?"

Warmth bloomed in Vivian's chest at the genuine concern in his voice. "Yeah," she said quietly. "We're okay. Will I see you tonight?"

"Count on it."

Vivian's hands were shaking with relief by the time she finally hung up the phone. There wasn't a good spot to wait in the restaurant, but she found an empty, round little table that was out of the way and settled in to watch the other diners until Florence made it down.

She couldn't stop herself from thinking of Honor just then—Honor, who seemed to find it so easy to write her off, to go on with her life. It was hard not to compare that to Danny, who had known Florence all of a handful of days before he was angling for any wholesome way he could to put his arms around her.

And Florence . . .

She never would have expected it, but Florence didn't seem to object. And Vivian didn't like how unhappy that made her. Maybe Bea was right. Maybe she was jealous. Maybe she was just looking for reasons . . .

No. That necklace had been exactly like the one Mr. Guzman had described. There was something fishy going on with Abraham. She was sure of it.

A man moving at a slow, stately pace cut across her vision, startling her out of her thoughts. He had just left one of the tables of elderly men. As he reached the door, he paused, turning back to say something to his friends.

Vivian caught her breath, half rising in her chair. She recognized that man. The last time she had seen him, she had held his head on her lap, and he had said her mother's name.

She was halfway across the restaurant from him, and the door was just swinging shut behind him, the bell jangling, when Vivian darted out of her seat, earning startled looks from the other diners. She hurried after him, but weaving between the tables and around one of Danny's cousins slowed her down. When she finally made it out the door, she glanced anxiously up and down the street, only to see the man's hat disappearing into the crowd. She tried to run after him, but by the end of the block, it was clear that he was gone.

Vivian clutched at a knot in her side, panting as she tried to catch her breath and ignoring the curious faces that turned her way. She could have kicked herself for being too slow.

But he had been sitting with friends. And if she hurried back, they would still be there.

The bell jangled again as she slipped back into the restaurant, and this time the faces that turned toward her were more than just surprised or curious. More than one looked downright suspicious. Vivian swallowed, giving the room a quick smile as Mrs. Chin stalked toward her.

"You're disturbing our customers, Vivian Kelly," she said quietly, but her frown was concerned, rather than accusatory. "Is there trouble?"

"No," Vivian said quickly. "Sorry. I didn't mean to . . . I just saw someone, is all, but I wasn't able to catch up to him in time."

"Someone you know?" Mrs. Chin looked around, clearly surprised. "Here?"

"Sort of." Vivian hesitated, glancing at the table of white- and gray-haired men who had gone back to their emphatic conversation. "Mrs. Chin, do you know any of the men at that table? They had a friend who just left, and I . . . I recognized him. Danny and I helped him out a few months ago, he got sick or something when we were passing by, and I think . . ."

"Yes?" Mrs. Chin prompted when Vivian fell silent.

"I think he might have known my mother," Vivian explained in a nervous rush. "Do you think you could ask them? About where to find him, I mean?"

"What if he doesn't want to talk to you?" Mrs. Chin asked, stern but not cruel. "You do not look like your mother was Chinese."

"No, she was Irish." Vivian swallowed. "If he doesn't want to talk to me, I'd be no worse off than I am now."

Mrs. Chin regarded her for a long moment, then nodded briskly. "I'll ask around. But now you need to go." She turned away as she spoke, her voice going a little cold. "You and that sister of yours need to get to work. And then I will need help with those dishes tonight."

"Mrs. Chin . . ." As soon as the words were out of her mouth, Vivian realized she shouldn't say anything. But Danny's mother had already turned back to her, an impatient, expectant look on her face, one foot just barely tapping.

"Yes?"

Vivian swallowed. "Have you changed your mind? Are you upset that we're here?"

Mrs. Chin sighed. "I do not like the way my son looks at her," she said at last. Seeing the defensive look that sprang to Vivian's face, she held up her hand. "I'm sure she's a very nice girl. But it is hard enough on our young men being here, and my son has made it harder for himself with his . . ." She considered her words. "His choice of work. I do not want his life to be harder still because he gives up his heart to someone who cannot hold his hand on the street without putting them both at risk. To someone who doesn't know how to be part of his world."

"Which world?" Vivian couldn't help asking. "This one? Or the one at the Nightingale?"

"Does it matter?" Mrs. Chin's brows rose. "Your sister isn't going to fit in either place, is she?" Her gaze went past Vivian's shoulder. "Time for you two to get to work."

She bustled back toward the kitchen just as Florence came downstairs and joined Vivian.

"Is everything okay?" Florence asked. "What were you and Mrs. Chin talking about?"

Vivian swallowed. "Nothing important. Come on. We're taking a cab to the shop today."

"Are you going to tell me why you changed your mind about us staying away from work for a few days?" Florence asked as they went out into the street.

"Well . . ." Vivian busied herself catching the eye of a cabbie so she didn't have to look at Florence. "That depends. How good of an actor do you think you can be, Flo?"

Things at the shop weren't quite as bad as Vivian had been dreading, but they definitely weren't good.

"An officer strolling by on his nightly rounds saw the damage and was able to summon assistance," Miss Ethel explained to the gathered seamstresses and shop girls, all standing quiet, obedient, and afraid in the back of the shop while she surveyed them like the teacher of an unruly class. Two sewing machines had been stolen, along with most of the pretty, expensive dresses that were waiting for their owners. Bolts of silk and velvet were gone, and the clock that Vivian had hidden behind so recently was knocked over, its face smashed. Someone had swept up the glass, but the shop was still a mess.

"Given the broken door, I think it is safe to say that some hooligan was responsible," Miss Ethel continued. "So I know I need not suspect any of you—" She paused, looking at each of them in turn as if to see whether anyone might look guilty.

Vivian kept her expression wide-eyed and guileless, praying that Florence was able to do the same. Under any other circumstances, she would have kept her sister in the dark about what she had done. But if Flo had arrived at work and heard that the dress had been stolen, she wouldn't have been able to keep her eyes away from Vivian. And they couldn't risk her giving the game away.

She had been furious, until Vivian had finally hissed, "What else was I supposed to do? I didn't do it just for fun, Flo, I did it to keep you alive. Are you saying I shouldn't have?"

There was no good answer to that, and both of them knew it. Florence had spent the cab ride to work practicing her surprised face while Vivian silently prepared for the worst.

"I need not suspect any of you," Miss Ethel said again, this time with more confidence. Vivian tried not to look relieved. "But I am . . . in a precarious position now. We all are. If you wish to continue being employed, we will all need to work twice as hard to make up the cost of what was stolen." Miss Ethel seemed to lose her train of thought for a moment, eyeing the damage to her store. Her chin trembled for a moment.

Vivian didn't want to feel sympathy for Miss Ethel. The woman was cruel and demanding, and she worked her employees to the bone. But Vivian could feel the guilt settling into her stomach anyway. This was her fault. And when she glanced at the faces of the other girls, the worry in their eyes at the prospect of finding themselves out of work, she wanted to cry.

She didn't, though. Vivian never cried.

"I will require everyone to work extra hours each week for the next month," Miss Ethel continued. "Especially you, Florence. You will come with me while we discuss what to do about Mrs. Blake's order." She cast another suspicious glance over her assembled workers, and the nine girls all held their breath as they waited. Finally she sniffed.

"Well, what are you waiting for? The work will not do itself. If you please!" She clapped her hands sharply.

There was a sudden flurry of movement as the girls hurried to their tables and tasks. "Oh, Vivian." Miss Ethel retrieved a folder of papers from the counter and began to flip through them. "A customer has requested that someone come by to take new measurements before we start on her commissions for the fall. I trust you will be on your best behavior." Her glance took in Vivian's bobbed hair and lingered on her cheap shoes. She sniffed. "I cannot afford to lose any business because you offend someone with your impropriety." Vivian bit her tongue to keep from giving a sharp reply as the shop owner turned back to her folder. "Here we are." She pulled one paper out and glanced over it. "Henrietta Wilson on Fifth Avenue."

Hattie Wilson. Vivian swallowed, forcing herself to smile as she took the papers Miss Ethel handed her. "Yes, ma'am. I'm sure Mrs. Wilson will have no cause to complain about me."

"You needn't shake in your shoes quite so obviously, Miss Kelly." Hattie Wilson's smile was mocking as she rose from her desk.

Vivian's jaw clenched, but she kept her face as impassive as possible and didn't move from the spot by the door where the housemaid had left her. "I'm not planning for any unfortunate accidents to find you today."

"But another day you might?"

"That all depends on you. For now, I believe our interests are still aligning nicely." She closed the heavy velvet curtains as she spoke. The room had once been her husband's study, and the last time Vivian had been in it, it had still reeked of masculine power. Mrs. Wilson hadn't softened the room—she was not a soft person—but she had made its opulence more elegant, with richer fabrics, new wallpaper, and crystal sconces that caught the light and sent it dancing across the walls and ceiling.

Coming around the desk, Mrs. Wilson strolled toward the large gilded mirror that leaned against one wall and began to unbutton the silk blouse that she wore. "And I do need my measurements taken, so you may work as we talk."

It should have made Vivian feel like she had more power, that Mrs. Wilson needed to at least partially undress in front of her. But the careless way that the woman tossed her expensive clothes aside, the fact that she could stand tall while Vivian would have to kneel to wrap the tailor's tape around her hips or make notes on her paper, made it clear who was in charge.

And Vivian didn't have a choice. She gritted her teeth and got to work, pulling her things out of the leather satchel she was carrying—shaped like a doctor's bag, but full of everything a seamstress would need to work on the go—and kneeling in front of the mirror, just as she was expected to.

"What interests are those, Mrs. Wilson?"

"That very curious note you showed me the last time we spoke." Mrs. Wilson held out her arms, looking as unconcerned as if she were bored by the conversation. But as Vivian stood to wrap the tape around her bosom, she caught sight of the mob boss's eyes glinting in the mirror. Mrs. Wilson was watching her every movement. "I might have been too quick to dismiss your theory about its origin."

Vivian's heart felt like it was speeding up, and her hands trembled a little. She kept her eyes on her task as she asked, as calmly as she could manage, "What's got you singing a different tune?"

"Snippets of gossip, the sort you hear in my line of work. About a new operation that seems to be springing up in your little corner of the city."

"What have you heard?" Vivian demanded.

"Not much. It's small, but perhaps not for long. And there are already whispers of a dangerous reputation. They seem to be a smart little group, because they have picked a very interesting calling card." She waited until Vivian looked up to continue. "It seems they have, rather elegantly, been using a drawing of a hemlock leaf to announce their presence."

Vivian bit her lip, then admitted through gritted teeth, "I don't know what that is."

Hattie Wilson made an amused *hmm* in the back of her throat. "The hemlock leaf can be used as a rather potent poison."

Poison. Vivian swallowed, sitting back on her heels. That was too much of a coincidence to be nothing. "Your measurements are done," she said quietly.

Hattie Wilson began dressing leisurely. When she was done, she held out her hand. "I'd like to see the designs Miss Ethel sent."

Vivian handed them over, and Mrs. Wilson took a seat behind her desk once more as she perused them. Vivian packed her things up slowly. "I'm guessing you're not sharing this with me out of the goodness of your heart."

"I don't know if you've heard the rumors, Miss Kelly, but apparently there is no goodness in my heart." Mrs. Wilson slid the sketches across the desk. "These are lovely. Tell Miss Ethel she may proceed." She pulled a stack of letters toward her and began to slit them open, one by one, with a silver letter knife. Vivian wanted to flinch with each slice. "As I said, our interests align. I have some business concerns not far from there, and a new outfit springing up, however small it may be for now, is bad for business. Particularly if they like to poison people. It risks the wrong kind of attention. So I'm sharing this with you, and in return, I expect you to share what you find out with me."

Vivian snorted. "Just a couple favors between friends."

"If you like." Mrs. Wilson set down her correspondence and met

Vivian's eyes, her fingers still resting on the letter opener. It wasn't quite a threat, but it was still a clear message. She was telling Vivian how things stood, not asking.

Vivian nodded slowly, her mind going to the Fitz Special that had made Honor look so scared. "You heard any rumors about cops being involved with this new little gang?"

"Nothing specific, but I wouldn't rule it out," Hattie said, her smile knife-edged. "Plenty of dirty cops out there."

"Any of them work for you?" Vivian asked, feeling very daring and very scared as soon as the words were out of her mouth.

Hattie looked at her for a long time, her face impassive, her fingers turning the letter knife over and over while she considered her answer. "Not directly," she said at last. "I have my friends, and I pay up, same as anyone else. But anything more than a favor here and there can lead to difficulties for everyone. Cop decides he doesn't want to work with you anymore when he already knows too much about how you operate? That can spell all kinds of trouble. And someone always ends up dead."

"Speaking from experience?"

"Just an observation." Hattie's smile was back. "Fella I know had a cop on his payroll until very recently, trying to work off some kind of family debt. And of course, the cop eventually decided that he could get rid of the debt faster if he shut down the fella's business instead."

"Who ended up dead that time?" Vivian asked, feeling sick.

"The cop." Hattie's voice was soft, but there was no gentleness in it. "It's not smart to cross someone in my line of work, Miss Kelly. I hope you'll remember that."

TWENTY-ONE

The mood at the Nightingale was wild that night. With Bea on stage and the band in fine form, the club's guests were in a dizzy, delighted mood, hollering and cheering as they danced and applauding wildly each time Bea finished a number.

It made Vivian's heart ache. She kept trying to catch her friend's eye, but Bea was avoiding her. And Vivian couldn't really blame her for that, even though she knew they desperately needed to talk.

"Hey there, beautiful girl." A grinning, tipsy young man who probably still shaved peach fuzz every morning caught her wrist as she finished setting drinks on his table. "I saw you dancing last time I was here and knew I had to take you for a spin. Kick up your heels with me?" His friends chortled as he teetered in his chair, and he shook his head, laughing at himself.

Vivian kept her smile in place as she gave her wrist a gentle tug, and to her relief he let her go. If he hadn't, she would have had to tell Honor that there was a boy who needed someone to teach him some manners. "You're sweet to ask, baby, but I can't dance unless I'm on a break," she said, letting him down easy, her eyes darting toward the bandstand.

Bea had just finished a number and was heading back to the dressing room for her break. "Maybe another time? I'm gonna be running my feet off all night with this crazy crowd." She pretended to give them all a stern look, one hand on her hip, while they grinned and chuckled. "Can I get you boys anything else?"

"You got a phone number?" one of them asked.

"Can't have a number without a phone," Vivian said honestly. She blew them a kiss. "See you boys later."

She dropped her tray off at the bar. "Back in a jiff," she called to Danny when he would have pushed another round of drinks toward her, and she scurried off toward the dressing room before he could tell her to stop.

Bea was just handing a cold, wet cloth to Alba, who was lying back with her feet propped up. Vivian's heart stuttered. "Everything okay?" she asked.

"Swell," Alba muttered, blowing out her cheeks as she laid the cloth over her forehead. "Just got dizzy, is all. This whole having a baby thing is a mess, let me tell you. I don't think I can work much longer, and God knows what'll happen to us then. Babies ain't cheap."

"We'll help you out," Bea said, going to her dressing table and kicking off her own shoes so she could stretch out her ankles. "And I'm sure Honor'll give you your job back once you can work again. She's not the sort to make a stink about a girl having a baby just because she doesn't have a fella to go with it."

"Thank God for that, because everyone else in the world sure is." Alba closed her eyes with a sigh. "Either of you gonna tell me why you're circling each other like alley cats tonight? It's not anything to do with Pearlie, is it?"

"You tell me, Bea," Vivian said, crossing her arms. "Did you talk to him?"

"Talk to who?" Alba asked, opening one eye. She glanced nervously between them.

Bea's jaw clenched, and her expression was hard as she met Vivian's eyes in the mirror. "Abraham," she said at last. "Vivian's got some wild idea that he had something to do with those letters."

"What? Your Abraham?" Alba sat up fast, then just as quickly lay back down, one hand over her mouth. "What?" she asked more quietly after swallowing rapidly several times. "That's crazy, Viv. Pearlie and Abraham got along great. And if he'd been involved with those letters, he'd have been involved with . . . with what happened to Pearlie. That's not possible." She glanced at Bea. "Tell her."

"I didn't realize you knew Abraham so well," Bea said, twisting around to look at Alba as she fiddled with her lipstick.

Alba shrugged, an awkward motion since she was still lying down. "Like I said, he and Pearlie got along swell. So I saw him around."

Vivian felt like someone was tying knots in her stomach. "So you didn't ask him about the necklace?"

"What necklace?" Alba interjected, trying to sit up again.

Bea sent an irritated look in her direction. "This one," she said through clenched teeth, touching the gold locket at her throat. "Viv's got some idea that it's like a necklace someone had to give up when they got one of those letters."

Alba's eyes were wide. "Did you ask him about it?"

For a moment, Vivian thought Bea wasn't going to answer, and when she finally did it was hard to tell whether she was more irritated with Vivian or Alba just then. "I did. He said he got it at a pawnbroker." For the first time, Bea hesitated. Then she nodded sharply. "He even told me which one."

Vivian let out the breath she'd been holding. "Then that's actually great news, isn't it? We can go talk to the pawnbroker and see if he remembers who brought it in."

"He might not be able to tell you," Alba pointed out, rising onto her elbows. "Legally, I don't think they can say. Especially if you tell him it mighta been stolen."

"Alba, isn't your break just about done?" Bea snapped, clearly out of patience. She shoved her feet back into her scarlet shoes, tying the ribbons with sharp tugs.

"Probably, but things aren't gonna be pretty if I stand up just now. If anyone asks for me, will you tell them I'll be out as soon as I'm steady?"

"Sure," Bea said, standing so abruptly her chair almost toppled over. She caught it just in time. "I need to be back on the bandstand in a minute anyway. You coming, Viv?"

Vivian was surprised that Bea would ask for her company when she was still angry. But Bea clearly had something she didn't want to say in front of Alba.

"I should, I'm not even supposed to be on a break right now. Need anything?" she asked, turning toward Alba, who was still stretched out on the room's tiny sofa.

"For five more months to be done," Alba muttered. "No, I'm fine."

When the dressing room door was closed behind them, and they were engulfed once more in the noise of the dance hall, Bea put a hand on Vivian's arm to keep her where she was. They stood there, in the corner just to the side of the bar, their eyes fixed on the crowd.

"Abraham was all cut up about what happened, Viv, you've got no idea," Bea said at last. "He even . . . he even thinks he knows how the letter writer found out about the money. He didn't want to tell me, but I could tell something was fishy, the way he was acting. And finally he let it out."

Vivian waited while Bea took a shuddering breath. She didn't want to push, not about something like this.

"Abraham said he picked Pearlie up from here after work once, him and some friend of his." Bea's hands, resting by her sides, were clenched into fists. "They were both roaring drunk, and Pearlie's talking a mile a minute at the top of his voice as they're staggering out, like he'd do when he was all worked up or excited. Bragging about how he's got his hands on some cash and there's more where that came from."

"And anyone could have heard him."

"Yeah," Bea agreed quietly. "I'm sorry I got so sour with you. Looks like you were right about the necklace."

"But not about Abraham," Vivian pointed out. "So I'm sorry I said anything about him."

"He's been so good through all this mess, Viv, you have no idea. He kept an eye on the kids when I was out yesterday so they wouldn't be alone. And he's been picking Mama up from work so she can get home quicker in the evening."

"Not to mention that he treats you real well." Vivian thought about saying more but kept her mouth shut in the end. She wasn't convinced yet that Abraham didn't have anything to do with the letters. She didn't want him to be in that kind of business. But until they talked to the pawnbroker, there was no way to know whether he had told the truth or not.

But her comment made Bea smile, though the expression was still haunted. "He does treat me real nice, doesn't he?"

"And now we've got something to go on," Vivian pointed out. "Tomorrow we can go to that pawnshop—"

Bea broke in, shaking her head. "Viv, you know better than that. What do you think would happen if I walk into a pawnshop and started asking questions about things that might've been stolen? Even if the owner is willing to talk . . ." She scowled. "All that would happen is I'd end up in trouble with the police."

The quickstep was racing toward its finish. It would be time for Bea to be back on the bandstand soon; Mr. Smith was already glancing her way with raised eyebrows, wondering why she was still hovering near the bar.

"Then I'll do it," Vivian said firmly. She thought about Florence, about that gun pointed at her on the dark street, Mrs. Henry's tired, sad eyes as she lost yet another member of her small family, Mr. Guzman saying he didn't want any more trouble. "This is the first chance we've really had to figure out who's behind those letters, Bea. I'm not sleeping on that."

Bea gave her a skeptical look, then sighed as she gave the bandleader a little wave to show she was on her way. "If you say so, Viv. But I'm starting to think this is something that can't be solved. We just have to survive it as best we can."

It was too similar to what Honor had said to her in that small, dark apartment. Vivian watched Bea cross the floor, weaving through clusters of patrons and hurrying waitresses, giving her hair a fluff and her shoulders a shimmy before she took her spot in front of the microphone, a wide smile on her face as the quickstep wrapped up. The bandleader gave a fast count—no mercy for the dancers tonight—and launched directly into the opening bars of "After You've Gone," played hotter than Vivian had heard it before. Bea's voice filled the dance hall, bold and beautiful and rich as honey. But in spite of the atmosphere of sweaty, stolen fun, Vivian shivered.

Just hoping to survive wasn't enough for her. Not anymore.

She was about to turn back to the bar—Danny was giving her a stern look, warning her it was time to get back to work—when a figure on the other side of the dance floor caught her eye.

Had someone actually let Bruiser George into the Nightingale?

Vivian craned her neck, trying to spot him through the crowd; when she couldn't, she began to push her way across the dance floor. Good-natured curses and an occasional sharp "Watch it!" followed her. But she dodged between the dancing couples, glancing around breathlessly as she reached the other side.

He wasn't there.

Vivian frowned, spinning in a circle as she stared at all the people around her. None of them were George. None of them even looked enough like him to have been mistaken for him from across a crowded, dimly lit room.

Had she imagined him?

"Viv?"

The quiet voice at her elbow made her jump. "Jesus, Mary, and Joseph, Ellie, don't sneak up on a girl like that," she gasped, trying to laugh off her nervousness.

"Sorry." Mousy, pretty little Ellie gave her a hesitant smile, but she couldn't manage to hold on to it for long. Her face fell into something far more serious as she scooted closer. "I heard you and Bea talking about some letters, just now. I think I know the ones you're talking about. Someone's making people—"

"Wait a sec," Vivian said quickly, glancing around. She still didn't see anyone who looked like Bruiser George, but she didn't want to take any chances. Across the room, she could see another waitress just ducking into the dressing room on her break. Vivian gave Ellie a little push toward the door to the back hall. "Let's talk out in the alley."

Vivian glanced around when they got outside, using her foot to slide a stray brick in front of the door to prop it open a little. The electric light from inside the club spilled out, jumping over stacked crates and colliding with the walls that surrounded the narrow, gloomy space. There was no one else out there, but Vivian pulled Ellie a few steps away from the door, just in case.

"What do you know about letters?" Vivian asked, keeping her voice down.

"I heard Alba talking about them a couple days ago," Ellie said quietly. "The ones that say to hand over something you own that's valuable if you don't want something bad to happen. That the same thing you and Bea were talking about?"

"Yeah," Vivian said cautiously. "Why do you ask?"

"I know someone who got one of those," Ellie said, wrapping her arms around herself as she spoke, as if what she was saying scared her. "I have a neighbor—you might've met her, she's been here a couple times. Anyway, one day I was over helping out with her sister's baby, and she had this paper that she was carrying around, a letter. She'd take it out and read it and look terrified every time she did. So I asked to see it. See, she used to have this really beautiful ring that she always wore, I think it was pretty valuable. And that was what was in the letter. Since I'd heard people talking about those letters, I told her to hand it over."

"That sounds . . ." Vivian trailed off, frowning. "Where do you live, Ellie?"

"About a mile north of here," Ellie said, looking confused. "Why?"

It wasn't in Vivian's neighborhood, but it wasn't too far away. That fit with what Hattie had told her about a new operation popping up in their part of the city. "Nothing. What happened to your neighbor? She okay?"

"So far. But I didn't know if she should still be worried. And since it sounded like you and Bea might know something . . . I don't know, I just want to be sure no one's gonna cause her any more trouble."

"I don't know anything for sure," Vivian admitted. "But could I maybe go talk to your neighbor? Could you tell me where she lives?"

"I mean, I could," Ellie said slowly. "But I'd probably need to go with you. Unless you know the signing language? She's mostly deaf."

"Oh." Vivian frowned. "I don't. Do you?"

"A bit. I asked Honor to teach me some when I started working here," Ellie said.

Vivian blinked in surprise. She knew there were folks out there who used signs to communicate. But it had never occurred to her that the club's hand signs might be part of that language—or that Honor might have a reason to know it. "Why does Honor know how to sign?"

Ellie shrugged. "Didn't ask, I figured it wasn't any of my business. I was just glad she could show me some, because no one else around here except my neighbor's sister knows them. I could take you to talk to my neighbor, I suppose. She can read lips pretty good. Tomorrow, if you want?"

"Yeah . . . yeah." Vivian nodded decisively. If she was going to talk to the pawnbroker about the necklace, she wanted to know what that ring looked like, too. She didn't need to keep wondering about Honor Huxley, who had made it clear how things stood between them. That was a brick wall she was tired of running into. Whatever Honor's secrets were, she could keep them. "Tomorrow, okay?"

When Vivian finally made it back to the bar, Danny raised his eyebrows at her. "Something going on that Hux and I should know about?"

"I don't think your Hux wants any more to do with it," Vivian said, trying to sound like she didn't care one way or another.

It didn't fool Danny. "She told me you two had a rough night," he said quietly, leaning his elbows on the bar. He had his serious face on, a rarity when he was working. "But if there's something more going on, she'll want to know."

Vivian shrugged. "Nothing new to worry about."

Danny gave her a long look, then nodded. "If you say so, kitten. But don't go getting yourself in a jam just because you're too proud to ask for help." He hesitated, then added, "She's hard to get close to, Viv. There's plenty even I don't know about her, and I know more than just about anyone. Don't take it personal."

Vivian held her hands firmly by her sides, resisting the urge to touch her lips as she thought about Honor kissing her in the street, scared and relieved and angry all at once. *I can't afford to give myself that kind of weakness,* she had said, with no regret in her voice, no nothing, just quiet and firm and resigned. "Nothing personal about it at all," Vivian agreed, smiling even as her chest felt like someone was squeezing it. She nodded toward the drinks he was fixing. "Where are those two headed?"

He smiled at last. "Fella in the corner table. Why don't you take them over?"

"Sure thing." Vivian took the tray bearing a glass of champagne and a whiskey cocktail, balancing it carefully as she wound her way through the crowd. The man at the corner table had his back to her when she arrived. "Ready for your order, mister?" she asked.

He tipped back his head to look up at her, a wide smile spreading over his face, and Vivian couldn't stop herself smiling in response. "Hey, Leo. Good to see you all in one piece."

"You too, Viv. That one's for you," he added, tipping his chin toward the champagne. "Danny said you could take ten for a drink and a dance if you wanted."

"Well, I won't say no to that. Lord knows I could use both after the last twenty-four hours." She sat, then leaned down to surreptitiously loosen the ribbons on her shoes under the table. "You sure you're okay after last night?"

"Right as rain," Leo said, taking a drink and leaning back in his chair. "Not much scary about the drunk tank when you know how to get out quick. And better I ended up there than you. Or Ms. Huxley," he added, almost as an afterthought. "Gonna tell me what else happened last night? I wasn't worried about me, but I was thinking about you the whole time."

"It was . . ." Vivian hesitated, turning her glass in slow circles. "It was quite a night. And it's been quite a day since then." She took a drink, then leaned forward, dropping her voice as she filled him in on what had happened after his arrest. Leo listened in silence, though she could see his hands tighten into fists, and when she mentioned almost being shot he was so agitated that he pushed back from the table and stood up.

"But you're all right?" he demanded, pacing two steps away, then coming back abruptly. Taking his seat once more, he downed the rest of his drink, grimacing at the burn of the whiskey before leaning forward to take her hands. "Viv, how could you—"

"I know," she said. She pulled her hands away, but she did it gently. "But it worked out fine, okay? And listen . . ." She hesitated, taking another drink before she leaned forward again. "Any chance you'd be up for a visit to a pawnbroker tomorrow?"

Vivian's deliveries were quick the next morning, and it was easy enough to hop off the elevated line heading south once she was done. She couldn't help glancing over her shoulder as she did, though, still checking the streets behind her as she walked and scanning the faces on the platform to see if anyone was following her.

She knew, logically, that the men from the other night had a history of using poison, or other deaths that looked like accidents, rather than following and attacking someone in broad daylight. But she kept looking over her shoulder anyway. She didn't want anyone to find her. And she didn't want to lead anyone to where she and Florence were staying.

But there was no one suspicious on the train platform, and no one who seemed intent on following her when she got off and hurried through the crowd back down to the street level. The rails clattered overhead as the train headed toward the next stop, and Vivian checked the scrap of paper that had the address she was looking for scribbled on it.

For all it was a different neighborhood, Ellie's home was practically a twin to Vivian's own. No matter where you went in the city, you could find buildings crammed with too many tenement apartments, laundry strung out of the windows to flutter about the alleys, children running barefoot in the street while someone kept an eye on them from the window.

Ellie was waiting for her outside, jiggling impatiently from foot to foot and yawning. "Come on," she said as soon as she spotted Vivian. "Golly, are you usually up this early? How do you do it after being up all night?"

"I'm usually up a lot earlier," Vivian said dryly. "I've been working all morning."

"Golly," Ellie said again, covering another yawn as she led the way into the building and up the stairs. "Glad I've got more than just me to bring home the bacon. I don't know if I could handle mornings after a night running off my feet. Are you just always tired?" She didn't wait for an answer but kept right on talking as they reached the fourth floor and a cramped, grimy hall. She pointed to the door just a few steps away from the stairs. "Beryl had to run out a few minutes ago, I passed her out front, but she said she wouldn't be long, so we can just wait for her to get back . . ."

Vivian didn't mind the chatter. There was something endearing about Ellie, barely older than a schoolgirl and enjoying every minute of her new grown-up life. It was easy for Vivian to let her mind wander while Ellie talked and they waited in the hall until the sound of footsteps made them both turn toward the stairwell.

A girl appeared around the curve of the stairs, out of breath and sweaty from hauling two large bags up the steps. She was young, probably close to Ellie's age, and had the same wholesome look to her. Her curly hair was tied back with a ribbon around her head, and her dress was pretty but too short in the sleeves. Her bags had groceries peeking out of them, and she jumped in surprise as she came up the steps and found them waiting, though Ellie hadn't been keeping her voice low. She flinched backward so sharply that she almost lost her footing, and Ellie had to catch her arm quickly. The girl gave her a grateful nod before she set down her bags and, turning toward Vivian with her eyebrows raised, made a quick, curious sign with her hands.

Vivian glanced at Ellie, who smiled encouragingly and said, "This is Vivian"—accompanied by a series of small motions with one hand that Vivian thought might have been spelling out her name—"who was hoping to talk to you." She made a few more signs as she spoke.

The movements weren't fluid the way the girl's had been, but the girl still gave Vivian a cautious nod and signed something slowly.

"She's saying it's nice to meet you," Ellie told Vivian. "Vivian, this is Beryl."

"Nice to meet you, too," Vivian said in reply, noticing that the girl was watching her mouth move closely. "Can I ask you some questions? About the letter you got a little while ago?"

Beryl's face went pale, and she shook her head rapidly. She would have pushed past them if Vivian hadn't held out a hand. "Please," she said. "It's real important." She hesitated, then said, "My sister got one, too."

Beryl glanced at Ellie, who frowned, thinking, before offering a few more signs. "Is your sister here, Beryl?" Ellie asked.

Beryl shook her head, and Ellie blew out a frustrated breath, glancing at Vivian. "I don't know as much of the signing language as Beryl's sister, but she's not here to help out. Maybe we could—"

She broke off as Beryl laid a hand on her shoulder, heading toward the door to unlock it. Gathering up her bags of groceries, she gave a little tip of her head to show that they should follow her.

Inside was a plain, unadorned little space, but there was a bright, hand-sewn quilt thrown over a rocking chair, and the smell of the morning's tea still filled the air. Along one wall was a row of four framed drawings, the kind that might have come from a book or a calendar, each one showing a different plant or flower. Beryl set her groceries down, then turned to give them a wary look as she held out her hand.

"Your letter," she said, slowly and carefully, pointing at Vivian.

Vivian pulled it from her handbag and held it out. Beryl took it, but as soon as she glanced down, her brows drew together and her expression turned belligerent. She thrust it back at Vivian, shaking her head.

"What?" Vivian asked, stunned and confused by the girl's sudden shift to irritation. Her hands closed around the letter again, and she glanced down at it before meeting Beryl's eyes again. "What's wrong?"

Beryl glared at her, then turned to Ellie. Holding one hand flat sideways, she dragged the finger of her opposite hand down the palm, then pointed at Vivian's letter in a gesture so abrupt it was like a stab. "What is that?" she demanded, each careful word bitten off and angry.

"Vivian, what did you do?" Ellie asked, her voice quavering.

"Nothing!" Vivian insisted. "This is the letter we got, honest."

Beryl shook her head again, signing rapidly, then abruptly turned on her heel and stalked toward the room's single, mostly empty bookcase. Taking a thick old book from the shelf, she pulled out a piece of paper that had been tucked between the pages and thrust it toward Vivian, tapping it rapidly as if to say, *No, this*.

Vivian stared at the paper Beryl handed her, then back at the one that had been sent to Florence. Both laid out simple directions and a simple threat. The phrasing was different, but that could be easily explained.

What was less easy to explain was the fact that the two letters looked nothing alike. Where Florence's letter had been written in blocky, poorly formed letters, Beryl's letter was neatly and impersonally typed.

And where the letter Florence had received had been unsigned, Beryl's closed with a simple sketch: a branch surrounded by triangular clusters of leaves.

"Golly," Ellie said, glancing over Vivian's shoulder. "Those don't look anything alike, do they? Are you sure they were sent by the same person?"

"No," Vivian said slowly. "No, I'm not sure they were at all." She glanced at the framed botanical prints on the wall, then at Beryl. "Any chance you know what kind of plant this is?" she asked, pointing to the sketch at the bottom of the letter.

Beryl nodded and spelled the word out with her fingers.

Ellie glanced at Vivian. "She says it's hemlock."

TWENTY-TWO

The pawnbroker that Abraham had pointed the finger at, located just south and west of the park, wasn't too shabby, as far as pawnbrokers went. There was no real sign out front, but the full window display and the three gold circles painted above the door said plain enough what it was. It was tucked almost under the rail for the elevated track and when they entered, the whole building was shaking as a train went clattering overhead.

Inside, a bell rang above the door as Vivian and Leo entered, trying their best to look like a respectable couple out doing a bit of shopping—or as respectable a couple as might be browsing in a pawnshop. Leo, hat tucked under one arm, smiled as he steered her toward the counter where the jewelry was kept.

"We're not here to buy anything," Vivian hissed at him.

"Doesn't mean we can't look at pretty things," he replied. "Unless you'd like to go examine the furniture? I see a very ugly chair over in the corner."

Vivian covered a nervous giggle, and the sound came out more like a snort, which made her clap her hand over her mouth. The pawnbroker glanced over at them, his expression considering. He was a plump, pleasant-looking man, with eyes that bulged a little too much and a chin that stuck out like a challenge. She had to fight the urge to fuss with her hat or tug her dress straighter, trying to look more worthy of attention. Or should they look more desperate and down on their luck?

The pawnbroker gave them a professionally courteous smile. "A moment, if you please." He turned back to the counter, where he was appraising a violin while a nervous-looking girl watched him, her hands twisting together. She was rail thin, as though she hadn't had a decent meal in days, and her eyes were wide and hopeful and sad all at once.

"It was my grandfather's," she said, her voice quavering as she watched the pawnbroker lift the instrument delicately in both hands. "He brought it over without a scratch on it, so I'm going to buy it back, you know, just as soon as I can . . ."

Vivian turned away, her gut twisting in discomfort. Leo was watching her. "Do you think you could do that, if you had to?" he asked with quiet curiosity. "Pawn something with that much meaning? I don't know if I could."

"Then you've never really been hungry," Vivian said, her voice equally quiet. She gave him a smile that had no humor in it. "Get poor enough and you'll sell whatever you have to sell to survive. It'll break your heart, but you'll do it."

She had never thought about it before, but for all he had been cut off from the wealthier side of his family, Leo must have grown up in relative comfort. He might live his life on the rough side of the law, but she had a feeling that hadn't been the only choice for him. "Did you go to school?" she asked abruptly, staring straight ahead at someone's tea service and silver candlesticks. She had never asked him much about his life before. Sharing personal stories wasn't the sort of thing that folks did at places like the Nightingale. And when he had taken her out before, he had been too busy trying to keep a lid on exactly who he was—and who his uncle was—to tell her about his past. "I mean college, or something like that?"

"My dad wanted me to," Leo said, lifting an old, gilded book with a title in a language that Vivian couldn't read. "He had hopes of me growing up to be something other than a tough guy on the street. But it would have been hard to pay for. And I had a hell of a chip on my shoulder once I found out who my mom's family was." He gave her a sideways grin, but there was an edge of regret to it, and he shook his head. "I lit out for Chicago almost as soon as my mom died. And my uncle found me there anyway."

"Do you wish you had?" Vivian asked, feeling a little in awe. She'd never known someone who might have gone to college before.

"Nah." He put the book down, slinging a friendly arm around her shoulders. "I like being a tough guy. And the company's pretty good."

"You'd probably be safer somewhere else, though."

"Anywhere can be dangerous," he replied, his expression growing more serious. "We both know that."

Vivian shivered, nodding in agreement.

"For God's sake, no, I can't wait any extra time."

The pawnbroker's irritated voice broke into their conversation. Vivian glanced over her shoulder, trying not to be too obvious. The girl had gone—she had left the violin on the counter, and the sight of it gave Vivian an ache of sympathy in the center of her chest—and a tall man had taken her place. He was scruffy looking, with hair that stuck almost straight up and clothes that were wrinkled, as though he had found them on the floor and pulled them on anyway. But he spoke forcefully as he leaned over the counter.

"One week extra, Mr. Joyce. You can give me that. They belonged to my wife. I just need one more week to pay you back."

"Poor bastard," Vivian muttered.

The pawnbroker scowled. "You're a cop, Arthur, you know how the law works. You have two more days. After that, they're no longer your property."

Vivian eyed the man, Arthur, in surprise. She never would have pegged him for a police officer. But she supposed even cops might fall on hard times. Especially if they were that rare thing, a cop who wasn't involved somehow in bootlegging.

"What if I come back with a few friends and get you shut down?" Arthur said belligerently, pulling himself up to his full height. Leo and Vivian weren't even pretending not to watch; they both stared at the sordid confrontation. "Everyone knows fellas like you run shady businesses. How many things here were stolen before you took them off someone's hands and put them up for sale?"

Vivian's breath caught and she glanced at Leo. That was exactly why they were there, after all. Should she try to catch the officer's attention, maybe talk to him on the way out? But Leo shook his head, tightening his grip on her arm to warn her to stay where she was. He clearly didn't like what was playing out there.

The pawnbroker sighed, looking far more bored than Vivian would have expected. "You could do that. Of course, your buddies would ask why you were pawning things in the first place, wouldn't they? And maybe I'd have to tell them all about your little gambling problem," he said, a cruel edge to his words. "I thought it had gotten better, since I hadn't seen you for a few weeks. Didn't need that extra cash for a little while, maybe? But it never lasts, does it? You always come back."

Arthur flinched, his face darkening with an embarrassed flush. "Lucky for you that I'm retiring soon," he snapped, sweeping his hand out to knock over a stand of silver spoons. It was the futile, destructive gesture of a man who had no other way to vent his anger. He pushed his way out the door, past another man just coming in, calling angrily back over his shoulder, "Getting out of this mess of a city!"

"See you next week, Arthur," the pawnbroker called as the door banged shut. He turned to Vivian and Leo, his cheerful salesman smile back in place as he came out from behind the counter. "My apologies for the unpleasantness. How can I help you this morning? I saw you were looking at our lovely selection of furniture? Or perhaps you seek something pretty for the young lady?" He gestured toward the jewelry display at the counter.

"As a matter of fact, we did want to talk to you about jewelry," Vivian said slowly, glancing at Leo. He nodded but didn't say anything, letting her take the lead. She took a deep breath. "A necklace that you sold a little while back, a gold locket with a rose on it."

The pawnbroker frowned. "A locket, you say? Was there something wrong with it?"

Vivian smiled, trying to look as sweet and friendly as possible so the man would be willing to talk. "A friend of mine showed it to me, and it was the prettiest thing. And I know—" She giggled. "I mean, it's a pawnshop, it's not like you'll have another. But if you've got good taste in one piece of jewelry, stands to reason you might have others I'd like, right?" She squeezed Leo's arm, giving him a flirtatious smile before turning back to the pawnbroker. "Does that sound familiar? A necklace with a rose etched on it? Did it come from here?"

"Well—"

"A necklace, is it?" a new voice asked. Vivian jumped, jerking around to stare at the man who had come in and was now watching them. Beside her, Leo tensed. The man eyeing them, his hat tilted low so most of his face was in shadow except for his smile, was Bruiser George. "That's what we're asking about?"

"What the hell are you doing here?" Leo demanded.

"Looking after my boss's interests, of course," George said, shrugging as he sauntered toward them.

Stopping by a display cabinet, he picked up a little wooden figure of a man and turned it over in his hand before tossing it back down so it clattered to the floor. The pawnbroker tensed, opening his mouth to object. But he closed it slowly without saying anything. Glancing nervously between the three of them, he began to inch slowly toward his counter.

George smiled at Vivian, and the expression made the hairs on her neck and arms prickle. "I hope you didn't think that she was cutting you loose after your little meeting. If there's a problem, she wants to make sure it's taken care of, even if she has to do it herself."

"You mean yourself," Leo said flatly.

George shrugged. "Same thing. Boss calls the shots. You can stop fidgeting, fella," he added, turning so suddenly to the pawnbroker that the man jumped. "I don't like fidgety little mice. Gives me an itch to make them stay still."

"I did see you last night, then," Vivian said.

"You might've." George smiled again. "So, what're we looking for today? A necklace, you said?" He turned to the pawnbroker. "Tell the girlie about the necklace."

The man raised his hands, shaking his head. There was sweat beading on his flushed face; he clearly knew the man in his shop was dangerous. "I'm afraid I don't know—"

"Leave him alone," Vivian snapped. "We don't need your help. And I'm not saying anything more with you here. So how about you shake a leg right on out the door?"

"You think not?" George ignored her and, keeping his eyes on the shop owner, stepped forward slowly. The pawnbroker stepped back. "You know anything about this necklace? What does it have to do with this hemlock group? Don't hold out on me now. I get angry when people hold out on me."

Vivian had no idea what to do, but Leo was already moving. He stepped forward just enough, putting himself in George's path. He didn't do anything threatening, but he planted his feet and smiled coldly. "She said this conversation isn't happening with you here."

"And I swear, I don't know anything," the pawnbroker stammered, glancing from one face to the next. Vivian could see his hands shaking.

Bruiser George pushed past Leo until he was right in the pawnbroker's face. "You sure about that?" he snarled.

Before either Vivian or Leo could react, George had grabbed the pawnbroker by the scruff of his neck and shoved him face-first into one of his display cabinets. The pawnbroker reeled backward and stumbled to his knees, stunned, as trinkets tumbled from the shelves, some of them shattering on impact. Bruiser George would have grabbed him again if Vivian hadn't pushed herself between them.

"What are you doing?" she demanded, shaking at the sudden burst of violence.

"Out of my way, girlie," he said, sneering at her. "I'm not being paid to stand around. I'm being paid to find out information. How I do it is my business." He took a step toward Vivian, who was still between him and the pawnbroker, one of his hands rising to shove her out of the way. Vivian tensed.

"Well, I'm not being paid at all," Leo said as he stepped next to Vivian, loose-limbed and ready for a fight. His voice was cheerful; his eyes were cold. "But I'll gladly smash your teeth in for free if you don't get out of here."

George, menacing and fearless a moment before, hesitated. Beating the pawnbroker was one thing, but he was clearly hesitant to mess with a man who moved like he knew how to defend himself. George was wiry and fierce, but Leo had several inches of height on him, and his shoulders were broader. The pawnbroker whimpered, but no one glanced his way.

Vivian drew herself up, hoping she didn't look as scared as she felt. "He said get out."

Bruiser George turned to glance at her, his sneer back. "She won't be happy if I don't come back with a full report, girlie."

"Poor her," Vivian said coldly. Beside her, Leo shifted, just the smallest change in how he held his weight, ready to move quickly if he needed to. "Guess she'll have to live with being disappointed."

"And it's you she'll blame for it, not me," George added, his smile twisting up at one side. "Trust me when I say you don't want to be on her bad side. She don't like it when folks she does a favor for throw it back in her face."

"We didn't ask for her help," Vivian snapped. "So she can keep her disappointment to herself. And you can do like I said and get out."

Bruiser George's hat had fallen to the ground in the scuffle; he picked it up now and dusted it off carefully before settling it on his head. "I'm going, girlie. Good luck to you." He glanced at the pawnbroker, who was still cowering on the ground. "You're going to need it."

Vivian didn't let out the breath she was holding until the door shut behind him, the ringing of the little bell sounding like a warning as it hung in the air.

For a moment, no one inside the shop moved. Then Leo turned to the pawnbroker. "You all right?" he asked, holding out his hand.

The pawnbroker didn't take it, scrambling to his feet on his own and staring at them fearfully. He inched toward the counter as he spoke. "You kick your friend out, then act all nice to make me talk, huh? Think you can play me like that? Get out before I call the police."

"We're not trying to play anything," Vivian insisted as the man took a sudden dive behind the counter. "We just have a few questions, that's all. About a necklace you sold—"

She broke off as the pawnbroker emerged, a shotgun in his hands. "I said get out of my store," he ordered, leveling it at them. His voice and his hands were both shaking.

"Easy, mister," Leo said, reaching out to grab Vivian's wrist and tug her toward him. "We're going, okay? No need to get jittery with that thing."

"Will you talk to just me?" Vivian asked, feeling desperate as Leo began to pull them both slowly toward the door. "I'm harmless, honest. Look at me, you can tell I got nothing on me. Please, I just need to ask one question."

"Viv," Leo warned, his voice low and urgent.

"Please," she begged, planting her heels and meeting the man's eyes. He looked as terrified as she felt. She wondered what had happened to him to make him keep a shotgun under his store's counter. "I'm worried about a friend."

The pawnbroker stared at her, considering, as he slowly lowered the gun. "He waits outside," he said at last, jerking his chin at Leo.

Vivian nodded. "Get gone, pal," she said, her attempt at a teasing tone getting stuck in her bone-dry throat. She swallowed. "I'll be okay."

"Viv—"

"Please," she repeated, turning her head just enough to meet his eyes.

He looked miserable and furious, but at last he nodded. He glanced back at the pawnbroker. There was a clear warning in his voice as he said, "I'll be just outside. And she's real important to me."

The pawnbroker jerked his head again. "Outside."

The menacingly cheerful bell rang out once more as Leo left, and then Vivian was on her own. She swallowed. "Thanks, mister. I won't take up much of your time."

He eyed her for a tense moment, then put the shotgun back under the counter. "Ask your question."

Vivian tried to smile, but the expression got stuck halfway and her lips barely twitched. "My friend's fella gave her a necklace, and he said he bought it here. Is it possible to check whether he was telling the truth?"

The pawnbroker narrowed his eyes at her. "Her young man gives her jewelry and this makes you worry? Why?"

"She thinks he mighta lied," Vivian said, telling part of the truth in the hope that it would be more convincing than an outright lie. "She's worried he stole it."

"If your friend worries her young man is a thief and a liar, she shouldn't be stepping out with him, no matter where the necklace came from," the pawnbroker said, starting to turn away.

"All right, *I* think he stole it," Vivian admitted, desperate. "I knew someone who had a necklace like the one he gave her, but someone stole it. It has me worried for her." She met the pawnbroker's eyes. There was a chance, if he had the transaction recorded, that whoever had stolen the necklace had pawned it, and Abraham buying it for Bea had been nothing but a coincidence. Either way, she had to know. "Please."

She held her breath while he stared at her. At last, he pulled a red handkerchief out of his pocket and ran it across his forehead. "Gold necklace, you said? Locket with a rose on it?"

"Yes," Vivian said, nodding. "Pretty little thing. Simple. Not cheap, but nothing real fancy either. The rose was kinda . . . like this?" She held her hands out in the shape of a wide cup, like a blossom that had fully opened. "Does that sound familiar?"

"No," the pawnbroker said at last. "I don't recall such a thing. But let me check my records." He gave her a stern look. "You don't move one inch, you hear?"

"Yessir." Vivian nodded quickly.

He disappeared under the counter for barely a moment before he emerged once more with a thick, heavy notebook. "When did your friend receive this necklace? Recently?" he asked, paging through it.

"This week," Vivian said. "Though I can't say for sure when he would have bought it."

He glanced at her from under bushy eyebrows, then turned back to his records, flipping through several pages, then scanning the closely written columns. At last he lifted his head. "Well, your friend's young man is lying about something. He didn't buy anything like that here."

Vivian felt as if her heart had suddenly stopped in her chest. "Are you sure?"

He gave her a sour look. "Yes. I keep very detailed records. I have to."

"Right." Vivian nodded rapidly, several times. What the hell was she going to tell Bea? And would her friend even believe her? "Thanks for your help, mister."

She turned away, and as she did so, her eye was caught by the silver candlesticks she and Leo had been looking at earlier. She froze, staring at them for a moment, before spinning back around. "One more question?"

The pawnbroker's jaw clenched, but he gave a single, curt nod. "One more."

"The candlesticks there, the silver ones with the filigree and the grape vines and poppies. Who brought those in?"

He raised his eyebrows. "You want me to look it up?"

"Please," Vivian said faintly.

"You think your friend's fella stole those too?"

"No, I . . ." Vivian thought quickly. If Abraham, or whoever he was working for, was using the pawnshop as a way to move goods, then there might be a record of who had pawned the candlesticks. But she couldn't tell the pawnbroker he might have taken stolen goods. If he thought there was a chance of getting in trouble with the law, he'd toss her out and cover his tracks as quickly as he could. "I think I know the girl who mighta had to pawn them. If they're hers and she can't buy them back in time, I'd want to get them for her. So they could stay in the family, you know?"

He eyed her suspiciously. "Out of the goodness of your heart?"

"That's what folks do for each other," Vivian said, scowling before she remembered that she was asking for a favor. "I just don't want to bring home the wrong pair if they're not hers."

He didn't look quite as if he believed her, but after a moment he nodded and flipped to another page in the book. "Well, you're in luck. Those ones are just for sale this week. And I remember the woman who pawned them." He gestured with his hand, indicating someone who was a bit shorter than Vivian. "Old lady brought them in a few months ago. Foreign name, but she spoke good English. Kaminski, or at least that's what I wrote down. That your friend?"

Vivian shook her head slowly, stunned. "No . . . no, that's not her."

Florence had been right. Mrs. Kaminski had pawned the candlesticks herself, probably a while before she even got the letter that had upset her so much.

"You okay?" the pawnbroker asked, eyeing her uneasily as he wiped his brow with the red handkerchief again.

"'Course I am," Vivian said, pulling herself together with an effort. She gave him a weak smile. "I'm always okay."

"Good." The pawnbroker slammed his book shut. "Then get the hell out of my store."

Vivian was up to her elbows in soapy water, but her mind was still churning over what she had learned at the pawnshop. Beside her, Florence was humming quietly, while Mrs. Chin, busy at the stove, glanced over at them every so often, a frown on her face. Vivian wondered if that was mostly directed at Florence or if it encompassed her, too. But Mrs. Chin didn't say anything, and Florence kept humming as she scrubbed, and Vivian still turned over half a dozen questions that she couldn't answer.

If the candlesticks were already gone, what had the letter writer wanted? Had they just not known when they sent the letter? But then why would they kill the old woman with a gas leak to steal something they would have been able to see wasn't there as soon as they entered the apartment? Did they just not know where it was kept?

And how did they find out their information, anyway?

"Viv, you gonna be ready to leave in half an hour?" Danny strolled into the kitchen, a towel over one shoulder as he dropped his tray and went to open the back door. A breeze snaked through the smoky room, and Vivian took a deep breath. Even Mrs. Chin stopped work for a moment to fan herself with the brown paper that had been wrapped around a bunch of herbs.

"That's up to your mother," Vivian said, glancing at Mrs. Chin. "All right if I take off?"

"Yes . . . yes. You go get ready for your job," she said, looking unhappy at the mention of the Nightingale. "We're closing soon anyway. Your sister and I can finish up. You're good girls, both of you," she added, a little begrudgingly. "You do good work without complaining."

"No chance of us complaining," Florence laughed. "I think staying here is the best we've ever eaten. You're a wonder at that stove, Mrs. Chin." She tried to brush a strand of hair out of her eyes with the back of her hand as she spoke, but ended up leaving a trail of soapy foam across her forehead.

"Here, I've got it," Danny said, grinning as he pulled the towel off his shoulder and flicked the suds away with it.

Florence squealed and tried to push him away. "Where has that towel been?" she demanded, laughing. "Don't you put it near my face!"

Grinning, Danny waggled it toward her once again. She responded by scooping up a handful of suds from the water and drawing her hand back, threatening to throw them at him. "Okay, okay!" he protested, laughing, holding his hands up as he backed away.

Vivian stared at them. Since when did her Florence, of all people, play and laugh?

"Get out of here," Florence ordered, putting her nose in the air, though she couldn't quite hide her smile. "I thought you had to get to work?"

"Sure do," he agreed, leaning against the wall as he grinned at her. Not even glancing at Vivian, he asked, "Half an hour, Viv?"

"Sure," she agreed, untying her apron, trying to ignore the hot, bitter feeling thrumming through her.

Had Florence completely forgotten why they were there? How

could she flirt and laugh when Vivian had been putting herself in such danger, night after night, trying to keep them safe? She knew it wasn't a fair thought; she had pushed her own troubles and worries down more than once with a dance or a drink at the Nightingale. She had often flirted with Danny to give her mood a lift when things were difficult or scary. She couldn't blame her sister for doing the same. And Florence *didn't* know how much danger Vivian had been putting herself in, because Vivian hadn't told her.

But the bitterness was still there.

"A moment, Vivian Kelly."

Mrs. Chin's voice stopped her just at the door, and Vivian turned quickly back. The last person she wanted to offend was Danny's mother, who had been so generous with them already. "Yes, ma'am?"

Mrs. Chin gave her son a look over her shoulder. "The trash needs to be taken out," she ordered, and he obeyed immediately, giving Florence a quick wink before hefting the bin and hauling it out the open door. Florence, smiling like she was keeping a secret, went back to the dishes. Mrs. Chin watched them for a moment, her mouth tight with worry, before turning back to Vivian, dropping her voice as she spoke. "His name is Mr. Sun," she said quietly, holding out a folded piece of paper.

Vivian took it automatically, but it was a moment before her brain caught up to what Mrs. Chin was saying. "That's . . . you mean the man I asked about? Mr. Sun, you said?"

Danny's mother nodded. "That's his address. It isn't very far from here, if you want to look him up. Please don't make me regret giving it to you."

Vivian held the paper carefully, not wanting to crumple it. "Thank you."

Mrs. Chin nodded. "You're good girls," she said again, this time with a sigh and a quick glance at Florence. "I need some fresh air."

Vivian watched her head out the back door. When she looked away,

Florence was watching her, her worry plain. "What was that about? Whose address, did she say?"

"Nothing," Vivian said, resisting the urge to tuck the paper behind her back. She told herself Florence wouldn't approve of her looking for someone who knew their mother, but that wasn't the real reason. The hot, bitter feeling made her want to keep a secret of her own.

"Vivian. Don't do this again."

She sighed. "I'll tell you later. I've gotta get ready for work."

"Okay," Florence said slowly. She didn't argue, but the concerned expression didn't fade as she watched Vivian leave.

And Vivian went, hating herself a little as the door closed behind her.

TWENTY-THREE

There was a storm hovering over New York that night, hovering but not breaking, and the heavy, charged air seemed to put the entire city on edge. Vivian was glad she had Danny by her side as they made their way to the Nightingale, dodging around staggering clusters of young men who were already drunk, high-spirited and belligerent in turn. As Silence opened the door to let them in, Danny glanced at the sky, dark with clouds and silvered with glances of moonlight. "Feels like we're in for an interesting night."

Silence grunted in agreement, and Vivian shivered.

The mood inside the club was equally tense. The tables were cleaned, the electric lights dimmed, the last case of liquor carried up to the bar. But it was all done in unusual quiet, punctured by sudden bursts of laughter or nervous whispers. The whole staff was on edge. Vivian wondered whether it was just the weather or something more.

"Everything ready?" Honor asked, stopping by the bar to check in with Danny. She glanced around the club. "Where's Beatrice? She's supposed to be on the bandstand tonight."

"We're missing Alba, too," Danny said, surveying the staff.

"They'll be coming together," Vivian said, arriving with a tray of sparkling glasses and handing them to the second bartender. "Alba's living with Bea's family for the moment."

Honor frowned. "Everything okay there?"

Vivian hesitated. She didn't know if Alba had yet shared the news of her pregnancy with Honor. And while there was no reason to think the Nightingale's owner would be prudish about the revelation, it still wasn't her news to share. "Far as I know," she said at last. "They might just be running a little late."

Honor was still looking over the club, but she glanced at Vivian out of the corner of her eyes. "You're doing okay? And your sister?"

"Just swell," Vivian said, a little more forcefully than she meant to. She smiled. "Probably moving back home soon, now the ruckus seems to have died down some."

"Like hell you are," Danny said, smiling cheerfully even as his voice was sharp. "You girls aren't heading back until we know for sure no one's coming after you anymore. Not when there might be a cop mixed up in this racket."

Vivian turned to glare at Honor. "You told him that?"

Honor raised her brows. "I tell Danny nearly everything, pet. You know that. And he does the same. It's how we keep our doors open and our people safe." Before Vivian could answer, she was moving off, gesturing to Benny and Saul at the top of the stairs so they would know it was time.

The band was just finishing warming up, discordant notes resolving at last as Mr. Smith counted off and they launched into a cheerful instrumental rendition of "Sister Kate." The electric lights dimmed, the first guests started to trickle in, and Vivian didn't have time to think about anything except work until she saw Bea arrive at last, tossing her things behind the bar and hurrying toward the bandstand.

Vivian managed to cross her path before she made it all the way there. "I need to talk to you," she whispered.

Bea took one look at her face, and her own grew far more serious than it had been a moment before. "It's not good news, is it?" Vivian shook her head. Bea plastered a smile back on her face, waving into the crowd as someone who had clearly started her drinking early yelled a welcome. "I'll see if I can just do a quick set, then tell them I need to powder my nose or something. Meet me in the dressing room."

Danny had been right when he said it would be an interesting night. The mood was high and wild, and Vivian was kept running around with almost no break. But it still wasn't enough of a distraction to keep her from replaying everything that had happened that day, starting with Beryl's letter. And when her mind jumped back to the memory of that revolver pointing at her . . .

Vivian shivered hard enough that the glasses on her tray clinked against each other.

Just as the first set was finishing, she noticed Alba at the bar, grimacing like someone who was trying not to be sick. She was speaking to Danny, looking apologetic; he gave her a nod and a comforting pat on the shoulder, jerking his head toward the dressing room.

Vivian watched her go, something tickling at the back of her mind. Something about the day they had gone to help Alba pack up.

She glanced at the bandstand. Bea was crooning her way through "What'll I Do," and couples were dancing with their cheeks pressed close together. The song was almost over. Vivian hurried toward the dressing room, wanting to beat her friend there.

She found Alba wiping her face with a damp napkin. A sharp, sour smell filled the air. "You all right?" Vivian asked.

"Never better," Alba said sarcastically, then sighed. "Ignore me. I'm fine. This is just no fun." She leaned over Bea's dressing table to reapply her lipstick. Glancing past her reflection, she saw that Vivian was still watching her. "Need something?"

"Yeah, I do," Vivian said. She bit her lip, not sure how to say what she needed to. Finally, she settled on, "I noticed that you like to draw, Alba. I saw your sketches when we helped you pack up."

Alba's hands stilled for a whisper of a moment, then she capped the lipstick with a decisive click and pressed her lips together to smooth out the color. "Yeah, I do. Is that a problem?"

"It might be," Vivian said quietly. "Because you had kind of a distinctive style of sketching. And I've seen something like that pretty recently."

Alba set down her lipstick and turned around slowly. "Oh?"

Vivian could hear the sound of applause through the door as the song finished. Alba didn't move, and neither did she. "You ever drawn a hemlock plant before, Alba?"

The silence in the room crackled as they stared at each other.

"Well?" Vivian asked. But she had to catch her breath to say it. Alba's silence had stretched out long enough to be its own answer. "We've only got a few seconds before someone comes through that door, so you'd better start talking."

Alba looked away long enough to scoop up a lighter and a package of cigarettes from Bea's dressing table. She lit one with shaking hands. "Have you told Beatrice?" she asked at last.

"Told me what?"

They both jumped. Bea was just closing the door to the dressing room behind her, her sharp brows pulled together in a frown. "Everything all right in here?"

"Of course it is," Alba said quickly, at the exact time that Vivian answered, "No, it's really not." They both stared at each other. Alba's eyes were blazing, and there was sweat across her forehead.

"If you don't want to tell her, I'm happy to do it for you," Vivian said coldly.

"Tell me what?" Bea insisted, glancing between them. "What the hell is going on?"

"Alba has something to tell you about those letters," Vivian said, not turning to look at Bea. She didn't want to take her eyes off Alba. "See, yesterday I finally saw one that had been written and sent weeks ago, and it looked nothing like the ones Pearlie and Florence got."

"Who's Florence?" Alba asked, but Vivian didn't bother answering.

"It was typed, not written. And it had a curious sort of signature. Someone had drawn a hemlock plant at the bottom. And a little bird told me recently that there're rumors of some new operation popping up around where we live. Apparently, they've got a thing for poisons, and they've got a little bit of style to go with it. So they like to use a little drawing just like that, a hemlock leaf, as a calling card."

"What does that have to do with Alba?" Bea asked, her voice shaking. Vivian looked at her friend at last. Bea's brown eyes were wide and wild. She knew exactly where Vivian was heading with this. But she didn't want to believe it.

"A little drawing just like the ones she does," Vivian said gently. "She's not denying it. Are you, Alba?" she added, turning back.

The three women stared at each other, none of them speaking for a painful moment. They could hear the music, a sultry, eerie tango, slinking under the door along with the heat from the dance floor. The cigarette between Alba's fingers was still burning, ash tumbling toward the ground, the glowing tip closer and closer to her fingers.

"I thought you loved Pearlie," Bea said, her voice cracking.

Alba gave her a pitying look. "Don't be stupid. He was a fun time, and so am I. It didn't need to be anything more than that."

"Tell me what happened, then," Bea said, her voice growing louder. Vivian put a hand on her arm to remind her where they were, but Bea shook her off. She took a step closer to Alba. "You were working with them, too? You the one who got Pearlie mixed up in all this?"

"No."

"What happened to my uncle?" Bea was practically yelling.

"Oh, for God's sake, Bea, it was Pearlie the whole damn time, okay?" Alba's voice cracked out like a whip, like poison, like a tray of crystal glasses smashing to the ground and leaving stunned silence in its wake. "I was just along for the ride. Your precious uncle was the one sending people letters and robbing them blind."

TWENTY-FOUR

The song in the next room slithered to an end, and the brief silence seemed to echo around them. Alba's words hung in the air. Vivian stared at her, just as much in shock as Bea was.

"No." Bea shook her head at last. "No, Pearlie wouldn't have done that."

"Of course he would have." Alba ground out her cigarette in the ashtray on the dressing table. The anger coiled in the gesture made Vivian flinch. "Did you know him at all, girl? He left Baltimore because he'd swindled too many folks there and had to get out of town. Why did you think your mother didn't ever want you asking him questions?"

Bea's face had crumpled. "No. No, he wouldn't . . . Pearlie didn't want to hurt people. I *know* he wouldn't do that."

"No, he didn't want to hurt people." Alba rolled her eyes, then grimaced, one hand going to the small of her back and the other gripping the chair next to her tightly. "But he didn't mind taking what was theirs. New York was a big playground to a fella like him, and he planned to set himself up real sweet here. He meant to take his time doing it, but he had to get creative pretty quick after he found out he'd be taking care of me and a baby, too. He wanted money fast, and we figured those letters were a way to get it."

Bea was still shaking her head, and she reached out blindly to take Vivian's hand like she was groping for a lifeline. Vivian squeezed it hard, wanting to comfort Bea, wanting to make it all go away. The band had struck up a waltz, and the sound of it—far too sweet for what was happening in the dressing room—made Vivian feel like she was floating in an ugly dream. She felt sick as she asked, "Whose idea was it?"

"Pearlie's." Alba was almost smiling, as if the memory amused her. "He asked me to draw the hemlock branch on it. He wanted some flair. Something that would make folks sit up and take notice, make them scared when they got it. It was working, too. Eventually, once folks got scared enough, he planned to start running a protection racket, and then he wouldn't need to bother with actually stealing anything at all."

"And what about Abraham?" Vivian demanded.

"What do you mean, what about Abraham?" Bea shook her head, hands raised as if to ward off whatever Vivian might say. "I can't believe . . . He couldn't have had anything to do with it. Not him too," she added desperately. "God, is every man I know a criminal?"

"He had something to do with it," Vivian insisted. "Isn't that right, Alba? You got all nervous when you heard me mention him last night. And he didn't get that necklace Bea's wearing from a pawnshop. So was he stealing things, too?"

"Not him," Alba sighed. Bea let out a long, shaky breath of relief, her hands rising to press against her eyes as though she were desperate to hide. "He's got a cab, right? And Pearlie needed a driver to get him out of places quick. Abraham didn't ask too many questions, because he's not stupid, but of course he knew something was going on. After a few jobs, he decided he wanted out. Pearlie didn't have cash to pay him that time, so he gave him that necklace."

Bea's hand went to her collarbone. "So it was stolen."

"Yes," Alba said, enunciating very slowly, as if spelling it out for them. "It was stolen, Beatrice. Your darling uncle stole it, and your sweet fella took it as payment, and he was smart enough not to ask any questions he didn't need to ask. Which is apparently smarter than you."

"But . . ." Bea pulled herself together with visible effort. "Pearlie couldn't have sent that letter to himself, then. Or the one that Vivian's sister got. And they didn't have the drawing, so you didn't send them either, did you?"

"Aren't you sharp as a tack." Alba regarded them scornfully, impatient with how long it was taking them to put the pieces together. "Why do you think I've been keeping my mouth shut? If it was someone else trying to weasel in on his game, it's not like I could bring Pearlie back to life by telling anyone what was going on and taking the fall for him. And if someone was trying to get back at Pearlie for what he did . . ." She shivered, looking nervous for the first time. "I sure as hell didn't want them to know I was involved." Alba lit another cigarette, inhaling shakily as if to steady her nerves. "He wasn't a bad man," she added, her voice growing more gentle.

"He was stealing from poor folks," Bea snapped. Vivian was glad; she had wanted to say it herself, but she didn't feel like she had the right to, not with Bea standing there. "From people who were already barely hanging on."

"If it makes you feel better, he'd have preferred to steal from rich folks. But he had to work with what he could."

"Oh, okay, then." The sarcasm in Bea's voice was painful to hear. She had loved her uncle. If Vivian had known what would come to light about him, she would have kept her mouth shut. But there was no going back now. "You trying to tell me that makes him a good man?"

"I'm telling you that makes him a person, same as anyone else, and a lot better than some. He treated me better than my own family does, and he was crazy about you and the kids. He meant it when he said he was taking you all out of here," Alba said, sniffing a little. "He mighta been a criminal, but family was everything to him. He was so excited when I told him about the baby. Said he always wanted to be someone's dad." Her mouth twisted as though she were trying not to cry, but her eyes were hard.

"So what am I supposed to do now?" Bea said, sounding lost.

"You move on with your life," Alba said. Her voice was relentless but not cruel. For all she had said she didn't love Pearlie, there were tears on her cheeks, and she brushed those angrily away. "Not many other choices."

"But someone killed him," Bea said. It sounded like a plea. "Don't we have to—"

"No," Alba said. "Yes, someone did it. And whoever it is, I'll hate them until I die, because it's their fault my kid's going to grow up without a father. But I'm not stupid. I've got a baby to take care of. And I don't have a death wish."

"Beatrice?"

All three of them jumped as someone knocked on the dressing room door. Ellie poked her head in. "They want you back on the bandstand." She frowned at the three of them. "Everything all right?"

"Everything's swell," Alba said, taking another drag from her cigarette. "Just a bit of girl talk, is all. Bea, you'd better hustle."

Without another word, Bea turned on her heel and followed after Ellie. She didn't look at Vivian or Alba as she left. Alba stubbed out her cigarette, then glanced at Vivian. "You coming?"

Vivian wondered if her friend would ever forgive her. She nodded and followed Alba out of the dressing room.

"Someone's keeping it going, though," she said. "They're still threatening people. You and Pearlie might have had some rules that you followed, but they sure as hell don't."

"Leave it alone, Vivian," Alba advised. "Your sister got a letter, right?

And you did what it said?" At Vivian's nod, she smiled humorlessly. "So she's okay, and so are you. Sometimes, that's as good as it gets."

"And what about the next person to get a letter?" Vivian asked softly.

"They'll figure out how to survive, same as you did. Come on. Danny's making eyes at us, and not the come-hither kind. Time to get back to work."

Up on the bandstand, Bea was belting her heart out with manic energy, the band exchanging worried looks as they worked to keep up with her. The dancers loved it, though.

Slowly, Vivian followed Alba back to the bar, wondering if she was telling the whole truth.

When Abraham strolled in that night, Danny had already rung the bell for last call. Bea was up on the bandstand, beginning a plaintive version of "Sinful Blues" for her last song of the night. Whatever anger or pain or sorrow she was feeling, it all poured into the music. The dancers on the floor looked happy for the reprieve from the fast pace the band had set all night. But around the edges of the room, the crowd murmured in a different kind of appreciation, eyes locked on Bea. Vivian was watching her too, her attention only half on her work, so she noticed the instant Bea's demeanor changed.

There was no change in her singing, but Vivian could see her tense as if an electric current had been run up her spine, and for a moment her gaze followed someone across the room before she remembered where she was.

Vivian turned to see where her friend had been staring and saw Abraham just taking a seat at the bar. He looked dapper as ever, his hat tucked under one arm as he ordered a drink, and he leaned back against the counter to smile appreciatively, his eyes half-closed behind his spectacles, as he watched Bea at the front of the room.

He was a man who didn't know he had been found out.

Vivian was in the middle of clearing glasses from the tables; as soon as her tray was full, she left it at the bar and made her way through the thinning crowd to him.

"Dance with me," Vivian said quietly. It was more of a request than an order, and he gave her a skeptical, almost suspicious look in response. They didn't know each other well, and Vivian had always thought he didn't really like or trust her. The feeling was mutual now.

He gave her a slow look up and down, his face impossible to read. Then he tossed his hat on the bar, unfolded his lanky body from the stool, and held out his hand.

Abraham wasn't a great dancer. He spent his nights in a cab rather than on the dance floor. But he clearly enjoyed the music, and in other circumstances, that might have been enough for her to have fun on the floor with him. But not this time.

"She knows," Vivian said quietly as soon as they were flowing through the line of the dance.

Abraham missed a step. "What, now?"

"Bea knows." Her head was close enough to his that she could keep her voice to a murmur. She didn't take her eyes off him as she spoke, wanting to see every flicker of his reaction. "She knows you lied to her about that necklace. She knows about the work you did with Pearlie."

He had a lousy poker face. His eyes darted toward Bea, then back to Vivian, but he looked away again as he replied, "I don't know what you're talking about."

How had Pearlie ever thought it was safe to get him involved in something illegal?

Vivian smiled sadly. "You're a terrible liar, Abraham. I wouldn't recommend trying that line with Bea. Not unless you want her to send you packing for good."

He looked around nervously again before turning back to her, and he scowled. "Look, I don't know what you've been telling her—"

"Alba told us."

He stumbled again. "Alba?"

"Alba," Vivian said relentlessly. He was sweating now, but she didn't let him look away from her. "You might not have asked Pearlie for details, but you had some idea what he was up to, didn't you?"

"Look—" As the music ended, he pulled her quickly off the dance floor. The dancers and drinkers were drifting out in ones and twos and threes, heading for cabs and home, ready to collapse into their beds. The band struck up one last song, a cheerful one for the end of the night, just instruments. For the moment, the corner that he pulled her toward was empty.

"I didn't do anything," he insisted. "Bea's got nothing to hold against me."

"You're sweating hard enough that I don't think you believe that yourself, Abraham. So why should I believe it?"

"Because I didn't—" He broke off, rubbing at his face with both hands. "I drove for Pearlie, all right? When he needed a car waiting for him late at night. And sure, I didn't ask what he was doing. I waited, and then as soon as he hopped in and said go, I went. But I was doing it for me and Bea, all right? Just a little extra dough here and there."

"What for?" Vivian insisted.

He sighed. "Just a little nest egg, all right? Fella can't ask a girl to marry him if he's got no money."

Vivian caught her breath, glancing over his shoulder for just a moment before her eyes fixed on him once more. "You're planning on asking her to marry you?"

"One day, sure." He scowled at her, not noticing her wandering attention. "I'm not just hanging around for fun, you know. Not like the sort of fella you find here. I'm not in any rush, but I'm gonna plan for the future. Or I was planning. If you and Alba ruined things for me—"

"I'm not the one who made you drive Pearlie's getaway car," Vivian said coldly. "If anything's ruined, you did it yourself."

"Well, I gave it up, anyway," Abraham said. "I got spooked when Pearlie crawled into my car bleeding all over the place, and I had to get him stitched up at three in the morning."

That made Vivian give him a considering look. "How'd he get hurt?"

"He wouldn't say, and I knew better than to ask," Abraham sighed. "And when I had to spend half the next day scrubbing blood out of my back seat, I decided I wasn't cut out for the criminal life. So that was that." He gave her a narrow-eyed look. "What tipped you girls off?"

"The necklace," Vivian said after a moment. Bea had talked to him about it already, so there was no point trying to keep it a secret. "Someone described a stolen necklace to me that was a little too much like the one Bea started wearing. And I knew she wasn't the one sending those letters or robbing folks. So that left you."

"Well, I didn't do either of those things," Abraham insisted. "I just drove the car, and I didn't much like how that ended up, anyway."

Vivian nodded slowly. "What do you think, Bea?" she asked, glancing over his shoulder again. "Do you believe him?"

A look of horror slowly crept across Abraham's face, and he turned to where Bea was standing just behind him, listening to their whole conversation. "Bea . . ." he began, then trailed off. None of them moved.

"Got anything more to that sentence?" Bea asked, tilting her head as she eyed him.

"I just . . . I'd never do anything to hurt anyone, you know that, right?" He gave her a shaky smile, but it faded when her expression didn't change.

"Then why did you lie to me?"

"I didn't . . . I was just . . ." He grimaced, looking toward the ceiling before meeting her eyes again. "Look, neither of us are saints. So now we've both had jobs that skirt the line of legal. Is it really worth getting so upset over?"

"Are you trying to tell me you think serving folks a drink or two is the same thing as stealing from a family with kids to feed?" Bea asked, her voice icy as winter.

Abraham winced. "I didn't know he was stealing. Not really," he said, starting to sound a little desperate. "Sure, yes, I knew it wasn't aboveboard, but I had no idea what was actually happening. I just drove the car. For all I knew, that necklace belonged to his mother. I just . . ." He sighed. "I didn't ask questions. I never ask a question if I don't want to know the answer."

Vivian had thought before that his poker face was terrible, so she wanted to believe that he was telling the truth now. But there was no way to know whether any or all of the night had been an act for him. She glanced at Bea, who was watching him impassively as Alba joined them, her hands full of her and Bea's things, glancing between the three faces.

"You finished having it out yet?" she asked, rubbing the small of her back. Her shoes were dangling from one hand. All around them, the last few customers were being shooed out to the street. "I'm dead on my feet, and Honor said I could skip cleanup tonight."

The last dancer was gone, and the lights began to flicker on one by one so the staff could clean up. The harshness of the electric bulbs, the stark way they illuminated the room and stripped it of its magic, felt only too fitting.

"Abraham was just about to take us home," Bea agreed at last. It was impossible to tell by her voice what she was thinking or whether she believed what he had told her.

"Yes, of course, absolutely," Abraham said quickly, nodding. "Happy to. It's why I'm here. You need a hand, Alba?" Taking their bags and shoes, he gave Bea a sad, hopeful smile. "I'm crazy about you, Bea. I'd do anything for you. You know that."

"Anything except tell me the truth?"

Abraham's smile crumpled. "I'd already decided I didn't want to be part of it anymore. The last thing I wanted was to put you in the middle of it, too." He shrugged. "I got around to the truth eventually, anyway."

"Eventually," Bea agreed. There was no sign in her expression whether she was willing to forgive him—or even believe him. Reaching behind her neck, she unclasped the gold necklace and held it out to Vivian. "Any chance you could get this back to where it belongs?"

"Sure thing," Vivian agreed, closing her hand around the locket and chain. She'd pop it in the mail or something—no sense letting anyone know she was more involved than they might already have guessed.

"You're right about one thing, baby," Bea said to Abraham, her smile sad. "It's a bad idea to ask a question if you're not sure you want to know the answer." She glanced at Alba. "And here I thought I was the sort of girl who didn't have any illusions left."

Alba's smile was somehow sympathetic and ruthless at the same time. "We all get there eventually."

Vivian watched them leave until she felt someone at her elbow. She glanced over her shoulder to find Danny standing there, frowning.

"What was that about?" he asked.

Vivian looked at him, wondering if she was brave enough to ask him about Florence, not sure whether it would be worse if he said his flirting wasn't serious or said that it was. "Nothing much," Vivian lied. There were some questions she didn't want to know the answer to either.

TWENTY-FIVE

What is going on with you this morning?"

Vivian jumped, realizing she'd been staring down at her shoes for over a minute without putting them on. When she looked up, Florence was frowning at her. "Did something happen last night?"

"No," Vivian said immediately. But she sighed when Florence gave her a pointed look. "Bea and Abraham got in a fight. She found out some things about Pearlie that . . . she didn't want to know."

"Anything to do with . . ." Florence trailed off, looking unsure.

"Do you want me to tell you?" Vivian asked, brows rising.

Florence sighed. "No, I really don't. Not if I don't need to know."

"Then come on," Vivian said, standing at last. "Mrs. Chin wanted us to mail a package on our way to work."

Mrs. Chin's errand took them along Greene Street, just past the address she had slipped Vivian the day before. Vivian wondered if that was on purpose or not. While Florence stepped inside the post office, Vivian lingered on the sidewalk, ignoring the sea of humanity that flowed around her, and stared at the building where Mr. Sun lived. There was a restaurant on the ground floor doing a bustling morning business. From above, she could hear shouts and laughter and children yelling in a way that was all too familiar.

"What are you staring at?"

Vivian jumped as Florence spoke next to her; apparently she'd been standing there for longer than she realized. She glanced around, worried that someone might have been able to follow them while she was distracted. But no one in the crowd stood out; in fact, they were the only ones standing still.

Them and one elderly man, with a head full of white hair and a neatly trimmed gray beard, who leaned on his cane and stared at them from the narrow doorway next to the restaurant's entrance.

It was the man she had seen that spring day on Baxter Street. And he was looking directly at them.

"Vivi?"

Vivian didn't answer her sister, too busy staring at the man, who stared right back at them as though he had seen a ghost. Vivian caught her breath and, without thinking, took a step toward him.

"Mr. Sun?" she whispered.

To her surprise, Mr. Sun reached out, his hand shaking, and laid a gentle palm against her cheek. His hand was rough, callused from years of work, but she didn't pull away. "My memory does not always do what I wish these days, and I cannot recall your name," he murmured. "But you look just like her." He smiled. "Aside from the hair. Mae had very memorable hair."

"How did you know her?" Vivian said, her voice hoarse. Next to her, Florence wasn't moving, and Vivian could almost feel the disbelief and hope radiating from her.

"I met her when she first moved to New York. She got lost riding the subway train and ended up in front of my door, asking for help. I was happy to rescue her." Mr. Sun dropped his hand slowly and turned to Florence, smiling. "I remember the first time I met you. Such a little bit of a thing. Such big eyes, looking at the whole world like you didn't trust it. I can see not much has changed." He chuckled at the memory. "And you . . ." He turned back to Vivian. "You could never stay still. Even when your mother carried you, she said you were always dancing and twirling."

"That hasn't changed either," Florence said, her voice shaking.

Mr. Sun's expression grew sad. "She disappeared when you were still so little. But here you are. I did not believe it when I heard you were asking about me."

Beside her, Vivian heard Florence's sharp intake of breath as she realized that this meeting wasn't a coincidence.

Mr. Sun was still speaking. "But I looked out the window, and there you were. I thought I was dreaming." He frowned. "Have I dreamed about you before?"

"In the spring," Vivian said, trying not to sound too surprised. His hair was white and gray, and there were some lines on his face, but his body did not look stooped or aged. He was not that old—perhaps in his fifties or sixties? But he spoke like a much older man. "You were sick on the street."

"Ah, yes." But he frowned and shook his head. "My memories of things that have happened a short while ago are much harder to find these days. But the things that happened many years ago . . ." He smiled. "Those I remember. I remember your mother. She was so pretty. And often so sad."

"Are you . . ." Vivian hesitated, not sure which answer she wanted. But she couldn't stop thinking of what Danny had told them. "Are you our father?"

He shook his head, but he was smiling. "No. I think I am old enough to be your grandfather, but I am not that either. She lived next door to me."

"Then do you know—"

"Yéye!" Mr. Sun had left the door open behind him, and the call came from inside its long, dark hallway. A girl came rushing out, breathless and looking worried. She was maybe a year or two older than Florence. And in spite of her hurry, she was still gentle as she took his arm. "Yéye, don't wander off like that, you scared me!"

"I had to speak to Mae's little girls," Mr. Sun explained, smiling as he gestured toward Vivian and Florence. Then he frowned at the girl. "Are you my nurse?"

The pain in her expression was quickly covered with a smile. "No, Yéye," she said gently. "I'm your granddaughter. Hu Dandan is your nurse," she added, beckoning toward the door. An older woman waited there, looking stern and competent and gentle as she took the man's arm to lead him back inside. "You know you're not supposed to go outside alone."

"It is hard for me to remember things these days," Mr. Sun said. He smiled as he said it, not seeming to be very bothered by the fact. But a moment later his smile faded, and he pressed one hand against his chest. "I remember this pain, though. I think I should go sit down."

His granddaughter looked worried. "That's a good idea. Hu Dandan will take you back upstairs. I'll follow in just a moment."

"Of course." Mr. Sun turned his smile to Vivian and Florence. "You will come see me again, I hope, so we can talk more of Mae Kelly." His expression became thoughtful as his nurse led him inside. "I have not talked of her in many years."

As soon as they had disappeared, his granddaughter's expression drooped, weariness showing through the patience and gentleness. "You will forgive me for asking, but what was he saying to you? His mind wanders these days, and we struggle sometimes to keep him safe."

"He knew our mother," Florence said faintly. She sounded like she couldn't believe it.

Seeing the woman's confused, slightly alarmed expression, Vivian added, "She died when we were very little. So to find someone who remembered her . . ."

"So it is not a coincidence you were standing on the street outside our home."

"No," Vivian admitted. "I was looking for him."

"Do you live near here?" the girl asked, her eyes narrowing a little.

"Just staying for a little while," Vivian explained, trying not to shift nervously under the girl's assessing stare. "Do you know Chin's Chop Suey?"

Some of the wariness faded from the girl's expression. "You know the Chins."

"Yes." Vivian nodded quickly. "I asked about your grandfather. He called me by our mother's name once, when we met before. He said . . . he said just now that he remembers things from the past better than those that are more recent," she added, hoping that it had been true.

"Yes." Mr. Sun's granddaughter sighed. "The past is like a moment ago in his mind. It is things like 'don't go outside alone or you may become lost' that he struggles to remember. At least he wasn't just wandering away."

"We're sorry," Florence said quickly, giving Vivian a quick, nervous glance. "We didn't mean to cause any trouble."

The girl sighed again. "He likes speaking of the past. Perhaps it would be good for him to talk of your mother." The glance she gave them was curious and a little disbelieving, but she shrugged. "Come by tomorrow. For today, he needs to rest."

"Of course," Florence said quickly, taking Vivian's arm and giving it a little tug. "We wish him well. And thank you."

"Yes, thank you," Vivian agreed. It was almost painful to be so close and to be sent away. But Mr. Sun hadn't seemed well, and she couldn't argue with his granddaughter. "We'll be by tomorrow."

Florence didn't speak again until they were sitting side by side on the streetcar, headed to Miss Ethel's shop.

"Flo?" Vivian asked cautiously. "You okay?"

"He knew our mother," Florence said quietly. Vivian's hand was resting between them on the seat; without looking, Florence reached out and took it, squeezing so hard it was almost painful. "I can't believe it. He knew our mother."

"We'll go back tomorrow," Vivian promised. "We have to."

The breath Florence let out was shaky, but she nodded. "Yes," she agreed. "We have to."

They saw the police cars parked outside Miss Ethel's shop while they were still down the street. Vivian's steps slowed, and Florence stopped completely, clutching her sister's hand. "Vivi, you don't think—"

"No, I'm sure not," Vivian said, even though she was far from sure. "Maybe—"

Before she could say any more, their attention was caught by a low whistle. Glancing in the direction of the sound, Vivian spotted a man in a suit, his hat pulled low, leaning casually against a lamppost near the entrance to an alley. He was almost directly across the street from Miss Ethel's store, but not quite; anyone glancing out the shop window would have to crane their neck just a bit to see him.

For a moment, Vivian almost stopped breathing. Then the man lifted his chin enough for her to see his face before gesturing with his head for them to follow as he ducked into the alley. Grabbing Florence's hand, Vivian followed him as fast as she could without running, keeping her head turned away from the store across the street in the hope that no one would glance out and see them.

"What are you doing here?" she demanded, while Florence looked around the alley uneasily. "What are *they* doing here?"

"I don't know," Leo said, glancing across the street where two officers were just entering the shop. "That's what I'm here to find out. And I wanted to try to catch you two girls first."

"How did you know they'd be here?" Florence asked, eyes wide and worried.

"Police use the radio like everyone else these days," Leo said with a shrug. "If you know what station they broadcast on, it's easy to listen in. Dispatcher gives out addresses where they need someone to go. I recognized this one."

"Should we . . . we have to go to work, don't we?" Florence asked, wringing her hands. Vivian waited for the lecture that she was sure was coming, but it didn't come.

"I don't think you should," Leo said, his expression very serious as he looked at Vivian. "I hate the thought of you taking a risk like that."

"I already took the risk," Vivian said quietly. "These are just the consequences. And we don't know for sure anything is happening." She peered out of the alley. "Doesn't seem to be any sort of big commotion, so they might not be here looking for anyone specific. And if they are, it'll look worse if we don't show up."

"It will, won't it?" Florence sighed. Her hands were trembling, but she squared her shoulders and took a deep breath. "Come on, Vivi. We've been through worse."

Vivian glanced at Leo again. "Can you stick around for a bit?"

"Sure thing. If I see you get carted off . . ." He had been trying to smile, but it didn't quite take, and he cleared his throat. Apparently that was a joke even Leo couldn't make. "If I see anything happen, I'll do what I can to get you out of it."

"Thanks," Vivian said, squeezing his arm. "You're a peach."

"Thank you," Florence echoed faintly. She reached out to take

Vivian's hand and held it tightly for a brief, comforting moment. Then they crossed the street together.

Heads turned to glance their way when they came in, but no one jumped up or pointed at them, and they weren't immediately arrested. The shop was in disarray, Miss Ethel fluttering her hands and her workers standing around as though they didn't know what to do with themselves. Vivian tried not to look too obviously relieved as she and Florence scooted their way back to where the other girls were clustered and waiting, all of them, she was glad to see, looking just as confused as she felt.

The commotion was caused by two different groups. At the front, a team of workers was repairing the door, which had been boarded up, and replacing it with a new one that lacked a window. But heading toward the basement were two police officers, flashlights in hand and grim expressions on their faces.

"I told Mrs. Blake that the dress disappeared the night of the robbery," Miss Ethel protested, wringing her hands and trying to stand in their way. "I don't see why she's . . . Why do you have to shut down my store?"

"To do a full investigation," one of them said. Vivian held back a quiet gasp. She recognized that gruff voice. "We can't do that if the place is swarming with customers. Or with your girls, there," he added, gesturing toward the huddle of anxious-looking workers.

"But there are very expensive materials stored down there," Miss Ethel protested, still trying to block their path. "And with the window broken up front, surely the basement isn't—"

"It pays to be thorough," said the other officer, his deep voice just as familiar as his partner's. "So we'll need you to stand aside. Unless there's some reason you don't want us down there?"

Miss Ethel sighed, pulling out a lacy handkerchief to pat at her flushed cheeks. "Just please be careful of my stock. I cannot afford to have anything else damaged."

"In fact, it would be better if you sent all these girls home," Deep Voice said. "Easier for us to work if it's less crowded."

His eyes drifted over the seamstresses clustered at the back of the shop. Vivian tried not to flinch as his eyes fixed on her before sliding to Florence. He hadn't seen her that night, she reminded herself. There was no chance of him recognizing her. Leo, on the other hand . . .

"But my business—" Miss Ethel threw up her hands. "Very well. Go home, girls. No work for the next few days while these gentlemen do their investigating. We'll reopen when they say we might. If there's anything to reopen when all my customers realize their orders will be late," she added acidly, glaring at the two officers.

A murmur of worry ran through the shop's workers, and Florence gave Vivian a panicked look. Vivian felt sick as she glanced at the girls around her. If her theft cost them all their livelihoods . . .

"And I'm not running a charity here," Miss Ethel continued. "You'll be paid for the hours you work, not the ones you sit at home. And Vivian." Her tone became sharp, but she looked almost pleased. "You have deliveries to make. If you were still a seamstress, perhaps you could have a holiday with the other girls." Her tone was mocking, but underlying it was a hint of satisfaction.

As much as Vivian bristled at it, she couldn't quite blame her for finding her triumphs where she could. She was already a mess of nerves and guilt—they hadn't left anything in the cellar, had they?—so she kept her head down and nodded obediently. "Of course, Miss Ethel. Right away."

There were three dress boxes on the counter, wide and flat and unwieldy. But Vivian didn't complain as she juggled them into place. The other girls were talking quietly as they gathered their things, wondering what the officers might find and what they would do if the store couldn't reopen. Florence kept darting nervous glances at the police, followed by one too many glances at her sister for Vivian's comfort. Clearing her throat to catch Florence's attention, she jerked her head toward the door, and Florence, after a last nervous look and gulp, hurried out.

"It doesn't help if you keep looking at me like I'm a criminal," Vivian muttered as they crossed the street, drifting away from the other girls.

"I'm sorry," Florence whispered back. "I'm just not used to . . . They're not going to find anything, are they?"

"Of course not," Vivian said, with more confidence than she felt. "Nothing to find." She glanced around. "Are you going to be okay heading back downtown on your own?"

"Are you going to be safe doing deliveries on your own?" Florence countered as they paused in front of the alley. "I know you said you took care of everything, but . . ."

"Let's walk, girls." Leo's voice was quiet as he fell in step beside them. "It never pays to linger when there are cops around."

"Pull your hat down a bit more," Vivian whispered. "The two cops in there might have a good reason to remember you."

Leo followed her suggestion instantly. "Now, where are you girls headed?"

There was a drugstore not far away with a telephone booth inside; Leo insisted that they call Danny to let him know Florence was on her way back. "And don't make any stops on the way," Vivian cautioned as they waited for Florence's subway train. "No sense taking any chances."

"And what about you?"

"I'll go with you while you do your deliveries," Leo said quickly. "Sound okay, Viv?"

"Fine by me," she agreed. Two sets of eyes were better than one. And while she didn't like the idea of Florence going off on her own,

Danny would meet her at the subway stop to make sure she got back safely.

She didn't mention the Fitz Special currently tucked into her purse. There was no reason to make Florence worry any more than she already was.

"All right." Once Florence was gone, Leo took the boxes from Vivian's arms. "Where are we heading first?"

"Upper East Side." Vivian rolled her eyes. "It's almost always Upper East Side."

"Great." Leo smiled. "Assuming we don't get murdered on the way, that means I can take you to lunch once these are off our hands."

"Sounds swell." Vivian couldn't quite match his lighthearted tone. "A few things happened last night that you might want to know."

"Pearlie?" Leo's fork hung frozen in mid-air as he stared at her. "Pearlie was writing those letters?"

"The original ones." Vivian nodded as she poked at her lunch. The place Leo had brought her was a cute little diner run by a Polish couple, both of them gray-haired and red-cheeked. The food was good, but thinking about Bea's face the night before had left her feeling like there was a pit in the bottom of her stomach, and eating just made it worse. She put her own fork down and leaned toward him. "And now there's apparently cops involved? It gives me the shivers. I want to think that since they got the dress, and I didn't see who they were, they'll leave us alone now. But how can I be sure?"

"It makes sense," Leo said, pushing his mostly empty plate away and setting his elbows on the counter where they were seated. The server was several feet away, helping another customer, and most of the other folks in the restaurant were at tables instead of the counter. But he still lowered his voice even further. "Someone got rid of that brandy bottle. The only people who could get close enough to evidence to do that either work at Bellevue or for the police."

"I don't suppose there's some unspoken list of dirty cops out there?" Vivian asked without much hope. The tables in the restaurant were covered with lace-edged tablecloths, and a cheerful yellow curtain hung over the bottom half of each window. The counter even had little jars full of flowers spaced along it, next to the morning's paper. But all she could see were the shadows in the corner of the room. "Guys that everyone knows about but no one talks about?"

Leo shrugged, grimacing. "Sure, to some degree," he said. His hat rested next to his plate on the counter, and he absently spun it in circles as he thought. "But I'm not in with them enough to know many details. The only guys I know are the ones my uncle has specifically asked me to work with, and even they don't like me much. But I don't think that'll help us narrow it down. Plenty of cops in bed with mobsters these days. Just look at today's paper."

"I didn't see it," Vivian said, shrugging. "Not much for keeping up with the news. Especially not this week. I always figure it doesn't have much to do with folks like me."

"Here." Leo stood, reaching out to snag one of the papers that was a few feet away from where they were sitting. He shuffled through the pages, then refolded it and slid it toward her. "See there, cop who was killed last month in a suspected mob hit. Young fella, too."

The article was a profile of the young officer's service, accompanied by quotes from his fellow officers. Most of the photos were from what looked like his funeral, full of flags and medals and a horse-drawn hearse. But one of the photos was him in uniform. He hadn't been a good-looking man; his nose was too big for his face, and his eyebrows gave his eyes a scowling expression, even though he was smiling at the camera. But something about the photo made Vivian frown.

"You knew him?" she asked.

"I worked with him when I first came back to the city, just a quick, one-night job for my uncle. And he was dirty as they come. If he got offed in a mob hit, it was probably whoever he was working for tying up some loose ends. Or someone sending the fella he worked for a message. Either way . . ." Leo shrugged. "Everyone's got a racket on the side. It's almost a job requirement."

It reminded her too much of what Hattie Wilson had described. Vivian shivered, wondering if it was the same man, trying to pay off his family debts and losing his life for his trouble. "He was real young," Vivian said quietly, glancing through the pictures, but she trailed off as one in particular caught her eye. "Hey, anyone in this look familiar to you?"

She slid the paper over so Leo could take a look at the photo from the funeral, and he frowned in thought as he stared at it. "That guy at the front, in the dress uniform. I think I've seen him before, but I couldn't say where."

"I think he was the one at the pawnshop," Vivian said. In the photograph, the man's face was drawn into a tight expression that showed no emotion at all. Serious and stoic, like the rest of the officers around him. "Arthur, the owner called him. Does it say who he is?"

"Caption says he was the poor bastard's dad." Leo let out a low whistle, shaking his head sympathetically. "Gambling problem and a son getting offed on a boss's orders? Tough time for him. No wonder he said he was getting out of New York."

"His dad?" Vivian pulled the paper back toward her to take a closer look. "Maybe that's why the dead fella looked so familiar . . ." Her voice trailed off again as she stared at the caption, which listed the names of the officers in the picture by initial and last name. *P. Rossi, H. Gonzales, G. Flannigan* . . . She looked back at the text of the article, scanning quickly to find the name of the dead man.

"Everything okay?" Leo asked when she stopped talking.

"Yeah." Vivian gave herself a little shake as the waitress behind the counter came to take their plates away.

"Anything else, kids?" she asked.

"I'm all set, thanks," Vivian said. She pointed to the paper. "Mind if I take a copy of this?"

"Help yourself," the waitress said cheerfully, beginning to stack their dishes. "They mostly just get read by the morning crowd. Anything else for you, sir?"

"Nah, that's it for today," he agreed, pulling his wallet out from inside his jacket. "Swell meal. Where to next, Viv?"

"That's all for my day," she said, folding up the newspaper and tucking it under her arm. Leo gave it a brief glance but didn't ask why she wanted to take it with her. She was glad about that. If he had asked, she would have had to lie to him. "I'm just going to go see how Bea and her family are doing."

"I'll keep you company on the way, if you don't mind?"

Vivian couldn't have said what they talked about as they caught the nearest streetcar and headed west and south past the park. She expected him to leave her at the station, but he insisted on accompanying her to the door of Bea's building, just to be cautious.

"We still don't know if someone might be keeping an eye on you," he pointed out as they walked. "Better safe than sorry."

"Sure," Vivian agreed, not meeting his eyes, her fingers clenched around the paper. "But probably best that you don't come up. Bea's not really your biggest fan."

"Still doesn't trust me?"

Vivian made a face. "Can't quite get past who your uncle is."

"And what about you, Viv?" he asked, stopping on the sidewalk in front of Bea's building and putting a hand on her arm. "Do you trust me yet?"

She didn't want to answer flippantly, but after a moment she nodded. "I think so. I think I got there."

There was a long pause, as though he were waiting for something else. "I sure am glad to hear that," he said at last, giving her a smile and a quick kiss on the cheek.

The spot where his lips had brushed tingled. Vivian hoped she wasn't blushing. There had been plenty of sparks between her and Leo not long ago, try as she might to ignore them. As he stepped back, she wanted to reach out and pull him closer, to bury her face against his jacket and pretend she was safe and cared for, that everything around her was simple.

But just at that moment, she couldn't afford to be distracted by a handsome smile or a fella who smelled like sandalwood and wintergreen. She couldn't afford the fantasy that anything was safe or easy. And she couldn't afford to let him know what she was planning, because there was no way he would let her go without trying to stop her. Her fist tightened around the paper once more.

Leo tipped his head toward the building's door. "Go on, get up there. I'm sure Bea could use a friend right now."

It took her a beat to find her voice. "Yeah. Thanks again for lunch. I'll see you around?"

"Count on it." He waited for her to go inside the building.

Before the door closed behind her, she saw him give a quick glance around, an instinctive gesture from a man who was used to trouble following him. Then he set off down the street. Vivian took a deep breath and began to climb the stairs.

Bea was usually home alone this time of day, with her family members at work and school. She crossed her fingers that Alba was out, too.

She and Bea had a visit to make.

"Girls." Dr. Harris stepped back from the door, looking surprised as he gestured for them to come inside. "This is unexpected. Is one of you sick? Is Alba all right?"

"We're just fine," Vivian said, her voice steady. Her hand was steady, too, as she pulled the snub-nosed revolver from her purse and pointed it right at him.

Dr. Harris's eyes went wide, and he held up both hands in front of his chest as he took a quick, stumbling step back. "What—"

"I'm here for the dress," Vivian said coldly. "It doesn't belong to you, and it didn't belong to me. And Bea—" She tilted her head toward her friend, who was standing just behind her, but she didn't take her eyes off the doctor. "Bea is here for some answers." She pulled the hammer back on the revolver. "So start talking."

TWENTY-SIX

Dr. Harris stared at the two of them, Vivian with the gun pointed unwaveringly at him, Bea blocking his path toward the door. He licked his lips and tried to smile, but the expression got stuck halfway across his face, and all he could do was eye them with increasing fear. "I don't . . . I'm really not sure what you're talking about. What . . . dress, did you say? What answers? Can you please put that down, Vivian? There's no cause for violence." Another attempt at a smile. "I'm a man of medicine, not . . . not whatever it is you think is going on."

"You're a man of a lot of things, all right," Bea said, tossing down the newspaper that Vivian had showed her. It was folded back to show the photo of the dead police officer. *Sergeant Paul Harris,* the article read. He smiled out of the page, looking remarkably like the man who was standing in front of them, glancing at the paper and then back at them with increasing horror. Further down on the page, A. Harris stared stoically at the camera in a line with P. Rossi, H. Gonzales, and G. Flannigan. "And apparently, so is the rest of your family. My condolences, by the way. You said your brother and father were caught up in mob business, didn't you? And your brother died because of it? Looks like Sergeant P. Harris got in a little over his head."

"See, when I saw Mrs. Kaminski's candlesticks in a pawnshop, my first thought was that whoever was writing those letters had gotten sloppy," Vivian said conversationally. "But when the pawnshop owner told me she had pawned them herself, I couldn't figure it out. After all, you had told me she was worried about a letter that came in the mail, right? And then there she was, a death that looked like an accident, just like Pearlie, and the most valuable thing she owned missing. And then when the letter came for Florence . . . God Almighty, I was so scared I could barely think. But that's what you wanted, wasn't it?" Her free hand tightened into a fist, but the one holding the gun didn't waver. He had threatened Florence. "You were a fast thinker that day to put it in my head that Mrs. Kaminski was another victim. Did you need the money the dress could bring in? Or did you just want me so scared that we'd stop trying to find out what happened to Pearlie?"

"Maybe both," Bea said, when Dr. Harris kept his mouth firmly shut. "I thought fellas like him were supposed to take some kind of oath not to harm people. But it seems like he's only out for himself."

"I am *not,*" Dr. Harris said at last, his voice rising angrily. He was shifting ever so slightly, as though trying to edge away from them, but Vivian turned to keep him squarely in her sight. "Do you have any idea how many people I've helped since I came here? But you think I did, what, just threatened and robbed the people around me? Just for the hell of it?"

"No," Vivian said thoughtfully. "I'm guessing it had to do with your father and his gambling problem."

"How did you—"

"Who did he need to pay off?"

When he didn't answer right away, Bea suggested, "I could start looking around, if you like, while you and Vivian stay here. I might find a real pretty dress that someone reported stolen recently. If your father has a gambling problem, I'm guessing you didn't trust him to hang on to it for you." She stepped forward. "How 'bout I do a little search?"

Dr. Harris seemed to crumple, his face falling and his shoulders slumping downward. He let out a long, shaking breath as he sank into a chair at the table. He dropped his head into his hands, his elbow knocking over his doctor's bag as he did and sending its contents skittering across the table. He didn't seem to notice, and his voice was muffled as he replied, "A man by the name of Clarence Earl. He doesn't matter, not really. My brother ended up working for him to pay off my father's debts. But Dad—" His voice grew bitter. "Dad couldn't stop, and the debts kept piling up. Finally my brother decided the best way to get out was a tidy little bit of blackmail."

"Got himself bumped off for his trouble?" Vivian asked coldly. She might have felt bad for the unknown Paul Harris under other circumstances. But all she could feel was rage at the man in front of her. She did lower the gun, though. They were between him and the door, and she hated holding it, hated what it meant.

Dr. Harris lifted his head just enough to give her a disgusted look. There was a hint of exasperation, almost a whine, in his voice when he spoke. "They were going to start coming after me, too. If I couldn't pay them off, I'd end up working for them, just like my brother. And I'd probably end up six feet under just like him, too." He shook his head. "My brother might not have been able to come up with a solution, but I am far more resourceful. I just needed to pay them back. I'd convinced my father to leave the force and move outside the city, too, so he wouldn't end up underwater again. It was all perfectly arranged."

"So you settled on my uncle as the last part of your *arrangement* and sent him that bottle of brandy?" Bea asked acidly, taking a step closer to him. "How'd you even know he had money?"

"Abraham said Pearlie got hurt one night," Vivian said, suddenly remembering their conversation with Abraham. "And they needed to get him stitched up."

Bea stepped close enough to nudge Dr. Harris, who still wasn't looking at her, with her toe. "That was you?" He nodded; his elbows slid slowly out until his head and hands were resting on the table, as if holding himself up even that little amount had been too much effort. "So you decided to do, what?" Bea demanded. "Take over his business to bring in a little cash?"

"No." Dr. Harris sat bolt upright at that. "I would never do something that cheap and desperate. I had no intention of writing any of those . . . those *letters*. I found the whole thing despicable."

He sounded indignant, as though she had accused him of something disgusting or indecent. Vivian and Bea both stared at him, waiting for him to realize the irony in his statement. But he just glared at them.

"But you did end up writing them," Vivian pointed out at last, when it became clear that he wasn't willing to acknowledge that murder was far more desperate and despicable.

"Only because I had to," Dr. Harris grumbled. "And how in God's name you realized there were two letter writers . . ."

"We saw one of the originals," Vivian said, with a mocking smile. "Either you never did, or you didn't think doing a good job copying Pearlie's style mattered."

"I didn't have time to do a good job," he snapped. "It's not like I could type out a letter in the middle of Beatrice's apartment."

"That was where you wrote it?" Bea demanded. "Right under our noses?"

"That was the day we told him we didn't think Pearlie's death was a suicide," Vivian said, nodding slowly. "He must have written it out quick and slipped it in with his papers. And then he brought up his patients who had received letters of their own—which I assume is how you found out about Pearlie's scheme in the first place," she added, not taking her eyes off the doctor, who watched her resentfully. "Though I doubt you knew he was the one behind it. I'm guessing you breathed a big old sigh of relief when Bea said she was planning to leave it alone."

"It would have been smarter for you if you had," he snapped. He turned away from her as though disgusted by the whole conversation. And as he did, his hand slid across the table to where things had spilled from his black bag. Vivian saw the movement just a moment too late. His fingers had already closed around a syringe; his other hand reached out faster than she would have thought possible to grab Bea by the arm and yank her off balance.

She stumbled toward him as he stood, just as Vivian was shouting a warning. And then they all froze, Vivian with the gun raised, Bea's eyes wide with fear, and Dr. Harris gripping Bea by the arm while he held the needle of the syringe against her neck.

"I wouldn't move if I were you," he said conversationally. "If I'm startled, my finger might slip. And I don't think either of you would like what happened next."

"Let her go," Vivian said through clenched teeth.

"I really don't think I will," Dr. Harris said, almost condescendingly. He shifted his weight, maneuvering himself and Beatrice around until he was closer to the door. He took a step back toward it, Bea shuffling with him. Vivian could see her friend's breath coming in quick, shallow gasps, could see her hands trembling.

But Bea's voice was steady as she said, "How do you see this working out, Doc? You could off me, sure, but you're not getting far before Vivian gives you a case of lead poisoning."

"She'd get arrested," Dr. Harris snapped.

"Sure, but you'd still be dead." For all her obvious fear, Bea's voice was steady, and Vivian could see how it was enraging Dr. Harris. "So what's the plan?"

Vivian gave him a mocking smile. "Guessing you don't have one, Doc. Just like you didn't for this whole thing. You thought you were in the clear when we said we were giving up, and then you found out we lied."

"You really should shut up soon." Dr. Harris gave Bea a shake as he spoke, condescension dripping from his words. Vivian held back a shudder as the needle gleamed mere inches from Bea's neck. But she wouldn't let him see her afraid.

"So you convinced me that Mrs. Kaminski had been one of the victims, too. And then I was ready to do anything to keep my sister safe when a letter for her showed up."

"Poor Florence." Dr. Harris shook his head. "I hoped I wouldn't have to do anything to her. I like her very much, you know." His smile made Vivian's skin crawl. "But you did what needed to be done. I have to commend you on your resourcefulness. Ah ah ah," he warned, pulling Bea closer. "Not another step."

Vivian, who had been inching toward him, froze in place. "Let her go."

"Put your gun down, or Beatrice is getting a dose of medicine I can guarantee she doesn't want."

Slowly, hesitantly, Vivian started to lower the revolver.

"Don't listen to him, Viv."

"I said, put your gun—"

The door burst open behind the doctor, smashing into his back and sending him stumbling forward. He lost his grip on Bea, and she yanked away, but not before Vivian saw his right hand move, the syringe plunging into Bea's neck before it was knocked out of the way.

"Bea!" she yelled. She swung the gun back up, but somehow Leo was there in the room, kicking the door closed behind him as he tackled Dr. Harris.

Bea had one hand clasped to her neck, her eyes wide but her whole body still, as though waiting to see what would happen. For a moment, there was nothing. "I think it's okay," she said, letting out a relieved breath and taking a step toward Vivian.

Then her legs seemed to give way, and she crumpled to the floor.

TWENTY-SEVEN

Bea!" Vivian shrieked, dropping to her knees next to her friend.

Bea's eyes were still open, but her lashes were fluttering. "Feel all woozy," she muttered. "Vivian? What did he . . ." She trailed off, blinking rapidly. "Viv?"

Vivian could feel the hot burn of tears like something at a distance. Clutching one of Bea's hands, she turned back toward the door, trying to aim the gun at Dr. Harris. But he was grappling with Leo, and there was no clear shot.

But Dr. Harris's only advantage was the wildness that panic gave him. He wasn't a fighter. When Leo's fist connected with his jaw, he went down in a crumpled heap, whimpering and clutching his face.

Leo shook out his hand, grimacing as he stood, and kicked the doctor in the ribs for good measure before hauling the other man up and shoving him toward the opposite end of the room, far away from the door and anything else he might use as a weapon.

Vivian stumbled to her feet, the gun pointed straight at the doctor. "What did you do to her?" she demanded. "What did you *do*? Fix it! Fix it now!"

Dr. Harris had to grab the edge of a chair to keep himself upright, wincing and gasping with pain. There were tear tracks on his cheeks, and his breathing was heavy, but he gave her a gloating look. "Kick that gun over here and I'll tell you which bottle has an antidote." When Vivian hesitated, he gave a chuckle, though it made him clutch at his side. "Ticktock, Vivian. Time's running out. Kick it over here. *Now*."

Vivian stared down at Bea. With a gasped sob, she started to place the gun on the floor.

"Don't listen to him."

Leo's voice made her jump. He came to stand next to her, the syringe dangling from two fingers. When Vivian gave him a quick glance, about to argue, she was stunned to see that he was smiling. It was not a kind expression.

"It's not a poison," he said. "It's a sedative."

"Are you sure?" Vivian demanded. Her hands were shaking now, the gun trembling as she pointed it at Dr. Harris.

"It says so right on the label," Leo said, calm and reassuring. Dropping the syringe, he crushed it under one foot, and the doctor flinched at the sound. "And he only got half of it into her. Keep that gun pointed at him." Kneeling down, Leo lifted Bea so that she was supported by one arm. With the other he gently patted Bea's cheeks. "You all right, Beatrice?"

"Don't feel so good," she mumbled. But she lifted her head, and after a moment Leo was able to help her to her feet, though she had to lean heavily on him. "Where'd you come from?"

"I can tell when Viv is lying to me," he said dryly. "And you girls didn't look behind you when you were heading this way. Figured I'd tag along and see if I was needed."

"Thanks," Bea mumbled. "Guess I owe you one."

"Don't mention it. So what're we going to do about him?"

Vivian stared at Dr. Harris, and he stared back at her, his expression equal parts sullen resentment and fear. "I don't know," she said at last.

Dr. Harris drew himself up, though it made him wince. "Look, I think we can all be reasonable here. Beatrice is fine, you've got the upper hand. Congratulations. But you know you're not going to shoot me. So let's—"

"I want that dress back, first of all."

"What on earth for?" Dr. Harris asked in genuine disbelief.

"Because it's not yours," Vivian snapped. "And plenty of girls could find themselves out of work because it's gone." Her voice was shaking, and she had to take a deep breath. "Why did you want it anyway? You paid off your father's debts. And you've made it clear that theft, at least, is beneath you. So why have me steal it? Were you hoping I'd get caught and arrested?"

"I wasn't hoping anything, Vivian, I just needed to distract you. I was in a panic."

"Really?" Vivian snorted in disbelief. "Because it seems like your father was hoping I'd end up dead. He almost shot me. I assume that was your father? And that he was the same helpful cop who snatched the brandy bottle from Bellevue?" She shook her head. "Can't believe I told you about that, too."

"He wasn't supposed to shoot at you." Dr. Harris sighed, but that made him wince too, and he prodded himself in the side carefully. "I think your bruiser there broke one of my ribs."

"Happy to break more of them," Leo said with icy cheerfulness.

"Charming company you girls keep," the doctor said. "My father's job was just to watch out and make sure no one tried to follow me. Bash them over the head or something." To Vivian's surprise, he smiled at them. "Look, girls, and you, whoever you are. I may have done a questionable thing or two, but I did it for family. And I honestly tried to warn you away. I didn't want anyone else to get hurt."

"Hurt," Bea said coldly. "Is that what you call what you did to my uncle?"

"Beatrice, your uncle was robbing his coworkers and neighbors," Dr.

Harris said, shaking his head as though he were deeply disappointed. "He was hardly a saint."

"Maybe not," Bea said. "But at least he wasn't a murderer."

Dr. Harris flinched, as if the word *murderer* was one step too far. His confidence wavered for a moment, and he glanced nervously at the gun that Vivian still held. But then he pulled himself together, his smile returning.

"You've got no proof," he pointed out. "Not with your bottle of brandy missing. You'd need the police to dig up some evidence, wouldn't you?"

"You think they won't?" Leo demanded.

"We can't do anything to him and he knows it," Vivian said through clenched teeth. "His dad's a cop. There's no way we can convince any of them to look into it. Unless . . . Leo?"

He knew she was asking about his uncle, and she could hear the grimace in his voice as he spoke, though she didn't take her eyes off the doctor. "I don't think he would. Not just on my say-so, not for something like this." His voice grew colder. "But I could probably get you off if you just shot him right now."

The revolver trembled in Vivian's hand. Dr. Harris saw, and he shook his head, still smiling. "Would you shoot me, Vivian? Do you think you could live with yourself if you did that?"

She couldn't, not like this, and she knew it. But she didn't lower the gun. "Tell me why I shouldn't."

"Well, because I would prefer not to die." Dr. Harris chuckled, but the sound faded quickly as he took in their stony expressions. "And because I'm a doctor. Helping people is what I do. Do you want to take that away from your neighbors, from all the people I help around here?" Dr. Harris's voice was pleading. But there was a note of confidence in it, as though he had her all figured out. She hated that he was probably right.

"Didn't do much to help Pearlie," Bea said coldly.

"I am sorry about your uncle, Beatrice, truly," Dr. Harris said softly. "But I was desperate, and it was the only thing I could think of. I didn't have the money I needed to bail out my father, and I wasn't going to come by it any other way. Most of the people I see can't even afford to pay me. Pearlie's death . . ." He shook his head. "It was awful, it was wrong, I know that. But because of it, I can keep doing the work I need to do. How many lives do you think I've saved, Beatrice? How many babies do you think I can save next?"

"Is that the story you told yourself to pretend you were the hero?" Bea asked, and her voice was shaking. "Vivian, just shoot him."

"She won't do that," Dr. Harris said firmly.

"No, she won't," another voice said from behind them.

Out of the corner of her eye, Vivian saw Leo spin around, Bea wobbling in his arms at the sudden movement, but she didn't take her eyes off Dr. Harris. She didn't need to. She recognized the voice.

"Hello, Dad," Dr. Harris said with a lopsided smile. "Not to worry, these folks are just leaving. We're all just going to pretend this whole thing never happened."

"And I just forget about Pearlie?" Vivian demanded. "Forget that you're a criminal and a murderer?"

"You hang out with plenty of criminals, girl," Arthur Harris said from behind her. "You even are one yourself now. Don't think we don't know how you got that dress. We've got as much dirt on you as you have on us. So yeah, you forget all about it."

"There's no need for that, Dad," Dr. Harris said. Absurdly, he looked embarrassed, as if his father had said something crude in the middle of a fancy restaurant. "Look, my father is retiring and leaving the city, so I won't need that kind of money again. That means no more letters. I'm not dumb enough to try this again when you'd know it was me, anyway."

"Better decide quick," Arthur Harris snapped. "I got a whole mess of buddies on their way from the station. I'd hate to see what happens if you're still hanging around when they get here."

He might have been lying. But they still had to give in, Vivian realized, her heart pounding. They couldn't risk messing with a crooked cop. Not like this. Leo had a free pass out of trouble, and he might be able to bring her along with him. But Bea . . .

Bea would end up in prison or worse. She couldn't risk that.

"If you ever come after my sister again, I will kill you." Vivian didn't stop to think if the threat was wise before she made it.

But Dr. Harris didn't seem offended. If anything, he looked disappointed, even a little hurt. "The letter was a threat to you, Vivian, not to Florence. I thought you understood that. I would never do anything to hurt your sister, she's a delightful girl. Before all this messiness, I was even thinking of asking her to the pictures."

"You don't come near her," Vivian snapped.

"No, I think that ship has sailed." He sighed, then shrugged. "Shame. But now that we have all that unpleasantness sorted out, you should get going before you end up arrested for assaulting me in my own home. It really is time to put this behind us."

Vivian stared at him, horrified by his pleasant tone. He was going to get away with it all. And she had to let him.

Slowly, she lowered the gun.

"I knew you were a smart girl," Dr. Harris said warmly, almost as if they were having a friendly conversation. He even smiled at her, but there was a cruel edge to it. "So you can go back to serving liquor to drunks and socialites. And I can go back to helping out folks who might die without me."

"Keep telling yourself whatever helps you sleep at night," Leo said. "Come on, girls. We've gotta get out of here."

Vivian glanced over her shoulder; Arthur had stepped to one side, gesturing toward the door with one hand in a motion that was almost a bow. The smile on his face was mocking. Leo still had one arm around Bea's waist and was hustling her out the door. Vivian looked back at Dr. Harris one more time. He raised his brows, an expression that was half question, half challenge.

The gun hanging by her side and her finger still on the trigger, Vivian backed up and followed her friends out the door.

TWENTY-EIGHT

They didn't stop moving until they were half a dozen blocks away, Leo and Vivian half carrying Bea to put as much distance between themselves and Dr. Harris's office as quickly as they could.

"I'm going to throw up," Bea suddenly announced, and Leo steered them into a gap between buildings where Bea sank to her knees, her hands braced against the wall. He politely averted his eyes, shielding them from view with his body. But Vivian held her friend's head between her hands as she emptied everything out of her stomach.

"Are you sure she's going to be okay?" Vivian asked, wiping Bea's face and mouth with her handkerchief and helping her stand. Bea was shaking, her eyes glazed and unfocused, but she didn't seem like she was about to collapse again.

"She should be, yeah. It might take a while to wear off, and she's probably going to want to spend the rest of the day sleeping. But I don't think we need to worry." Leo put one arm around Bea's waist. "Whistle us up a cab, Viv. She needs to get home, and if we carry her all the way there we're going to get attention we don't want."

"We can't just let him go," Bea insisted, her anger clear in spite of the slur to her voice. "We've got no reason to trust him. He could change his mind. He could be planning to get rid of us all to keep his secret."

"Don't worry, this isn't done," Leo said firmly. "I've got people I can talk to. I'll figure out a way to nail him. I can talk to the coroner again. And if I need to, I'll drag his name into it next time my uncle asks me to look into something." He reached out to give Vivian's hand a squeeze. "I'm not going to let anything happen to either of you."

"He's already got the cops on his side," Bea pointed out as a cab pulled over for them.

"Yeah, but his dad's leaving the city. And I know the commissioner," Leo quipped as he opened the door.

"Not her," the cabbie said, glaring suspiciously as they were about to help Bea slide in. "I'm not taking her if she's going to be sick all over my car."

"She just fainted is all," Vivian said quickly. "Too hot out here."

"Not my problem," the cabbie sniffed.

Leo wordlessly handed over a few bills. The cabbie counted the money, sniffed again, and shrugged. "Fine then, load her up."

"Guess I'll have to start liking you after this," Bea mumbled once they were all in the back seat, leaning unsteadily against Leo's side, her eyelids drooping. She glanced at Vivian. "And I guess maybe you and Florence can head home."

Vivian sat with her purse in her lap, heavy with the weight of the gun. She didn't want to live with the guilt of killing a man in cold blood. But now she had to live with the guilt of letting him get away with what he had done. And he would always be there, a threat hanging over their lives.

She stared out the window as the buildings began to slide by. "We'll need to keep our eyes out," she said slowly. "But I think you're right. Tomorrow, it'll be time to go home."

She knew she couldn't have shot him. But part of her still wished that she had.

Vivian was on edge when she got to the Nightingale for her shift that night.

Abraham had been at the Henrys' house, waiting to talk to Bea, when Vivian and Leo hauled her up the stairs. Whatever had been said between them before, he hadn't asked questions or hesitated before swooping in to carry her to her room and sit anxiously by her side as she slept for the rest of the afternoon.

When she woke up at last, she was still woozy, but there were no other lingering effects from what Dr. Harris had given her. Luckily, Mrs. Henry had been at work all day, otherwise Vivian would have had to decide how much to tell her, and that was a call she didn't want to make on her own. It had been hard enough choosing to tell Abraham, but he wouldn't be satisfied with less than the full story. And as worried as he was, Vivian didn't feel right keeping him in the dark.

Alba, whose pregnancy was just beginning to show, had alternated being sick and caring for Bea all day, and she announced that neither of them were coming to work that night. "But Abraham will drive you, Viv," she said, giving him a pointed glance. "I don't know what you girls got up to today, but you should maybe not be wandering around at night by yourself."

"Sure thing," Abraham agreed, though he didn't look happy about it. Vivian wondered if he would ever forgive her for her suspicions, justified though they had been.

It probably depended on whether Bea forgave him or not.

But he had taken her home to get ready for work, then to the Nightingale, driving in heavy silence that Vivian was too nervous to break. She felt odd and uncomfortable, sitting alone in the back seat, sure she was costing him a fare that he could have put to good use. But he didn't protest. And they both knew it could have led to trouble if someone peeked into the car and saw her sitting next to him in the front seat.

It wasn't until he had parked a few doors down from the Nightingale's back-alley entrance that Abraham finally spoke. Lighting two cigarettes, he handed one to her and took a long drag of his. "You think she's going to be okay?"

"Right as rain in a day or two, I'm sure," Vivian said quickly. She trusted Leo's assessment, though she couldn't shake her own worry for her friend. "I'm just worried about what she's going to want to do afterward."

All the windows in the car were rolled down, and Abraham slowly blew a stream of smoke out his. "I won't let her do anything that'll get her hurt."

"You're a good fella, Abraham," Vivian said, meaning it. Everyone kept secrets. Everyone did things they weren't proud of. He was no different. And he loved her friend.

He met her eyes in the mirror. "We'll see if Bea agrees with you."

When Vivian finally made her way inside, Danny was in the middle of doing inventory. Most of the staff hadn't arrived yet, but the band was running through a couple new songs. They had a new bass player, a skinny kid with thick glasses who looked extra scrawny next to his instrument but played with plenty of style. Danny listened to Vivian in silence, then wiped the sweat from his forehead. "Damn. Mr. Smith won't be happy," he said, glancing at the bandleader. "Bea's a real draw now; there's folks who come just to hear her sing." He shook his head. "One of these days, some big-name place is going to snatch her up." His gaze sharpened. "Is there more to it than just her being sick?"

"Yes," Vivian said quietly.

Danny nodded. "Any of that trouble likely to follow you here tonight?"

Vivian shivered. Dr. Harris had as much reason to avoid her as she had to avoid him. If he wanted to make trouble, she suspected he was more likely to wait a few days until she let down her guard. But his father had been a cop. And she had no idea whether he knew where she and Bea worked. "Maybe tell the boys on the door to keep an eye out for any plainclothes trying to sneak in. Just in case."

Danny's expression grew alarmed. "Kitten, don't tell me you and Bea were messing around with the police? What were you thinking?"

"Not on purpose," Vivian said, wincing. "But sometimes it's hard not to stumble over a crooked cop in this city."

Danny blew out a slow breath. "All right. Hux has a few friends of her own on the force. I'll tell her to give them a call and keep an eye on things for us. And I'll go tell Mr. Smith his star isn't coming tonight." He headed toward the bandstand, giving her shoulder a comforting squeeze as he passed. "Cheer up, kitten. We'll keep you safe. It's what we do around here."

"Did you see Florence before you came to work tonight?" Vivian asked.

He paused, giving her a worried look over his shoulder. "Is she in danger?"

"No, I just wanted . . . never mind. We've got work to do." Vivian managed to give him a smile. "Thanks, Danny-boy."

She didn't have Danny's knack for spotting an undercover cop, but Vivian still kept an eye on the door and her things behind the bar, in case she needed to make a quick getaway. But the night unfolded with the Nightingale's normal playful, sultry energy. She overheard a few grumbles as she wove through the crowd, from folks who were disappointed not to hear Bea sing. *Beatrice Bluebird,* she heard more than one person call her, with no idea where the name had come from. Danny or Honor, she suspected, trying to capitalize on Bea's growing popularity.

By the time her second break rolled around, she had relaxed enough to accept an invitation to dance, just as the band struck up an easy foxtrot. It was one they played nearly every night, and it had become a running game at the Nightingale that every time the chorus rolled around, everyone had to switch partners. It was just the distraction that Vivian needed for a few minutes.

When the last chorus began, there was a wild scramble. Laughing, Vivian's current partner twirled her toward someone new, who caught her around the waist before she could see who it was. A little dizzy, she blinked rapidly and shook her head to clear it.

And then she froze. The man who had caught her was Bruiser George.

"Hello, there, girlie," he said, smiling. "Surprised to see me?"

Vivian tried to push away, but he had one arm locked around her waist and the other one holding her hand, and he wasn't letting go as he steered them back into the dance. With anyone else, Vivian would have been pleasantly surprised by how good a dancer he was, but she wasn't interested in any more surprises from George. She didn't like causing a scene, but there were times when it was necessary, and she was confident that Danny would have her back if she did. She planted her feet and took a deep breath.

But before she could say anything, George jerked his head toward the back of the room. "Boss is upstairs waiting for you."

Vivian stumbled as he pulled her out of the way of another dancing couple, who gave them an odd look as they went past. To her relief, he let go, and she took a quick step back to put distance between them. Bruiser George gave her an amused look. She had the feeling that he enjoyed knowing he had flustered her. "Let's go, girlie."

"Not likely," Vivian snapped. "I'm not going anywhere with you."

He sighed, looking hurt. "Mistrusting girl."

"You're damn right I am."

"Fine." He was starting to look irritated with her, Vivian was pleased to see. "Then I'll go sit at the bar, and you can go up on your own. Excuse me for trying to be a gentleman."

"You're not, and we both know it."

"Just get on up there, will you?" he growled. "She doesn't like to be kept waiting, and I don't need her thinking I'm the reason she has to."

In spite of her nerves, Vivian felt a small smirk creeping across her face. "Guessing she wasn't happy with you, then, about that dustup at the pawnshop?" she asked with mocking sympathy. "Poor George. In trouble with the boss."

He glared at her. "I'm going to the bar. You're going upstairs."

"You can't make me. Not here," Vivian taunted. She saw his eyes narrow, but before he could do more than draw a deep breath in, she smiled. "But I'll go to be nice. Get yourself a drink, George. You look like you need it."

"One day, girlie," he said softly as she turned away. "One day, that smart mouth is gonna get you in trouble. I just hope I'm there to see it."

Vivian didn't give him the satisfaction of turning around, but the back of her neck prickled all the way to Honor's office.

"Come in," Honor's voice called when she knocked.

The tableau was eerily familiar: Honor behind her desk, Hattie Wilson seated in front of it. An empty glass waiting for Vivian.

But she was already on edge from the day, and her conversation with Bruiser George hadn't helped. So when she came into the room, she didn't take the seat that had been left for her. Instead, she stopped a few feet from the desk and fixed her eyes on Mrs. Wilson. "Did you need something from me?"

Hattie Wilson gave her a slow look, then took an even slower drink from her glass. She was elegant as always, in a dress of black-and-gray silk, a white fur stole wrapped around her shoulders in spite of the heat. The veil on her tiny confection of a hat left her eyes in shadow, and Vivian wondered uneasily what they might have revealed about what she was thinking.

Vivian didn't look at Honor, though she desperately wanted to.

At last Mrs. Wilson spoke. "You know what they say about if you want something done right. Since you managed to send George packing—I won't say I'm not impressed, though I am curious about this young man he says you were with—I decided I needed to find out what you've learned myself. About *your* little problem with *my* competition. So tell me, Miss Kelly." She took another sip. "What news is there for me?"

"The kind you don't need to worry about anymore," Vivian said slowly. Out of the corner of her eye, she saw Honor lean forward, though she doubted her boss would let any of the surprise she might be feeling show on her face.

Mrs. Wilson raised her brows. "Oh?"

"Yes." Vivian hoped her expression was as impassive as those of the other two women in the room.

"Just poof, it's gone away?" Hattie pursed her lips. "I'm going to need more than that."

She couldn't name Pearlie and Alba as the criminals using the hemlock calling card. There was no point. Pearlie was gone, and she didn't want to drag the rest of his family into it. And Alba . . . Vivian didn't like her much, but she clearly had no plans to keep going with what she and Pearlie had started.

She could have named Dr. Harris. For a moment she wanted to. She had a feeling that pointing the finger at him would mean the doctor was no longer a problem or a threat she needed to worry about. But she couldn't do it.

She hadn't been able to pull the trigger. And she couldn't pretend, even to herself, that naming him to a woman like Hattie Wilson wasn't as good as the same thing.

"No," Vivian said, surprising herself with how cool her voice sounded. "You really don't."

Hattie looked genuinely surprised. "Do you not know who was behind it, or are you not going to tell me?"

"I'll let you wonder which one. But it isn't a problem you need to worry about anymore."

"I don't like it when people keep information from me," Hattie said, her voice all the more menacing for how soft it was. She set down her glass and stood. "I did you a favor. I expect something in return."

"Your return is that you don't have to worry about this hemlock group anymore," Vivian said, holding her ground through sheer stubbornness and hoping Hattie didn't see her trembling hands. "That's all I'm saying."

"Miss Kelly, I hope you're paying very close attention because I—"

"She's not yours to order around."

Vivian jumped. She had almost forgotten that Honor was still in the room. Hattie turned more slowly, but she looked just as taken aback. "Excuse me?"

Honor stood. Her smile was friendly, but her voice held a clear warning. "You've said your piece, Mrs. Wilson. I'm sure Vivian appreciates your favor. But she doesn't work for you. She works for me. And around here, when a woman says she's done talking, we respect that."

Hattie seemed about to reply. But then she stopped, her lips slightly parted, staring at Honor. "I just realized who you remind me of," she said. A slow smile spread across her face, and she began to laugh. "Oh, that's rich. And yet not." Her voice grew a little mocking. "It isn't as if you'll ever see any of that money."

"I have no idea what you're talking about," Honor said, her voice so even and cold that Vivian suspected she knew exactly what Hattie Wilson meant, that Vivian herself was the only one in that office who was still in the dark.

"Of course not." Hattie gathered her fur around her, still laughing, as she made her way toward the door. "Very well, we'll leave our business here. Perhaps we'll cross paths again in the future." She took one more look at Honor and laughed again. "Have a good night, Ms. *Huxley*."

They could still hear her laughter drifting up the stairs as she left.

"What was that about?" Vivian asked Honor.

"I could ask you the same thing. What do you mean, it isn't a problem anymore?" Honor came around the desk, then seemed to think better of it, stopping several feet away from Vivian. But her worry was still there, peeking out from under her usual cool expression. "Does it have something to do with why Beatrice isn't singing tonight? What happened?"

Vivian shivered and wrapped her arms around herself. Part of her wished that Honor would reach out again to comfort her, wrap an arm around her the way she had in the cab that night. But neither of them made any move toward each other. "It's kind of a long story."

Honor went back to her desk and poured an inch of liquor into the empty glass. She held it out to Vivian. Their fingers brushed against each other as Vivian took it, but Honor's face stayed impassive. Vivian hoped hers did, too. "We've got time," Honor said softly, leaning back against the edge of the desk.

She stayed that way while Vivian spoke, her voice sometimes speeding up with excitement or shaking with remembered fear. Vivian didn't look at her, and when she had finished, she downed the entirety of the glass in one gulp, then coughed, her eyes watering at the bitter sting of the liquor. When her vision cleared again, she found Honor watching her, jaw tight and fingers clenched around her own glass.

"Do you feel safe, knowing he's still out there?" Honor asked quietly.

"No." Vivian shivered again. "I mean, I do for now, I think we're kind of . . . we're stuck, aren't we? Him and me and Bea. We all know too much that can hurt the others. I don't trust him, so I don't know how long that will last for. But I don't know what to do about it, either."

Honor nodded, staring into her glass, but Vivian had a feeling that her mind was elsewhere. At last she looked up. "But safe for now," she said quietly. "Which I'm glad to hear." She took Vivian's empty glass before heading back around to the other side of her desk. Setting them both to the side, she pulled out a few papers and began to sort through them. "I'll have one of the boys tailing you and your sister for a few days, just to be sure. Indulge me," she said, glancing up from under her lashes as Vivian started to protest. "I keep my people safe."

"All right," Vivian agreed. At least Honor thought she was worth that much. She hesitated, then asked, "What did Mrs. Wilson mean, at the end there? Who did you remind her of?"

Honor's eyes were back on the papers. "I already said, I have no idea what she was talking about."

She wasn't telling the truth, Vivian was sure. But if there was one thing dancing and working at a place like the Nightingale taught her, it was that the roundabout approach was a much better way to get folks talking than pressing them for details that they didn't want to share.

"Ellie said you taught her some of the signing language, and that's how she could talk to her neighbor. How do you know it?" Vivian asked instead. "That's how you came up with the club's signals, right?"

"My sister," Honor replied after a long pause. She kept her eyes on the papers as she said it.

Vivian stared at her. Somehow, she had never thought about whether Honor had a family or not. It was impossible to picture her in any other world than the one she had created at the Nightingale. "You have a sister?"

"Had." Honor looked up at last. Vivian realized she must be getting used to reading Honor's nearly inscrutable expressions, because she could see the edge of sadness that was lurking there. "She died a few years back. Influenza."

"I'm sorry."

"Me too." Honor shrugged, back to her search. She must have found the papers she wanted, because she pulled several out, though she kept them turned away from Vivian. "She had pretty limited hearing. A neighbor taught her and me so we could sign to each other. The schools for deaf kids don't like to teach signing, but there're everyday folks that know."

"Not your parents?" Vivian asked softly. She didn't want to be fascinated by the rare glimpse behind the curtain of Honor's private life, but she couldn't help wanting to know more. Without meaning to, she took a step closer.

Honor must have heard the interest in her voice, because she glanced at Vivian again, a wry smile on her face. "If you're very good, pet, maybe, *maybe* one day I'll tell you about my parents. For now . . ." She tapped the edges of the papers in her hands against the desk, two sharp little thwacks, knocking them into a neat line. "It's time for both of us to get back to work."

Vivian wanted to ask more, but she made herself nod and turn to go.

Honor's voice stopped her just as she reached the door. "Vivian . . ."

She glanced back over her shoulder. Honor was watching her, not speaking. Then she gave a sad smile. "I'm glad you're okay."

"Me too," Vivian agreed.

And she made herself leave.

TWENTY-NINE

Vivian glanced out the window. Benny, one of Honor's bruisers from the Nightingale, was still there, lounging against a streetlamp on Spring Street and reading a newspaper. But he glanced every so often at the door of the Chins' place, then up and down the street, keeping an eye out for trouble. His presence eased some of the worry that had tightened up her shoulders. She turned back to her sister, who was packing.

She didn't want to ask. She was scared of the answers she might get. But she knew she couldn't bear putting it off any longer.

"Flo, are you . . ." Vivian hesitated. Her eyes were fixed on the dress she was folding, but she could feel her sister staring at her. She swallowed. "Tell me about Danny."

Florence let out a breathy little laugh, an embarrassed, delighted sound that Vivian couldn't remember ever hearing her make before. "I don't know what you mean."

"Yes, you do." She lifted her eyes at last to find her sister watching her. "It's all right, Flo. I just want to know what you're thinking. Or if the two of you have . . . what you've talked about."

"What I'm thinking . . ." Florence crossed to the washstand to pick up her hairbrush. But she stood there, turning it over in her hands as she replied. "I've always felt like all I could do was survive, to just struggle through each day and hope I made it. Things started to get better for us—I haven't felt so desperate or exhausted these past few months—but still, it was . . ."

"Hard," Vivian said quietly. "It's hard."

"It's hard," Florence agreed, crossing back to the bed and placing the brush with the rest of her things. "But Danny . . . He doesn't just survive, does he? I mean, he does, we all do, none of this is easy. But his heart is thriving. He's so alive it feels like he glows sometimes." She turned to look at Vivian at last. "And then, for whatever reason, he turned that glow on me. Being around him feels like . . . like being in the sunshine after living in the dark my whole life."

"The reason is pretty obvious, Flo," Vivian said, her throat so tight she could barely get the words out. "You're a hell of a girl. And you're as sweet and pretty as they come." She hesitated, then added, "It doesn't bother you that he's Chinese?"

"I can't imagine it makes his life any easier in this city," Florence replied quietly, looking down once more. She had picked up a dress and was folding far more carefully than it needed. "But no, it doesn't bother me."

She glanced up at her sister. "Does it bother you?"

"Me?" Vivian asked in surprise. "Of course not. I've known Danny for ages."

"But knowing someone, and seeing him with your sister . . ." Florence bit her lip nervously but pressed on. "That's two different things. There's plenty of people would be bothered by it. And you've been acting odd ever since—"

"I'm not bothered by you being sweet on him," Vivian interrupted, her voice catching in her throat. She closed her eyes, unable to look at her sister as she forced the admission out. "It's just hard to think about losing you." She opened her eyes again, meeting her sister's shocked gaze. "It's been just you and me for so long. I don't . . . I don't know what I'd do without you."

"Oh, Vivi." Florence put aside the skirt she was folding and reached for Vivian's hand. "You can't get rid of me that easy. You know that. I'll be pestering you to watch your language and go to bed for the rest of your life."

That made Vivian smile. "You would," she said, shaking her head. "But you know . . ." She hesitated. "If anything comes of it—of you and Danny I mean—"

"It won't be easy?" Florence asked. Vivian nodded. It was an understatement, and they both knew it. It was hard enough being a poor Irish girl. Being an Irish girl stepping out with a Chinese man could be downright dangerous for both of them. "Nothing's ever been easy in our lives," Florence said. Her hands were trembling, but her voice was firm. "But if something does come of it . . . I think it might be worth the risk. And at least with a dead mother and no father to speak of, I don't have to worry about my family objecting."

"Does that mean . . . ?" Vivian hesitated again. "Have you and he talked about . . . anything?"

"No, not really." Florence turned back to her careful folding, a blush spreading over her cheeks. She seemed about to say something else, but she closed her mouth quickly.

Vivian wondered if her sister was lying. She wondered what she had missed these last few days. But she couldn't bring herself to ask. "Well, he's a swell fella," she said, turning away so Florence wouldn't be able to see the pained expression on her face. "Whatever happens next, I'm glad he's making you so happy now."

"Yes," Florence said quietly. "It's nice to feel happy." She gave her head a little shake, then smiled. "And it's nice to have the day free from work, even if we're going to miss the money. Should we—"

But whatever she might have said was lost as someone knocked sharply at the door. When they opened it, Danny was there. Florence greeted him with a bright smile.

"Hello, sunshine," he said, but he didn't quite smile back. "Viv, this just arrived for you."

It was an envelope. Her name was written in English on the front, but below that were a series of Chinese characters, some that she recognized from the front of the Chins' restaurant. She frowned, her stomach fluttering with nerves. "It came in the mail?"

Danny shook his head. "Some local kid brought it. I don't think . . ." He glanced at Florence and cleared his throat. "I don't think it has anything to do with the other thing."

Vivian nodded. She didn't think so either, but her hands were trembling, and she couldn't bring herself to open it.

"Here." Florence eased it out from between her fingers, which were gripping it hard enough to crumple the edge of the paper. "Let me." She ran a finger under the flap and pulled out the letter. As she read it, she let out a gasp, one hand rising to cover her lips as the envelope fluttered to the floor.

"What is it?" Vivian demanded, feeling like the bottom had just dropped out of her stomach.

Florence glanced up, and her dark eyes were full of tears. "It's Mr. Sun. He . . . he had some trouble, they think maybe with his heart. His granddaughter sent it." She looked up, her trembling lower lip caught between her teeth. "He died, Vivi."

"Does she say that he . . ." Vivian swallowed. "Did he say anything about our mother before . . ." She couldn't bring herself to finish the sentence.

Florence shook her head slowly. "She says he went to bed and didn't wake up. But she sent . . ." She handed the letter to Vivian and bent to retrieve the envelope from the floor.

It was only a few lines, a note written in kindness by someone who didn't have any reason to remember them. But at the very end was a single line that made Vivian's heart skip a beat. *After we spoke, I remembered seeing this with some of my grandfather's papers. I thought you should have it, in case my guess about it is correct.*

"She sent a photograph," Florence said quietly. She stared at it for a long moment, then handed it to Vivian.

The woman in the image stood in front of a nondescript building, its sign written in Chinese characters. Her hair was pinned back, and the shades of gray in the photo hid what color it might have been. But looking at her face was like looking at Florence, like looking in a mirror. She held a round-cheeked baby on one hip. Her other arm hung down so she could clasp the hand of a tiny girl with her thumb in her mouth.

"That's us," Vivian whispered. Her voice trembled. "That's our mother."

"She looked like you," Florence said, coming to stand next to her.

"She looked like you," Vivian said. She wasn't sure whether she wanted to laugh or cry. Florence's hand slid into hers, and for a moment they stood there together, greedy eyes tracing every line of their mother's face.

"I know what we should do today," Florence said at last. "Since we don't have to work. I know where we should go."

"I'd offer to come with you girls," Danny said, and Vivian jumped a little. She had forgotten until that moment that he was still in the room. "But I've gotta put in my hours in the kitchen."

"That's all right." Florence gave him a sweet smile. "This is something we should do just the two of us."

"Well, us and Benny," Vivian said, remembering.

Florence frowned at her. "Who?"

The ferry ride to Hart Island had been an odd one, with Benny sitting behind them, awkward and silent, while the sisters clasped hands and braced themselves against the rocking of the boat, both of them still staring at the photograph of their mother. Florence had been unnerved to find out that they needed someone to keep an eye on them, but she didn't argue.

And now that they were there, he had slipped outside like a shadow, waiting while they went to check the records office to find out which part of the island held their mother's body.

The clerk frowned when they gave him the year and month and said it would take a few minutes to locate the right entry. He had to pull several old ledgers out of storage, and they waited together, hands still clasped as they watched with eager eyes while he flipped through the pages. They had never visited before. But with the photograph still clutched in Florence's hand, it felt like they could finally face it. Vivian even felt a flutter of anticipation, almost excitement. Her mother had never felt more real than at that moment.

There would be no headstone for her, of course. There wouldn't even be an individual grave. But there would be a place, a spot that they could look down on, and know that was where Mae Kelly rested.

"I'm sorry, miss," the clerk at the office said, his voice recalling Vivian to where she was with a start. "There's no record of a Mae Kelly being buried here."

The sisters glanced at each other, and Vivian could see her own confusion mirrored in her sister's expression. "Do you think you could check another—"

"I checked 'em all," the man said. He had tufts of hair sticking out around his ears and a bushy white mustache that twitched when he talked. His words were clipped and professional, but his eyes were unexpectedly kind as he shook his head. "I checked the months around it, and the same month the year before. I checked by day and I looked up the name. There's no record. She wasn't buried here." He shut the record book firmly, dust flying from its pages in a little cloud.

"But . . ." Vivian shook her head, confused. "But where would she have been buried?"

The man shrugged. "Can't help you there, girls. This is where the unclaimed bodies ended up. If she's not here . . ." He shrugged again.

Vivian was too dazed to respond; as if from far away, she heard Florence thank the man for his help. It wasn't until they were back outside that she spoke.

"Flo, do you realize what that means?"

"I think it means that someone claimed our mother's body." Florence was trembling all over. "Which means that someone knew her, and cared enough about her, and had enough money to give her a proper funeral. But not enough to find us."

"Maybe they didn't know where to look," Vivian whispered. "Flo . . . we have to find out who it was."

"There's no way for us to do that, is there?"

"Maybe . . ." Vivian spoke slowly. "Maybe the place to start looking is at the coroner's office. And luckily, I know a guy who might help us." She gave Benny a wave, and he nodded, falling into place behind them as they made their way to the ferry launch. "I'm going to be heading out tonight."

"But it's not a night you're supposed to . . ." Florence trailed off. "You mean you know someone at the Nightingale who might be able to help us?"

"Leo got me into Bellevue once," Vivian said thoughtfully. "He might be able to help me out again."

"All right." Florence nodded as Benny followed them onto the ferry. There were no other passengers this time—the island wasn't a popular destination—but he still sat just behind them as it puttered into motion. "I hope you still have a dress I can borrow, because I'm coming with you."

Vivian gave her a sideways glance. "Are you coming because you want to hear what Leo says or because you want to see Danny?"

Florence didn't answer, just smiled as she turned to look out the window. And Vivian's heart gave a little lurch inside her chest as the boat began to take them away.

THIRTY

It was a beautiful night outside, fluffy clouds flirting with the moon, glowing silver in its light. And it was a wild night inside, the smell of smoke and champagne hanging in the air as they made their way down the stairs toward the dance floor. The sultry, humid heat of the night had made its way onto the dance floor, too, in spite of the electric fans that sent the fringes of their dresses trembling and raised goose bumps on Vivian's arms.

The dancers spun around the room, heels kicking toward the ceiling and light flashing from their rhinestones. On the bandstand, Beatrice Bluebird broke hearts and mended them with every note she sang.

Vivian wound her way through the crowd, Florence's hand in hers, until she reached the bar where Danny was making a group of girls blush and giggle. She glanced at Florence, but her sister put her chin in the air and marched straight to the bar, plopping herself down on a stool and waiting for Danny to notice her.

It only took him a minute, and his expression softened when he saw her, as though he were looking at something rare and precious.

It made Vivian's heart ache, but underneath the pain was a feeling of relief. She didn't want to be left behind, but Florence deserved to be cherished. And even if it didn't last, Danny was the sort of fella who could do exactly that.

Leo was waiting at the bar, exactly where she'd asked him to be when she called. He bent his head to say something to Florence, who blushed and nodded, then he gestured to Danny, who produced two glasses of champagne a moment later. Handing one to Florence, Leo spun around on his stool and held the second one out to Vivian.

Her fingers brushed his as she took it, and the heat of even that brief touch was like a breath of comfort going through her. He gave her a smile, but he looked her over at the same time, as though checking to see that she was still in one piece. "You all right?" he asked. "No trouble from . . . No trouble?"

"Not yet, anyway," Vivian said, ignoring a little shiver of unease. She was getting too used to looking over her shoulder. She took a sip of her drink. "I wanted to talk to you about something else, though."

He gave her a considering look. "Tell me on the dance floor," he suggested.

Vivian hesitated, then nodded. "Flo, you gonna be all right until I get back?" she asked, setting her glass on the bar next to her sister.

"Mr. Chin will keep an eye on me," Florence said. Danny, who was busy mixing up a pitcher of drinks, smiled.

The band was playing a smooth foxtrot, slow and sweet, that left plenty of breath for talking. Vivian settled against Leo, glad for the warmth of his palm at her back, the soft pressure of his hand holding hers. For a moment, she could forget everything that had happened since Pearlie's death. For a moment, the only thing that mattered was the music and the man she was dancing with.

Closing her eyes, she fell into the rhythm of the dance, trusting Leo to guide them. She liked being able to trust him. There was so little in her life that felt easy or simple, but somehow, leaning on Leo had become both. As he turned them across the floor, their bodies fitting together like the notes of the music, she told him about her mother and what they had learned that day at Hart Island.

Vivian's voice broke a little as she explained about the missing record, and she had to stop talking. For a moment, a gentle silence hung between them. Leo didn't press her for more, just held her close and waited until she was ready to continue. "And I was thinking," she said at last, "if we want to find that kind of record, maybe the best place to start would be the coroner's office. They've gotta keep track, right, of who comes to claim bodies?"

"I guess so." Leo looked thoughtful. "I never considered it before. But sure. I can get you in there to find out." He smiled, and his voice grew a little more gentle. "You know I'm always happy to help out a friend."

"What if . . ." Vivian didn't have the courage to finish the question. She didn't know what she would have done that day without Leo. What if she wanted to be more than just his friend?

The ache was there behind her heart again, and she had to look away. As she did, she caught sight of Honor, shaking hands and schmoozing a table of suited men. It was the sort of thing she did every night, the way she kept her club in business. There was nothing remarkable in it at all, except for Honor herself, who moved like silk and jazz, who didn't care what anyone else thought of her or her life. And who made it plain that she wanted to live that life alone.

Vivian was tired of being alone.

"Leo," she began, turning back, then hesitated. He raised a brow at her but said nothing. Afraid of what he might say, afraid of being told once again that she wasn't enough, Vivian had to take a deep breath before she could continue. "Leo, would you like to go see a picture this weekend? With me?"

She had caught him off guard; she could tell by the way he stumbled, the only time she had ever seen him clumsy while dancing. The song ended as he was recovering his footing, but he didn't let her go as the other dancers applauded and Bea took a bow, preparing to go on her break.

"I'd like that, Viv," he said at last, smiling at her. "I'd like that a lot."

They were still staring at each other when someone squealed his name. "Leo!" called a girl with dark hair and a dress so stylish it made Vivian want to squirm with envy. "Leo, you owe me a dance, cruel man. Where have you been this week?"

"Around," he said, grinning as he let go of Vivian's waist and turned toward the girl. But he was slower to release her hand, his fingers lingering on hers as though he had to force himself to let her go. "Don't leave before I see you again," he murmured to Vivian.

"Count on it," she replied as she stepped back and the band started on a quickstep. Bea had disappeared back into the dressing room, and Vivian would have followed. But she spotted Honor going after her star singer. So she turned and headed back toward where Florence waited at the bar, chatting with Danny as he filled a tray of glasses with gin and champagne.

"They said it looked like a suicide."

Vivian stopped in her tracks, trying to figure out who had said it.

"How awful," another voice replied with gruesome relish. "Did they say how?"

"Arsenic."

Vivian spotted the speakers, two well-dressed women with jewels in their hair and cigarettes dangling from their fingers who were just heading toward the ladies' powder room, gossiping as they went. Vivian changed direction quickly to follow them, her entire body jangling with sudden nerves.

"Absolutely tragic, for someone so young. And so promising, the papers said! He had set up his practice in an absolutely impoverished neighborhood, just a bit north of here, in fact."

"How selfless," the second woman agreed. "A handsome young

doctor, done in by despair . . . that Fitzgerald fellow should write a book about it . . ."

The door to the powder room closed behind them, cutting off the rest of their conversation. But Vivian had already frozen where she stood.

Then she spun on her heel and ran back toward the dressing room.

"Bea!" She threw the door open, panting. "Bea, did you hear—"

She broke off. Bea was at her dressing table, turned around in her chair to look at Honor, while Alba stood nearby. All three of them were speaking in quiet voices, their heads close together. And all three looked up as Vivian burst into the room.

Honor's face was impassive as always. Alba had a slight smile, sarcastic and brittle, and she lifted her chin as though daring Vivian to finish her sentence. And Bea . . .

Bea just watched her, waiting.

Vivian swallowed and let the door swing shut behind her. "Did you hear?" she asked quietly. She glanced at both of the other women, but it was Bea that her eyes settled on at last. "Seems that Dr. Harris is dead."

"Really?" Alba drawled. "How did that happen?"

Something clenched inside Vivian's chest like a fist, hard and angry and scared. "Seems he got his hands on some arsenic. Which is pretty easy to do, of course. Heard some gossips calling it a death of despair."

"Imagine that," Bea said softly. She turned back to her dressing table, but her hand trembled as she picked up her lipstick. "Guess that'll be in all the papers tomorrow."

Wading through the tension that crackled between the three women was like walking into a puddle and discovering it was actually a fast-flowing river. Vivian couldn't find her footing. She didn't know where to look or what to think.

"What—" she began, then stopped.

"I should get back to work," Honor said smoothly. She headed toward the door, pausing by Vivian on the way. "Don't be too upset about the doctor, Vivian," she said softly. "I hear he wasn't a nice fella."

Before Vivian could think of what to say in response, she was gone. She turned back to Bea and Alba, who were exchanging a look. Alba grimaced and rubbed the small of her back. "My poor puppies are howling, but I've gotta get back out there if I want to be able to afford this kid," she said, giving Bea a pat on the shoulder as she went past. At the door, she turned back and smiled, one hand on the jamb. "By the way, there's something over there for you, Vivian," she added. "Bea mentioned that it was important to you." She gave another mocking smile before the door closed behind her.

She had been looking toward one of the sofas, where a small package lay, wrapped in brown paper and tied with string. Vivian hesitated. She knew what she would find in it, but the thought of seeing it was more than she could bear. She took a deep breath, then unwrapped it quickly, before she had the chance to talk herself out of it.

The deep blue fabric of the dress seemed to glow against the plain brown paper, and the tiny dots of topaz and aquamarine caught the light until the whole thing shimmered like blue-and-gold fire. Vivian stared at it, until it slithered from her nerveless hands and pooled back on the paper. Quickly, shivering with dread that someone else would come into the dressing room and find her holding it, she wrapped it back up and tied the string once more.

Only then did she raise her head, unsurprised to find that Bea had stood up and was watching her.

"He killed my uncle," Bea said quietly. "And I think he'd have done the same to us if he had the chance."

Vivian nodded.

"We're burying Pearlie tomorrow. Right next to my father," Bea added, her voice breaking. She had to take a shaking breath before she could continue. "They sounded like each other when they laughed."

Vivian stared at her. She hadn't been able to pull that trigger, but she had wanted him gone. She couldn't tell whether the sick, light-headed feeling rushing through her was guilt or relief. "Bea." She could barely get the words out. "Which one of you—"

"You remember what Abraham said before?" Bea interrupted. "Don't ask any questions unless you're sure you want to know the answer. Are you sure?"

She wasn't. She desperately wanted to know. And she desperately wanted to stay ignorant, to stay free of the burden that knowing would be. For a moment, looking at Bea was like looking at a stranger. Slowly, Vivian shook her head. "No," she whispered.

Bea gave her a crooked smile. "They're expecting me back on the bandstand. Why don't you find yourself a partner, and I'll sing a Charleston just for you?" She headed toward the door, but she turned back before she opened it, her hand on the knob. Her voice was quiet as she spoke. "And thanks, by the way. I can't say I like everything I found out. But you were a hell of a pal to help me find it."

Vivian nodded again, not quite trusting herself to speak.

Bea seemed to understand. "See you out there, Viv."

She left the door open behind her, and the brassy swell of the music filled the room, floating on the sultry summer air. Vivian paused there and took a deep breath.

Then she made her way toward the dance floor.

ACKNOWLEDGMENTS

Writing a book is a joy and a disaster every time, but the process for this one was particularly grueling. Luckily, while I may have been the one typing, I wasn't alone. Putting a book out into the world is a team effort every time, and I'm always afraid I'm going to forget someone when it comes time for acknowledgments (especially because the acknowledgments must be written before the process is fully done). So let's call this an incomplete but heartfelt list of thank-yous:

To Nettie Finn, who loved these characters from day one, believed in this book before it even existed, and made every iteration of it better.

To Whitney Ross, agent extraordinaire, who is the sort of guide and advocate that every writer should be lucky enough to have in their corner.

To Brian, a partner in every way, who rearranges everything to give me time to write when I'm up against a deadline and believes in my work as much as I do.

To Reagan Ralston, Mary Ann and Joe Paljug, Laura Helferstay, Ryan Jackson, Natalie Nhan, a small army of daycare teachers, and everyone else who makes up our child-rearing village. And to the kids, for being good sleepers. (It makes everything easier.)

To the amazing Minotaur/Macmillan team, including Sarah Haeckel, Allison Ziegler, Christina MacDonald, Rena Segall, Hector DeJean, Sara LaCotti, and the many others who have helped this series make its way into the world. And to my authenticity readers—Dee Hudson, Zhui Ning Chang, and D. Ann Williams—who gave invaluable feedback.

Thank you, each and every one of you.

And to you, reading this today—my endless thanks to you.

AUTHOR'S NOTE

While putting together a presentation on the world of the Nightingale, I came across the surprising statistic that at the height of the Jazz Age, there were about 32,000 speakeasies in New York City. That becomes even more impressive when you consider that the city had about 120,000 blocks. You could walk less than four blocks and find a place to buy a drink in the middle of Prohibition. (In Washington, D.C., you didn't even have to walk two.)

Another fun fact: around the same time, organized crime in the United States (which became profitable for the first time due to the demand for illegal liquor) made as much money as the entire federal budget. While the Nightingale itself may be my own invention, there was plenty of real-life crime, big and small, for me to draw on when creating it.

The rise of organized crime in the Jazz Age led, unsurprisingly, to a rise in murders, assisted by the illegal movement of weapons and the flood of modern poisons that industrial developments unleashed on the world. And the rise in murders led, in turn, to the extraordinary growth of the field of toxicology.

The medical examiner that Vivian meets, though I didn't use his name, was Charles Norris, a pathologist and the first trained medical examiner in New York City. Together with chemist Alexander Gettler and his team, he worked against incredible odds (and a whole lot of local political corruption) to trailblaze the science of forensic chemistry, making it a vital part of both crime solving and courtroom arguments. These forensic detectives changed how poison cases were investigated in New York City and around the world. If you want to learn more about Norris, Gettler, and the poisoners of the 1920s, I suggest picking up Deborah Blum's *The Poisoner's Handbook: Murder and the Birth of Forensic Medicine in Jazz Age New York.*

However, the everyday people of New York couldn't fix the problem of mob bosses and poisoners. So they often turned to an age-old scapegoat to vent their fears and frustrations: immigrants.

Chinese men were a particular worry to white Americans at the time. The American economy needed the labor of Chinese men, but people didn't want Chinese families settling down. The Page Act (passed in 1875) was supposedly about limiting forced labor, human trafficking, and prostitution. In reality, it was used to keep Chinese women out of the United States for exactly the reasons that Vivian, Danny, and Florence discuss. In 1882, the Chinese Exclusion Act prohibited the immigration of Chinese laborers—though there were already many in the country at the time—and made it easier to deport Chinese immigrants. This law was later extended as the Geary Act, which was still in effect well into the Jazz Age. And while white women did marry Chinese men, due to the exclusion of Chinese women, these marriages could bring both social stigma and legal risks. Women who married Chinese men took on their husband's nationality and could lose their U.S. citizenship if their husband hadn't been born in the U.S. or if he left the country for any reason and was denied re-entry. I highly recommend *The Chinese Must Go,* by Beth Lew-Williams, as a resource for learning about the history of Chinese migration in the United States.

There was a particular immigration workaround that became popular in the 1920s, discussed in the excellent research of Heather Lee: restaurants. The owners of certain types of businesses were allowed to sponsor immigration for laborers who would then work for them, and restaurants fell into this category. Many Chinese residents already in the country took advantage of this loophole, opening restaurants so they could hire friends and family members and bring them to the United States to work. This led to the proliferation of Chinese restaurants, particularly in cities like New York.

These restaurants were found all over the city, not just in the areas where Chinese immigrants lived. They ranged from cheap "chop suey joints," where you could get a meal for under a dollar, to upscale dining rooms. Many were considered among the finest restaurants in the city.

I've tried to stay true to the historical realities of things like policing, forensics, and immigration in the 1920s, but there are times when I did fudge the facts a little. For example, the Fitz Special, also called the "FitzGerald Special" or "Fitz Colt," was indeed a custom Colt revolver made to be easily concealed by undercover police officers. John Henry Fitzgerald began working on the Fitz Special sometime in the early to mid-1920s, but there's no record of when the design was completed. There's a good chance that I have Vivian pocketing her Fitz Special a year or two before it was actually in use by police.

But tweaking the truth to make the story work is one of the fun parts of writing fiction.